EARTHQUAKE ETHAN

FORCES OF NATURE BOOK THREE

R.L. MERRILL

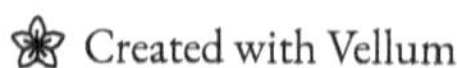 Created with Vellum

ONE

January 2017
Los Angeles, California

The morning after Ethan Bradley landed at LAX, the earth shook. Literally. Being from Iowa, he'd always been afraid of earthquakes. He remembered watching footage when he was probably four years old of the one that hit Northridge, and it stayed with him. He'd even turned down a part in the 2015 film *San Andreas* because he was terrified of the real thing.

Plus, at the time, he'd been fresh out of college and wanted to be considered a serious actor, and accepting a role in a Hollywood disaster blockbuster didn't fit in with his professional goals. Instead, he'd done stage in New York, then ended up going to London to film a clever romantic comedy. Then came more stage, a period film, and more accolades at the age of twenty-six than he'd imagined possible.

When his hotel room rattled his first morning in LA and sent him diving under the desk in the early hours, he'd wished he'd been able to stay in Europe as planned.

But London had nothing to offer him after the paparazzi ruined his life. And he couldn't go home. So there he was, back in the States, and ready to grovel before his former producer—and crush—for a role, *any role*, that would allow him to get back to doing what he loved...acting, singing, performing.

Love was a strong word. It was what he knew, what he was good at, where his God-given talents lie.

He'd come to LA with a plan. Sort of. Go see Reese Matheson. Pray he opened the door and took pity on him. And that he didn't hold a grudge.

He plugged the Malibu address he'd gotten from his London manager's office into the Lyft app and went outside to wait for his ride. And prayed.

If Reese wouldn't see him, he had a plan B.

He'd go see Reese's business partner, Toby Griffiths. Which was probably a terrible idea, but the best he had.

Because there was no plan C.

He had exactly fifty dollars cash on him and a credit card dangerously close to being maxed out. Rock Bottom was flying up to meet him fast.

The Lyft driver dropped him off at the end of a long driveway leading to a quaint little house that backed up to the Malibu shoreline. He knew nine o'clock on a Sunday morning was early, but the earthquake had shaken him so much that he couldn't wait to get out of his room at the Holiday Inn. He'd been to LA before to promote his films, but he'd never felt comfortable among the glitz and glamour of Hollywood and Beverly Hills in the limited time he'd been there.

Malibu had the scenery people thought of when they imagined Southern California. Palm trees, mountains that broke off into the sea, miles of sand with beautiful people jogging along the water's edge. It was picturesque, and sometimes cliché. For Ethan, it represented his last hope.

He climbed the steps, cleared his throat, and reached for that enthusiastic confidence that used to come so easy for him once upon a time—

The door opened before he even had a chance to knock.

The short Filipino man standing there in a pair of scrubs had one eyebrow raised and a hand on his hip. "Can I help you?"

His tone didn't come across as helpful, despite his words.

"Yeah, sorry. I'm looking for Reese Matheson? My name is—"

"I know who you are." The man's raised eyebrow turned into a frown. "Just a minute," he said before closing the door with a little less force than a slam.

Breathe. It's fine. Reese is a good guy. He won't be angry that I showed up. He's a generous, kind person—

The door opened again.

"He just finished surfing. He's showering. You can come in and wait for him."

The man's gaze dropped to Ethan's duffle on the porch next to his feet and *both* eyebrows shot up behind the black hair that fell across his forehead.

Ethan picked up his bag. "Thank you so much. I'm sorry to drop by unannounced."

The man held open the door and gestured toward the living room to the right. A familiar jingle played in the next room, and he heard someone cough. There was a doorway that looked as though it led to a kitchen directly in front of him, and a hallway off to the left probably led to bedrooms. The house felt small but homey.

"He'll be in shortly," the man said before walking through the doorway Ethan thought might lead to the kitchen.

Ethan turned the corner and set his bag down. He looked around the small living room with wood-paneled walls. Several black-and-white pictures hung above the leather couch. The place had a definite vintage surf movie vibe. To his right, a pair of French doors were open to a bright room. An older man wrapped in a blue plaid bathrobe lay on a hospital bed. He coughed once more and then noticed Ethan standing there.

"You one of Reese's friends?"

Ethan put on his best smile—it had been called dazzling by many an entertainment reporter—and took a step forward.

"Yes, sir," he said, remembering his manners. "Is that...are you watching—"

"*Sex and the City*. Yeah. Reese bought me the DVDs. I'm on Season Two. That Samantha is a fox."

Ethan chuckled. Kim Cattrall. A fox indeed.

"It's a great show."

The old man looked him up and down once more, gave a grunt Ethan assumed was in agreement, and went back to his program.

A door slammed, and Ethan recognized Reese's voice.

"Hey babe? I'm going to shower inside. It's a bit chilly out there."

He heard the lowered voice of the man who'd let him in and then Reese's. It sounded as though an argument ensued, taking some of the wattage out of Ethan's smile.

"I promise, I won't get sand everywhere," Reese said, and then he came through the doorway. In a towel.

"Ethan! Wow. This is a surprise. How've you been?"

Ethan felt a bit of that old flutter he'd get whenever Reese was around. He'd gotten over his crush, but Reese was still a lot to behold. Ethan wasn't sure of the welcome he'd receive, so he held out a hand.

Reese took it, shook, and then instead of the usual hearty hug he'd always given with a firm pounding on the back, he kind of awkwardly gave Ethan a side hug.

Over his shoulder, Ethan saw the man in scrubs standing in the doorway with his arms crossed.

"Good. Well, I've been okay. How are you?"

"Great," Reese replied, though it sounded forced.

The man in the doorway cleared his throat.

"Oh, Ethan, this is Jude, my boyfriend."

It took every ounce of Ethan's acting talent to keep his smile in place as he held out his hand to Jude to shake. Jude. A dude. *Reese is with a guy.*

Ethan of a year ago simultaneously sighed with relief that he hadn't read the guy wrong and sighed with disappointment that his flirting hadn't managed to nab the gorgeous fish.

"Great to meet you," Ethan managed to say before he stepped back and shoved his hands in his pockets.

"Wow, I didn't know you were in town. Come in, come in. Sit down."

Reese held out a bronzed arm toward the couch and he took a seat in a recliner at the other end. In just a towel.

"Reese." Jude had that eyebrow raised again.

"Yeah, babe?"

"The shower?"

Reese looked down at himself and chuckled. "Oh. Yeah. Hey, uh, let me take a quick shower. I'll be right out. You, uh, want anything? Breakfast? Jude was just—"

"No, no, I'm fine. I ate already." *Yeah, my last protein bar.* "I don't want to trouble you."

Jude turned on his heel and headed back into the kitchen.

Reese glanced in the direction Jude just left and winced. "No problem. Uh, I'll be right back."

He turned and trotted down the hallway to the left and closed a door.

Ethan dropped his head into his hands and blew out a breath. He'd fucked up. Again.

He saw Jude's feet in front of him before he heard him place a glass on the table.

"We have plenty for breakfast," he said, his tone kinder. "At least have some juice?"

"Thank you so much," Ethan said.

"Where's mine, Jude my boy?"

Jude walked over to the man in the hospital bed. "I'm just finishing the bacon," he said as he rearranged the pillow behind the man's head. "I made you French toast," he said. "And I bought you some more applesauce."

The man rubbed his hands together. "Sounds great. How about you get it for me before I waste away, huh? You trying to starve me?"

Jude patted his arm and walked away. "I have coffee, too, if you'd like," he said to Ethan as he passed.

"Juice is fine, thank you."

Jude passed through to the kitchen and was gone for a few moments, long enough for Ethan to take one more look around the room. He noticed a laptop on a table by the entryway. A pair of earbuds lay on top and a backpack leaned against the table leg.

A door opened in the hallway and a younger Filipino man appeared.

"Hey Jude? Can I grab some breakfast? Jane's picking me up to study."

Jude appeared in the doorway carrying a tray loaded with plates, a glass of juice and mug of coffee. His eyes darted toward Ethan and then back to the younger man. Who noticed him.

"Oh, I didn't— Hey, are you—"

Ethan stood from the couch. "Ethan Bradley." He held out a hand and the young man hurried to reach for it.

"Cool. I'm Bailey."

The kid smiled with an eagerness Ethan knew to be that moment when someone recognized you but they didn't know whether to say something or—

"Hey, Bails, you out of here?" Reese called out from the hallway.

Reese appeared in a pair of sweatpants and a long-sleeved Quicksilver t-shirt. It was weird seeing him in a beach setting wearing surf attire after the last evening they'd spent in London, all wrapped up in formal clothes. Reese definitely seemed more at home in California.

"Yeah, Jane's coming to pick me up. We're going to study. Jesse is making me take my finals tomorrow." He rolled his eyes.

Reese patted him on the back. "School first, dude. You know that."

"I know," Bailey grumbled. He darted into the kitchen and was back in a second with a handful of bacon in a napkin. He scooped up the laptop, stuck an earbud in and left the other to hang, and then slid the strap of the duffle over his shoulder. "Bye, Jude. I'll be home for dinner."

Jude met him in the hallway. "You better be ready for those tests tomorrow. You know Mom and Dad will freak out if you don't—"

"I know, I know, jeez." He kissed Jude on the cheek. "Nice to meet you," he called to Ethan.

"You too."

Reese lowered himself into the chair once more. Jude approached him with a cup of coffee. He handed it to Reese and started to walk away, but Reese grabbed his hand and tugged on it until Jude leaned down so Reese could kiss him.

"Thanks, babe."

Jude's gaze met Ethan's and then he excused himself.

Reese set the coffee cup down on the side table and crossed an ankle over his knee. He was barefoot.

Ethan had to remember he wasn't here to renew his crush on Reese. He needed the man's help.

"So, what's going on? What brings you to town?"

Ethan swallowed hard and said a silent prayer.

Please let this work.

"It's kind of a long story."

Two

Arthur woke with a start and sat up straight. Elvis, his twenty-pound furry roommate, launched himself off of Arthur's bare leg.

"What the—"

The window rattled ominously and the bed felt as though someone had kicked it. Hard. The framed print of Elvis Costello's debut album that he'd hung up hastily next to the bathroom—the one he knew he should have used molly bolts to hang—swung back and forth before crashing to the ground, the glass shattering.

Fuck.

An earthquake was a helluva way to start his day. All signs were pointing towards trouble and he hadn't even stepped foot out of bed.

He cursed when he remembered he'd left his slippers in the living room and therefore would have to walk past the glass to get to the broom and dustpan.

Fuuuuuck

Elvis howled from the kitchen to announce that morning had broken and it was time to break his fast.

"Don't worry, my friend. The ground quakes, the path is strewn with danger, but I shall sacrifice it all for your care and comfort, your majesty."

It was silent for exactly three seconds before a louder howl was heard.

Fucking fuckshit fuckery of fucks.

Arthur swung his feet over the edge of his queen-size bed and stepped down. In something squishy.

The amount of *fucks* that spilled from his normally curse-free mouth were numerous and passionate. He walked on the side of his foot to keep from spreading the foul substance on his laminate floor and spotted another pile just outside his doorway.

"At least you didn't vomit on my duvet again," he said, counting his one lucky star that the infuriating feline hadn't soiled his bedding. Removing the cover from the duvet without spreading the mess was difficult, but replacing the cover after a thorough wash and dry in hot water was an ordeal.

Arthur carefully stepped around the pieces of glass that thankfully remained in a small pile in the doorway and entered the bathroom. He stuck his foot in the shower and turned it on, cursing colorfully once more when he remembered he still wore his satin pajama pants. Removing them now would most definitely bring them in contact with the disgusting substance on his foot, so he pulled the leg up and did his best to rinse the muck off without getting water all over his floor.

He failed.

While removing his pants, he stepped in a puddle and slipped, catching himself on the counter and smacking his funny bone in the process.

Yeeeooooooowwwwwwlllllllllllllll

"Oh, I'm coming, you insufferable menace!"

Arthur stomped into the kitchen. He turned on the Keurig to warm and then opened a can of prescription cat food, because of course his feline ward had delicate sensitivities. The lid snapped off and flicked the gooey mess onto his bare stomach.

"Really?" he shrieked.

Mrrrrrroooooooowwwwwwwwwlllll

Elvis sat on the counter next to his bowl like the prince he was, swishing his fluffy gray tail back and forth, knocking yesterday's mail onto the floor in the process.

"Honestly, I was going to move that—"

The plus-sized cat brought a giant paw up to lick.

Arthur sighed and scooped the food into the cat's bowl. Elvis was supposed to be a temporary resident in his home when his best friend Patricia walked in on her now ex-husband mid-blow job with a drag queen in Las Vegas, and subsequently went on a much-needed sabbatical followed by an amicable divorce, but when she returned, she asked if her cat could remain with him until she found a new place. By then, Arthur had grown accustomed to Elvis's peculiar behaviors. He voiced his concerns about how another move would affect the feline menace, and Patricia asked if he wanted to keep him.

That was four years ago.

Arthur adored Patricia—and Elvis, if he was being honest—and would do anything for her, although on mornings like this, when he was supposed to have a blissful day of no commitments ahead of him, he wondered why he was so loyal.

But the fact that he *was* loyal had him running for his phone when he heard it ringing on the table next to his bed. The ringtone—"Good Vibrations"—let him know it was Reese Matheson, and if Reese was calling today after he'd promised Arthur a day off, something might be amiss.

It was an appropriate theme song for this morning, Arthur thought with a smirk.

Arthur jogged through the doorway...and forgot all about the broken picture frame.

Glass crunched under his left foot, a stabbing pain shot up his leg and he fell onto his hip and slid across the floor on his left butt cheek.

No amount of swear words would save him from the sting, the ache, or the prospect of cleaning the trail of blood off his floor.

He sat with his back against the bed and tried to catch his breath, afraid to look at his foot. The ringtone stopped for a few beats and then started again. Of course. Reese was persistent.

Arthur grabbed the phone, shouted more fucks to the heavens above as loudly as possibly, his neighbors be damned, and answered.

"Hey, Reese. What's up?"

"I have a situation."

Reese frequently had a situation. First it was the sordid pictures, then the disaster breakup, then complications with his grandfather, then his whirlwind affair with his grandfather's caregiver...all while they were in production for their new musical, which was set to open in two weeks. *What could it possibly be this time?*

"One that couldn't wait until tomorrow?" He wanted to take the words back as soon as he'd said them. Reese was a great guy, one of his best friends as well as a client, and he'd been through a world of shit in the past couple of months. Arthur prided himself on always being there for his clients, a trait that made him one of the top managers at Slade Artist Management, alongside Patricia. Losing his temper with his bread and butter was a no-no.

"Yeah. I'm sorry about that. Uh, I have a visitor."

Arthur frowned. "Okay?"

"It's Ethan."

"Oh. Kay. Well."

"Yeah. He came to the house."

Arthur winced. With the pictures and stories that came out in the UK tabloids, Ethan's presence might not go over smoothly in Reese's domicile. "Awkward much?"

"He doesn't have anywhere to go," Reese said, his voice low. Arthur imagined that was a delicate situation for him and his live-in boyfriend, Jude.

"How did he find your address?"

"His former manager in London gave it to him. Why, I have no idea. Look, he's in a bad way. You think you could meet with him?"

"Me? And do what, give him counsel? Offer him confession? The guy caused major problems for you."

"Arthur," Reese said, frustration evident in his voice. "It's not his fault what happened."

Arthur squeezed his eyes shut and pressed his lips together to keep from uttering another string of fucks. He never swore in front of anyone else. He was a professional. A problem-solver, and a good one. Protecting a client's image was one of the most important parts of the job, whether he liked it or not. He always did his best to insulate them from scandal. Unfortunately, scandal had found Reese during the London run of his last musical, *Ruby in Red Plaid*, which starred one Ethan Bradley.

"I'm sorry, Reese. What can I do?"

"Well, for starters, the only place I've got for him to sleep is my couch."

"Right. Bailey's got the spare room. Okay, what about Toby?"

Reese must have covered the phone with his hand, as Arthur heard muffled voices on the other end.

"Sorry. I can't get ahold of Toby. He and Spencer are working like mad on the book."

Right. Arthur's even higher-maintenance client and friend, Toby Griffiths, had a tight deadline and a slew of problems of his own. Toby was Reese's business and creative partner and, lately, a walking soap opera. Arthur had done all he could to be there for emotional support, but his first priority was their professional matters, and right now those required the two to remain focused on their musical production and the accompanying book. Toby had stepped back from his involvement in the current production and Arthur'd had to step in to assist Reese.

"I promised Grandpa I'd stay with him today since I've been gone so much—"

"What do you need me to do?"

There went his day off.

It took Arthur an hour to remove the glass from his foot, clean up the shards and blood, and sop up the water he'd gotten all over the floor before he fell again. He'd been looking forward to a day in his pajamas, full of Netflix and junk food—two indulgences he rarely allowed himself. Instead, he put on a no-nonsense suit and tie and laced up his most comfortable dress shoes, praying he didn't bleed through his Band-

Aids and ruin his Allen Edmonds, and he climbed into his hybrid Volvo to face the Sunday drivers.

If it had truly been his day off, he might have taken out his pride and joy: his 1971 Triumph Vitesse, fully restored and converted to an electric motor. Driving the tiny convertible, a college graduation gift from his father, was the only indulgence in his carefully constructed life.

The ride to Reese's Malibu bungalow from Arthur's townhouse off Sunset in Hollywood took him over an hour, and by the time he arrived, he'd listened to the entire 1977 Elvis Costello classic album *My Aim Is True* twice, substituting the song titles for ones that matched his fucked-up day.

"Welcome to my Working WEEKEND."

"Miracle Man ON MY DAY OFF."

And the one that got his ire up...

"Blame It On ETHAN BRADLEY THE SPOILED PRETTY BOY WHO CAN'T KEEP HIS HANDS TO HIMSELF AND JUST FUCKED UP MY DAY ON THE COUCH WITH NETFLIX."

He parked behind Reese's and Jude's matching Teslas. Boy, had Jude thrown a fit when Arthur had done as Reese asked and had the car delivered. It was sometimes difficult to handle Reese as a client. He imagined having him for a boyfriend would be a massive undertaking.

Arthur adored Reese and Toby. They'd become more than clients. More like family or the kind of best friends who always needed to be bailed out of something. They were the perfect example of why Arthur would never become involved with an artist, but he loved them all the same. He'd seen several managers come and go at Slade, many of them seduced by the allure of dating a model/actor/musician. It never ended well, and often they became fodder for tabloids. He knew of a few managers who'd *married* the talent, even, only to find out that artists were fickle and rarely were in it for the long haul.

Arthur would rather step on glass and cat puke every morning like *Ground Hog Day* than go through a public breakup. Hollywood was full of cautionary tales, and Arthur had always avoided such entanglements.

He'd rather be single forever than go through that kind of hell.

He knocked on the door and Jude answered with a forced smile.

"That good, huh?"

Jude looked over his shoulder and then stepped outside the door, closing it behind him. "I appreciate you coming. Mr. Matheson is having a rough day. I'm afraid he's coming down with pneumonia. It's been hard to get him up and around these days. Reese is worried."

Thomas Matheson had been a phenomenal musician and song-writer from the days of the Rat Pack and Frank Sinatra. Arthur always felt a little star struck around him...and he had a lot of sympathy for him and Reese and Jude. Dementia was an evil disease and it wasn't fair. Poor Thomas was slowly being robbed of his quick wit and dry sense of humor, as well as recognition of the people around him.

"I'm so sorry, Jude. I came as soon as I could. Is he...Ethan's here?"

Jude's eyes darted toward the closed door. "He's in bad shape. The poor man had nowhere to go. If we didn't have our hands full here—"

"Of course, no. I know Reese would do anything for a friend, but—"

"We're just not in a position to take him in."

Take him in?

Arthur blew out a breath. "Alright. You know I'll do whatever I can. Reese can't afford the distraction right now." This was beyond terrible timing.

"I know you were supposed to have a day off today," Jude said. "I appreciate you coming over. So does Reese."

They exchanged a solemn look, and Jude turned to enter the house.

Arthur stiffened his back and prepared for full damage-control mode. He wasn't an actor like his clients, but it would behoove him to at least pretend to not intensely dislike Ethan Bradley.

Fucking Ethan Bradley.

"Hey, Arthur," Reese called out. "You remember Ethan?"

Ethan stood from the couch and his smile could have lit up Dodger Stadium.

"Hello, Ethan," he said, forcing himself to reach out for a handshake he had no desire to give.

"Mr. Frye. Thank you for coming. I'm sorry to take you away from your Sunday."

So he was playing the part of the all-American, clean-cut, corn-fed Iowa boy. How charming.

"Sit down, sit down," Reese said, shooting a glance at Jude, who in turn gave Arthur a knowing look.

The doors to Mr. Matheson's room were closed. Arthur unbuttoned his suit coat and sat in a wingback chair across from the couch.

That was when he recognized the gravity of the situation. If he had been paying attention, he would have noticed right away and not been blinded by Ethan's smile.

He wore Nike tennis shoes that looked as though he'd trained for and run several marathons in them. His jeans were worn at the knee, and not as a fashion statement. And his fingernails were chewed to the quick.

The golden boy had sure seen better days.

THREE

E^{than}

"So what's been going on, Ethan? How did that Anna Kendrick movie turn out?"

Ethan dug deep for those acting chops to answer Arthur's question. He had to play this cool.

Screw that, Ethan. It's time to be honest.

"I hear it turned out great, but I, uh, was let go."

"What?" Reese looked genuinely concerned. Thankfully. "What do you mean, you were let go?"

"Um, so the producers thought the pictures and stories in the papers would hurt the film..."

Reese cursed and looked away.

Arthur stared. And kind of smirked.

Ethan knew a lot of folks didn't like him, and that was okay as long as he got work. He'd asked his acting coach once long ago why he seemed to face so much hostility from people he thought he'd been perfectly kind to, and his coach told him, "Ethan, you're beautiful. People can't stand that. They will tear you down any chance they get, so you have to have thick skin if you're in this business for any length of time."

"I got locked out of my studio housing. And my manager dropped me."

"Jeez, why?" Reese asked.

Ethan felt his jaw muscle twitch. "He said he didn't represent artists who couldn't handle themselves in a respectable manner."

"Jesus," Jude said and shook his head. He stood behind the recliner where Reese sat. "How bad were these pictures?"

Reese looked at Ethan, his cheeks reddened, and then he reached for Jude's hand. "Well, you saw how Jada reacted."

Jude rolled his eyes. "Yes, and? Her reactions obviously don't hold a lot of weight with me. Are we talking blow jobs in public? Full-frontal nudity?"

Reese barked out a laugh, seemingly relieved by Jude's lack of concern. "No, there was no nudity—"

"It was a drunken embrace," Arthur interrupted. "It was easily misunderstood."

Reese frowned at Arthur. "We were laughing, that's all. And yes, we had our arms around each other, but—"

"And the tabloids posted stories about how I supposedly got the role in *Ruby* and that I'd done it again with the movies. It got worse after the initial pictures." His cheeks flushed and he felt sick to his stomach. "It was my fault," Ethan said. "I'm sorry to have caused problems for you."

Reese shrugged. "Everything happens for a reason." He smiled up at Jude and tugged his hand to pull him down for a kiss. Jude lost his balance a little and pulled away before Reese could deepen the kiss.

"You're impossible," Jude whispered, but he grinned. "I'm going to check on Grandpa."

Ethan was glad to see Reese so happy. That was what mattered most. Any lingering crush Ethan had on the man was better off forgotten.

"That sucks about your manager," Reese said. "Do you have any contacts here in the States? Anyone you've worked with?"

Ethan shook his head. "I only did the one Broadway show before I did *Ruby*. I went to London. I did the two movies before we did *Ruby* there, but that's it. I had two film projects lined up and after the pictures and stories came out, everything dried up. Look, I'm not afraid to get my hands dirty or take small parts, I just want to work." It hurt to smile, but damn he'd do it. "I *need* to work. Reese, you told me once that if I was ever in LA to look you up, that you'd hire me again, and I know it's unprofessional to show up at your house, but I didn't know how else to get ahold of you."

"Calling his manager is usually a good way," Arthur muttered.

"Arthur," Reese admonished. He was being so nice. Ethan felt even guiltier for being there. "What kind of work are you looking for?"

Ethan exhaled. "I'm literally up for anything: theater, film, voice work... I heard you had a new show—"

"Which we cast already," Arthur said.

"Arthur!"

"Reese, can I speak to you for a moment?"

Reese and Arthur exchanged a long look, and then Reese stood from the chair. "Will you excuse us, please?" He held a hand out and gestured for Arthur to follow him out back.

Arthur gave Ethan a frown on the way out.

"I have never seen that man be nasty to anyone," Jude said, returning to the room with his eyebrows raised. "And normally I don't engage in gossip, but I'd love to hear just what happened in London."

Ethan smiled. "The show was great. We had such a great cast. It was my first time onstage in London and the audience was so polite. But at the wrap party, we'd all been drinking, and I'm not much of a drinker. I remember Reese and I singing together, which was when the pictures were taken I think, and then I woke up with...well, anyway, they left and I was scheduled to start shooting the next week, which was the end of October? Things really went downhill from there. I've been trying to line up auditions on my own, but no one will speak to me after Randolph Winthorpe, my UK manager dropped me. I've never really worked in LA so I thought maybe I could have a fresh start here."

"I'm sure Reese and Arthur can figure something out. Would you excuse me? I need to get Mr. Matheson his medicine."

Ethan faked another smile and then slumped back against the

couch. Maybe he should have worn his suit, but it didn't fit right anymore after he'd lost weight. He hadn't been working out and he hadn't eaten much.

This had been a mistake. Why did he have to come and disrupt someone else's life because of his problems? He should just start hitting the job placement centers, maybe do some temp work, or he could check with the carpenters union and see if they'd accept him, since he'd been a member years ago back in Iowa, although he'd let his membership lapse.

If only he could have gone home...

His to-do list became this swirling monstrosity that wrapped him in a cocoon and threatened to blot out the light until he couldn't breathe. He debated on standing up to leave, but then he close his eyes for just a minute, thinking maybe it would all go away.

FOUR

"What's wrong with trying to help this kid, Arthur? He did good work for us in New York and London. He was a little goofy and distracted at rehearsals sometimes, but his performances were top-notch. He earned us great reviews and a freaking Tony award."

Arthur looked at Reese with his hands on his hips and he had to fight not to raise his voice.

"He also hit on you and slept with Toby. He's baggage you don't need right now, especially with the show in high gear." He ran a hand through his hair, hoping to calm himself, but he was just so irritated. Reese was such a nice guy and he wanted to take care of everyone. As far as Arthur was concerned, he should tell Ethan to look for a handout elsewhere. It was Arthur's job to protect his clients, and it was difficult to do that for a guy like Reese, who had a heart like a dump truck.

Reese rolled his eyes. "Everyone sleeps with—or *slept* with— Toby, or tried to anyway. I certainly don't consider that a character flaw. And now that Toby has Spencer, we don't have to worry about that anymore."

"Are you sure about that? Whatever, even leaving Toby out of this, *you* don't need the hassle."

Reese frowned at him and crossed his arms over his chest. "Arthur, I'm sorry I pulled you into this on your day off, but is there something else bothering you? It's not like you to be so negative."

Arthur had a lot of comebacks on the tip of his tongue, none of which were typical of him. What *was* wrong this morning? Was it the earthquake? The puke? The glass? He really was feeling foul, but that didn't change the matter that Ethan Bradley was potentially trying to take advantage of his client, one of his *favorite* clients, and he wasn't about to let that stand, no matter how damned talented or attractive he was.

"Reese, I'm just trying to look out for you. I don't appreciate this guy showing up on your doorstep looking for a handout."

Jude opened the slider.

"Reese, we've gotta help this guy. He's in there asleep on the couch. What the hell happened to him?"

Great. Looked like Arthur wasn't going to be able to pull Jude over to his side for backup.

"Poor guy. Listen, Arthur, put him up at a hotel for a few days, charge it to my account, and see if you can find anything for him. Can you do that? I'm not asking you to babysit—"

"That's exactly what you're doing," Arthur muttered. When Reese started to protest, he raised his hand. "Fine, I'll get him a room and I'll check with my contacts, see if my assistant can get him some auditions set up. But I don't want him around the show, Reese. Or you, for that matter."

Or me.

Reese flinched at Arthur's last statement. "Fine. Thank you. Sorry to put you out."

Arthur exhaled harshly. "You're not. I just...you've got a lot on your plate and I hate to see you take on another problem."

Reese pulled himself up to his full height. "I appreciate your concern, Arthur, but I don't see Ethan as a problem. I've been lucky to never have fallen on tough economic times, and I refuse to let anyone in my circle suffer when there's something I can do about it." He looked over and took Jude's hand. Jude's cheeks flushed and he gave Reese a small smile, one of appreciation.

Arthur could keep arguing, but it was obvious he wasn't going to win. Reese with his mind set on something was nearly impossible to budge.

"All right. I'll get him set up and then I'll see you tomorrow at the theater. Remember, you've got press set up all week, so maybe don't wear your flip-flops or your SpongeBob t-shirt."

Reese groaned. "Aw, man, I hate wearing real shoes."

Jude shook his head. "I'll make sure, Arthur. And thank you again for coming over."

The three of them went inside and, sure enough, Ethan's head lolled toward his shoulder and his eyes were shut.

Arthur cleared his throat and Ethan shot up off the couch. Reese threw out an arm to steady him.

"Whoa. You're okay, man."

Ethan's eyes were wide and Arthur's irritation eased a bit. The guy really *was* in bad shape. This wasn't the cocky and arrogant kid he remembered from New York. The one who he'd heard bragging backstage about how being the lead in *Ruby in Red Plaid* was really opening doors for him, that he was already getting A-List offers.

No, this version of Ethan Bradley looked like he'd been through the wringer. And now it appeared Arthur was stuck with him.

"I'm sorry," Ethan said with a nervous laugh. "That earthquake messed me up this morning. I still feel like my legs are wobbly."

Reese frowned. "We had an earthquake?"

"Yeah, you were out surfing," Jude said. "Your grandfather slept through it but Bailey came running in and dove under the kitchen table."

Arthur stepped on his foot wrong and winced. "Yeah, I had a little damage."

Reese's eyes flew open. "Are you okay?"

"Yeah, just a picture frame. Stepped on the broken glass." *My brand-new framed and signed Elvis Costello print that I'd finally decided on the perfect place for.* Arthur had quite a collection of 1980s-era album and movie art. Music and film from that era represented everything that was good about his life, and his home showcased the things he loved most.

Jude frowned. "Want me to take a look at it?"

"I'm fine," Arthur protested, but then Reese and Jude were pushing him onto the couch and Reese had his shoe off—

"Dude, you're bleeding through your sock."

And next thing he knew, Jude had his sock and bandage off, had sent Reese for the first-aid kit, and the two of them were doing minor surgery on Arthur's foot. His cheeks were hot. He hated having the attention on himself.

"It doesn't look like you need stitches, but you should stay off of it and leave the bandage off as much as you can."

Arthur gritted his teeth. "I'll do just that as soon as I get home." Where he would still be if it weren't for Reese's fire drill this morning.

"Great. And hey, why don't you set Ethan up near the theater so he can come on over tomorrow. You're not going to believe this show, Ethan. Jude's brother is one of the leads and he's great. The show is going to be fucking fantastic."

"That's great. I'd, um, love to see it."

Reese beamed and Arthur internally groaned. So much for keeping Earthquake Ethan away from the production. *God, let's hope he doesn't shake anything else up.*

"We'll get out of your hair," Arthur said, putting back on his shoe and sock. "See you and Toby tomorrow?"

Reese frowned. "I'm not sure if he's coming, but I'll give him a call."

Arthur and Ethan said their goodbyes. Ethan picked up a well-worn duffle bag, and he followed Arthur outside.

"Thank you, Mr. Frye. I appreciate it. I'm sorry if this caused you any problems today."

"It's fine," Arthur said. He opened the rear hatch of his Volvo and gestured for Ethan to drop his bag in, but as they stood next to their doors, he finally spoke over the top of the car.

"Look, Reese is a great guy, but it's my job to take care of him. Protect him. You understand?"

Ethan nodded in small, jerky movements. "Sure I do."

"Then next time you find yourself out of work, try not showing up on Reese's doorstep. I'm going to see what I can do, but no one's going to hand you anything. You're going to have to earn it."

It was the tough-love speech Arthur used to give new clients. Not that Ethan would ever be his client, but it was obvious this guy didn't know the unwritten rules of Hollywood, and before Ethan made a bigger ass of himself, Arthur felt compelled to give him a few lessons.

"I understand, Mr. Frye—"

Arthur slid into the driver's seat and had the car started before Ethan opened the door. He got in and tried to make himself small, or maybe he just *was* small. Arthur was tall, 6'3" on a good day, and he'd thought Ethan was as tall as him. He sure seemed like it when they'd met in New York two years prior. He'd taken up all the space—as well as all the air in the damn room—with that dazzling smile, his twinkling pale blue eyes, and those broad shoulders, which framed a well-toned, prominent Superman-sized chest. And no, Arthur hadn't been checking out his long legs, nor the six-pack that was visible under the open vest he wore for the final scene in the show.

Reese and Toby had had plenty of folks working with them on *Ruby*, so Arthur had stayed in LA, only coming out for the dress rehearsals and opening night. He'd been introduced to Ethan then, but they'd never had much opportunity to get acquainted. After he'd seen Ethan's performance, it turned out to be a blessing.

Arthur had been thoroughly enchanted, and that didn't happen to him. As a rule, he wasn't attracted to performers of any kind. He avoided dating them, though his personal life was filled with entertainers he knew through his parents. And then there were clients who were friends, like Reese and Toby.

There was one surefire way to get him to *not* click on a dating profile on the rare occasions he looked for company, and that was to have "actor" or any permutation of that word in a bio on a dating app. Not that he had much time to date—no, not with Reese and Toby deciding to throw together this musical in just six weeks so that Reese's grandfather would likely be able to see it.

"Mr. Frye? I just want you to know that I was raised to never take a handout by my parents. I was also told once I left home not to bother coming back, otherwise I'd have gone back to Iowa. I'm not proud about any of this. I swear to God, I'll pay back every cent Reese spends on me."

The indignation Arthur was trying to hold on to cracked and started to flake away.

"It's fine. There's a decent hotel near the theater. I'll get you set up there for the week." Arthur pulled out of Reese's driveway and headed back toward Hollywood. At least it was on the way to his place and traffic wasn't horrible. The less time he had to spend in the car with Ethan, the better.

"And I'm willing to do anything. I can do construction, wait tables, *anything*. I don't want to put you out if there are no auditions."

Arthur glanced over at him. That was a surprise. Where was the prima donna he'd met previously? "I'm assuming you have headshots, reels, and a resume ready?"

He nodded. "If I can get access to a computer at the hotel, I can send them to you."

Arthur frowned. "You don't have a computer?"

Ethan shook his head and wrapped his arms in front of him, clutching his elbows.

"Okay, then, I'll have my assistant Audra check tomorrow. If there's anything you'd be right for, I'll let you know. And listen, I know Reese invited you to the theater—"

"I won't get in the way, I promise."

Dammit. If he kept this up, Arthur might actually like the guy, and he had no room in his life for—

"And if they need any help with anything, I'm happy to do it."

Arthur snapped his jaw together and ground his teeth.

What was wrong with him? Ethan had said he wasn't brought up to take handouts, and Arthur hadn't been brought up to ever be cruel. That didn't mean he hadn't been on the receiving end.

"And did I hear you say you had some damage from the earthquake? I'd be happy to take a look. I'm handy with—"

"It's fine. I've gotta get a new picture frame. No big deal."

"Oh."

Arthur stopped at an intersection and turned to look at Ethan, gearing up to give him a little more tough love, but the guy was smiling so hopefully at him.

"I really want to thank you, Mr. Frye. I didn't have a lot of hope when I landed here in LA last night, but I do now."

Arthur took in his genuine smile, which was somehow more attractive than his leading-man smile; took in his slightly shaggy hair that looked as if it could use a deep conditioning and a cut. He started making mental lists.

If he's going for auditions, he's going to need a haircut and a facial. Probably wardrobe assistance. Sky blue would look great on him with those eyes. Black was always a good color with his dark hair and tanned, freckled skin, although he's much paler than he used to be.

"Mr. Frye?"

A horn honked and Arthur nearly missed the light, he'd been so preoccupied. It definitely helped to look at Ethan as a potential client, even though he had neither the room nor the desire to take him on. His roster was full, thank you very much. But if he looked at him as a potential client, he wouldn't, you know, *look* at him.

"Call me Arthur," he said with a sigh. "Mr. Frye is my grandfather."

"Great. Thank you."

So polite.

Fucking fuck fucked. Why did he have to be so polite?

Five

E^{than}

Arthur pulled his Volvo up to a massive five-story cinderblock building with brightly painted murals called The Hollywood Spot Hotel and parked in the covered loading zone.

"We've been working at a smaller theater for rehearsals, but the show is going to be at the Pantages. They'll be working there starting tomorrow. It's just up the street."

Ethan had spent the past six years between New York and London, but he'd only been to LA twice and it always surprised him. The glamour wasn't visible in most of Hollywood with the exception of during special events. In New York, you knew what to expect, but Hollywood seemed like it would be so dreamy and glitzy. Even Malibu had been different than in the movies and on TV, but then it made sense.

He'd learned fast that the places where the movies were filmed weren't even like the movies. He'd fallen in love with acting and thought the life of an actor would be full of hard work, of course, but also fancy parties, jet-setting...

There'd been a few parties, but he'd spent them posing for photographers and taking interviews rather than dancing and drinking with his co-stars. And he couldn't eat or drink any old thing he wanted. He had to maintain his physique, which prior to New York had been acquired through physical labor on the family farm, not working with a trainer until every muscle stood at attention. He missed hamburgers.

Well, right now he missed real meals in general. What he wouldn't give for his mom's pot roast. He could kick himself for being in such a hurry to leave, for looking down on the hearty home-cooked food he'd been raised on. He could sure use it now.

Ethan grabbed his bag from the trunk and followed Arthur into the hotel lobby. The stone building was decorated in a Hollywood theme and he found himself gazing in awe at all of the portraits. He'd foolishly thought for sure his face would be up there with the greats someday soon when he signed his contract for his first movie. Okay, maybe his second movie; the first one was definitely geared toward young adults and he'd only gotten as far as *Teen Vogue*. They'd compared him to Ashton Kutcher and Jason Momoa, who'd left their Iowa roots far behind to become bona fide sex symbols.

He'd been a lead in a highly acclaimed musical that won a Tony and starred in two British films, one as the hunky American love interest and the other as a member of the British nobility. And now he was flat broke. Not exactly up there with Kelso and Aquaman.

"Here," Arthur said, giving him his room key and one of his business cards. "If you have any emergencies, you can call me. You've got the room through Friday at this point and then we'll see where we're at. Please remember that this is on Reese's dime and don't go trashing the place."

"I won't do anything to tarnish his reputation."

Any more than you already have, and yeah, Arthur was staring at him as if he were having the same thought. Ethan wondered whether Arthur was this serious all the time, with his dark blue eyes behind stern glasses and a permanent frown line between his carefully manicured brows. Shockingly red brows that matched his fiery red hair. He had an angular jaw and cheekbones that made him look intense, but then his mouth was soft, with puffy pink lips. And the whole package was covered with freckles. He seemed older than he looked, but then he was just so...commanding.

"Rehearsals start at eight tomorrow. Feel free to come over whenever and as soon as I have the opportunity to get with Audra, I'll let you know what I find out. We have an agency we work with. Give me your number so I can call you in case something comes up."

"Uh," Ethan said, and then winced. "My cell service got shut off. I can only use my phone with Wi-Fi. I have WhatsApp. I'm EthanB1992."

Arthur gave him such an incredulous look that Ethan wished he could take his last words back. He sounded like a disaster. How unprofessional to not even have a cell phone.

"How about email? I don't use whatever you just said."

"Oh, sure. My email is EBradley at AOL-dot-com."

Arthur typed it into his phone, shaking his head. "AOL. Wonderful. Okay, see you tomorrow."

Ethan stood there holding onto his bag with both hands as if it were a life preserver, and he sucked in a breath. "Thank you again, Mr.— I mean, Arthur."

He was trying his damnedest to be nice and humble with this guy who obviously hated him. It made sense. Now that he knew those pictures had been a huge problem for Reese, well...he'd probably hate himself too. He'd just have to take it. But that didn't mean he didn't want to run up to his hotel room and curl up in a corner and cry.

Arthur gave him one last look, and Ethan wanted to believe it was one of support, or maybe "it gets better" or something other than pity, but what he saw in Arthur was...indecipherable.

Was it hatred? Was it dislike? Or was it discomfort, as though Arthur had thoughts and feelings about this whole mess that he was holding back?

Ethan had no clue. What he *did* know was that Arthur was one of those people who'd probably never been embarrassed in their life, who always had their stuff together and knew what they were doing. Ethan envied people like that. He was competent in certain things. He was good with his hands, his singing was above average, he could dance, and he could act well. He couldn't always talk to people well in real life, though, unless he was pretending. Sometimes he pretended so much, he didn't know who he truly was.

Until the ground opened up and he fell into purgatory, and then obscurity.

He'd had to accept things about himself, things like he didn't have the skills needed to live on the streets, nor was he willing to be dishonest or steal to get what he needed. He discovered he wasn't proud, that he was willing to admit he was lost in order to get help. He'd had to come back to America because without a manager, agent, or any job prospects, he couldn't renew his visa. At least back here he could get a job, even if it paid only enough to eat.

Speaking of, his stomach, which had been satisfied after Jude fed him breakfast he wished he hadn't needed so much, was full for the first time in weeks. So many things he'd taken for granted in his life, like food, were now in hyper focus.

Watching Arthur walk away gave Ethan a sinking feeling. The manager carried himself like a busy man, someone on the go who was always thinking about the next thing on his to-do list, always solving other people's problems.

Unfortunately, Ethan had become a problem he needed to solve. Which was too bad. It would be nice for a together man like Arthur to see Ethan as more than a hassle, more than a client. Maybe a friend? It had been a long time since Ethan had one of those.

He clutched his room key card in his hand and tried to remember which floor he was on.

"Second floor. Got it." He went up the stairs, his legs had finally quit shaking from the earthquake. But then he started thinking...was *this* place safe in an earthquake? Was he going to get crushed in a pile of stones if another one hit?

He reached the landing on the second floor and heard hoots, hollers, and a whole bunch of water splashing. His room was right in the middle of the landing, so he set his bag down and peered over the railing.

There were four guys floating in the middle of the pool in giant floaties that took up most of the water, and they were currently filling up water cannons and shooting each other, and then shooting them up in the air, alarmingly close to where Ethan was standing. He stepped back and thought, *Well, at least it won't be boring?*

He opened the door to his room and stepped inside to be greeted with a print of Elvis Presley from his movie *King Creole*, in a frame with the vinyl next to it.

He dropped his bag, his shoulders, and his head. Figured. Of all the stars...

He'd been told he had a voice like Elvis by a talent agent his choir teacher had introduced his mother to after his school play his freshman year. His mom had been intrigued enough that someone thought he had a talent worth developing that she was willing to make the investment, hoping it would pay off for the family.

That probably sounded worse than it actually was. Ethan's mother, Kathy Bradley, ran their household as efficiently as a small business. Each of her four kids was allowed one extra-curricular activity, either music or whatever sport was in season, and they were all enrolled in scouts. She'd never been willing to break that policy until she met with his first talent agent.

The other Bradley sons had been skilled enough at sports, and Ethan had gone along with whatever made people happy. Which was why he'd agreed with the plan to turn him into a triple threat. Vocal lessons, dance lessons, acting lessons...plus sports, because the talent agent thought his physical agility and sporty all-American appearance would help him stand out.

He did admire Elvis. *King Creole* was a fun movie. And heck, all the hard work kept him busy and, he thought, made people like him. That's really what he wanted, that reaction, that swoon, that applause, the cheering. He loved that his performances touched people. That wasn't so wrong, was it?

Ethan took out his clothes and hung up his dress shirt and slacks. He laid out his second pair of jeans, hoping the wrinkles would shake out of everything. Then he sat in the chair and exhaled.

It was one in the afternoon. He had no plans, no money, no prospects.

But he did have his two feet. Pacing the floor of his hotel room was a waste of time and would likely lead to him finding a corner of the room to hide in and cry.

"Nope. No more moping. Time to see what Hollywood has to offer."

An hour later, he was thoroughly amazed and entertained. How could this part of Hollywood that contained the Walk of Fame, the Pantages, the Dolby, and the Chinese Theatre also have massive cheesy tourist shops, a mall-type shopping center, and a Ripley's Believe It or Not Museum? And the Jimmy Kimmel show was filmed right there? While Spider-Man and Captain America posed with families from the Midwest and dancers shot choreography on their iPhones in the middle of the sidewalk. It was the wildest collection of activities happening in one spot that he'd ever seen.

Everyone has a hustle.

The guy in the tin suit and silver paint stood frozen until an unsuspecting passerby would become part of his schtick. There were guys handing out cards with info about the nudie bars, flicking them as you walked past, the clicking sound grabbing your attention. They knew just how close to get without harassing passersby. And the street artists with their airbrushing kits sold unbelievably cool pieces for a few bucks to young girls while asking for their numbers.

Tourists were shelling out ones, fives...a few twenties, all to get their pictures taken with celebrity look-alikes.

How ironic that an actual celebrity was walking among them with holes in his shoes and not enough food to eat past his next meal.

A group of dancers had a piece of cardboard in the middle of the sidewalk and they were taking turns breakdancing and facing off against each other, then working off each other to do complicated partner stunts. Ethan watched them do their fifteen-minute routine three times before he got a chill. It was January, not as cold as Iowa of course, or New York or London, but breezy, and he hadn't brought his only jacket. The sun was low in the sky and he figured he should get back to his hotel before it was dark. He bought a two-dollar kid-sized hotdog off a street vendor and ate it in three bites as he walked, shivers rattling his teeth.

The hotel was less than a mile from the brightly lit center of Hollywood, and he had to pass through a street with few lights and a couple of burned-out cars. Two young teens sat on the sidewalk with a sign asking for a dollar to help them get some food.

Ethan didn't have much, but these kids had less.

"Here," he handed them each five bucks. "Find some dinner, all right?"

They nodded at him blankly and thanked him in hushed voices. They headed in the direction he'd come from, and he sighed.

He'd been in that same place in London. Relying on the kindness of strangers for a week before his flight to LA, and he prayed he wasn't recognized. How awful would it be to see the next tabloid headline: "Boy Toy Bradley Destitute after Sacked from British Period Film over Rumors of Impropriety." Or something equally awful like "American Playboy Matheson Heads Home, Ditching Gay Paramour Bradley."

He entered the hotel lobby and gazed longingly at the attached bar and lounge, thinking a meal and a few beers would be a nice way to end his day, but he needed to save the last few dollars he had. Besides, they had continental breakfast in the morning. He could make it until then. He'd eaten more that day than he had in the past two weeks.

He climbed the steps to the second floor and smiled when he heard a guitar being picked.

"See, baby, that's how you play the blues."

"What do you know about the blues, Cosmo?"

Ethan turned the corner to see a tall guy sitting on the landing with a tiny woman sitting behind his guitar and between his legs as he tried to teach her.

"Oh, what's up man? Sorry, are we in your way?"

"No, no," Ethan said, trying to get around them, but they were blocking the steps and landing. They stood up, and he scooted awkwardly past them.

"Thank you—"

"Hey, man, everything okay for you so far?"

"Yeah, he's the manager of the place," the woman said. "You need anything, he's right in this apartment here."

Sure enough, one of the units kitty corner from Ethan's room had the door and drapes open, and Ethan could see that it had been connected to the room next to it. There was a kitchen and everything... and apparently, a party going on.

"Thank you, I'm just going to my room. Early morning tomorrow."

"You got an audition?"

Ethan blanched. Did this guy know who he was?

"Just guessing because I saw you in here with Arthur Frye. I'm Cosmo. I'm the manager, as she said. I'm, ah, acquainted with Arthur's business partner, Patricia Wilson."

He looked nothing like any hotel manager Ethan had ever met. But he didn't want to be rude. He shook the man's hand. "I'm Ethan. Nice to meet you."

"Far out," Cosmo said, giving Ethan a curious onceover. "Have a restful sleep. We'll try to keep it down. Make sure you grab some of the continental breakfast in the morning. We aim to have the best waffles in LA. Not sure we're there yet, but we aim."

He winked and went back to noodling on the guitar with the woman staring at him dreamily. He was wearing cutoff jean shorts and no shirt. His hair was long, dark, and super curly. It almost looked like a wig it was so...perfect.

"Maybe he'd like a drink?" The woman was smiling at him, and Ethan knew that was his cue to get lost. Whenever he got attention like that from a woman, her man tended to get aggressive, and Ethan was not in any position to—

"You're welcome to come on over, if you want. My advice though? Get your beauty sleep if you've got an audition. You want to be in your best frame of mind."

Ethan held up a hand. "Right, I don't have anything lined up yet. Just, uh, gotta get an early start." He sure as hell hoped he did soon. "But thank you. Enjoy your night."

He waved and went into his room, resting his back against the door when it closed.

He'd spent so much time alone lately, a party sounded nice, but then people would ask questions or he'd get noticed and it would be awkward.

No, sleep was a good idea. Or it would be if his mind wasn't racing. Instead, he lay there for hours listening to the party across the hall...the music, the laughter...the sex. All of it was loud, and he might have been irritated with the lack of sleep. Instead, he found himself wishing he could be partying with them. Not as Ethan Bradley, but just one of the guys, having a good time.

He hugged a pillow close to his chest and squeezed his eyes shut. Crying would definitely not have him looking his best in the morning.

A jolt to the bed sent him scurrying to his feet just as the window rattled and the hotel information booklet fell over on the table. There was a squeal from outside.

"Another earthquake! Man, that one almost knocked me over."

"Nah, the news app says it's only a 2.9. It just felt strong because it was close by."

But Ethan didn't care whether it was 2.9 or 10.0, he needed solid ground beneath his feet. He'd had enough upheaval to last him a lifetime. If the earth kept shaking here in Los Angeles, maybe he would have to start over somewhere new. Someplace where nobody knew his name. He'd rather face hurricanes or tornadoes than earthquakes in LA.

Six

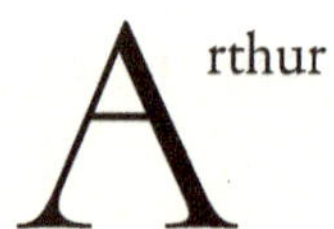rthur

Arthur woke up once more cursing. The earthquake last night sent Elvis running from the room and he'd spent an hour looking for him. He finally found him wedged behind the couch, where he couldn't get out without Arthur moving the whole thing, which was murder on his cut foot. He tried to make it up to his feline friend by giving him an extra serving of cat food, but that meant leaning on the counter and watching him eat. Elvis was weird like that. He wanted you to stay with him while he ate. Otherwise, he'd leave his food untouched but yell at you for hours that he was hungry.

Arthur had learned how to tell the difference between the hunger yowls and the "clean my cat box" shriek and the "I'm bored, entertain me" squawks.

After Elvis had eaten, Arthur went back to his bed in a foul mood, only to think of the cause. Ethan Bradley. Although, Ethan was only a portion of the problem.

Arthur was the bigger part of the problem.

He was angry with himself for being so rude, so mean. He'd returned home and done a thorough internet search on Ethan Bradley, only to become even more disgusted with his own behavior.

The guy had been through hell. The pictures taken at the show's wrap party were only the beginning. A story came out that said Ethan had promised sexual favors to the director in order to be cast as the lead in a big-budget historical film that some felt would have been his ticket to the Oscars and the BAFTAs. His female co-star had come out in support at first, but then admitted she didn't really know him, nor did she know anything about who he was actually dating.

There was also an article touting additional rumors, these ones with pictures. Ethan hanging on both Toby and Reese, him cuddling with a female co-star in a restaurant booth, and one of the two of them supposedly arguing, that accused him of dumping her to pursue Reese. They were brutal. He'd known the British tabloids were more salacious than in the US, but this was awful.

"Disgusting." Arthur had tossed down his phone in frustration. He felt as though he should take a shower after reading such trash. Then he'd proceeded to go through his email and see if there was anything there that would work for Ethan. The sooner he got the guy hooked up with a job, he wouldn't have to worry.

But he *did* worry. He'd left the kid on his own at a barely above-seedy hotel and taken off because he couldn't handle his own feelings about him.

Monday morning, he was up before the sun. He worked out while Elvis hollered, drank his first of many coffees while Elvis ate, showered while Elvis watched him from his perch behind the toilet...

"Why are you so judgy this morning? I said I'd make things better."

If it were possible for the cat to look even more disgusted, Elvis could do it. If he could speak, he'd probably remind Arthur that he'd taken Elvis in when he was down on *his* luck and look how good that had turned out.

"Fine." Arthur reached over and turned the music up on his water-proof speaker. The Clash's "Train in Vain" echoed throughout the bathroom suite, and Elvis blinked his eyes closed. He almost had a satisfied smile on his smug little face.

Arthur arrived at the theater shortly after ten, cursing his tardiness but there'd been a broken water main on Hollywood Boulevard and he'd been stuck in traffic for forty-five minutes to go the two miles from his office to the theater.

"What did I miss?" he asked choreographer Jesse Martin-Black as he took a seat beside her. The tall blond had a look of concentration that didn't fit with her usual warm and friendly personality.

"We've done one full run-through this morning, and I'm giving them a break before we do it again. Besides that? I'd say we need more than two weeks to get this production show-ready. But it's gonna be *fiiiiine*." She laughed and made a face. She'd been an absolute godsend to this production and Arthur was so glad to count her as a friend. And if this production hit as big as he thought it would, he might just sign her as a client. The world needed more Broadway-style choreographers.

Arthur groaned. "Tell me about it. I've gotta spend a bit more time at the office later today and try to salvage my thriving management business. Besides these two geniuses, I've got a reality-show dancer who's decided that he wants to make me earn my paycheck while I sort out his schedule so he can potentially meet up with an admirer. I've got a music producer I just took on from one of our retiring partners who needs to reschedule her spring gigs because she's fallen in love with a pop star and wants to go on tour with her. Everyone's in love and it's not even Valentine's Day yet."

It was true, this musical had required much more of Arthur's attention than his clients' usual projects. Reese and Toby had been in a hurry to open the show because Reese wanted to make sure his grandfather would be lucid enough to see it. After Thomas fell back in November and had to spend a month in a rehab facility, Reese felt a sense of urgency. Thankfully everything had come together with a minimalist stage setup up and a small cast. Most of the work had been the choreography and making sure the band was solid. Tickets were going on sale tomorrow and then they'd get an idea of how well this limited engagement was going to do. Then they'd shop it to Broadway or do a national tour...

Yeah, it was a whole lot of loosey-goosey planning that gave Arthur hives. He'd do anything for these guys, and he'd done a lot, but *man* this was shaky.

"And I met our guest." Jesse's brows rose dramatically.

"You mean the uninvited guest," Arthur muttered.

Jesse elbowed him, and he held up a hand. "I know, I know. I'm being a dick and I don't even know why. He got dealt a shitty hand, I get it. But he thought *this* was the right way to handle it?"

Jesse looked to her right and behind, and Arthur followed her gaze to where Ethan was sitting by himself. His hands were folded in his lap and he was just taking in the activity around him with a curious look on his face.

"He seems really nice," Jesse whispered. "I didn't know what to think after seeing him in *An Affair by the Thames*. I love that movie, but he was so dastardly in it."

"Yeah. If I've learned anything it's that you never quite know what you're going to get with Ethan Bradley. Have Reese and Toby shown up yet?"

"Reese, yes," she said, pointing down to the orchestra pit, where he was chatting with Dwayne and the other folks in the band. "Toby texted me and said they uploaded the final draft of the book to the editor last night—well, early this morning—and that him and Spencer would be over a little later."

"Wonderful. Let's just hope Toby doesn't go on walkabout again."

"Arthur! What's got into you?"

He leaned forward and rested his forearms on the seat in front of him. "Besides my newest pseudo-client showing up unannounced, my folks left a message to tell me they're coming to town this week."

Bernard and Ella Frye had an uncanny knack for letting Arthur know at the last minute that they'd be dropping by and that they expected him to take them to dinner at their favorite local haunt, The Dresden. They'd invite all of their friends, and expect Arthur to handle transportation, reservations, and entertainment.

Arthur loved his parents to pieces, but their timing wasn't always great, and sometimes it felt a bit like they were just another pair of clients, not the people who'd brought him into this world. Bernard Frye was a famous director, and Ella Bowman-Frye had been a Hollywood starlet in the seventies and eighties. They were immensely talented, both of them, when it came to film. Not so much at raising a child, but then, that was tough when you were beloved by American society and globe-trotted for work. Whenever they'd been at home, however, Arthur had been the center of their universe.

Arthur had pursued a career in talent management after earning his BA and JD from USC as a way to be a part of their world in the capacity he knew best—caretaking. His parents bragged about him, which he supposed meant he was a success in their eyes. They'd retired a year ago and moved to Palm Springs, and now he rarely saw them unless they had business in LA. Then they'd put his management skills to the test.

"I take it that's not a party?"

"A party, yes, but not for me, it's not. I love them, don't get me wrong. I'm just not the actor/filmmaker son they anticipated, and I've had to live with that for...how old am I? Thirty-seven years?"

"Really? I thought you were my age. But Arthur, come on. You're a genius and one of the most competent men I've ever met. How could any parent not be proud as hell of you?"

Arthur dipped his head and smiled at Jesse. "The kind who are Hollywood royalty. It wasn't their fault their son turned out to be an ugly duckling."

Her jaw dropped open and she reached for him, starting to scold him, but her husband, rock star Danny Black, plopped into the seat next to her...with a maroon beret on his head and an unlit cigar between his lips.

"When am I going to see some action, people?"

Jesse pushed his shoulder and he cracked up.

"Oh come on, I want to be where the magic happens."

Jesse blew up her bangs. "Magic. Yeah. We could use some."

Danny plopped the beret on her head and leaned around her with his hand out for Arthur to shake. "What's up, Art? How's business?"

Arthur shook his hand and then fell back in his seat. He rubbed his face, pulling it downward. "Aging me rapidly."

Danny barked out another laugh and pulled Jesse to him for a kiss. "Look, I just stopped by to drop off Jane. She and Bailey are going to study when he has a break. That's what she says, anyway. I'm a little concerned but I'm trying to be one of those enlightened dads."

Arthur frowned. "She didn't go to school?"

He shook his head. "Winter break. All of her friends went skiing, she didn't want to go. Said she wanted to hang out around the theater." Danny shrugged. "I guess she kind of digs this scene. Or maybe she digs Bailey." He frowned at that and crossed his arms over his chest. "Maybe I should stick around and supervise."

Jesse rolled her eyes. "It's fine, Danny. Don't you guys have rehearsals?"

Danny was the lead singer of the multi-platinum hard rock band Blackened, which happened to be managed by Arthur's best friend Patricia. Hollywood really was a small world.

Danny sighed. "I guess. Anyway, I wanted to see if you guys needed anything before I take off."

Jesse shook her head. "I'm good. Arthur?"

He blew out a breath. "Actually, you need a roadie? I need to do something with *him*," he said, tilting his head. He turned to glance back, and Ethan was watching them with an eager smile, like the kid hoping to get chosen for the kickball team.

"Hey, I recognize that guy," Danny said.

"You do," Jesse said in a conspiratorial whisper. "Jane made us watch *Take My Hand* about a thousand times when it came out."

"No way! Ethan Bradley? Holy shit. What's he doing here?"

Arthur groaned, and that earned him a smack from Jesse. "Arthur! It's kind of a long story, babe, I'll fill you in later. Right now, I need to call an end to this break and get them moving again."

Jesse stood and Danny took her in his arms, dipping her low and then kissing her neck until she squealed.

Arthur sighed. *Love. Ain't it grand?* Everyone seemed to have found it lately. He couldn't get away from lovebirds. Reese and Jude, Toby and Spencer, then add in Jesse and Danny...Arthur was surrounded. And on the outside looking in. Like with everything. He was good enough to have around to take care of everyone, but apparently not to date.

Ugh, why all this self-loathing? That wasn't his usual M.O.

"Woman, you have to let me get to work, damn," he said as he kept kissing Jesse. She finally got loose from him, and she shook her head as she waved and blew him a kiss before heading down the aisle to the stage.

Danny sucked in a breath and pressed a hand to his chest. "I am one lucky son of a bitch." He turned and smiled at Arthur. "You take care of her for me, will ya? Don't let her work too hard? She's only just getting better from that nasty flare-up of her rheumatoid arthritis. I can't have her sick like that, you feel me?"

Arthur nodded. "Of course. I'll keep her hydrated and sitting down as much as possible."

Danny patted his shoulder. "Good. It's scary, you know? When you love someone like that. You want them to do what makes them happy, and yet you know it's not always good for them."

"I'm sorry, Danny. I'll do the best I can."

Danny squeezed his shoulder. They watched Jesse wrangle the dancers, and Arthur felt Danny's pain. Jesse was an incredible dancer. It wasn't fair that she couldn't perform anymore due to her illness, but to see the joy she had working on this show was infectious.

"Hey, Daddy? Can I have your keys? I need to grab my guitar out of the trunk."

Danny handed the keys to Jane and patted her on the head, which did not go over well with his sixteen-year-old daughter. She batted his hands away and took off at a jog for the outside of the theater.

"Excuse me, Mr. Frye?"

He turned to find Ethan had moved to the row behind him. He was smiling nervously.

Arthur had left a message for his assistant Audra to get to work on finding something for him, but hadn't heard anything yet. He didn't have high hopes that she'd find anything immediately. But he'd woken up this morning determined to be less of a jerk, so he put on his most pleasant face and answered him. "Hey, Ethan."

"Sorry to interrupt, I just wondered if you knew whether or not they need any help with anything? I'm not real good at taking up space."

"Oh, Ethan, you know what?" Jesse came trotting back up the aisle. "I wondered if you might give me some notes for the actors on this run-through? Would you mind?"

SEVEN

E ^than

Ethan gave a relieved sigh. He hadn't wanted to intrude, only, A. he was *dying* to meet Danny Black; but more importantly, B. he'd noticed a few things while he was watching their first run-through and he thought he'd try to be useful.

"That's actually a good idea. Ethan's got a lot of stage experience. He could probably give you some good notes," Arthur said.

Ethan felt his cheeks flush. It was the first truly nice thing Arthur had said to him since they'd met.

That wasn't true. He recalled Arthur complimenting his performance in *Ruby in Red Plaid*, but it wasn't said directly to him. It was in an interview with *Broadway Magazine*.

"Ethan Bradley as Randy in the show embodies every young person with hopes and dreams in Los Angeles. You can't not *root for them to come to fruition. He's such a passionate performer, so compelling, you'll believe in his character's journey."*

It was obvious he didn't feel the same about real-life Ethan.

Arthur stood and gestured for Ethan to take his seat. "Here, you take this seat next to Jesse. My dear, can I get you some water?" he asked of Jesse, giving Danny a knowing look.

"I've got water, thank you, but I'd love some pork rinds and a big giant Coke." She gave Danny a sneery smile as she sat down.

He grimaced and held a hand to his stomach. "Oh, God. No. I swear sometimes I think I married a frat boy."

Arthur cracked up, and Ethan felt a little relieved. The man could actually laugh, and he was so much more relaxed today than yesterday. Maybe Ethan hadn't made things quite so bad.

"It's a good thing you aren't *my* client, Danny. I'd do just about anything for your wife. If she wanted to dip French fries in her milkshake while eating crackers and sardines, I'd get it for her."

Jesse burst out laughing and kissed him on the cheek, turning his ruddy cheeks redder. He kind of reminded Ethan of Prince Harry, with his boyish good looks and his barely tamed red hair that was perhaps a few shades darker and thicker than his royal doppelganger. And with those smart wire-rimmed glasses, Arthur managed to pull off sophistication and innocence at the same time. It was sexy as hell.

"Oh, come on, we ginger brothers need to stick together, Art."

Arthur rolled his eyes and planted his hands on his hips. "You can at least pass for blond, man. Bet no one called you Carrot Top in school."

Danny lifted the corner of a lip. "If they did, I kicked their asses and shut them up. There's a reason I got kicked out of school at fifteen and ended up on the streets of LA."

Ethan's eyes bugged out. "Really? You?"

And then he wanted to die. Danny being a homeless kid was nothing like Ethan being a twentysomething has-been with no place to go.

Danny laughed. "I guess it's a good thing, too. I'd never have met my beautiful wife if it hadn't been for my wayward youth."

He bent down to kiss her as a third redhead joined the group.

"Here's your keys, Da—" She froze and her eyes went wide.

"Janey," he said, taking the keys. "Have you met Ethan Bradley yet?"

She shook her head and lost her cool for just a second, long enough for Ethan to worry his presence was going to be a problem. Then she stuck out her hand.

"Jane Black. It's nice to meet you."

She was so poised for a teenager. Ethan couldn't have pulled that off. His palms were sweaty just being five feet from a rock star like Danny Black. He took her hand and shook it.

"Nice to meet you, too." Ethan let go and rubbed his hands on his thighs. He sat down with two seats between him and Jesse, not wanting to be considered inappropriate. But no, Jesse grabbed his hand and pulled him over.

"No, sit here. I don't want Reese to yell at me if I'm talking too loud. Sometimes I forget my teacher voice."

Ethan felt his cheeks get hot, and he looked to Arthur to see his reaction. He didn't want to intrude or be a pest—

"How about you, Ethan? Can I get you anything?"

He stared at Arthur for a long moment, too long, before he cleared his throat.

"I'm okay, thank you." He could have used some water, for sure, but he didn't dare ask Arthur to go out of his way for him. He could tell he was treading on thin ice with the intimidating man.

Arthur patted Jesse's shoulder. "I'm just going to check in with Reese before they get started again. Ethan, as soon as I hear something from my assistant, I'll let you know."

Jesse, Danny, and Jane all looked at him, and all he could do was smile sheepishly.

"Thank you. I appreciate it."

Arthur nodded, shoved his hands in his pockets and strolled with purpose toward the orchestra pit. Ethan tried not to notice how that action pulled the material tight across Arthur's backside. The guy was just so put together. His suits all fit him just right, as though they'd been lovingly tailored to hug his every sharp edge and rounded curve.

Ethan had never been a clothes horse. He wore whatever he had. Right now, he was surviving with two pairs of jeans the costume department had given him from his films and a few shirts. He'd wear those or plain t-shirts. He only had two pairs of slacks and dress shirts left, and everything he had needed to go to the cleaners. He wondered if there was one nearby. How much would it cost to get them done? Would it be cheaper to wash the stuff and iron it himself?

"Ethan?"

Jesse had been talking to him and, like a dolt, he'd been staring after Arthur.

"I'm sorry."

She smiled at him and then glanced in Arthur's direction. "I wanted to ask you what shows you've done besides *Ruby*?"

"Oh," he said. "Well, I did some local theater in Iowa, then in Chicago during college, and then I went to New York when my agent thought I was ready. I made my Broadway debut in *Hands On A Hardbody—*"

Danny coughed. "Excuse me? Did you just... That doesn't sound like a Broadway show I've ever heard of."

Jesse rolled her eyes. "It's about a truck, Danny. Don't be gross."

He shrugged. "What do I know? I've never even been to Broadway."

"Oh, well, it was a pretty awesome show. Trey Anastasio wrote the music for it. The play is about a real-life group of people in Texas competing to win a Nissan truck. They had to stand around with their hand on it, and whoever did the longest won. The music was super fun and the cast was great. After I had a supporting role in *Hands*, I auditioned for the lead in *Ruby in Red Plaid* and I got it. That changed everything for me."

"And then you did the movies, right?" Jesse asked. Jane pushed past her father and sank into the seat on the other side of Jesse, curiosity on her young face.

"Yeah," he said, clearing his throat. "I did two films. Then they brought *Ruby* to London." And he really didn't want to talk anymore. Thankfully, Reese signaled from the pit that they were about to start and the dancers took their places.

"Oh my God," Jane said. "I'm so excited to see the whole thing! Bailey was so nervous for today."

"I'm gonna run, guys." Danny kissed his women and ran off just as the house lights went to black.

Jesse leaned over toward Ethan and whispered, "*Boy* is Bailey's first show ever. He actually cut school to come for the audition. Reese and

Jude had just gotten back together and Bailey had just moved in with them, so he'd heard all about the musical. It was a big mess, but his parents agreed to let me homeschool him until the show is over. Our other lead, Sean, has only done high school shows and one community college performance. They're phenomenal dancers, but I don't know. Something's missing. Can you help?"

Ethan nodded and straightened in his seat. "I'll do whatever I can, yeah."

Jesse smiled and patted his knee just as the music started up.

Ethan loved the swing vibe, loved watching Reese on the piano on the corner of the stage. He'd gathered that the dancers wouldn't be singing, that instead Reese, a bass player named Dwayne that Ethan recognized from *Ruby*, and a drummer would be set up on the side stage and would be performing the songs. He'd always loved Reese's voice, and the Dwayne guy sang great, but he couldn't help but wonder where Toby was, why he wasn't in the show. He didn't want to ask too many questions and figured he'd just see what was what.

The show began with the Boy getting fired from his job washing dishes and wandering the streets of Las Vegas in what appeared to be the early 1960s, until he found himself in front of the Firelight Lounge. He leaned against the street sign all forlorn-like, and he's hanging his head just as a group of guys burst out of the club nearby. They all give each other shit, make catcalls at women walking by, and end up following a group of girls off, but one member of the group, Bailey's character, sees the Boy and pretends to be tired. He waits until the others leave and then he makes his move. He's drawn in by the Boy's red hair...

And Ethan clearly saw the problem.

"Bailey has never acted before, huh?" he whispered to Jesse.

She shook her head without looking. "No. And he nails the dance parts, but he's not...*going for it* with Sean. It's like he's intimidated, but he's supposed to be the one who's the pursuer."

"Right. Okay." Ethan kept watching as they went from meeting on the street corner to going for coffee, then Bailey gets the Boy a job at the club where he plays with his band, and the two of them make eyes at each other across the room. But then Bailey ends up sitting with a young woman and her family while eating dinner, and the Boy is their server. He spills water on another customer and he gets shouted at by the manager. Bailey consoles him, and they go to Bailey's room.

The pivotal scene where the seduction takes place was so well choreographed, Ethan forgot to breathe. At that point, there was a break where the band played, and Ethan leaned over to Jesse.

"Wow. That scene was...you really...*wow*. And they pull it off, but there's just..."

"*Right*? They just need..."

"Yeah." He blew out a breath. The scene was so moving, it took Ethan back to the first time he'd had to be intimate with an actor onstage. It had been his co-star Emily, in *Ruby*, and while they'd been friends, he was not attracted to her in any way. It had been a true test of his acting ability to create the chemistry needed to play the role of the cool young guy showing up in LA with his band to make it big and meeting a cool young chick who was way more worldly than him but hadn't made it yet. The two of them bond over their desire to be stars, and she stands by him as his confidant while he gets his world rocked, first by an older woman manager, then a rock star he idolized. When he decides he really wants Ruby, she's slipped through his fingertips and he's got to fight to win her back.

Ethan had been very much like Randy in that show. He'd thought he was hot shit after doing *Hardbody* but then when he won the lead in *Ruby*, the *other* offers came in. He'd been a little careless with people's feelings in the beginning, and his life mirrored Randy's a little too closely. He let the popularity go to his head and made some bad choices.

The music cut off, and Reese proceeded to have a heated discussion with the musicians.

"Well, we made it through once and a half," Jesse said with a sigh. "I guess that's decent. It's lunchtime anyway. Let me go check with Clora and see if the food's here yet. Would you excuse me?"

Ethan nodded to her, and then he could feel Jane watching him.

"Not more drama," she said. "I get really tired of hearing adults complain about how dramatic teenagers are all the time. Being around this group?" She made an explosion sound with her mouth and an accompanying hand gesture.

"Yeah, I think it goes along with the whole theater thing. Most people I know who are involved in theater in any way have some kind of drama." Ethan didn't want to admit that he certainly had his share, but then she might have suspected something if she was privy to why he was there.

"Hey, Jane. Ethan. Jane, do you want to have lunch outside? I need to get out of here for a bit." Bailey was a sweaty mess but his smile was genuine.

Ethan remembered being so excited about being in *Hardbody* that he couldn't sleep most nights. He'd lie in bed thinking about what he'd learned that day, what he'd learn the next day. He went over his lines in his head and sang the songs until he knew them forward and backward.

Bailey didn't have lines, nor would he be singing, but he did have to act, and that was what Ethan realized he could help with. He needed to come up with the best way to broach the subject so as not to negatively impact the kid, but he knew he could help him.

"Let's go grab some food," Jane said. She stood, grabbed her guitar case, stepped into the aisle and then turned to frown at Ethan. "Aren't you eating?"

Ethan swallowed with a dry mouth. "I'm not part of the cast—"

Jane shrugged. "Neither am I. Come on, there's always plenty. You're here with Arthur anyway, right?"

"Not technically," he said under his breath, but he stood. "I'm just here—"

"Come on," Bailey said, a knowing look on his face. *Awesome.* His brother or Reese probably told him why Ethan was there. "I wanted to ask you some questions if you have time."

Ethan breathed a sigh of relief. Hopefully Bailey would ask, so Ethan wouldn't have to trounce on his developing ego.

"Sure. I could use some water," he said. But he didn't want to take food that didn't belong to him. Cosmo hadn't been entirely right about the quality of the waffles, but Ethan had enjoyed the continental breakfast all the same. He'd eaten two servings and then grabbed a couple of apples and a granola bar for later, which he had in his coat pocket.

He followed the teenagers down the aisle toward the stage and through a doorway that led to the bowels of the theater. Raucous laughter came from the green room, where tables were set up with catering.

"Oh, yum, tacos! These are so good," Bailey said, grabbing a plate overflowing with taco fixings. Jane grabbed one too, and they both took cans of soda.

"Ethan, help yourself," Jesse called out.

Ethan cringed as several people looked around to see who she was talking to. Then the murmurs started, the whispered voices.

"Hey," Reese said, coming over and patting his shoulder. "What did you think so far?"

Ethan beamed. "The music is brilliant, Reese. And the choreography is stunning. Congratulations."

Reese smiled and patted his shoulder twice more. "Thanks," he said as he gazed around the room, distractedly. "No Toby yet, huh, Jesse?"

She shook her head. "I didn't see him, and I left my phone up in the seats."

Reese pulled out his phone and swore when he found no messages. "Hopefully he makes it after lunch." He walked away tapping out a message to someone on his phone, and Jesse leaned in toward Ethan.

"Please eat, Ethan. I hate to see the food go to waste."

"Thank you," he said. He helped himself to a plate and a bottle of water and then joined Jane and Bailey.

"You guys going outside?" Jesse asked them.

"Yeah, we'll be out back," Bailey said.

Sean walked past him with a nod, but Bailey only gave him a blank look and then went back to speaking to Jesse.

"Okay. Take until one and then we'll regroup to start up again. I want to do the second half and at least one more run-through today."

Bailey's jaw ticked but he smiled. "Yes, ma'am."

Jesse rolled her eyes and then flicked a hand at them. She went to join Reese and Dwayne, and Ethan felt torn. Should he give Bailey notes without telling her first?

He followed the kids outside and the bright sun caught him off guard. He'd spent so long in London, the sun seemed foreign, making this whole experience seem unreal.

Jane and Bailey sat on the back steps, so Ethan joined them and rubbed at his eyes.

"I have a million questions for you," Bailey said, "but I'll let you eat first."

Ethan barked out a laugh. "It's fine. Ask away."

"Okay," Bailey said, taking a huge bite of taco. Which meant he then had to hold up a finger so he could finish chewing. Jane laughed hysterically and nearly choked on her food.

"Ready when you are," Ethan said. Bailey continued to chew and make faces before he finally swallowed.

"I always do that," he said. "Take a bite when I have something to say and then forget what I was going to say. But now I remember. How do you, like, know how to act? I mean, I get the whole 'go there, do this move, you're sad, you're angry, okay now you're angry but you're pretending to be okay but you're really not, and then you'...you know what I mean?"

Ethan chuckled and set down his plate. He wanted to savor those tacos. "First of all, have you ever taken any acting classes?"

Bailey shook his head. "No way. And the only dancing I've ever done was color guard at school. I have no idea why they even picked me."

"They picked you because you're amazing," Jane said, smiling at him. "Jesse says all the time what a natural you are, that she hardly has to correct you because you pick things up right the first time."

Bailey blushed and pushed his hair out of his face. "She's had to show me things more than once."

Jane elbowed him, and he laughed.

"You're doing incredibly well for not having any training. Honestly, acting is mostly intuitive. I think some people have extra intuition in that area, and that makes them predisposed to having the ability to act. Some actors are also just super in tune with their emotions, and they can call on that whenever they need to for a scene. The truth is, I've taken a bunch of classes and workshops, but I learned the most just from working with others and actually being onstage. And from having brilliant directors."

"Well, we don't really have a director for this show besides Jesse and

Reese—"

"And Reese is a great director," Ethan said. "He tells you how you should feel in each scene, how the *music* is supposed to feel, and that's all you really need for his work."

Bailey frowned. "I mean, I guess. I know what's happening in the scenes, but I don't know how to *feel*."

Ethan breathed a sigh of relief. That was exactly what he was going to talk to Jesse about. The kid was just confused.

"That's the first step," he said with a laugh. "Let me ask you this... have you ever been in love, Bailey?"

He blushed again, and his eyes darted toward Jane before he spoke. *Interesting.*

"I don't know. I'm only seventeen."

Ethan laughed. Oh, he'd had plenty of crushes by seventeen but he still hadn't truly been in love. He could fake it onstage, though. He knew that he was in love with the *idea* of being in love.

"Perfect. What do you think being in love feels like?"

He glanced at Jane again, and she shrugged. "What are you looking at me for? I've never been in love either. The only thing I know of it is from watching Dad and Jesse." She stuck a finger up to her mouth and stuck her tongue out like she was making herself puke, and Ethan laughed.

"Yeah, being around lovebirds can be tough."

"My brother and Reese are usually so busy with Mr. Matheson at home that they don't really show much, but there are the quiet moments where, like, Reese pulls Jude in and kisses his forehead, or Mr. Matheson will be having a bad day and Jude will give a small smile across the room to Reese. My parents are like that, like a team. They do everything together; cook, clean, take us places. That's how I see love. Like teamwork."

Jane groaned. "That's better than googly eyes, making out on the couch, flowers, and writing songs. Four years, that's all I've seen with no signs of letting up."

She may have been complaining, but it was half-hearted. It was more...admiration and envy than teenage disgust.

"Okay. Let's talk shop."

EIGHT

Arthur had left the theater briefly to run to his office, check in with Audra, and make a few phone calls. He definitely was motivated to get Ethan some work and get him the hell away from the production of *Boy*. Reese was at his wits' end worrying about everything, Jesse's health was fragile, and who knew what Toby's reaction would be to Ethan's arrival.

"Hey," she said when he arrived. "I told you I'd call you. You didn't have to come all the way over here."

He kissed Audra's cheek. "Please tell me you have some news."

She rolled her eyes. "Touchy this morning. What's the deal with this guy? Half the people I called practically hung up when I mentioned his name. The other half were ready to sell their firstborns for a meeting."

Arthur sighed and rested his hands on his hips. "Let me guess, the ones ready to sell were not the most upstanding?"

She made a face that confirmed his suspicions. "Not all of them? There are a few promising leads."

Arthur had worried that Ethan would be in demand for folks looking to capitalize on his notoriety and would be avoided by those with so-called reputable projects. He had to spin this just right...or get Audra to do it. Which he should. He should let her handle it all.

"Well, we'll keep looking. Is Patricia in?"

Audra nodded. "She is. She got flowers. She was arguing on the phone. She came storming out, growling, and when she went back in there, she shut the blinds."

Arthur dropped his hands and let his shoulders hunch. "Ah," he said, pulling himself up to his full height. "I'm going in."

Audra laughed and waved as she picked up her ringing phone.

Arthur strolled across the office space he shared with Patricia and four other agents. They each had their own assistants in a common workspace and the enclosed offices were around the outside of the space. Patricia's was across from his. After the managing partners, they were the senior members of the Slade Management team, outlasting some of their close friends.

There'd been Maggie Boudreaux Stone, who was a fantastic manager, a real star catcher. She'd been on track to go far...but then she married another agent at their firm, Thomas Stone, who turned out to be a real scumbag. He was fired after killing her in a single-car accident. No one had been sorry to see him go, and none of them had ever completely gotten over the loss of their teammate and friend.

Then there was Sherry Jordan, who broke Arthur's golden rule— don't date the talent. Well, she hadn't just *dated* the talent. She'd eloped with Marcus Lambert of metalcore band Maggie's Bones, after the band imploded. Now she managed Marcus's solo career as an independent operator and was still close with her friends at Slade. She was missed, but she certainly had her hands full.

And then there was Patricia, who Arthur assumed was growling because of her own dating dilemma.

"You busy?" he asked her as he knocked on her office door. She left it open a crack if she ever shut it at all. Patricia was a people person and one of his longest and bestest friends. They'd been pups together at Slade and she understood him better than anyone. Especially understood the purpose behind his rules.

"If by busy you mean irritated, frustrated, and annoyed? Yes, yes I am, Arthur. How are you?"

He fought a smile as he entered her office cautiously and took a seat, unsure whether or not he was going to be a shoulder to cry on or...a body for target practice.

"Well, since Audra hasn't found a way to make my current situation disappear, I'm right with you."

Some of her ire bled out and she gave him a sympathetic look. "Ethan is still here?"

"He showed up to rehearsals this morning, as directed. When I left, he was sitting with Jesse and she asked him for notes on the run-through." He pressed a hand to his forehead. "The show opens in two weeks, Patricia. What am I supposed to do with a tainted celebrity?"

Patricia sighed and came to sit in the chair next to him. "You could sympathize with him, for one. I don't understand why you're so angry with this guy. Sounds to me like all he did was flirt a little heavy-handedly—"

"And slept with Toby—"

"Which is entirely Toby's situation to deal with. Your dynamic duo are doing great. This musical is going to be great. I don't see how Ethan showing up is going to be a problem. Folks here aren't quite as engaged with the paparazzi shit as they are in England. That story barely made a blip over here."

Arthur sighed. "You're right. He just...I don't know. There's something about him. I'd just rather not have him here."

Patricia frowned. "Because?"

It was Arthur's turn to groan. "Because! I could see myself breaking my rule with him and it pisses me off."

Patricia covered her mouth with both hands before grabbing his forearm. "You *like* him!"

He frowned at her and ran a hand over his face. "I don't like him."

"But you do."

"But I don't."

"You don't."

"I can't."

"But you do."

"But I can't! I refuse." Arthur stood up to pace.

Patricia sat back in her chair. "You refuse? Oh, sweetheart. Refusing doesn't quite work. If it did, I wouldn't still be getting flowers from you-know-who."

Arthur rested his hands on his hips. Oh yeah, he knew who. "Speaking of, I dropped Ethan at you-know-who's hotel yesterday."

"That...could be bad. You do realize that you-know-who still throws the occasional parties where things get wild, right?"

Arthur threw up his hands. "As if that could make it worse? If I'd taken him to any of the upscale hotels, the paparazzi would be watching. If I'd taken him out of town, then I'd have to play chauffeur. And if I brought him to my place..."

Patricia pressed her lips together and gave him an evil smile. "You'd be tempted to break your rule."

"Yes! And I can't do that." Although now that he'd said it aloud, something relaxed inside his tightly-coiled conscience.

He'd admitted he was attracted to an actor to his best friend and the ground hadn't cracked beneath him and swallowed him whole. There'd been no lightning strike, no clap of thunder. No, just a warm sensation tingling in his heart where he wasn't used to such an occurrence.

Maybe it wasn't a terrible thing, to feel something for Ethan. Several images of Ethan's smile, his bright eyes, the cut of his jaw, even his freckles, flashed in Arthur's mind. The way his voice hitched when he'd called him Mr. Frye, so eager to please, so...adorable.

But no. He couldn't. Right?

He flopped down in the chair and they both leaned forward with their elbows on their knees and their chins in their hands.

"We can't, can we," she said, sounding just as conflicted as he was.

"We can't."

"Yeah, we shouldn't." That sounded less convincing.

"Oh, come on, Patricia. Are you really letting the flowers wear you down? It's been three years!"

"He's writing poems now, too. Really good ones."

Arthur groaned. While still smarting from the collapse of her marriage, Patricia made the snap decision to run off into the sunset with Jesse's former neighbor and Danny's protege, Cosmo Grammatica.

What was supposed to be scratching an itch turned into an obsession on Cosmo's part, and for the last three years, he'd been sending Patricia flowers, serenading her outside her window, and now...poetry? It sounded like he was wearing Patricia down.

"Not you, too. Can I not have one person in my life who isn't swayed by love?"

She actually giggled. "Oh, Arthur. Has it been so long since you've gotten that...*feeling*...over someone?"

"You're beginning to sound like you're going to break out in song."

"And what's so wrong with that? You and me, we've held out for so long, trying to be levelheaded. Don't you get tired of always doing the smart thing? The responsible thing?"

"Not until lately. Speaking of the responsible thing, did I mention my parents are coming this week?"

Her playful expression was gone. In its place was the business face that he counted on when his parents were coming.

"The usual? The Dresden? Need anything?"

"No, I've got it. I'm going to see if Danny will play."

"That's a good plan. Friday night?"

"Yeah."

"Want support?"

He shrugged. He should be able to do this on his own, but having Patricia there always made him feel better. "If you don't have anything better to do."

She stood up and moved back behind her desk. "I don't have anything scheduled and I'd love to see them."

"They'd love to see you, too. You can do no wrong in their eyes. Mine either, to be honest. Look, if you want to bring Cosmo..."

"I might. He wants to take me away for another weekend. Things are so much simpler when it's us away from the world." She frowned. "What about you? Seriously. How long has it been, Arthur? You haven't dated anyone since—"

"Yeah. Since Raul the chef. He thought I was too boring."

Patricia rolled her eyes. "What the hell does he know? He was so in love with himself that he didn't even pay attention to you, and his food sucked. It was too bad that schoolteacher didn't work out."

Arthur sniffed. "Clarke? He was sweet, but I started to feel like I was one of his third graders. When he cut up my steak at dinner, I just knew. I might be boring, but I am not helpless."

"Arthur, please. You are not boring, nor are you helpless. Are you particular? Yes. Are you structured? Sure—"

"I know. I ooze sex appeal, Patricia. You can say it."

She came from around her desk and gave him a big hug. "You deserve a special man, Arthur. He's out there. I just know it. You won't settle; you'll wait for the one man who shakes things up, shakes you to your core, and you'll know he's the right man."

"Dramatic much?"

She pulled back and mussed his hair. "Do you know how many thousands of dollars I spend to get my hair the color you wear so naturally?"

Arthur shrugged. Being a ginger was always easier for women, or at least that's what he'd told himself. "It makes you special," his blond mother had said. Sure, but being special when you're a star is one thing. When you're ordinary, it's better not to stand out.

"And you look fabulous, my dear. I've got to get back to the theater. Thank you, by the way, for arranging the ticket sales and all of the venue issues. I know the guys are doing their best to take care of everything, but without a true production staff, I'm worried we're going to drop the ball on something."

"No problem," she said. "I love the theater. I miss my days at UCLA in the theater department. I just didn't want to spend my entire adult life broke and on a diet."

Arthur burst out laughing. "Good point. Alright." He kissed her on the cheek. "Let me know if anything comes up."

He waved as he went out the door and into his own office. He checked his messages and straightened a few papers on his desk until he realized what he was doing.

He was avoiding being in Ethan's orbit.

Why was he letting this guy get to him? He'd been around beautiful people all of his life. He knew better than to think of them as anything other than business.

It was time to face the music—musical.

His cell phone buzzed.

"Mother, hello. How are you?"

"Darling, I just wanted to make sure you had all of the arrangements for this weekend?"

Hi, I'm fine. It's nice to hear from you. "I've got The Dresden's party room booked and I'm working on entertainment—"

"And you'll arrange for that cake from your friend, won't you? From Harvey?"

Work is great, Mom. Thanks for asking. It was easier for Arthur if he just filled in the gaps of his mother's conversations. "I will check in with Harvey, yes, but this is short notice for her."

"Oh, but she's so good. I really hope she can do it."

Yeah, I'm actually quite busy with the new show. "I'll call her today."

"Excellent. And you've reserved our bungalow?"

In between running errands and dealing with the bomb that has been dropped in my lap, sure I've... Shit. He hadn't called The Beverly Hills Hotel yet. "I'll get on that, Mom. I'm sorry, I've been very busy with the show—"

"You have assistants for that sort of thing, don't you, Arthur?"

He crushed his fist against his forehead for making that slip. *I do, but I have my hands full...* "Are you driving in or do you need me to arrange a pickup from the airport?"

"No. Your father wants to drive the Alfa Romeo out."

Arthur stood up straighter. "*What?* He never drives that car, especially not in LA. Are you going to be comfortable in it for the drive?" This was going to be a disaster. His mother would complain, his father's gout would act up or something...

"It'll be fine, dear. Just make sure the other arrangements are made, would you? I want this to be a peaceful weekend for your father. You are a dear! Looking forward to seeing you. Goodbye!"

Ella hung up before he could say goodbye. Yes, she was probably busy and didn't mean to be rude, but honestly, Arthur should expect this treatment by now.

He took a moment to breathe and then went back to see Audra. "I have one more favor to ask," he said as she hung up the phone.

Audra Diaz always gave him a cheerful smile, even when he knew he was asking a lot of her. She was a fellow graduate of USC and had strong ties to the Latine community in Los Angeles. She was a go-getter, organized beyond belief, and never shied away from a challenge. He was damn lucky to have her.

"Sure thing. Still working on Ethan."

Arthur shook his head. "Believe it or not, I have bigger issues. Can you call The Beverly Hills Hotel and see if the bungalow my parents love is available this weekend? They're coming into town and I need—"

"Already on it," she said, picking up the phone. "And dinner on Saturday at the Polo Lounge, correct?" Audra was truly a godsend. She'd make a great manager, and soon he'd talk to Patricia and the board about promoting her. She was more than ready to take on her own clients. Until then, Arthur would breathe a little easier knowing she had his back.

"You're a peach," he said, kissing her cheek. He left the office, walking through the atrium and out to the parking lot to his Volvo. For once, he didn't break any land speed records. He took his time, stopping at every yellow light, pissing off the hurried drivers behind him, all because he wasn't ready to face the music. Instead, he hid out as long as he could in his safe car listening to The Plimsouls' "Oldest Story in the World" and bopping his head along.

In fact, he was still sitting in his car, tapping his fingers along to the music on his steering wheel, when the car's sound system shut off. Strangely, he still heard music, though. He looked around and gripped the steering wheel hard.

"No no no no...this is not happening."

The music drifting in through his cracked window came from none other than his biggest problem.

Ethan Bradley.

Playing a guitar and singing.

To an audience on the corner of Hollywood Boulevard and Argyle.

NINE

E^{than}

"Ruby, baby, it's your time to shine. Come home with me. Say you'll be mine. Cuz tomorrow, baby, you never know, where that road will take us, where we'll go."

The guitar strings felt so good under Ethan's fingers. He was a little rusty, but he felt invigorated to be playing, singing, and just plain *living!* He'd thought maybe he could show Bailey what it was like to emote while performing a song, and Jane had suggested he do a number from *Ruby* as an example.

Jane Black sang Ruby's part and it was just like old times, but with a much younger co-star who happened to be the teenage daughter of rock star Danny Black, one of Ethan's favorites. She had a fantastic voice, and she'd let him play her insanely cool guitar. Ethan was flying high.

"You're right. It may be my time to shine. So why would I go with you, not leave you behind? Cuz tomorrow, baby, I'll be a star, and I'll forget you, wherever you are."

They harmonized on the chorus while Bailey kept the beat by slapping his thigh. They'd moved around to the side of the theater because it was chilly in the shade, and that meant they were now within view of folks on Hollywood Boulevard. It was a little weird, but Ethan was just so happy to be playing guitar again, he was barely aware of his surroundings.

"Whatever's out there, wherever we stay, I'll always remember, our time in LA,

"Where nobodies line every corner every day."

Jane let the final note carry while Ethan played the last few bars, ending with flourish.

"Wooo!" Bailey jumped up and was clapping and whistling for them.

A couple walked by and dropped some change in Jane's open guitar case, and Ethan waved as Jane and Bailey burst out laughing.

"Uh, thanks?" Ethan called after them.

"That was really cool," she said. "I don't know if I'm any good as an actress, but I sure love this kind of music."

"You could totally do theater, Jane. You can sing your ass off, and you've had lots of dance lessons," Bailey said, nodding. "She's been helping me with some of the choreography. Especially the tap. I've never tap danced before."

"Well you certainly cover it up well," Ethan said. "You dance great."

"Thanks," Bailey said, rubbing his neck. "I don't know, though. I feel like there are parts that are really serious and we're just going through the motions, you know? And it's kind of awkward, you know—"

"The hands-on scenes?" Now they were getting to Jesse's concern. He was glad Bailey had brought it up.

"*Right.* Yeah. Sean keeps to himself during rehearsals, and when I ask him what he thinks, how we could maybe make it stronger, he just shrugs and says, 'It'll be fine. Jesse will tell us what to do.' But the show is in two weeks, and I want to do good for Reese and Toby. They have a lot riding on this."

Ethan had gathered that the two chose LA for their opening for personal reasons, but they hoped that this limited run was the first stop on their way back to Broadway.

"I can't help you with the tap, Bailey, but if you want any notes, or want to go over any of the scenes with me, I'm happy to help. I remember being so nervous the first time I had to touch my co-star."

Bailey swallowed and nodded. "Yeah, like, it's not like I don't want to touch him." His eyes bugged out. "Wait, that sounds..."

He glanced at Jane, and she had her lips pressed together and her eyebrows raised as if she were trying not to laugh.

"There are two levels to the scene, the actual physical touch, and then there's the emotional impact the scene is supposed to be portraying. If that makes sense. Actually, have you worked with an intimacy coordinator?"

Bailey shook his head, and Ethan thought, perhaps, this would be a great suggestion for Jesse.

"It would be helpful for both of you."

"Did you have one for *Ruby*?" Jane asked.

He shook his head. "No, not until I worked on my first film. It was super helpful though." He snorted. "I was so nervous in *Ruby*. Especially doing the scenes live. Thankfully they weren't super involved, but singing while snuggling was challenging."

Jane laughed. "It always seems so natural watching actors, but like, I've heard how loud my dad sings. I can't imagine being that close to his mouth while he's belting out a song. Oh! Speaking of which, can you play that one song from *Ruby*, the one when they kiss for the first time."

Ethan checked the tuning on the guitar once more. "Wow, it's been so long since I sang these songs." And so much had happened. He'd taken off like a rocket and then crashed...whether he'd burned or not was still to be determined. He started to play the song, and Bailey and Jane swayed together on the step.

"What would it be like?
Would it feel the same?
When you love someone
It's no longer a game
I thought I loved him
But the more I'm with herrrrrrr

The more I'm surrrrrre
It's gonna be everything
She's come to be my everything
I can feel her, smell her,
Want to taste her
Will she feel the saaaame?"

He glanced around and blushed when he noticed that people had stopped on both sides of the street to watch. He smiled bashfully and continued the song.

"I thought that it felt right
When it was him
I wanted to be close
I wanted to kiss him
Again and again
But he doesn't make me
Feel like I do
When I'm with herrrrrrr
This time I'm surrrrrrre
It's gonna be everything
Will she be my everything
Want to feel her, smell her,
Long to taste her
Does she feel the saaaame?"

Ethan opened his eyes and continued strumming, smiling at the latest addition to the audience. He moved to stand in front of Arthur and kept smiling as he sang the chorus once more. He wanted to make him smile, wanted to get some sort of reaction other than disgust out of him. He'd been told that his voice, his singing, made people happy. It used to make his parents happy. It was the only way he knew how.

He finished the song, still staring at Arthur as people whooped and hollered, all of them dropping money in the guitar case. Okay, that part was weird, but man, he felt great. He—

"Happy?" Arthur did not appear to be happy. He spoke in a low voice. "At least half of those people just posted your impromptu concert on social media. I'd think by now you'd learn to be more careful about what you do in public."

Ethan never wanted to get used to the sick feeling he got when he thought about those pictures, about how people looked at him and whispered when he went into a pub, or when he's shown up on set to film his third film, only to have them send him packing, saying he was damaged goods.

Jane and Bailey were counting the money and giggling, so Ethan set the guitar in the case and stepped back, rubbing his hands on his jeans.

"I'm sorry," he said, but Arthur's jaw twitched and he gestured for them to go inside. He stormed in around back of the theater and Ethan watched his retreating back with a sense of doom.

"Oh man, I'm sorry, Ethan," Jane said, but he waved her off.

"It was fun. Thanks for letting me play your guitar."

"Oh, there you are," Jesse said as they came in. "I was just coming to find you, Bailey. Let's have a little group huddle and then start the second act."

Bailey's eyes darted to Ethan before he nodded and then trotted off toward the stage so he could get warmed up.

Arthur was talking to Reese and...Toby. He'd apparently arrived while they were outside. But instead of being excited to see him again, Ethan just felt sick. Especially when the three of them seemed to be having a heated exchange.

"Hey, Jesse," a man said as he approached where they stood in the middle of the seats.

"Spencer, hi," she said, accepting his embrace and kissing his cheek. "I'm glad you're here. Have you met Ethan Bradley?"

The man turned a kind smile on Ethan and held out a hand. "Spencer Hart," he said as they shook. "Sometime dance stand-in, significant other of the *other* force of nature around here. Oh, and therapist to angsty teens, at your service."

Ethan was happy for Toby—he desperately needed someone, that was for sure. The guy had some serious issues, though Ethan had been flattered at the time that Toby had paid attention to him. Jude had been understanding about Ethan being there, but would Spencer if he realized who Ethan was? Seeing as Ethan had actually had sex with Toby? This could add even more stress to their show.

He felt himself pulling away, taking a step back, wishing he could disappear.

But Jesse grabbed for his arm as she snorted at Spencer's words.

"I'm surrounded by angsty teens, I tell you. I even married an overgrown angsty rock star! Thank goodness for your particular skill set and calm demeanor."

Spencer laughed. "I guess I've missed some fireworks?" he asked, and then his eyes bugged out. "Wait! You're *the* Ethan Bradley! I loved you in *Hands on a Hardbody*. I saw it in New York when I was there for a conference. What a fun show." He shook Ethan's hand again enthusiastically.

"Actually, speaking of fireworks," Jesse said. "I wanted to ask your opinion. You too, Ethan. I want you guys to watch this next part with me." She shooed them over to the spot she'd been camped out in and Jane approached, picking up her backpack.

"I'm going to go work on my homework in the office, in case anyone asks. I think I need a break from all this testosterone." She flung her long red hair over her shoulder and strolled up the aisle.

"Well," Spencer began, his smile nervous when he saw the hands flailing in the conversation going on below them. "I wonder what that's about?"

Ethan tried to sink into the chair, grateful it was semi-dark.

"Whatever it is, we don't have time for it. Hey everyone? Let's get back to work. I want to see Act Two in its entirety. Sean? Bailey? You ready?"

They both nodded and took their positions.

Reese held up his hands and turned to trot over to his spot onstage.

Toby and Arthur had a few more words before they both turned and approached them.

"Holy Mary, mother of the unholy ghost. Ethan Bradley, whatever are you doing here?"

Ethan hoped Toby was more shocked than disturbed, so he decided to answer that way.

"Surprise?" He shrugged. "I, uh, I'm between gigs, and I decided to come see what you and Reese were up to." He offered his most winning smile, and Toby did that thing where he tried not to look aghast.

"Ethan is going to help me with notes for the dancers," Jesse said to Toby in that way you try to talk someone into acting normal again.

"Riiiight," he said as he took the seat next to Spencer. Arthur sat on Toby's other side, looking cautiously between Toby and Ethan.

Ethan stared straight ahead from the other side of Jesse, wishing he were anyplace else.

TEN

Arthur

Sitting in the same row with Toby, Spencer, and Ethan was even more tense than arriving at Reese's house that morning to find Ethan there. Toby was balancing on a fine edge with his mental health and sobriety, and Spencer had a huge job holding him steady. Thankfully, the even-keeled guy didn't seem to mind. Arthur had no idea if Spencer knew all about Toby's past, but since Toby was flagrantly open about his flaws, he was pretty sure Spencer at least had an inkling of what he'd gotten himself into.

Spencer took Toby's hand and smiled at him like the sun rose and set in Toby's eyes. It was ridiculous how quickly Arthur's closest friends —had fallen gobsmackedly in love with the two most patient men on the planet.

It was also awesome.

And Arthur knew he should first and foremost be happy for his friends, not sitting here in the dark feeling envious of their joy...and irritated with the man whose presence could harm that joy. Whose presence was threatening to upset Arthur's carefully constructed...celibacy? Yeah, that's what it was. Arthur had chosen to take himself out of the dating pool after a lackluster effort and he hadn't thought twice about it until Ethan came waltzing in looking like a tarnished fallen angel, a bit worse for wear.

Toby had been shocked to see Ethan, but mostly he was worried Spencer would be upset. Reese told him to get his head out of his ass.

"Spencer is the most mature of all of us," he'd said. Spencer knew exactly who he'd gotten involved with.

"But, like, he knows about my past, but like, not *everyone* in my past, you know?"

"Come on," Reese said. "Do you really think it matters? I don't get the sense at all that Ethan is here for any other reason than he had no place else to go." He put his hands on his hips and sighed. "He's in rough shape, man. And after he acted his ass off for us, we can help him out, you know? Look, we both know what it's like to have folks turn their backs on us, don't we?"

There was a lot that passed unsaid between them before Toby nodded. "Whatever you want, Reese."

Then he'd trudged back up the aisle and Arthur had dutifully followed him.

"I just don't want to hurt Spencer," Toby whispered to Arthur before entering the row where Jesse wanted them to sit and watch.

"You can't change your past, right?" he whispered in Toby's ear as they took their seats. "Do right going forward. That's all you can do."

Toby patted his leg and then turned to kiss Spencer's cheek and splayed his hand possessively on Spencer's thigh, however, the grip told Arthur that Toby's hold was more to keep himself steady.

Earthquake Ethan strikes again.

Arthur couldn't take his eyes off their joined hands, though. What would that feel like? Having someone who accepted you for who you were, warts and all, tumultuous past and all. All Arthur had ever gotten was questions.

Why aren't you in showbiz like your parents?
What's your talent?

Where did all that orange hair come from?

As if he'd failed the genetic lottery somehow. Or hadn't tried hard enough, and therefore wasn't valuable.

So he'd set out to make himself valuable to the people who had what he didn't have. At least that way he could still fit in with his parents' circle. And he'd been very successful. His clients had won many industry awards and made mountains of profits. Arthur had been instrumental in that success, and he was confident in the notion that he was very good at what he did. He may not have talents that people paid money to see or listen to, but people paid him good money to manage *their* talents.

"Okay, Ethan and Spencer," Jesse said as the music started up. "We need some work. These boys look like they're going to jump out of their skin when they touch each other. We gotta get past this."

Arthur watched as Spencer and Ethan leaned forward, engrossed in the action onstage. Reese was singing about love and longing, and Bailey was attempting to seduce Sean. Their *characters* were. Seducing. Arthur glanced at Spencer and saw him moving in his seat with the boys, and he recalled that Spencer helped Jesse with the choreography. He was frowning slightly.

Looking past him, Arthur spotted Ethan. His legs were crossed and he leaned forward as if trying to get closer. The fingers on his right hand were stroking his throat as he sat deep in thought, his lips parted, eyes narrowed.

Those lips.

It was easy to see why Ethan had scooped up big roles after Reese and Toby discovered him. He was classically handsome, sure, but he was just *so compelling* to look at. More than beautiful, his face drew you in, his movements were like art brought to life by a divine kiss, and Arthur was grateful that here, in the relative darkness of the theater, he could watch him undetected. Study him. If he were caught, he could pass it off as professional interest. He was a talent manager after all. He could profess to be observing Ethan Bradley as part of his duties, to find the young man with the incredible physique, the heartbreakingly beautiful voice, and the Matt Bomer ice-blue eyes...

Well, that didn't sound like a professional observation.

Arthur hadn't dated anyone in an embarrassingly long time. What was he supposed to do? Anyone he went out with in LA likely knew who he was or who his clients were, and he'd had too many dates that ended in, "So, can you get me an audition?" or "I'd love to meet your parents." It was infuriating. Even friends had used him.

It wasn't until he'd met up with his current Disastrous Duo that he'd met men who appreciated his managerial skills, but also just seemed to like having him around. He'd traveled with them, and though he naturally fell into the caretaking role, they'd handled their own personal business. Other than them and his client Joe Judd, Arthur didn't fraternize with his clientele. Toby and Reese were almost his age and they treated him like a peer. And man, had it been nice to be included.

The scene onstage ended and everyone stood up to clap, including Ethan. He glanced over to smile at Jesse, and he caught Ethan's focused gaze.

And Arthur couldn't look away.

The next scene started up onstage. This time it was the morning after the Boy and his seducer had spent the night together for the first time, and Bailey's character was trying to figure out how to escape, though he didn't want to. Torn between his ladykiller musician persona and the Boy, who he's head over heels for, he leaves to rejoin his band... heartbroken he can't stay and claim the one he really wants, but he leaves a note sealed with a kiss before he exits the stage in tears.

Bailey nailed that part.

He was so believable as he played the role of the swinging band member, they even had him pretending to play a piano with his puffed-up chest, but as the band's performance goes on, he spots Sean waiting tables and his expression is...forlorn. The longing is so potent, it tugged at Arthur's own...need? Desire? Hope for some kind of connection in his own life? Those feelings were especially raw sitting next to one of the two new love stories in his immediate circle.

The rest of the second half was finished twenty minutes later with the leads in a giddy embrace as they prepare to run off into the sunset. Jesse stood and trotted down the aisle to the stage to debrief with the exhausted dancers.

"What do you think?" Toby stood and rested his hips on the seat-back in front of him with his arms crossed over his chest. He addressed the question to Spencer, but Spencer's eyebrows shot up.

"I mean, I can only comment on their technical performance, which they certainly have down. I mean, wow. Bailey leaps so high, I can't believe it. And for two guys who haven't tapped much before, they really picked up the steps. But I see what Jesse's saying...there's something missing, but I don't know. I think they're just shy with each other."

Toby snorted and Spencer huffed.

"Oh, come on," Spencer said. "It's not like Bailey's going to manhandle Sean like you manhandled me when you first saw the choreography."

Toby touched his fingers to his lips in a mock demure expression. "Whatever do you mean?"

Ethan sat quietly while they made their exchange, but his gaze bounced between them, and a couple of times he looked as if he had something to say but thought better of it.

"Okay, I gave them fifteen," Jesse said. "What do you think?"

Spencer threw his hands up. "I don't know what to say."

And Jesse's shoulders dropped. "Ethan? What do *you* think?"

He smiled brightly as if he were thrilled to be called upon. "I think someone needs to talk to them about the birds and bees, so to speak." He chuckled. "Bailey's fantastic, but he just looks so happy to be there, he's missing the part about being *happy*, if you know what I mean?"

She blew out a breath. "*Yesss*, and I'm not real sure how to give those notes to a couple of young guys...I mean, Sean is nineteen, but Bailey's seventeen. His parents know the story, thank God, or this would be even more awkward, but the scene is quite...frank." She tapped her lips with her fingers. "I wish they could have seen you do the scene with Julian, Spencer." She sucked in a breath as Toby growled.

"That's not happening again," Toby said. "If y'all want me to keep my head from exploding."

Jesse turned a pleading gaze on Ethan. "Ethan? I've seen videos of you in *Ruby*...do you have any wisdom to impart? Without help, I'm afraid the show isn't going to pack that emotional punch, you know what I mean?"

Ethan looked at Toby with huge eyes and swallowed hard. "I'm happy to talk to them, as long as Toby and Reese are okay with it." He fidgeted with his hands in his lap, and Arthur wondered if this was all a show...but no. Ethan's leg was bouncing. He looked like he'd jump out of his skin if someone said boo to him. Had Arthur really gotten it *so* wrong about him?

"Please," Toby said. "Help."

Ethan gave a timid smile. "All right. Jesse? You want me to talk to them now?"

"*Please*," she said, gesturing for him to follow her.

"Reese is okay with this?" Ethan asked before he moved.

"*Yeeeeesssss*," she said. "*Come onnnn.*"

Spencer and Toby moved their legs to let Ethan pass them in the tight row. Ethan managed to move past Toby without touching him, without making eye contact, and only murmuring "pardon me."

It was strange to see Toby so uncomfortable around someone. He was normally so cocky, and Arthur had even been present when Toby had encountered an ex. He was never so...awkward. It spoke to how much he loved Spencer, how much he adored the sweet man.

As soon as Ethan moved past him, Toby whispered to Spencer. The two of them stood and, holding hands, walked the opposite way out of the row.

"Excuse me, Mr. Frye," Ethan said, waiting for Arthur to pull his legs in or stand up.

"Hmm? Oh." Arthur started to open his thighs, but at the last minute, he stood—and collided with Ethan, their groins brushing as Ethan nearly toppled into his lap.

"I'm so sorry, Mr.—"

Arthur caught him by the arms and decided then and there to drop the asshole facade.

"Ethan? Call me Arthur. I'm sorry...I've been... Look—"

"It's okay. You have every reason to not want me here. I apologize if I've made a difficult situation worse." His stunning blue eyes were wet as he gave Arthur a sad smile.

"You haven't. And I promise, I'll take care of you." Arthur's eyes bugged out as he realized what he said, but the effect his words had on Ethan stabbed at his heart.

Ethan sucked in a shaky breath. "I appreciate that more than you know."

He moved past Arthur and hurried down the aisle toward the stage, rubbing at his eye.

Arthur cursed as his phone rang.

"Hey, Audra. You have some good news for me?"

His assistant laughed nervously. "One piece. I got your parents' suite, but The Dresden had to close for emergency renovations. I'm sorry."

Arthur plopped down in his seat and sighed, rubbing his forehead. "So you're telling me I need to find another venue for their friendly gathering."

"I'm sorry. Also, I looked through all of the requests and I see a few acting roles that might work for Ethan, so I've got a call in to the casting director. I also have a car commercial, a watch print ad, and there's an AIDS charity variety show that's looking for some theater names. He's out, isn't he? It's the show where they flip the songs?"

Arthur felt hot all of a sudden. Watching Ethan sing traditionally straight songs in a celebration of queer love onstage, dancing, that smile of his... He stood and began to pace the aisle, unable to contain his angst any longer.

"Let me ask him. Thank you. That's great news. Hey, why don't you draw up a contract, you know, just in case."

His assistant was quiet for a minute. "You're going to take him on?"

"No. Well, I don't know. But if we land him something, they're going to want to know he has representation. I don't want him turned down if any of the UK nonsense blows back."

She was quiet for a minute. "I really loved him in *Take My Hand*. You can't take your eyes off of him onscreen."

Not in person either.

"I know. Listen, he's in the middle of a conversation. Let me talk to him and you get the paperwork drawn up."

"Great. You want me to look around for a venue for your parents?"

Arthur cursed again and his assistant laughed.

"No, let me think about it. It can't just be anyplace."

"Not if you don't want to upset your mother."

He huffed out a breath. His whole life was surrounded by drama. Oh, who was he fooling? He was just as guilty as his friends, allowing his angst over Ethan to affect his normally staid demeanor. The last thing he should be thinking of is how much he enjoyed having the focus of Ethan Bradley on him.

"Oh my God, can we keep him?"

Arthur spun around to find Jesse bouncing on her toes. "He's so good with the boys. And he suggested we get an intimacy coordinator. Do you know Charlie Sampson? He said he worked with her on one of his films."

Arthur planted his hands on his hips. This was the problem with them not having a true director for this play. It was going to be beautiful, no doubt, but things like an intimacy coordinator weren't first and foremost in their minds. "Right. Yeah, I have heard of her. I should have thought of that myself. Let me see if I can get in touch with her."

He ran a hand down his face and tried a few deep breaths. Nope. Didn't work.

"Hey," Jesse said. "What else is going on? You look like you're about to—"

Arthur groaned. "I'm fine," he said, as his phone rang again. He held up a hand to Jesse and answered the call. "Hello, Mother."

"Do you know, Arthur, I just heard The Dresden is closed, isn't that terrible?"

Arthur winced. "Yeah, me too. Don't worry, I'm working on another venue for your party."

Jesse's eyes widened, and she started to step back, but Arthur reached for her arm.

"Oh, it's not a party, really," his mother said. "Only a few friends. Maybe ten people altogether. We could have it at your condo."

Arthur swallowed.

"Oh, Mother, I'm not set up to entertain." Sure, his house was immaculate, but he'd have to take down his wall art, and hide his music collection to avoid comments from his father. He had bought the place thinking someday having a pool party would be fun—

Jesse waved and stage whispered, "What about our house?"

Arthur's eyes flared and he covered the phone. "Oh, no, I couldn't put you guys out—"

"Who is that, darling?" his mother asked.

"It's Jesse Martin-Black. I'm at the Pantages. Reese and Jesse are in final rehearsals for the new show."

"Oh, how lovely. We'll have to put it on the calendar. Your father is dying to see it. He just loves Reese, and Thomas, of course."

Bernard Frye knew everyone in the Hollywood scene and had a special place in his heart for the celebrities he grew up worshipping, including Thomas and the other musicians who'd played with Frank Sinatra.

Jesse was still gesturing. "We'd love to have your family over," she said, tugging on Arthur's suit. "Danny loves flirting with your mom." She started making faces and gestures that had Arthur shaking his head.

Of course. Everyone loved Arthur's parents.

"Mother?" Arthur began, squeezing his eyes shut. It really would be a huge weight off to have his parents over to Danny's. The Blacks lived in what had once been the home of Director Roland Curtis, who'd been Bernard's mentor and was still a close family friend. It was amazing just how small a world Arthur existed in. "The Blacks have invited us to gather at their house. What do you think?"

"That would be lovely! Oh, Bernie! Jesse and Danny are going to host us, won't that be wonderful?"

Arthur heard his father mumble something and his mother answered, "Of course, dear. Arthur will arrange everything, won't you, sweetheart?"

"Yes, Mother." And he would because as much as his parents' visits stressed him out, he also wanted them to be happy, to be proud.

"Kiss kiss, darling. We'll be driving in Thursday and will look forward to a soiree on Friday with the Blacks. And be sure to let Reese and Toby know we would love for them to come by if they have time. I know they're busy with the show. Ta-ta, my darling."

"Love you," Arthur said as his mother disconnected. He sighed and slid his phone in his pocket.

"Oh, Arthur," Jesse said, giving him a hug. "Let me call Nora. She hasn't thrown a party in a while. She'll love to do this. Let us handle all the food and drinks—"

"No, Jesse, that's too much."

"Nonsense! It'll be a good way for everyone to blow off steam before we head into dress rehearsals next week…I think we're all going to need it. Danny and the guys have also been in rehearsals all week. They'll be ecstatic to have a diversion."

Arthur rubbed the back of his neck. Having a full house would definitely take some of the pressure off. Patricia said she could come. She always knew how to placate his parents. It would be fine.

He looked toward the stage with Jesse waiting on his answer, and saw Ethan giving the boys a talking to.

Ethan. What was he supposed to do with him? About him? About how he couldn't stop thinking about him in ways that had nothing to do with business?

He was starting to think less in terms of what to do with him and more in what he wanted to do *with* him. Watching him earlier had been a high note, a momentary break from being so on top of everything.

What would happen if he ignored his rules?

ELEVEN

E^{than}

Being helpful was giving Ethan a rush. He'd watched the boys fumble with each other like the nervous teenagers they were and thought *aw*. He remembered those days. Ethan had been totally closeted until he'd gone to college, and there he'd met boys like him. He'd been beyond naive, flirting with his fellow cast members while reading pamphlets at night about safe sex and PrEP. He had condoms and lube in his bag at all times, determined to lose his virginity, but the first time he'd found a willing partner, he hadn't known what to do. Neither had the other guy. They'd jerked each other off clumsily and said awkward good nights before going their separate ways.

The first time he'd tried to top, he couldn't get hard enough and the guy was too tense for things to work out. After that, he'd exchanged plenty of blow jobs, but he hadn't felt like his tutelage had gone far enough. His night with Toby had been the first time he'd bottomed, and he'd been scared half to death. It had taken all of his acting ability to get through it without throwing up.

He hated even thinking about it because it was the last form of intimacy he'd had, and it had been a pretty awful experience. He'd realized quickly that what he'd been doing wasn't what he really wanted, wasn't healthy for him. He wanted affection, he wanted to please someone, and not just because he was good in bed.

He wanted what he pretended to have in the movies and onstage.

He wanted to be in love.

So he channeled that desire as he spoke to Bailey and Sean.

"Bailey, what do you think your character wants?"

Bailey's deep brown eyes were wide as he looked between Sean and Ethan. They'd gone backstage to a dressing room while Jesse worked with the rest of the cast.

"I, uh, think he wants to figure out why he likes this person? I mean, he likes Sandra, so, um, why does he feel some kinda way about the guy, you know?" He swallowed hard and his gaze darted toward Sean.

Ethan didn't think Bailey got it, and why would he? He was young.

He turned to Sean. "How about the Boy? What does he want?"

Sean gave Ethan a flirty smile. "He wants to be chosen. At first, he wants to know why he's got this guy's interest, but then he wants the guy to choose him. Once he's had his attention, he doesn't want it to stop. He wants the guy to pick *him*." Sean smiled at Bailey, but it was fleeting and the two dancers laughed awkwardly.

Ethan nodded. They got it on a surface level. "That's all well and good, but—"

A memory flashed, and it took his breath away. He didn't want to go there.

Shit. He couldn't have this conversation with them. Not with just the two of them and him in the room, anyway.

"Actually, you two hang on one minute, okay?" He needed reinforcements.

He poked his head out into the hall and when he saw no one around, he went in search of the guy who was much better suited to have this conversation.

Spencer and Toby were sitting in the audience, so Ethan skirted around the edge of the stage, catching a curious glance from Jesse, and he took the steps carefully. He didn't like the expression Toby had when he saw him.

"Hey, Spencer? Can I talk to you a minute?"

"What's up?" Toby asked.

Ethan didn't want to make an awkward situation worse. "So, without confirmation, I'm pretty sure neither of these two have...um... experience." He raised his eyebrows hoping the two men got what he was saying.

Spencer crossed his leg and tilted his head. "You mean, sexual experience?"

"I do," Ethan said with a wince. "Look, I'm just an actor. I know what worked for me when I needed to get into the right headspace for an intimate scene, but I also don't want to say anything inappropriate..." His face flushed and he shook out his hands, his heart suddenly suffocating him. "I want to do this right and not make anyone uncomfortable. Would you mind?"

Spencer hesitated only a second before he popped up. "Oh, oh. Of course. Toby? Do you mind?"

Toby gave an exaggerated sigh. "I suppose you are the best person since you actually do this shit for a living."

Spencer gave him a sarcastic smile. "Thank you. I'll be back."

Toby held up his hand. "I'll be here." But his gaze followed them, and when Ethan looked back at the stairs, Toby was frowning at him.

"I'm sorry," Ethan said to Spencer as they got near the dressing room. "I just...I've had a few bad experiences, and I don't want to do the same to these boys."

Spencer stopped him with a hand to his arm. "Are *you* all right talking about this?"

Ethan gave him a shaky smile. "I hadn't thought about it in a long time. I'm fine, just brought up some squicky feelings."

Spencer smiled. "Let's make this a positive for the two boys, shall we?"

Ethan nodded and gestured for Spencer to step inside the door.

"Hey, there. I'm Spencer Hart. Ethan asked me to be present while he talks to you, as I'm a licensed therapist and I spend most of my time working with teens discussing issues of sexual orientation and identity. If you have any questions, I'm happy to answer them as best as I can."

Bailey and Sean looked at each other, and then looked at Ethan and then Spencer, and the questions started flying.

"Whoa, okay," Spencer said with a chuckle. "Let's start at the beginning."

Spencer was magic, and soon he had the boys feeling way more comfortable with their scenario.

"I think I wasn't thinking about this show as anything other than being an opportunity to dance and to support my brother and Reese," Bailey said. "I'm just a nerdy color guard kid who's never had a girl-friend or a boyfriend and never really cared." He swallowed and blushed. "I've been worried maybe I couldn't pull this off because I don't know—"

"No way," Ethan said. "Look at it this way. Robert DeNiro has never been a mob boss...that we know of. Leonardo DiCaprio has never been a cop or, well, probably any of the things he's done before. Inti-mate scenes are just that, they're pretending. You don't have to have experience, but you do need to find a way to know what your character wants and needs. And it doesn't have to be, like, specific. You don't have to be like, 'I want him to touch me, I need him to kiss me.' But more like, 'I need *him*. I need him to love *me*. I need him to want *me*. So whatever you have to picture to get there...'"

Spencer smiled at Ethan. "It might help to think less 'how can I relate to this person's experiences,' and more 'how can I relate to feeling this way?' And it could be a desire to prove to others that you can do what you set out to do, or a need to be taken seriously, which I think we can all relate to, in or out of a relationship with anyone."

Sean raised his hand, and they all laughed, letting go of some of the tension. Ethan was so grateful to have Spencer there. The boys really opened up with him in the room.

"Sorry, habit." He turned to smile at Bailey. "I also think it's weird because you and I haven't had a chance to get to know each other. Like, at first I thought, well, we're just like our characters. But I don't know what's okay as far as how to touch you... I know Jesse told us what things should look like, but—"

"Ah. Yes. Consent." Spencer nodded.

"Right," Ethan agreed. "And to help with that, I mentioned to Jesse a woman I worked with before who's an intimacy coordinator. I'm hoping she'll be able to come down and go over the scenes with you. She was a lifesaver for me in *Take My Hand*. I..." He couldn't believe he was going to admit this. "I kept getting, um, hard? Whenever we had to get close in our scenes? There were a couple of heavy make-out scenes, and while I'm as gay as the day is long, and my co-star was one of my best friends at the time, it was like, the more I told myself 'don't get hard, don't get hard,' the more it happened. I was so worried I'd make her uncomfortable, but then we talked about it, and she was like, 'Dude, if it happens, it happens. Do you want me to, like, eat onions before we do the scene? Maybe not wear deodorant?' And just like that, I was over it."

Bailey snickered, and then they were all laughing. Ethan was really happy to see Bailey and Sean actually talking to each other, admitting how nervous they were about doing the scene in front of others, and how grateful they were that they would have most of their clothes on. He figured the intimacy coach would still be a good idea, but this was a good start.

There was a knock at the door, and Arthur gestured for Ethan to come out into the hall.

"Hey," Ethan said, himself now feeling awkward. He hated that he and Arthur were on this weird footing. Not only did Ethan wish he hadn't had to come here destitute and desperate, but he also wished he and Arthur could have met on better terms. Both times. Because Arthur was exactly the kind of man Ethan wished would pay attention to him.

"How did that go?"

Ethan glanced back in and grinned. "Great. I think. They're finally talking to each other. I think they've both been so nervous they hadn't had a chance to really talk to each other or about how they felt. Spencer is great, though. He talked to them about the biology involved with arousal and how it's not always... Sorry. You probably don't need a physiology lesson. I'm just glad I could help."

Arthur cocked his head to the side and narrowed his eyes. "You mean that, don't you?"

"Yeah," Ethan said, his smile slipping. "I do. This show is really important, not just to Reese and Toby, but to everyone who's going to see it. I would do whatever I could to help, and not just because Reese is helping me, um, out of...yeah."

Arthur blew out a breath and pulled out his phone. "Right. Well, Charlie said she can come by Wednesday, so thank you for that suggestion. Also, I had my assistant put together some paperwork for you to fill out."

Ethan's nose and eyes burned, but before he could ask, Arthur gave a quick shake to his head. "I'm not ready to offer you representation. This is temporary. I have a full slate of talent and after what happened, there are a lot of folks who won't even consider you. I have a line on some auditions, commercials and print ads, but in order to inquire for you, I need—"

"Whatever, I'll sign it. I'm sorry to be putting you out."

"No, that's not—" Arthur began.

He reached for Ethan's arm, and Ethan pulled away, his eyes filled with tears. He was so ashamed. He should just put an end to all of this.

"Mr. Frye, I'm not proud of *any* of this. I think it's better if I leave. I'll find something else. Please apologize to your assistant. I'm sorry to waste your time."

"Hey," Arthur said, his voice softer. He put his hands on Ethan's biceps and backed him gently to a corner, away from the open dressing room door. "Look, I haven't handled this well, all right?"

Ethan crossed his arms, but Arthur didn't back away. "No, you're right. Maybe I should just forget all this. Actors fail every day, right? I had a good run. I should just go get a regular job. I'm not cut out—"

"You should do no such thing. You're a natural, Ethan," Arthur snapped. He blinked as if he'd surprised himself. "No, you just hit a bad patch and fell victim to the tabloids, but giving up now lets those assholes win."

Ethan let his head fall, as well as a couple of tears. He couldn't believe he was showing his underbelly in front of this together man. "You probably think I'm such a loser," he breathed.

TWELVE

Arthur may have been tough as nails and damn good at his job, but he'd never made someone cry before.

"I absolutely do not think you're a loser. And I wouldn't blame you if you quit and left LA. Nothing wrong with it, people do it all the time. This business isn't for everyone, that's true, but Ethan...please don't take my hesitation as a lack of faith in your abilities. Sometimes it has nothing to do with your talent. Timing and who you know matters, right?"

"And I had lousy timing." He shook his head and wiped at his face. "I feel like such a jerk. I was just scared, you know? I tried everything in London. I talked to everyone. I had so many doors closed in my face. But then my visa ran out, and I only had enough money to fly here. I've never been this close to, like, nothing. I didn't eat, I slept outside...I was embarrassed. Ashamed. Like, what's wrong with me? Why can't I make something work? I didn't want anyone to know.

"And now I'm...a cliché. It killed me to show up at Reese's. Now I know how those actors who...you know the horror stories you hear? I think I know how they felt, how they could just give up on life."

"Hey, come on," Arthur said, and he was really worried now. Did he need to get Spencer out here? "You've hit a bad patch—"

"Oh, I know. I'm sorry. I don't...I'm okay, I'm not going to hurt myself, I swear. I realize how it sounds. Seriously, though, Arthur. I appreciate everything you've done, but I don't know if I should—"

"Yes. You should. Let me work my magic. Give me...a month. If by the end of a month, you're ready to move on to something else, we'll shake hands and part. Don't pack it in yet, okay?"

Why did the idea of...parting...feel so wrong?

Where this enthusiasm came from, Arthur wasn't sure. Maybe he wasn't ready to have Ethan out of LA. Maybe he wanted the challenge, to remake this man into the star he should have been before those stupid fucking pictures ruined his chances.

Maybe Arthur was a sucker for a pretty face, and what a pretty face Ethan's was. His smile was that of an excited kid, not that of a seasoned actor or a jaded Hollywood star.

He'd moved so close to Ethan that their knees brushed, and Ethan's eyes went wide. He backed away, but bumped into the wall as if he hadn't realized where he was. He laughed nervously.

Arthur was looming. He had a few inches on Ethan, and while he never considered himself a big guy, Ethan didn't seem so larger than life up close like this. He coughed into a fist before stepping back. That brush of the knees? Made his mouth water. The contact sent a shiver through Arthur, waking him up for the first time in recent memory. That alone should have been warning enough.

Danger.

"So I sign the papers...and then?"

Arthur blinked. Were eyes really that shade of blue? Was it humanly possible?

"And then...?" Arthur was confused. Had he missed something? "And then..."

It would be so easy to press up against Ethan, maybe place a hand on his waist, tousle his hair...

And then *what*? Arthur would find work for Ethan, Ethan would make a little money, make some connections, and have a path forward. He'd be on his way, hopefully, back on that star trajectory he'd been on when *Ruby* wrapped. He'd soar...and Arthur would be happy. Of course. He always wanted the best for his clients. And after a month, if Ethan wanted representation, there were others at Slade trying to build their lists. Arthur would be back to business as usual.

"And then?" Ethan asked again, chuckling this time. He brushed his dark curls out of his face and fixed Arthur with that megawatt smile, the one that had been all over the ads for *Ruby*. The face that brought in the crowds, the voice that wowed the award-givers, and the emotion and acting range that had casting directors fighting over him at one point.

"And then, hopefully, you'll be back on track." Arthur smiled woodenly and the electricity faded from Ethan's smile.

"Great," he said, his tone flat. "Thank you. What do you need me to sign?"

Arthur looked at his watch. "Why don't I pick you up in the morning and bring you to the office? You can sign the papers, we can get your resume and headshots together, and Audra can go over what she's found for you. Now, remember. I'm not going to throw you at just whoever, and you can certainly say no to any of our suggestions. For any work we find, we'll connect with an agency we partner with. I'd advise you to be somewhat selective. It may mean things are lean for a while, but I don't want to do anything more to harm your chances of scoring bigger roles, do you understand? So if I seem picky, that's why. We need to repair your image, and I have a reputation—*Slade Management* has a reputation for guiding the careers of our clients in a professional and beneficial manner. We'll look out for your best interests, Ethan, and you need to trust me to do that, okay?"

Ethan nodded. "Thank you, Arthur. I promise, I'll do good work for you."

So eager, and so innocent. Was this all a put-on? Arthur had a hard time accepting this version of Ethan. He'd have to trust that the guy wouldn't leave him high and dry, or worse, engage in more public bad behavior.

"I won't let you down. I'll be good for you." Ethan blushed as he spoke the words, and gave Arthur a shy smile.

God, that sounded hot.

Arthur exhaled.

Yeah. *If only.*

If only Ethan wasn't an actor. If only they hadn't met in the business. If only—

"That's a wrap for today," Jesse called out. "See you all at early o'clock tomorrow. Get rest. Get hydrated. Eat a good dinner."

Dancers and crew filled the hallway, and Arthur stepped back from Ethan, rubbing his mouth with his hand.

"Jesse's so good with the cast," Ethan was saying. "It's lucky Reese and Toby found her."

"Yeah, it was kismet. My partner Patricia is Danny's manager, and so when Reese and Toby decided to fast-track the show, her name came up. And Spencer knew her through one of his friends. It's amazing how small the world really is out here."

Ethan shoved his hands in his pockets. "I wouldn't know. I never spent much time in LA."

Arthur couldn't believe the guy hadn't made a gazillion friends, or broken as many hearts. "No? Well, there are great people, and then there's everyone else. Thankfully for you, the ones you know are in the first group. Listen, can I drop you off?"

Ethan shook his head and shoved his hands in his pockets. "I can walk. You've done enough already, Arthur. Thank you." He smiled once more, but those eyes...while they usually sparkled and stabbed right through to your heart, now they were red and glassy.

The man was tired. He needed to be at his best if they were going to pull off his resurrection. Arthur would need to arrange a spa trip, haircut, facial, and a shopping trip. Those were the parts of the job he loved. Would he love doing them with Ethan?

"You're welcome," he breathed, and part of him wanted to continue that statement. *You're welcome to come home with me. You're welcome to sit on my lap and let me—*

"Arthur!" Jesse walked with a bounce in her step as she approached.

"Danny and Nora are totally excited for Friday! She wants to know about any dietary issues or any foods your parents don't eat."

"Oh, sure. I'll give her a call."

He turned back to say goodbye to Ethan, but he was walking down the hallway toward the exit. Alone. His head down, shoulders slouched.

That was so wrong. Ethan should be walking proudly, that strong jaw out, chest and shoulders high, and those long, muscled thighs... He'd made Arthur weak when he first met him, made him trip over his words. Then Arthur had observed Ethan in his element, and he'd thought, yeah, he was just like all the rest.

Had he been so wrong?

Now, Arthur wanted to skin those paparazzi alive. Wanted to throat punch anyone who'd ever said an unkind word to Ethan Bradley, even himself. There was no reason a man that beautiful, that talented, should ever be treated as anything other than a gift.

And Arthur Frye was going to work hard to make right the wrong way he'd treated Ethan. Starting tomorrow morning, Ethan Bradley was going to get the full Arthur Frye treatment. He would bring the pride back to that man's walk, the swagger that made men and women swoon. He would make sure Ethan never went hungry ever again.

Thirteen

E^{than}

Ethan waved goodbye to all the folks he'd met that day and walked the couple of blocks back to his hotel. From across the street, he was greeted with the sound of loud voices coming from the pool area once more. He wasn't sure he was up for more peopling, but he put a smile on his face just in case.

He'd talked to more people today than he had since *Ruby* in London, and it had been awesome to feel useful. He'd had fun sitting outside with Jane and Bailey at lunch. It was a bit awkward hanging around teenagers, though he'd been the teenager once upon a time, looking for any help he could get, and he'd appreciated the older actors who were happy to give pointers and advice.

But every time he had to interact with Arthur, he'd wished he'd learned a long time ago to keep his mouth shut and stop being an over-sharer. It had been evident in the manager's face that he wasn't impressed.

Ethan was a nuisance.

Ethan didn't belong there.

Ethan was a problem to be dealt with, nothing more, which sucked.

Ethan admired Arthur and wanted to impress him, but what would it matter? After a month, even if he managed to land some sort of a job, Arthur would wash his hands of him. Better to not let this spark of a crush develop into something bigger. A time of crisis wasn't the best time to be trying to find a...someone. Especially given what happened the last time he'd had a crush.

He'd pulled out the apples he'd had in his pocket since breakfast on the walk, planning to have them for dinner, but when he'd passed an ancient old man sitting with his dog under the overpass, he'd given the fruit to him, along with the last ten dollars he had in his pocket. He'd seen a potential future in which he'd have to beg for food again, or dig in trash bins for leftovers. He'd like to think someone would take mercy on him.

When he reached his hotel, he climbed the stairs rather than taking the elevator and found that no, it wasn't a party going on, but the manager, Cosmo, was trying to replace a window.

"Need a hand?" Ethan asked as he trotted closer.

Cosmo was straining under the weight of the window. The other guy with him, Jinx, was not being helpful at all.

"Thanks," Cosmo said, shooting a dirty look at his friend. "I meant to get this done before Jinx arrived with the beer. We're all useless after the beer arrives."

"What?" Jinx cried out. "Last time I helped you replace a window, I dropped it on my thumb and couldn't play guitar for three months. Want me to do that again?"

Cosmo exhaled and gave Ethan a grateful look. "I'd love some help."

Together, they got the window into the opening and Cosmo checked to see that it was level. He drilled in the screws while Ethan kept the window from shifting.

"Perfect. You're good at this. Do you have, like, experience in construction? Or maybe only on TV? Or the movies? Wait, have you done TV? I think I've only seen you in that one movie with the hot British chick."

"Take My Hand? Or *Affair on the Thames*?"

Cosmo scratched his head. "The one where you and the chick were banging on the stairs—"

"Ah. *Take My Hand*. Yeah. My dad's in construction. I worked with him for years before I went to New York. Stage and film. No TV yet, but I'm open to anything. Are you an actor?" Ethan knew he was the manager of the hotel complex, but he also knew that most people in LA had lots of hustles.

"Nah, man. I'm the other end of the starving artist segment of the entertainment spectrum. Musician."

"Oh, cool," Ethan said with a smile. "Would I have heard any of your stuff?" He tried not to let the starving artist remark sting.

Cosmo wrinkled up his nose. "Not yet. We just about had a record deal and then half my band quit. It's just Jinx and me now. We're still playing together and working on music, but I took on this gig for my uncle after the apartment complex I co-owned burnt to the ground. Jinx went back to school after that, so we're biding our time, ya dig? It'll happen when it's meant to."

"How awful! A fire? Was anyone hurt?"

He laughed. "Just me and Jinx. My building was toast. Insurance covered the loss. I still manage the other units, but I'm living here now for my uncle. Keeps me busy. Socking some money away for a rainy day."

"That's great. I'd love to see you guys play sometime." Cosmo had such a positive outlook. Ethan wished *he'd* been a little more resilient instead of freaking out.

Cosmo gave him an appraising look. "No offense, but we don't usually get talent of your caliber staying here. Not that we don't provide top-notch service, but—"

"Oh, well, let's just say I'm here in town for a fresh start." The tears burned his eyes once more but he wasn't going to break down again. No way.

"Far out. Hey, listen. Thanks for the help." He leaned close, and Ethan was momentarily mesmerized by his swirly hazel and greenish eyes. "Some of my friends still get a little wild. Someone did a Tarzan move off the floor above us and swung through the window in the wee hours. Not sure if you heard. Sorry if you did."

Ethan looked up and then back at Cosmo. "Like, from up there? What, did they swing on a rope?"

"Tied up a bed sheet to the railing, leaped out over the pool, and meant to land on the walkway here, but the railing snapped off. It wasn't rated to hold the weight-in-motion of one Cletus Bukowski, former tight end for the Chargers. He overcompensated, came through the window, and landed in my living room, even took out my kitchen table." Cosmo shook his head, his long mane of curls falling over his bare shoulders. He was wearing a tool belt, cutoff jeans, and nothing else. "I wanted to at least get the window in tonight. I can fix the table in the morning."

"I can help," Ethan said. "I have a meeting in the morning, but that's probably it for the day." He smiled hopefully at Cosmo, who seemed surprised.

"Aren't you in town for work?"

Ethan sighed. "It's a really long story."

Cosmo put a firm hand on his shoulder. "Come in and have some steaks with us," he said, gesturing to his unit.

As much as Ethan was feeling raw, staying in his room alone would likely mean crying again. He wasn't sure he was strong enough to be alone with himself.

He beamed at Cosmo. "I'd really appreciate that."

Dinner was indeed steaks, along with Greek salad and...potato chips?

"Sorry, man," Jinx said with a laugh. "I get leftovers from this food delivery business I work for and they don't always go together."

"Yeah, like last week we had so many peas, dude," Cosmo said. "We started to make split pea soup, but then someone put on *The Exorcist* and we just couldn't do it. So we put them in quesadillas, man. That's some good shit."

"Ramen too," Jinx said. "Peas have a lot of protein and fiber, you know. Or like two weeks ago it was beets."

They sat on the dining chairs holding their plates, which made cutting the steak interesting. Jinx and Cosmo entertained him with stories about the wild parties they'd had at their old apartment.

Ethan offered to wash dishes, but Jinx waved him out of the kitchen. Ethan took a seat next to Cosmo on the couch.

"Hey, Cosmo. You heard from Jesse?" Jinx asked from the kitchen. "Man, I miss her."

Ethan frowned. "You mean Jesse the choreographer? I met her today."

Cosmo nodded, flicking his hair over his shoulder. "She's great, huh?" His laugh lines and crow's feet placed him somewhere in his thirties. His lifestyle and dress code seemed much younger, but his gaze held a lot of life experience.

"Yeah. Super talented." Ethan was surprised at yet another connection.

"Jesse was my neighbor. She went to work with Danny, they fell in love, she moved up to the hills with him, and they got hitched. Thankfully she was with Danny when the fire happened." He let out a breath. "Thought she was the one who got away...until I met the *real* one who keeps *trying* to get away."

"Funny how that happens. How things aren't always what we think they are when we're in it." Boy, Ethan wished he could tell the Ethan of last summer to make some much better choices.

"Getting distance is good, but yeah. I'm on the long campaign with my lady now." Cosmo winked and clicked his tongue against his teeth.

Ethan felt himself growing sleepy and zoning out of the conversation a bit. "Hey, I think I'd better go before I fall asleep," he said, standing from the couch. "I really appreciated dinner. I haven't shared a home-cooked meal with folks in a long time."

They all laughed, and Ethan feared he'd offended them.

"If that's what you think is a home-cooked meal," Cosmo said, "I'll have to bring you to the next Grammatica family gathering. My big fat Greek family will feed you so thoroughly, you'll need to be rolled out the door."

"Oh, I couldn't impose."

"Nonsense," Jinx said, putting a hand on Ethan's shoulder. "Cosmo and his family take care of their people. And if Arthur put you here, you're our people."

"You know Arthur? Like, personally?" Ethan couldn't see how these relaxed rocker guys and Arthur ran in the same circles.

"It's one of those six degrees of separation things. I know Jesse," Cosmo said, counting on his fingers. "Through her, I met Danny, and through him, Patricia, my future wife, though she's determined to resist...where was I? Ah, Mr. Frye." He held up four fingers. "Four degrees. He's Patricia's business partner. A little uptight, but he's a huge music geek, mostly a New Wave aficionado, but he loves all the good stuff. We bonded over a shared love of Elvis Costello."

Ethan felt his jaw threatening to fall open. "Oh yeah?"

"He's a diehard fan. He doesn't talk about it much, doesn't talk about himself much at all, but we got him drunk one night at Danny's house and he begged us to keep playing 'Watching The Detectives.' It was hilarious."

Ethan's mind kicked into gear. He'd met Elvis Costello at an event for *Take My Hand*. He'd contributed some of the music to the film. Ethan was a huge fan of the Americana album he did. He wondered what else they might have in common. He wanted to talk to him, spend time with Arthur when he wasn't groveling for help.

"Hey, how long you going to be in town?" Cosmo asked.

That was a good question. "Depends? Oh! You mean for the room?"

Cosmo snorted. "I'm not worried about the room. We stay pretty booked but I always keep a few rooms vacant for friends. No, I was thinking more like taking you out on the town."

Ethan's eyes watered, and he knew it was time to go. Any kindness would break him right now. "That sounds fun. Let me see what happens at my meeting tomorrow?"

"Sure," Cosmo said. "And don't worry about the table."

Ethan frowned and walked over to look at the table, which had been pushed into a corner.

"The legs busted off on one side. I think it's toast."

"Actually, have you got some wood glue and clamps? That and a few screws should do the trick. This is good wood, not the fake stuff."

"I think I can scrounge those up tomorrow. Maybe swing by when you're free. If not, though, don't worry. If you've got an appointment with Arthur, that means he's got plans for you. Patricia's told me about his meetings. He's intense but a really good guy. He'll make you a star, baby."

Ethan laughed but he felt warm inside, and it was more about seeing Arthur than it was about landing a new project...and wasn't that something? He knew he needed to be focused on his career, but what good was finding success if you had no one to share it with?

Arthur's whole demeanor had changed toward Ethan by the end of the day. Perhaps he'd been pleased that Ethan was helping the boys? Whatever the reason, it had Ethan anxious to see what tomorrow held.

Ethan said goodbye to Cosmo and Jinx, thanking them again for the meal, and he went to his room. He was too tired to do more than strip down to his boxers, set the alarm for six in the morning to give him plenty of time to iron his clothes, and fall into bed.

And pray.

FOURTEEN

Arthur typically had a period of time to research his clients thoroughly, and with Ethan going into the office with him first thing in the morning, he was going to have to cram it into one night. Thankfully he'd called on his way home and had Audra send him everything she could find on Ethan, including audition recordings, video clips of his performance in *Hands on a Hardbody*, and interviews in print and on video that he'd done. Arthur needed to know how Ethan had handled himself, whether something could come back and bite him in the ass for helping the guy.

Three hours after he'd parked his Volvo at his condo off Sunset, Arthur was curled on the couch with Elvis, the last of a full bottle of wine he'd opened in his glass, crying into a bowl of gummy worms. He'd already had popcorn, which everyone knew had to be followed with a sweet, and he'd used half a box of tissue.

Damn. He had no idea *An Affair on the Thames* was so fucking sad!

The story of an American heiress about to debut in London society in 1897, and the cunning and conniving Lord Harrington—played by a well-coiffed Ethan Bradley with an impeccable British accent—who blackmails the heiress into working as a team, only to discover the truth of her motivations in a heart-wrenchingly beautiful scene.

And then there was the audition tape he'd done for another historical film that he'd ultimately been cast in and then dropped from, which had Arthur ready to throw the remote at the screen. How could they have let him go? He'd nailed the role, emoting on screen as if his life depended on it. Which apparently it had.

Now, Arthur may have kept a stoic facade around his clients and co-workers. He had to be the consummate professional at all times. But at home? With no one around? He frequently indulged in tearjerkers, and *Thames* was one of the tearjerkiest films he'd ever seen.

"Look at him, E," he scoffed to his feline friend. "The guy goes from gas station attendant chic in *Hardbody* to nobility in *Thames* and manages to pull it off! The aw-shucks farm boy to a perfectly done British accent! How could anyone *not* hire him?"

Arthur pulled his fuzzy blanket closer around him as he seethed with indignation. Elvis gave him a dirty look for upsetting his lap. He stood on the most painful spots of Arthur's inner thighs until he made himself comfortable.

Arthur's phone buzzed on the side table, and Elvis gave a loud *rowl* as Arthur leaned over to grab it, once more disturbing his comfort.

At this hour and on this particular occasion, he wasn't surprised to see it was Audra.

"Which did you watch?" he asked before giving her a greeting.

She sniffled loudly into the phone. "Oh my God, how had I not seen this movie?"

"Which one?"

"*The Thames*!" she cried. "Oh, it's so sad!"

"I know!"

They shared their impressions, hers being how good Ethan looked in period wear, how believable the chemistry was with his co-star, Felicia Swann, who she had a major lady boner for. Arthur kept his opinion to himself for the moment. His opinion being that Ethan needed a good fucking by a capable man...his character in the film, of course. Not that Arthur was volunteering to do it himself. But oh, how Lord Harrington's smart mouth made Arthur want to kiss the sass away. He tended to feel that way about historical romance heroes. All that haughtiness made him want to take them down a peg.

There's an idea. Perhaps if there was more pegging in historical romance...

"I don't care what those tabloids said about him," Audra was saying. "He looks like he wants to eat her for dinner *and* a midnight snack. Maybe even have leftovers for breakfast. I don't blame him. She's so hot. And the two of them are my sexuality explained for real."

Arthur chuckled but he was in the zone. "All right, so we know he's got period film potential—"

"And with his shirt off in those trousers? Moving a whole-ass tree by himself, he certainly could pull off the shirtless rom com hero vibe—"

"Have you watched *Take my Hand* yet?"

"Please. I saw that in the theaters. A panty-melting experience for sure. What I'd like to see him do is something a little grittier. Get his pretty face dirty."

Arthur's mouth watered thinking of Ethan a little scraped up, those faint freckles covered in grime, maybe some wet clothes that would cling to his shapely thighs. *Stop that right now, Arthur Emmanuel Frye.*

"What about a Netflix gig? What was the one we got info on...the espionage one," Audra said. "You think he could pull off something like that, in the same vein as *The Night Agent* or *The Recruit*?"

Ohhh, the suit porn. Arthur could picture it now, and he caught a bit of drool with his finger as he shoved another gummy worm into his mouth. "There's potential. He's got the physicality for it." But the fact that Arthur was having fantasies of peeling a suit off of Ethan and using his tie to—*no*. He cleared his throat when what he needed to do was clear his dirty mind. "These are all good places to start. After we get him to sign the papers, let's run all of these by him. Then you can start setting up some meetings. He's also going to need a whole spa and style treatment."

"I'm happy to schedule all that. I wouldn't mind taking him—"

"I can handle it. You've got your hands full with the documents and looking for leads. I also want you to look into his finances. With the success of his projects, there's no reason he shouldn't be receiving at least some residuals. Also, we need to do a thorough social media audit. I don't want any surprises."

She was quiet for a minute. "That's...you've been so busy, I figured you'd want me to help out with that kind of stuff. Did I not do a good job last time?"

"God, no. Audra! You are amazing. It has nothing to do with you. In fact, I was thinking that he could be your first solo client. What do you think?"

Audra gasped. She'd gone from his assistant to an informal internship over the past year. He'd been planning to promote her in the first part of this year anyway.

"Do you really think I'm ready?" she asked.

"I do. But let's see how this goes, okay?" he hedged. "He's bringing some baggage with him, and I don't want to saddle you with that." *Sure. That's why. Not because you want to keep him...close.* But then, not being his direct manager left a door open...

Who was Arthur fooling? He was already over a line he couldn't uncross when it came to Ethan. He had feelings. Whether he acted on them or not, he needed to put Audra in place to avoid any impropriety.

"Okay," she said, her voice lowering. "Tell me you didn't cry at the part in *Thames* when—"

"When Josephine admits to Lord Harrington *why* she's willing to risk everything to pull off the heist? Oh, God—"

"And he takes her hand and tells her—"

"*'Have the jewels, milady. You've already stolen my heart.'*"

And they were crying and laughing together at their ridiculousness.

"That smile alone should have been enough for those stuck-up British execs to forget about the scandal," Audra said, huffing her disdain into the phone.

Arthur knew, though, that there were still some film companies that wouldn't touch an out actor, especially for a cis-het period film. It was bullshit, but Arthur had learned how to play their games to ensure that his clients got the best deals. Besides Reese and Toby, Arthur carried several other queer clients on his roster, and he'd been quite successful in getting them where they wanted to be in their careers with hard work, good connections, and a little manipulation where needed. He'd learned from his mentor, Horace Manning, one of the founders of Slade, how to get what he needed for his people.

"Yes, well, wouldn't it be great for Ethan to blow up here in the States? Not only as a snub to the Brits, but also to be embraced by America? We all know that the execs don't always have their pulse on what the people want, and there are plenty of examples of gay actors who have continued to have success in both queer and straight films. Luke Evans, Matt Bomer, Zachary Quinto...Ethan Bradley could handle himself with the best of them."

"If anyone can make that happen, it's you," Audra said, and then Arthur heard her yawn.

"You mean *you*. You're going to steer things for Ethan. And for that, you need to get some rest," he said to her. "It's only Monday. It doesn't do for us to lose sleep so early in the week."

She chuckled. "True. And you decided to give up caffeine for your New Year's Resolution. How's that going for you?"

Arthur grunted. "At this very moment? Fine. Don't ask me about yesterday and no promises for tomorrow."

"Moderation, my dear Arthur. Even giving up the Red Bulls and your iced coffees is a great start."

"Yeah, well, my doctor about had a coronary of his own when he got a load of the results from my heart monitor." Arthur had experienced a few occasions of heart palpitations over the summer, and so his doctor had required him to wear a monitor for twenty-four hours. The results hadn't been good, and when his doctor asked him about his caffeine intake, he'd immediately told him to cut it out.

Easier said than done. He'd started his bad habit as a college student, slamming espressos and energy drinks. Starbucks made it so easy to overdo it with their iced coffee bottles sold everywhere. Coffee was more prevalent in society than water, it seemed, and between morning coffees, late-morning lattes, after-lunch dessert cafés, afternoon Rockstar pick-me-ups, and Red Bulls with dinner when he needed to work into the night... Well, he could blame his work all he wanted, but he was an addict and his addiction had caught up with him.

Patricia and Audra were the only two who knew about his little heart hiccups, and he intended to keep it that way. He hadn't even told his parents. He couldn't afford to show any weakness, nor let his clients see that he wasn't 100% focused on their careers.

"You're too young to be having heart issues, Arthur," Audra said. "And I say that as an unrepentant Diet Coke-a-holic."

Yeah, and Patricia had taken up smoking again after her divorce. They were all a mess, but they hid their bad habits fairly well and enabled each other in the name of productivity.

"Yeah, well, talk to me about it after my parents are back home. By the way, Danny and Jesse Black, bless their hearts, volunteered to host my parents' soiree this weekend. If you have other plans, I'm envious, and if not, please come suffer with me."

"Arthur, your parents are adorable, but I know it's not the same for you."

Arthur was grateful there were some folks who saw it his way. That his parents, America's Sweethearts, were also a lot to take.

"I equally adore and dread their visits. I know. I'm a terrible son."

"You are no such thing," Audra said, this time yawning loudly into the phone. "You are a good son, a great boss, and a phenomenal talent manager. Get some rest and be ready to put Operation: Put Lord Harrington's Saucy Mouth to Work into play first thing tomorrow."

"Thanks," Arthur groaned, however he wasn't sure if the groan was about her bad joke, or the fact that he had an idea of how he wanted to put that mouth to work—and it wasn't auditioning for acting jobs.

They hung up, and Arthur did his nightly hygiene routine. He then attempted to do his mindfulness practice, which the doctor strongly encouraged as a way to lower his blood pressure without medication. He had a couple more weeks before he was due to go back to see the doctor to determine whether his attempts at lifestyle changes had made a difference.

Had they? Not really. There was always something going on to send him running for his vices, and this week it was Ethan and his parents' impending visit.

Ethan.

He was the main thing interfering with Arthur's mindfulness exercises.

Because his mind was full of thoughts about the handsome, enigmatic actor.

Which version of Ethan was the real deal? What would it be like to have his full attention? To be the one to help resurrect his career?

To be the one to take care of him? Find pleasure with him?

Arthur stumbled to his feet and began to pace, though his foot was still angry with him.

"Why has this man turned you into a raging, hormonal teenager?"

And then he thought of the scene from Ethan's audition. He'd darkened the skin around his eyes, his curly dark hair was longer, and he'd fought with it while giving his monologue to the camera. Arthur replayed it one last time, his body heating as he watched Ethan chew on his lips before he pleaded with the person his words were directed to.

"To hell with you for making me want more for myself. I was content —no, I was blissfully happy in my self-indulgent world, and you come along, tearing me away from that place where each day was predictably the same, to a world where my heart is shredded repeatedly, every day, knowing I can't have you. My only relief is putting quill to paper, and even that slices me open. It's you. It's always you. And I can't take it anymore."

An actor was only as good as the writer's words. But Ethan had it in him to send any piece of work into the stratosphere with tangible emotional strength.

And Arthur needed to put that goal front and center.

It had to be about Ethan.

His dreams, which featured him and Ethan alone, walking along the beach, talking and laughing, maybe kissing under the warm California sun, had something else to say about that.

When Arthur woke to his alarm Tuesday morning, he could hear victory music in his head. His foot was still tender as he climbed out of bed and did his morning feeble attempts at fitness, crooning lovingly to Elvis, who was out in the kitchen yowling the song of his people, or all the domesticated house cats in the world who were currently starving as their humans went about their self-centered morning rituals.

"Patience is a virtue, E," he called to him before going to the bathroom to shower, rebandage his foot, and style his unruly bright red hair. He chose a slim-fitting, black, pin-striped double-breasted suit with a matching vest, a sharp white shirt, and a skinny cornflower-blue tie. Gray wingtips rounded out the look, and Arthur knew he looked like the Hollywood power broker he had to be for his clients.

He was Arthur Frye on a mission, and today's mission included keeping his clients' show on schedule, preparing for his parents' imminent arrival, and setting a career revival in motion for one dazzling Ethan Bradley.

He opened his coffee cabinet and his hand flitted between the decaf and regular espresso, wondering if today was the day he chose to make a difference with his health.

The buzz of his phone gave him pause.

It's very kind of the Blacks to offer to host. Please order one of those bouquets from Grammaticas that Roland loves so much. I understand he's arriving Thursday. Be a dear and make sure to get a bottle of the scotch that he loves as well. And a gift for Danny and Jesse. You'll know what's best.

The text went on screen after screen, with requests and guests to invite. It was literally three days away. But Ella knew Arthur would move heaven and earth for his parents, and therefore she made sure he knew just how many and what kind of bricks were involved. By the time Arthur had fed Elvis, made his fully caffeinated espresso and downed an everything bagel with cream cheese, he had a list of ten items to somehow complete while making Ethan Bradley a star once more.

Arthur collected his laptop in the crossbody leather satchel and shoved a Rockstar in the side pocket, thought for a second, then added a can of water, feeling proud of himself. Espresso in hand, he made his way down the back steps to the garage. Flicking on the light, he knew exactly what would make him feel powerful today.

He grinned like a cocky bastard.

Fifteen

Ethan

Ethan waited in the lobby of the Hollywood Spot Hotel in his too-big navy-blue suit, which was hanging weirdly due to the apples and oranges he'd shoved in the pockets. He'd eaten breakfast, sticking to yogurt, shredded wheat, and a banana instead of the waffles—better to get in the mindset of clean eating. Most roles he'd likely be reading for would require him to be in tip-top physical shape. He had to be ready to show most, if not all of his body, and potentially be able to meet rigorous physical demands.

All of that would be work. He wasn't in terrible shape, but he'd lost a lot of muscle mass from not eating well. Well, not eating much at all.

George Michael was playing over the lobby speakers while guests went in and out of the dining room with cups of coffee and attempted, like Ethan, to sneak out as many provisions as possible, although most of the others looked ready for the area's theme parks, like Universal

Studios or Knott's Berry Farm, or perhaps a day of touristy activities like wandering along Hollywood Boulevard.

Ethan wondered if he'd enjoy a day like that, if he had the extra funds, or perhaps it would be fun to visit more local-favorite joints like Cosmo had suggested. He hadn't had much time to do any touristy things in London, as he'd been working the whole time. Ethan liked to work. He liked the work of being an actor. He'd been grateful for the jobs...and at some point he supposed he began to assume he'd always have work.

Big mistake.

He caught a glimpse of himself in the mirror and decided he needed to divest himself of his fruit. No way did he want to be extra lumpy in front of Arthur. He left the apples, oranges, and even a banana in his room, but he kept the three granola bars he'd grabbed. He could hide those well enough. *Sorry for the food theft, Cosmo.*

He made it back down to the lobby, but his stomach was doing flip flops, wondering how he was going to act normal around Arthur all day, pretending like everything was okay. He started to tremble, thinking once more of that moment when he'd checked his bank account from his phone right before it had been switched off, only to find he was down to less than a hundred euros and he couldn't pay the rent on the room he'd let since he'd been locked out of his flat, got dropped by his manager and lost his contracts—

"Don't go there," he whispered to himself. He shook out his hands, feeling the granola bars thunk and crinkle in his jacket pocket with his movements. He wished he had some sort of backpack or tote bag, but then he would look even less like the hot young actor he was currently attempting to play.

Since when had living his life turned into another role to perform?

A shiny, flashy, metallic blue vintage sports car pulled into the hotel parking lot entrance and squealed to a stop under the archway. It was stealthy, there was no engine rumble nor exhaust smell. There was no familiar logo on the car, and Ethan had never seen anything like it, not that he was a big car expert. The man opened the door and stepped out wearing a pair of sleek sunglasses and a mouthwateringly fitted suit. The sun caught his fiery red hair—

Ethan found himself gawking at Arthur Frye.

Who smirked and gave him a beckoning gesture with his two fingers.

Ethan sucked in a breath, attempted to stand up a little straighter to hopefully hide the terrible fit of his suit, and he plastered on a brave smile he didn't feel in the least.

He pushed open the lobby doors and whistled. "That's a stunning car you've got there, Mr.—I mean, Arthur."

Arthur started to smile, but then he gave him a onceover and that disappointed frown was back.

"I'm sorry. It's the only suit I have left."

Arthur sighed and gave a resigned nod. He seemed more positive—and way less snarky—than he had been up to this point. And standing next to his sporty car, he was debonair. It was all Ethan could do to smile and not let the granola bars fall out of his pockets.

Arthur's face softened, and he chuckled. "Well? Are you ready?" He gestured for Ethan to climb in the car.

"Sorry. It's just...it's beautiful."

"My father gave it to me from his collection when I graduated from college. It wasn't running, the interior was trashed, but I had a dream," he said as he lowered his relatively tall frame into the incredibly compact car. Thankfully Ethan's suit was bigger now, because at one point it was so tight, squeezing into a small space like this would have caused him to Hulk out of his clothes. As it was, the material stretched over his knees as he attempted to fold them into the car and close the door, the sound of fabric stretched to its limits covered by the music playing low.

"Tight, huh?"

Ethan swung his shocked gaze to Arthur, and the man's eyes went wide, his cheeks the brightest red Ethan had ever seen on a person not straining at the gym.

"The fit. *The car.* Sorry. I'm used to it being a squeeze." Arthur laughed again and shook his head. His knees barely cleared the dash, but he looked so good behind the wheel. Arthur put the car in gear and pulled forward with more force than Ethan thought possible.

"It's so quiet," he remarked, bracing a hand on the dash, then he pulled it back and tried to pull his shirtsleeve down enough to buff the fingerprints off the wood.

"Oh, don't worry about that," Arthur said with a smile. "This car gets lots of affection from me after I drive it, which isn't often. And as to your other comment, it's quiet because it's been converted to electric. I tried for nearly ten years to get a new engine for it, but finally when these EV conversions became common and affordable, I went for it."

"Nice," Ethan said, rubbing his hand over the leather seats. "It's like new. And still good for the environment. I love that idea. I've never had a car of my own." He winced at that admission. "I mean, I learned how to drive in my dad's pickup and got my license in Iowa, but I left home and moved to Chicago, then New York, and the only other place I've lived is London, so...yeah."

Arthur had that frown going again. Would he ever *not* have it where Ethan was concerned?

"That's...wow, so different. We were a car family. My father *looooves* his cars. Growing up, we had a sensible car always, but my father has a whole collection of toy cars." Arthur shook his head and laughed. "I almost became a mechanic so we'd have something in common."

"I did construction with my father, but I wouldn't say we had anything in common. I didn't really have a choice. It was either that, or he wouldn't let my mother put me in dance, vocal, or acting lessons. I liked it, don't get me wrong, and I'm not afraid to work hard and get my hands dirty..."

"But you like being onstage more?" Arthur asked sincerely. Ethan had thought Arthur didn't have a single iota of interest in anything about him.

"I do, yeah. I felt more understood, sort of. Well, like, people were more accepting of me in theater than on a construction site. And while there's a certain joy in making something with your own hands, I love making people happy. When you're onstage, or even in film I suppose, you get to entertain a lot of people at once, you have more potential to make people happy. Building a house? Sure, it makes the homeowner happy, but I never got to see that part of the work."

Arthur glanced at him. "Well, you do good work on both stage and screen."

Ethan couldn't help it, his smile bloomed like a bud that had finally gotten some much-needed water and was no longer in danger of shriveling up. "Thank you."

Arthur frowned again. "It's true. And you've got a proven track record of excellent performances." He made a left turn and sighed before muttering, "Let's hope it's enough."

Ethan's stomach lurched as he thought once more that this trip, coming to LA, had been a terrible idea. Perhaps he should have gone back to Iowa, groveled to his father and brothers to forgive him, let him come home, and go back to work with them. He shuddered thinking about how that would have gone.

"Hey," Arthur said gently, placing a hand on his forearm and pulling his hand away from his mouth. He hadn't even noticed that he was chewing on what was left of his nails. His hands were a mess. "It's going to be okay," Arthur said, his usually stern voice sounding soft.

Ethan let out a long, shaky breath.

"Yeah. Sure. Thank you, again, Mr.—I mean, Arthur."

Arthur laughed. "You're going to give me a complex. Mr. Frye is my grandfather, I told you."

"Not your father?" Ethan asked, hoping maybe he could learn a little more about Arthur in the process.

"My father is Bernard Frye, the director? He's Bernie around here, or Bernard. Not Mr. anything, except maybe Mr. Hollywood in the seventies."

"Oh wow, you mean...he directed *Let it Go*! I love that movie."

Arthur smiled. "Yup. That was dear old Dad."

"That was my mom's favorite movie. I swear that movie was why she wanted me to be an actor to begin with."

"That's..." Arthur started to say something else but then he stopped himself, shook his head, and the frown was back. What did Ethan have to do to get past that frown?

Ethan had no idea where they were but some of the buildings looked familiar, as if he'd seen them on film at some point before. After about twenty minutes, Arthur pulled into a parking garage and parked in a reserved spot. He turned the car off and sat for a moment, his hands twisting on the steering wheel.

"Arthur? Did I do something wrong?"

He glanced at Ethan and grinned. "No. In fact, I think my father would be happy to hear that his film inspired your career."

Ethan wasn't sure how to respond, but his smile could not be contained. Until Arthur noticed him fidgeting in his suitcoat and heard the tell-tale crinkle of wrappers.

"What have you got there?"

Ethan's face flushed, and he was glad that it was fairly dark in the garage.

"Oh. Um, I kind of smuggled some granola bars of the continental breakfast. I know they don't allow that, but I wanted to make sure I had..." Was he really about to admit that he'd become quite concerned about where his next meal was coming from? Would a guy like Arthur understand? Ethan certainly never imagined he'd experience food insecurity. He was grateful to Reese and Arthur for putting him up at the hotel, and he would never ask for anything more. He was determined to pay them back every cent, and if...*when*. He had to think in terms of when, his fortunes changed, he was going to do anything he could to help those who needed it.

"Ethan?"

Arthur's tone was incredulous, and Ethan couldn't face him. Not this close, in this tiny, fancy clown car. But Arthur wasn't moving to get out of the car, and Ethan didn't want to come off as dramatic by fleeing.

"Hey," Arthur said, putting a hand on Ethan's arm. "Normally I wouldn't pry, but if we're going to be working together, I have to know things. About your financials, that kind of thing."

Ethan nodded and looked down at his hands, which he smashed together to keep Arthur from seeing them tremble. "I'll tell you whatever you need to know." He'd hate every minute of it, but he had no more pride.

"What happened to your earnings from *Ruby*? From the films? I know it wasn't life-changing money, but surely you had enough—"

"Any extra I had, I sent home to my folks. My mother...she was sick. Hospice. Not everything was covered."

"Oh, God. Ethan, I'm sorry. Did she pass?"

He nodded. "Two days before opening night in London." He offered Arthur a sad smile.

Arthur's eyes bugged out, and he placed a hand on his throat. "Why didn't you say anything?"

Ethan shrugged and looked down at his hands again. "I spoke to her every day until she couldn't anymore. She didn't want me to come home. She said I was doing exactly what she wanted me to do, that it was important I stay, that there was nothing for me to do at home." He let out a long breath.

"So you weren't there for her services?"

"Oh, there wasn't a service. My father and brothers had her buried, had our priest bless the grave. They said it wasn't necessary for me to come back. Ever." He laughed, and it sounded awful even to himself. "Mom was the one keeping us together, and without her... My father assumed I'd fail at acting in college and would come home. He was angry I chose not to stay in the family business and contribute, you know, since he'd paid for all the lessons and such. He basically told me if I was going off to New York, to not bother coming back. That was before Mom was sick. After? He wouldn't speak to me."

Ethan had never told another person about what happened when he left home. He dodged questions about his family in interviews, kept the conversation on whatever project he was working on at that time.

"I don't know what to say." Arthur's voice was barely above a whisper. "My parents are certainly a handful, but they've always supported me. In their own way." He chuckled and Ethan wondered what Arthur's upbringing was like.

Ethan smiled at him. "I'm glad." He hoped his smile didn't appear like it was about to fracture into a million pieces. "I think if I ever have kids, whether they want to be professional video game players, mimes, or clowns in the circus, I'll support them no matter what."

Arthur burst out laughing. "I'd have to draw the line at mimes. They're just so...have you ever actually watched mimes? We have several street performers on Hollywood Boulevard who do that stuff and it always annoys me. I want to pay them to stop. The only mimery I can stand is the Albert Brooks bit."

Ethan laughed, and it was a little easier to breathe. "I think whatever people can do to make others happy, that's good. That's all I've ever wanted to do."

Arthur placed his hand over Ethan's, who sucked in a breath, startled by his kind touch.

"We're going to make sure that you do. And I don't want you to worry about a thing, okay? Not food, not your hotel, nothing. After we sign the documents today, we're going shopping, and tomorrow I'm taking you to a spa. You need to look and feel your best when you take meetings, you got it?"

"No, Mr.—I mean, Arthur. I'll be okay. Please. I can't pay for—"

"Not now, but you will when you get work. Look, my assistant and I spent hours last night brainstorming, and we have plans. This is what we do. I just need you to trust me."

Ethan mustered up the bravest smile he could. "I do," he breathed.

Arthur's gaze dropped to Ethan's lips, and suddenly the car felt even smaller. Ethan's clothes felt tighter. He couldn't breathe. Arthur was still holding his hand, his deep blue eyes, surrounded by thick reddish lashes, only a tad lighter than his bright red hair, that gaze locked on his. Were they having a moment? Was this a test? What was the right move here?

A car honked somewhere in the garage, and Ethan jumped, banging his elbow on the door.

"We should—"

"Yeah."

Arthur scrambled out of his door and Ethan did the same. They walked around to the back, and when they stood in front of each other, Arthur gave Ethan an awkward shoulder punch, which seemed totally out of character for him.

"We're going to find the right work for you, I promise. I've been doing this a long time, and I know talent when I see it. If you're willing to put in the effort, I'll make sure you get what you want."

Ethan smiled, unsure if Arthur could deliver on that last one.

What Ethan really wanted? Besides enough money to live on? Was to have someone like Arthur Frye looking at him with pride, with appreciation. With love. And Ethan wanted to be worthy of that. So work he would, all the effort plus an extra hundred percent. He would make sure Arthur Frye was never sorry for backing him.

SIXTEEN

Arthur didn't think he actually took a deep breath until he was safe and secure in his office. When he'd left home that morning and chosen to take out the Triumph Vitesse, he'd been looking for that winning mind-set, that confidence boost he sometimes needed before taking on a new challenge, and wrangling Ethan Bradley's career back into some sort of successful trajectory was not going to be an easy task.

He hadn't thought, however, how he'd be affected being crammed into the tiny car with the once-larger-than-life actor. Or by the heart-breaking story he'd told. Of course, the professional side of Arthur's brain knew he'd be researching those details as soon as humanly possi-ble. He wasn't about to get roped in by a sob story that was all fiction, but there was no denying the pain Ethan tried so hard to hide behind that dazzling smile. If what he was saying was true, if this guy truly had no one to care for him, well...didn't that just amp up Arthur's protective streak?

He let Audra handle all of the paperwork with Ethan while he checked his email to see if any of the folks he reached out to had answered him. He had three positive responses who were willing to take meetings with Ethan, which was a good start. Arthur would have Audra set them all up, let her run with the scheduling. He just hoped he could make it through the shopping and spa trips without losing it.

Why did the guy have to be Arthur's catnip? Not that he had one particular type of guy he went for. He only had one *absolutely not* category, and that was artist. Ethan Bradley fit squarely into the no-no zone. Only Ethan was turning out to be nothing like he'd thought, and that was messing with Arthur's head.

That moment they'd had in the car? What had he been thinking?

He's the most beautiful human being I've ever seen.

Those lips are bliss in the flesh.

His voice makes my heart dance in my chest.

So it wasn't his head doing the thinking, it was his heart doing the feeling, and his heart was woefully out of practice. While he hadn't been celibate by any means, he'd kept his heart out of any relations. There was no room for feelings. Dates were strategic, sex was biologic, and work was no place for either.

That was when he realized he should not be the one to take Ethan shopping, because holy mother of the redeemer, he hadn't quite thought about the implications of such a trip.

Being fitted for clothes meant removing them first.

His phone buzzed, yanking him out of yet another panic when it came to Ethan.

"We're done here," Audra said, a smile in her voice. Arthur had heard them laughing together in the bullpen the whole time. It seemed Ethan had won over another member to his support team.

"I'll be right out."

But before he could stand from his desk, his cell phone buzzed. Mom.

"How can I be of service, Madame?" he answered, and his mother laughed.

"My darling boy, is this a bad time?"

He peeked through the window to see Audra and Ethan with their heads together, giggling. It was nice to see Ethan a bit more relaxed, and he knew Audra would boost his ego without making him insufferably arrogant. He could use the boost. Clothes always fit a man better when he felt good about himself.

"Never for you. What's up?"

"Oh," she said with a sigh. "I'm just worried about your father, and I wanted to talk to you about it before we come to town. He's been... restless lately. You know how he gets, and lately he's been trying to micromanage my book club meetings, and he turns his weekly lunches with the guys into an aria...I'm just...worried."

Arthur had worried, like his mother, that their decision to retire out to Palm Springs was premature. While Bernard had had some health issues, he was nowhere near depleted of creative juices. And while Palm Springs was a happening place, Bernard Frye wasn't happy unless he had a project to work on.

"How much of this is him driving you nuts and how much of it is him not being happy?"

She laughed softly and spoke closer to the phone. "More the latter, son. I know he'll be sixty-six this year, but he doesn't like feeling like he has nothing to offer. I don't know, what do you think?"

Arthur picked up a pen and flicked it between his fingers. "I think Dad has run through all of his hobbies and he needs something new."

"Well, what do you suggest, darling? We're sitting out here watching all of our friends get old."

Arthur sighed. "Are you happy out there?"

"I can be happy anywhere your father is, darling, you know that, and as long as I'm not too far from you."

"That doesn't answer my question. You know I'll do whatever's in my power to make you and Dad happy."

"What about you, Arthur? Are you happy?"

Ethan's full laugh filtered in, and he peeked out the blinds again to see him with his head back and his hands over his eyes as he laughed at something Audra said.

"Am I happy?" *You know, I thought I was fine, but I don't know that I know exactly what happy feels like?* "That's a good question, Mom. What I am is about to take a new client out for the treatment."

"Ooo," she murmured. "Who is your new client?"

Arthur found himself grinning. "Do you recall the actor who played the lead in Reese and Toby's *Ruby*?"

She gasped. "Oh, you mean that adorable young man Ethan Bradley? The one that was in that terribly sad British film, what was it called?"

"*An Affair on the Thames.*"

"That's the one." She made a purring sound. "He's *wonderful*. And he's your client now? He's a great catch for you. Does he not have an agent already?"

And this would be the true test. If he told his mother and she agreed with him, he'd feel vindicated in taking Ethan on. If she didn't...

"You recall the fallout Reese had from those pictures in London?"

She made thinking noises for a moment and then, "Ohhhh. That's right. His girlfriend. Poor man. You know, the British press is notorious for printing the most outrageous falsehoods. That was Ethan in those pictures then?"

"Yes. When those pictures came out, he was dropped from a couple of pictures and his management as well."

She growled. "Those pompous, arrogant, dimwitted fools. The poor man. Well, he's in the best possible hands now. Oh, darling, you should bring him to the soiree at the Blacks' on Friday! I would love to meet him."

Arthur shifted in his seat. Having Ethan there, around his family and their friends, where Arthur wouldn't necessarily be in the background like he was at official events...that seemed too close.

Maybe you just don't trust yourself to keep things aboveboard with him.

Which is exactly why you're having Audra handle his business.

"I'll see if he's available," he eventually said, laughing when his mother squealed in delight.

"Oh, that will be so fun! I can't wait to ask him what it was like working with Dame Judi Dench."

"I'm sure he'd be delighted to tell you."

"Wonderful. Now, you be a dear and think about what I said in regard to your father. If something were to come along, you know, that would catch his attention and perhaps give him something to bring him back his fire, you can maybe just mention it casually...without mentioning this conversation?"

"Yes, Mother. You taught me how to be discreet."

She chuckled. "Yes, I did. I taught you all I know. I hope it's served you well."

"It has, Mom. Thank you." His mother was in a mellow mood today, which was always Arthur's favorite, but if she was worried about Bernard, Arthur needed to be too. His mother didn't worry for no reason. Was dear old Dad up for a new project? Perhaps a mentorship? Possibly teaching classes or...

Arthur had an idea. He'd bring it up to his father on Friday, but for now, he needed to get on with Ethan.

Arthur opened the door to find Audra and Ethan huddled over her tablet, looking at the screen together. Ethan had his forearm on the desk and was looking down, his brows pinched in a look of concentration, his shirt pulled tight across his broad shoulders, his knees splayed out as he attempted to look closely.

"I just wanted you to have a look at some of their previous print campaigns to see the kind of vibe they're going for."

He nodded, the back of his crooked index finger stroking his chin. "Wow, I hadn't really thought about doing anything like that. Those guys are like...models, though."

Audra sat back and her eyebrows shot way up. "You could model too, my dear."

"You should listen to her," Arthur said as he approached.

Ethan gazed up at him with those eyes full of wonder...and hesitation, like a dog who's been abused. Like any word from Arthur's mouth could crush him. This man had really been to hell and back.

Arthur had seen actors get crushed and wash out early. The fact that Ethan hadn't given up after what happened in London gave Arthur confidence that he was resilient, and that would bode well for his career. Arthur wanted to be sure they picked the perfect projects for him. He'd have to make contact with the agents he routinely worked with, but first he wanted to introduce him around...

And his parents' soiree Friday would actually be a great opportunity for Ethan.

"Are you ready to go?" he asked him.

Ethan stood from the chair and tried to smooth down the front of his suit coat. "Sure."

Arthur pressed his lips together to keep from laughing at the crinkling sounds coming from his pocket. He reached for Ethan's biceps. "Audra, he's all set? All the papers signed?"

She nodded. "Yes, and I explained to him that you will be supervising me and I will be working for him."

Arthur nodded. "Good plan. Ethan, Audra is one helluva go-getter, and I think she'll make a great manager for you. I'll be here to oversee everything, but the two of you will be working closely together."

Ethan grinned widely at her and held out his hand. "Thank you, Audra, for taking a chance on me. I won't let you down."

He glanced back at Arthur as if to convey the same feeling.

"Well, the first thing we're going to do," he said, guiding Ethan over to his office door. He opened it and gave him a gentle push inside before he closed the door. "Is to divest you of your stolen goods."

Ethan's eyes went wide and he blushed. "Oh. Yeah, probably I shouldn't bring them shopping. They'll get crushed. Do you have someplace—"

Arthur pointed toward the tray on the top of his cabinet. "I think they'll be fine over there."

Ethan shuffled over and started pulled three granola bars out of his pockets. When he turned back around, Arthur noticed just how much the suit didn't fit him. He'd lost a lot of weight.

"Let's add lunch to our plans. I think we can hit one or two spots to shop before we grab you some sustenance."

"Oh, I'm fine. You don't—"

"Ethan," Arthur said, tilting his head. "You signed with Slade, with Audra and me. I'm going to take care of you, okay? No arguments. You signed over your right to argue about what's best for you."

Ethan's eyes went wide. "But—"

"I'm exaggerating," Arthur said when it seemed the poor guy was about to freak out. "But I'm your— *Audra* is your manager, and in order for us to make money, you've got to be in the best position to work. We can't have you going into meetings with your stomach growling."

Ethan looked down at his feet and nodded. "I just hope someone will hire me. I don't want to be indebted to you."

"Well, I do have a favor to ask you." He shoved his hands in his pockets. "I'll explain in the car?"

Ethan stood a little taller, his smile gone. "Okay." He started for the door and moved around Arthur, making extra effort not to touch him.

Well, shit. What had he said this time?

SEVENTEEN

Ethan

Ethan strolled out of Arthur's office, doing his best impression of someone who wasn't balancing on the edge of a chasm. He focused on breathing, just like he was taught in his acting workshop. In for three, hold for three, out for three, repeat as long as necessary to keep yourself in the moment, in control of your body, your response to stimuli. All that matters is the triangle. He continued his exercise through the lobby, and down the hall to the elevator, while in the elevator, while Arthur chatted with a colleague. Ethan was glad for the moment to collect himself, and to prepare to respond to whatever Arthur meant by a favor.

He thought he'd taken Arthur's measure, but what if he hadn't?

Ethan had decided he would never compromise himself for his career. He'd been asked for a "favor" before. At first, Ethan had told himself it was part of the job, or at least part of landing a job sometimes. He'd tried to convince himself that giving of his body wasn't any different than exposing himself in a role. It was a job, it was an act, and some acting required more sacrifice...But he'd ultimately gotten himself out of the situation before anything more traumatic happened. It was exactly the situation he'd thought of when he asked Spencer to be with him when he talked to the boys.

He didn't want to think Arthur would ask him to compromise himself.

The thought left a bad taste in his mouth.

They arrived in the parking garage and he let Arthur lead the way to the Triumph, which Ethan loved so much, but he was anxious about getting in the car, getting that close to Arthur again.

"We can grab something hearty at Nate'n Al's. How does that sound?"

"Sure, thank you."

Arthur unlocked Ethan's door and opened it, smiling brightly. "Hey, you look like you're headed to the firing squad." He chuckled. "Don't like shopping?"

Ethan blinked; he didn't want to seem unappreciative. "Shopping is fine, I guess. I'm not really...I haven't really done much. Just wear what I'm told."

Arthur closed his door for him after he folded himself into a pretzel. He trotted around and climbed into the driver's seat.

"Well, you're in luck. I happen to love this part of the makeover, and that's what we're doing today. I want to craft an image for you that is comfortable but flexible enough for formal events or casual outings. Sound good?"

Ethan put on a friendly smile, not wanting to offend. "Whatever you think is best."

Arthur nodded but his frown was back.

More breathing, E. Just breathe. In two three, hold two three, out two three.

Arthur talked a bit about the area they were driving in. "Patricia really helped me find all the good spots. I used to go out with my mother, but our tastes are quite different. I'd prefer to find locally owned shops with an up-and-coming designer than blow my wad at a name-brand designer showcase."

Ethan shrugged. "I grew up wearing whatever my mom could get from catalogs, as our biggest city was Des Moines and not a high-fashion place. We went to Chicago for some auditions and we'd go shopping there. She knew how to stretch a dollar, that's for sure." He smiled, remembering how much fun those trips were, just him and his mother, away from the judgy comments from his father and brothers. "Most of my stuff I lost when I got locked out of my flat the studio had let for me. All I've got left is a few of the items I was able to take from wardrobe after my projects and some second-hand stuff I picked up in London."

"I'm going to have Audra look into that situation for you. If at all possible, we'll get your stuff back, okay? They can't just confiscate your belongings. I'm sorry you had go through that."

"Thank you."

Ethan felt some of the tension leaving his limbs as Arthur talked about the places he liked to go in London. Ethan hadn't gotten to see a lot, but he'd been within walking distance to Camden from his hostel, and he'd enjoyed walking around and people watching.

"The Sky Garden is pretty amazing," Arthur said. "I took my parents there last time we went— Oh! That reminds me...the favor."

Ethan stiffened in his seat, his hands balling into fists.

Breathe.

"What's wrong?"

"Nothing. What do you want?"

He knew he sounded off, and by Arthur's wide eyes, he was not doing a good job of keeping it together.

"Ethan..." Arthur pulled the car over and turned as much as he could to face him. "We obviously need to clear the air here. If I'm going to be your manager, you need to be able to trust me. If that's not—"

"Look, it's just...when people I've worked with have asked me for a favor, they had something *specific* in mind. I didn't want that to be the case with you."

He forced himself to look Arthur in the eye as he spoke, so he saw the moment it dawned on him what Ethan's perception had been.

Arthur put a hand over his mouth, and his face paled.

"Ethan, no. I would never...I would never do that. Ever. Has that... that's happened to you?"

Ethan nodded and turned to face the window. He hated having to admit any of this to Arthur. He also hated that his mind had immediately gone somewhere so dark. He knew he should be careful who he trusted, but he wanted to trust Arthur.

"Listen to me, Ethan. I will never, ever let that happen to you, and if I or anyone I put you in contact with ever puts a toe out of line with you, I want you to tell me. Sexual harassment and assault are intolerable. I protect my people. Didn't Audra give you our company statement to look over?"

Ethan nodded and wrapped his arms around himself. He turned to give Arthur a look. "I don't put a lot of trust into pieces of paper."

Arthur narrowed his eyes. "I mean what I say, and that includes every piece of paper that comes out of my office. You've been dealt bad hand after bad hand, and that stops now. Do you understand? Ethan, I won't—"

"You can't undo what's been done, and I've learned my lesson. I'm more careful now. I'm sorry I even said anything.

Arthur exhaled and put the car in gear, his expression pulled tight. He didn't speak until they pulled up to what seemed like a strip mall, only it was a little more upscale. Once he had the valet park the car and they were walking toward one of the shops, Arthur stopped Ethan with a hand to his elbow.

"I heard what you said, okay? I'll drop it for now, but I want you to trust me. If you want to speak to any of my other clients, or if you want me to set you up with a therapist, whatever you need, I'll do it for you."

Ethan's chest unclenched and he could breathe deeply for the first time since Arthur's office. "Thank you."

Arthur nodded once and then pulled open the door to the first shop they came to. "Welcome to Miracle Merv's."

Mervin Serrano was a short, older Filipino man with brown skin, silver hair, and the most welcoming smile Ethan had seen since leaving home. He was a quick and efficient tailor and at the end of an hour, he'd fitted Ethan for three suits, and he'd outfitted him in surprisingly affordable casual wear.

Despite Arthur's assurances not to worry about the prices, Ethan appreciated Merv's careful selections. He even kept Ethan's suit and said he'd have his people make it look like new. A few dress shirts, undergarments, some trousers, a baby-blue wool sweater, and a rose-colored cashmere V-neck had him feeling like a million bucks when they left. Arthur carried one garment bag and Ethan another as they left the shop with plans to return in three days. It seemed Arthur and Merv had a relationship that involved quality expedited service.

"You bring me the most handsome customers, Mr. Frye."

Arthur gazed at Ethan approvingly. "And you do magic every time. He looks great, and it's all thanks to you, Merv."

Merv preened under Arthur's compliments, and they hugged before leaving his shop with Arthur's assurances they'd be back Friday.

"Let's get you fed."

Ethan stopped Arthur before they reached the valet stand. "I can't thank you enough for all of this."

Arthur grinned. "You look a million times more comfortable. It was worth it to see you smile like that."

"Like what?"

"Like you believe in yourself. In your worth. I like putting that look back on your face."

Ethan felt his cheeks flush. He'd left on the rose cashmere, with the sleeves pushed up on his forearms, and charcoal-gray slacks that hung perfectly from his hips and were so silky smooth against his legs as he walked, he really did feel like a million bucks.

He looked like he belonged in Hollywood, with a man like Arthur by his side, about to take him out to lunch.

And while he appreciated what Arthur said before, he couldn't help but feel disappointed.

There would likely never be an Arthur at his side as more than associates. How could there be when Ethan was such a mess? Arthur was a mature, successful man who could do so much better than a struggling actor who couldn't take care of himself. At least for today, he would soak up every moment he got to spend with Arthur.

Lunch was delicious. Ethan was grateful there had been healthy portions of salad full of proteins and all the vegetables he'd been missing. And the fresh-baked sourdough made his mouth so happy he had to hold back his moans.

"You probably should have gotten the steak," Arthur said with a laugh as Ethan used his bread crust to sop up what was left of his salad.

"I'm sorry. I'm being ridiculous, it's just so good."

Arthur rested his chin in his hand and gazed at Ethan with a warm expression.

"What? Do I have food in my teeth?"

"No," Arthur said. "It's been a while since I've been out with someone who takes the time to appreciate their food, who gets excited about new clothes. I think sometimes we take for granted the joy that comes from the small things in life, you know? Especially here in LA."

"But nothing today has been a small thing for me. Nothing you've done for me since I was dumped on you has been small. You're so good at what you do, Arthur. I'm so grateful."

"Stop it already," Arthur said with a laugh, his freckled cheeks growing rosy as he glanced away. "I like making my clients' lives better, maybe even make a few dreams come true in the process. It makes me happy to take care of things." Then he cleared his throat. "And now that I hopefully have proven myself to not be a total creep, the favor?"

"Sure." Ethan sat a little taller in his seat. *Truth time.*

"You already know that my parents are semi-Hollywood royalty?"

Ethan nodded, curious.

"They retired to the desert a couple of years ago, but they make regular trips into town and when they do, I'm expected to lay out the red carpet, so to speak."

"That's...wow, so you're close?"

"Oh yeah," Arthur said. "As close as I can be to them and still meet their expectations. They're coming to town this weekend, and they always like to have a good old-fashioned soirée with their Hollywood pals, both old and new. The Blacks offered to host, since I usually rent out the banquet room at their favorite restaurant, but it's closed for renovations. Anyway, I told my mother that you were in town and she'd love to meet you. Will you join us? There will be some folks there who would be great to get you face time with and... What?"

Ethan's chest bloomed with hope. "You'd want me to meet your parents? Wait, how does your mom know who I am?"

Arthur blushed again, and for the first time, he seemed a bit bashful, not like the man in charge. "She loved *Affair on the Thames.*"

"*Really*? Your mom saw my little movie?"

"We *all* loved it, Ethan. You were so compelling, it's like, impossible to look away."

Ethan was used to fans approaching him with shy requests for autographs, which he always gave. He'd be nowhere if folks didn't like his movies, but to have someone he respected so much admit to watching his film...and liking it?

"I'd be honored," he breathed. "Tell me where and when. And what can I bring?"

Arthur chuckled. "Yourself. Danny's assistant already has the menu planned. My friend Harvey is making my father's favorite cake. Everything's set. I'll pick you up. Or actually, I'll have Audra bring you. I need to be sure everything's settled—"

"Of course! Thank you. I'd be honored. And at least now I have decent clothes to wear."

Arthur let his gaze travel over Ethan's shoulders. "That sweater is perfect. It really makes your smile even more dazzling."

Ethan couldn't help his grin.

Okay, maybe he was off limits to Arthur, but he'd like to think he'd had a little effect on such a competent, professional, and attractive man. It was harmless, wasn't it, to have a crush? He wouldn't act on it, of course. Shouldn't. Look where that had gotten him! But he wanted to make Arthur proud, wanted to find work and repay him for his kindness. If part of that was entertaining Mrs. Frye, he'd do his very best.

"So, tomorrow?"

Arthur continued to gaze at Ethan as if he had something important to say.

"Tomorrow..." He left that word hanging there between them.

"Ye-es?" Ethan asked finally. They were back doing this again. Arthur leaving off in the middle of a thought, Ethan waiting for instruction. "Tomorrow? Is there a plan? Where do you want me?"

Ethan watched as Arthur's pale neck and cheeks flushed. "Want... you? Yes."

Ethan's own face flushed with Arthur's admission. Surely he meant—

"At the theater! Yes. I'd love for you to be there, to help Jesse and the boys. With the intimacy coordinator. Yes, that would be wonderful. And oh, here." Arthur handed Ethan an iPhone. "So Audra can get ahold of you. Our numbers are programmed into it, in case you need... anything."

It was odd to see Arthur get flustered. Ethan didn't dare hope that it had anything to do with him.

He took the phone, though he nearly dropped it when he touched Arthur's fingers. Arthur reached for the phone with his other hand to keep it from dropping and then they were sitting there, both of them holding onto the phone with both of their hands.

Arthur chuckled first, and when he was sure Ethan had a hold of it, he let go, carefully.

EIGHTEEN

rthur

Past Arthur made a good decision when he'd decided to have Audra pick up Ethan, take him to get his suits, and bring him to the Blacks for the party Friday night. Even though he'd been counting the hours, foolishly, until he could see him again after their trip to the salon Thursday, he'd anticipated a chaotic day on Friday, and he'd been right.

But Thursday...*ohhhh, Thursday* Arthur feared he'd lost the battle between his professional, rule-following side and his ridiculously romantic side. All it had taken was two smiles from Ethan: the one he wore when Arthur dropped him off at Emil's Salon and Spa, and the one that had greeted him when Arthur came back to pick him up three hours later.

"This really isn't necessary, Arthur," Ethan had pleaded. "I hate for you to spend your money—"

"You need to stop thinking of it that way. *We* are making an investment in your career, that's what all of this is about. You looking as polished as possible when Audra starts taking you for meetings next week will be more check marks in your favor with these people. While you're naturally beautiful, there are expectations—"

"I know, I've just never been that good at the physical fussing. Things were easier when my mom cut my hair—" He sucked in a sudden breath and turned to look out the window.

"Your mom sounds like she was a very resourceful woman who cared about you very much."

A smile played at Ethan's lips, and he sighed. "She saw something no one else did, and then made sure that *everyone* saw it. She believed in me." His voice sounded like he probably had when he was still a child.

"And we're going to make sure everyone here sees that *it* she saw in you, all right? If that means cucumbers on your eyes and a percussive therapy gun to remove stress in your facial skin, or even an IV drip of vitamins and minerals to have you glowing, we're going to do it."

Ethan had chuckled and turned to grin at Arthur. "I'll do whatever you say. It seems silly, but I'll do it."

"Haven't you ever had spa treatments?" Arthur asked, curious about his previous working experiences.

"Reese and Toby had massage therapists come in when we were working on *Ruby* at one point. Students, I think. That was nice. And my costar in *Take My Hand*? She and I used to get together at her flat and do masks and manicures. She had one of those paraffin wax things." He shrugged and chuckled. "It was fun."

Arthur still couldn't get over that *this* was the real Ethan, the real deal. So unassuming, so not like the narcissistic performers he'd known all of his life. And it didn't seem to be a show at all. The question was, could he turn on the confident actor when he needed to? He must have done it before to gain the roles he'd had, as casting directors were not known to suffer an insecure actor.

And when he'd walked out the salon door while Arthur was taking a call, with his loose curls bouncy, tossing his jacket over his shoulder and cocking a hip out as he looked around for Arthur's car, Arthur had hung up on Audra mid-sentence and leaned against the wall to keep from listing as his tongue nearly rolled out like a cartoon character.

Could this man *really* not have a clue?

When Ethan spotted him, he'd approached with that smile that had gotten him into film in the first place, the smile that had wowed audiences, earned *Ruby in Red Plaid* a Tony award, and made *Take My Hand* and *Affair on the Thames* box office hits. Absolutely, breathtakingly stunning. Arthur had given up trying to hide his approval. Ethan apparently needed reassurance, and Arthur wanted him feeling as confident as possible.

It helped that Arthur's reassurance was an understatement. He'd watched this man who'd been knocked down a peg or five start to crawl back out of the hole those damned pictures and stories had put him in and start to regain his shine. Arthur had been partially responsible, but he'd also seen firsthand how resilient Ethan was.

Jesse had called Arthur Thursday morning to gush about how awesome Ethan had been with Charlie, the intimacy coordinator, the day before. Reese had texted that he was grateful to have Ethan's help, and see, wasn't it a good thing that Reese had insisted Arthur take care of him? And Toby had texted to say the show was coming together swimmingly and that Spencer was super impressed with Ethan.

Audra had planned to take Ethan to lunch Friday and then spend the afternoon brainstorming the kinds of projects and goals Ethan had for his career. Arthur taught her how to do these sorts of intakes and prep sessions, and he wished he could watch her, but he thought it would be best for her to fly this one solo. Honestly, he didn't need to fall any harder for Ethan.

It was going to be hard enough to be around him on the periphery, but he knew he needed to back off. For Audra. But also for his own self-preservation.

He told himself that inviting Ethan to his parents' soiree would be good for his career facelift. There were folks in his parents' entourage who could put the word out about him, who might even be working on projects he'd be good for. And Ethan needed friends if he was going to stay in LA even for a little while. You couldn't be a solo operator here.

Arthur knew that firsthand. He was grateful for the network he'd created, especially considering what it took to pull off this event. It had required all of his powers of people herding, event organization, and personal flair to get his parents picked up from the hotel, taken on the five errands they needed to run, and to the Blacks' home fifteen minutes before their friends were set to arrive, and then he had to run back out and pick up Harvey and the cake, because Harvey's van broke down and Jinx was already picking up the catered food from The Dresden in his van, so Arthur's Volvo was going to have to work.

His mother was disappointed the cake wouldn't be set up before the company arrived, but Nora assured her that they could put it together on her rolling cart and present it after dinner to all the *oos* and *ahs* she wanted. Harvey had created a jungle-themed cake with vines and a waterfall effect to celebrate Bernard's 1977 adventure film, *Tropical Pursuit*. It was his first blockbuster hit, and it led to him getting tapped for so many projects that he called it the start of his career, even though it was his sixth feature. Harvey had outdone herself, if the pictures she'd sent Arthur were any indication of how awesome the cake would be.

Bless Nora Benson. If Arthur hadn't known how much Danny paid his assistant, he would have insisted on a raise for her. As it was, he kissed her on the cheek as he arrived and said, "Tickets to any show you want for the entire season, I swear to God."

Nora rolled her eyes and swatted at him. "You think this is the most extra thing I've had to do this week? Think again."

"That's right. Roland's here."

Roland Curtis, the legendary, multi-award-winning and well-respected film director, was the original owner of the beautiful mansion atop the Hollywood Hills. Nora had been his assistant until he decided to retire and move to Spain. When Danny bought the house from him, she stayed on, and she'd been working with the Blacks for several years now, though recently it was on and off. Nora was engaged to Roland's current assistant, Amalia, who now traveled back and forth between Spain and LA to be with Nora. That would be their lives until Jane graduated from high school in two years, and then Nora would retire as well.

Funny how it all worked out for Arthur's friends, this whole love business.

Well, not quite for Cosmo and Patricia, although Cosmo continued to be persistent while also giving Patricia space. It had been difficult to watch how hard Patricia took the end of her marriage, though every little bit of time she spent with Cosmo brought back more of her spark. The guy might look and sometimes act like a slacker, but he was one hundred percent all-in when it came to being everything Patricia needed, which for now meant being patient.

Speaking of, Arthur's best friend and business partner came rushing to his side to offer assistance with the cake, followed by Cosmo. Jinx, whose arms were full of catering trays, called out a hello as he brought in the food from The Dresden.

"Harvey's getting the pieces out of my car. Nora? Is the cart in the garage?"

She nodded, and Patricia and Cosmo darted away to grab it, him whispering something to her, Patricia giving him a sideways smile that Arthur knew meant she was enjoying the banter. Regardless of what Patricia thought about her need for time and space, she and Cosmo had a ridiculous amount of chemistry. The problem was that she had lost her confidence when she split with her husband, and though she'd done a lot to work on herself and had bought a new condo down the road from their office in Beverly Hills, she still resisted the idea of any sort of permanency with Cosmo.

Cosmo had committed to taking the ride with her, and Arthur had grown to appreciate how much the odd man doted on his best friend, even if their relationship was unconventional and his life choices were somewhat peculiar.

Bronson and Julian Manning—members of Danny's band, and the sons of Arthur's mentor, Horace (see, such a small world)—and Jesse were setting up gobs of food in the great room next to the kitchen. The doors were open to the outside patio, where tall gas heaters were lit, and Arthur spotted his parents holding court around the fire pit, fruity drinks in hand.

Danny and his drummer, Alex, were playing bartender, doing some sort of complicated moves a la Tom Cruise in *Cocktail.*

Lord, please don't let them get injured, Arthur thought, as they tossed glasses to each other. The bar was set up near the walkway to Nora's cottage. It was a tiki setup that Arthur hadn't seen before.

"Where did the *Forbidden Island* set come from?" Arthur asked Nora as he noticed the tiki torches around the pool, the straw mats on the patio, and the tropical flowers and leis distributed about the place.

"Danny has been watching too much YouTube, that's where. He and Alex have even been talking about buying property and opening a tiki bar with their 'signature recipes'." Nora put her hand to her forehead and gazed up at Arthur. "Please help Patricia put the kibosh on that."

Arthur chuckled. "You seem to think the term 'manager' means we actually can manage our clients when they get a wild hair."

She sighed loudly. "You'd think I'd know that by now."

"Thank you again for hosting my parents," Arthur said, giving her shoulder a squeeze. "You saved my life."

"That's an exaggeration, but okay."

She might have thought so, but Arthur would've been devastated if he'd had to tell his folks they couldn't host an elaborate soiree for their friends. Admittedly, their last-minute antics made things difficult, but he'd never failed to provide a great time for them. It took a lot of maneuvering to set these gatherings up three or four times a year, but he enjoyed spending the time with his parents and their often legendary guests. Thank goodness he had such great people in his life to assist or else his perfect streak would have crashed and burned.

"Darling, come over here."

Arthur paused for a deep, fortifying breath and then approached his mother.

"Hello everyone," he said as he neared the group of folks his parents had invited this time to say hello. There were the usual suspects: Rob and Michele Reiner, who'd brought Albert Brooks and his daughter with them; Arthur's aunt and godfather, screenwriting team Susie and Michael Bowman; acting/producing/directing power couple Kevin Bacon and Kyra Sedgewick; retired director Roland Curtis and his partner, Fernando; and producers Rebecca and Norman Reynolds. Tatiana Richmond, one of the best casting directors working today, rounded out Arthur's parents' crew this evening.

There were others who came to their soirees, sometimes up to fifty or even a hundred folks would pile into The Dresden to hang out with Hollywood royalty like his folks, and thankfully they all tended to be truly good human beings. Yes, there were still some of those to be found in LA.

"I hear you've been busy," his father said, taking Arthur's hand and drawing him over to sit beside him on the arm of the outdoor couch.

"Helping Reese and Toby with the musical, yeah. They're doing the fastest fast-tracking I've ever seen fast-tracked."

The group chuckled. Then they wanted to know about the show.

"Well, as you know, Reese got the inspiration from his grandfather's music and the story about how his grandparents met in Vegas in the sixties, but he added a queer spin to it to reflect, well, reality."

There were lots of murmurs of approval, and Arthur was once more darn proud to be working with such fantastic and talented people.

"Reese and Toby will be coming by, won't they?"

Arthur squeezed his father's hand and smiled at his mother. "Yes, they will. Toby and Spencer are picking up the first proofs of the books, and Reese, Jude, and Bailey are waiting until after Thomas retires for the evening to leave him with the night nurse."

"Poor Thomas," Roland said, and the others crooned. "He's such a force of nature on the piano. You know he performed on the scores for several of my projects."

"I didn't know that," Arthur said. "I'm sure Reese knows. He's a walking wiki page of his grandfather's accomplishments."

"No wonder you two are friends," his mother said. "You're a walking database about all things Hollywood in the eighties."

He felt his cheeks warm and wondered if he was standing too near one of the tiki torches. "Seeing as my parents were everywhere during that decade, it just feels like family history to me."

Roland chuckled and held up his drinks to those gathered. "A golden era indeed."

And it was. Between Bernard, Roland, Rob and Albert, not to mention Kevin Bacon, this circle of friends had been present for so many of the memorable movie moments in the '80s. His collection of stories and history of the era had been Arthur's way to connect with his parents, since an acting career hadn't in his future. He'd been an awkward kid, not traditionally handsome as he matured, and while he probably could have had a career as a Seth Green or Courtney Gains kind of character actor, he didn't particularly like being the center of attention, and pretty soon his parents gave up trying to make him that way. Dance, music, and vocal lessons had all been flops, so he did his best in school, becoming an honor roll student, a theater geek who was decent onstage, but thrived in the behind-the-scenes roles.

In college, he'd shown a knack for business that his parents steered toward talent managing alongside colleagues they'd known for years. He'd launched the careers of several A-list actors, and now he had his hands full with folks like Reese, Toby, Joe, Lydia. He was ready to concentrate on setting Audra up for success with Ethan, along with the up-and-comers he mentored through several workshops he participated in with his agent pals.

"You know, I wonder what Reese would think about doing a documentary about Thomas," Roland said. "He's led such a colorful life and with the success of *The Wrecking Crew* documentary and some others from that era, it might be a good time. Might even help get the play to Broadway."

Arthur beamed. This was one of the reasons why his parents' soirees were such a great idea. Putting the best minds of Hollywood together had netted some fantastic results, including a few Academy Award-winning films and several box-office successes.

Roland's suggestion kicked off a whole conversation about funding and what projects they were all working on, and it gave Arthur an opportunity to excuse himself to go check on the food and cake setup.

"Oh, Arthur dear," his mother called. "Isn't Audra coming?"

"She should be here soon, Mom. She's bringing her new client."

He swallowed hard, holding back the other titles he'd love to apply to Ethan...*love interest, leading man, plus-one.*

Could he honestly see himself having any of those? With an *actor*? Could he break his rule for Ethan Bradley?

"Oh, that's wonderful! She's ready, don't you think?" his father asked. "Who is she working with?"

Just then, he heard Patricia squeal, and he turned to see her hugging Audra. And behind the women...

"Ethan!"

Jesse trotted over to him in her bare feet and tiki print dress and hugged Ethan tightly. "So glad you made it."

There was a flurry of whispers from his parents' circle, and he felt his mother's hand at his back, but he couldn't tear his eyes away.

"So you gave him to Audra, huh? Probably smart."

"Yeah. It's good for her."

"Uh-huh," his mom said, patting his back. "Good for you, too."

Arthur turned to protest, and his mom winked at him.

Mom knows best.

NINETEEN

Ethan

Walking into a rock star's house in the Hollywood Hills that was full of more celebrities than any award show party he'd ever been to had Ethan's knees knocking. Jesse's hug grounded him, thankfully, until he spotted Arthur.

Who was staring at him with that expression Ethan had yet to decipher.

"Let's get you introduced—" Audra began, but his stomach had been off all day, thinking of this event, plus he had a bit of an allergic reaction going on, and he felt a sudden urge to flee.

"Actually, Jesse, can I use your restroom first?"

She gave him a knowing look, and Audra patted his back. "Don't take too long. It's better to show the sharks you have no fear first and *then* run away."

He hip-checked her, relieved that they'd hit it off so well, and then took Jesse's hand as she led him back into the house, hoping she wouldn't be grossed out by his sweaty palms.

"We can't have you meeting all of these people while you're green around the gills. Do you need to spew?"

She pulled him into a bathroom near the front door and he chuckled. "I don't think so? I just...needed a minute. Wow, I was not expecting to see faces I actually recognized. Kevin Bacon, are you kidding me?"

Jesse's eyes bugged out. "I know! But you know, since I met Danny, I've had my mind blown many times. The first time was Nikki Sixx, you know, from—"

"Yeah! I love Motley Crüe. You met him? Oh man, I would have totally freaked out."

She laughed. "I did. And Danny loves to tease me about it, but then we had a graduation party for Danny here, and Bronson got Alice Cooper to come! I got to see Danny stumble over his words and it made me feel better. I think everyone gets starstruck and freaks out at some point."

Ethan scoffed. "Except Arthur. He's so perfect. I bet he's never embarrassed himself in his life."

Jesse put a hand on Ethan's shoulder. "Arthur's a sweetheart. What do you mean?"

He flinched when she touched him. The baby-blue sweater, the one Arthur picked out specifically to match his eyes, was itchy under her palm, and he prayed he wasn't blotchy all over his neck. He hadn't realized it was made of wool until he'd gotten it back to the hotel. He hated showing weakness for any reason around Arthur, loathed that he'd had to meet this incredibly smart and competent man while he was at his lowest point. But Arthur had complimented the sweater, more than once, and Ethan wanted to do whatever it took to get Arthur to see him as an equal. Which wouldn't happen if he was scratching.

"I got this when he took me shopping and...well, he liked this one, and I wanted—"

"Oh God, Ethan, your neck is all red! Are you okay?"

"Yeah, I...um...I'm allergic to wool."

Jesse tilted her head to the side. "And you're wearing a wool sweater? I...*ohhh*."

He gave her a shrug, and she gave him a knowing glance before she nodded.

"Here, get it off." She grabbed for the hem and yanked the thing off before he could protest. "I think I've got some Benadryl."

"Oh, no, I don't want to be any trouble."

She rolled her eyes. "Stay here. I'll grab you one of Danny's shirts."

"But Jesse—"

"Hey, what's— What's wrong with your neck?"

And Ethan deflated.

Arthur had obviously come to see why he was being rude and running back inside the house instead of meeting his parents. He'd come clean and then take his punishment.

"I'm sorry, Arthur. I have a little wool allergy."

Arthur blinked at him in disbelief, but then his eyes widened as they traveled over the skin left uncovered by his white tank undershirt.

"You've got hives. That's not a little allergy, Ethan. Why didn't you say something?" Arthur's voice was gentle but his frown was severe.

Ethan figured it was time to fess up. "It was the piece of clothing that got the most reaction from you." He shrugged, shoved his hands in the pockets of his slacks and leaned a hip against the counter. "I figured...if wearing it could keep you smiling at me the way you did in the store, it would be worth a little itching."

There. He'd said it. He hadn't completely admitted to having a crush on the man, but he'd shown his hand.

Crush wasn't the right word. Crush was how he'd felt about Reese last summer. It didn't describe the deep admiration and attraction he felt for Arthur.

Arthur's jaw dropped, and Ethan wasn't sure which of them was redder at that point.

Jesse returned as Arthur was pulling the bathroom door closed. "Thank you, darling," he said, taking a pill bottle from her.

"Oh! Here," she said, passing him a black long-sleeved turtleneck. "It should fit. They're about the same size. It's Danny's wardrobe, though, so there aren't a lot of color options. It's cotton, Ethan, so it should help with the itching. Let me know if I can get you anything else."

"You're a peach," Arthur said to her. "Please let my parents know I needed a moment with Ethan and that we'll be right out."

"Sure thing," she said, peering through the crack curiously before Arthur closed the door rather firmly.

"I'm sorry," Ethan said. "I don't mean to keep you from your party."

Arthur shook his head and popped two pills out of the bottle. "Don't be. It's my parents' party. I've made sure they have everything they need. You're my priority now. Here," he said, dropping the pills into Ethan's hand.

He took them and bent forward to drink from the faucet, trying not to get water everywhere.

"You probably shouldn't drink alcohol tonight with those pills," Arthur said, stepping closer as Ethan straightened.

"Oh, it's okay. I don't drink. Not after...well, you know. That was the last time I had a drink."

"Here," Arthur said, presenting the turtleneck. "This will hide the redness. It's probably worse because the sweater hadn't been washed before you wore it. Oh, take off the tank, it's got bits of wool on it."

They both reached for Ethan's shirt, and Arthur's eyes went wide. He stepped back, holding the turtleneck to his own chest as if for protection as Ethan pulled the tank off. He tried to look away, but the giant mirror that took up the entire wall meant he couldn't *not* see Ethan shirtless.

"I didn't mean to cause a fuss. I didn't think it would be that bad. Guess I haven't worn wool in a while."

Arthur glanced at Ethan's shirtlessness and his cheeks grew redder. He shoved the turtleneck back at him and Ethan reached for it, but it slipped. They both went to grab for it and knocked heads.

"Oh, Arthur, are you okay? I'm not usually this clumsy!"

"I am," Arthur said, holding a hand to his forehead and wincing before he laughed. "It's my fault. I, uh, well, it's one thing to see you shirtless onscreen, but in person...it's overwhelming."

Ethan's smile fell. "Arthur, I know you don't want me..."

Arthur put his hands on Ethan's arms and they both froze at the contact. "I *do*, though. Very much. That's the problem."

Ethan sucked in a breath, terrified to believe his ears. "You do? But—"

"I do. Ethan, come on. You have to know."

"Know?"

"Know...how attractive you are. How I'm... That I'm attracted to you, okay?" He turned and placed his hands on the counter. "And I can't be. I shouldn't even be saying this to you, in here, with you..."

"Covered in hives? Because I was trying to impress you?" His heart was pounding. "I'm not sure I heard you right. Did you say—"

"You heard me right." Arthur let his head fall, and then he looked at Ethan in the mirror, over his glasses. "I'm sorry, Ethan. I'm being honest. I'm attracted to you, and that's wrong, especially after what you told me in the car the other day. I'm being completely unprofessional."

"You *would* be," Ethan said, allowing himself to give in and move a step closer. "If you were my *actual* manager. And if I hadn't been wishing for you to feel that way about me since you picked me up from Reese's."

Ethan loved that when Arthur stood and faced him, he had a couple of inches on him. Add on that thick, carefully tamed pompadour that Ethan wanted to muss, he was perfect. Lean, probably he struggled to keep weight on, with more freckles than Ethan had, and his skin was so pale, his lips so pink.

Ethan stepped closer, studying the swirl of color on Arthur's cheeks.

"But I don't...I don't *do* this, Ethan. And why would *you*? You could have anyone."

"Because I want *you* to see me."

Arthur sucked in a breath as he stared at Ethan's lips. "I do. But I can't. *We* can't."

Ethan willed Arthur closer, and for a moment he thought maybe it worked. Arthur leaned in, his breath ghosting across Ethan's face. Ethan lifted onto his toes, leading with his lips, slowly so as not to spook Arthur. He slid his hand forward and his fingers brushed Arthur's on the counter. He linked them, and sighed when Arthur did the same, giving Ethan's hand a squeeze.

"I want to be good for you, Arthur. I want you to..." So close their lips nearly brushed as Ethan spoke.

Arthur gasped.

Ethan placed his other hand on Arthur's chest, feeling his heart pounding beneath his touch.

"Ethan," he whispered.

There was the lightest of brushes, lip against lip, but it sent a shudder through Arthur's frame.

"God," he whispered, and Ethan moaned as Arthur's other arm went around his waist, pulling their bodies close, making light contact from pectoral to pelvis. It was agony to be so close and—

"Forgive me."

Arthur jerked Ethan closer, their torsos now pressed tightly, his grip on Ethan's belt so strong. He licked his lips, his tongue brushing Ethan's bottom lip and then it was happening. There was no denying the contact. This kiss was for real, the glide and pressure of his lips on Ethan's was intentional, insistent, and intense. He felt the tips of Arthur's long fingers digging into his side and loved the small sounds of desire Arthur let escape.

Ethan's legs nearly gave out, they were shaking so badly. He clung to Arthur's shoulders and dragged his tongue over Arthur's, relieved at his accepting moan. And just as he felt himself begin to—

The lights went out with a pop.

Surprised screams followed by laughter filtered into the bathroom.

They stood clutching at each other and panting in the dark as Ethan realized the shaking wasn't him.

"Shit," Arthur said. "This is a big one. Hold on." He turned Ethan and pushed him against the door, pinning him there with his back to the wood as Ethan began to hyperventilate. The house made a groaning sound, something glass broke on the counter, and Ethan jumped.

"Hey, shhh. It's okay, it's just an earthquake," Arthur said, stroking Ethan's hair. "You're safe. The doorway is a good place to be."

Ethan pressed his face into Arthur's chest and tried to slow his breathing.

When it finally stopped, there was another burst of laughter outside.

"How can they be laughing? Don't we need to—"

"Shhh," Arthur cooed into his hair. "Let's stay here for a minute, make sure it's actually done." He pulled his phone out of his pocket with one hand, still holding Ethan tight with the other, and he flicked on the flashlight. "Looks like a bottle of essential oil fell off the shelf onto the counter, that's all that happened in here."

The scent of lavender hit Ethan's nose and he sneezed.

"Bless you." Arthur chuckled, and Ethan could finally breathe.

"Are we all right?" Ethan whispered.

Arthur set his phone down on the counter with the light up so Ethan could see his intense expression.

"I should be asking you that question. *Are* we?"

"Are *we*?" Ethan asked right back.

Arthur sighed, and the crease was back on his forehead but he hadn't let go of Ethan for a second. "I'm sorry, Ethan. I should never... especially after what you told me."

Ethan smiled up at him and pressed his palm to Arthur's cheek. "I'm glad you did. *We* did. Kiss, I mean. Although I'm not happy the Earth moved."

Arthur ran a thumb over Ethan's lip. "Then I must be doing it wrong. The Earth *should* move."

"Oh, it moved," Ethan said, his breathing nearly back to normal. "And I'd like it to move some more, but..."

Arthur pulled back just enough to give them some air. "But we probably should check in on everyone, make sure the place is safe."

"And then?" Ethan asked hopefully.

"And then...we should socialize. I did bring you here to network."

"Mmm, you did. But then..."

"Then...I don't know, Ethan, I—"

"Don't answer yet. Think about it. Get back to me. But don't *not* think about it."

"I won't be able to not," Arthur said, his gaze back on Ethan's mouth. "Not that I should."

"Oh, you definitely should. Again. More. Many times more."

Arthur blew out a breath and ran a hand through his gorgeous hair. "You...Ethan."

Ethan admired the hell out of Arthur's seemingly unshakeable composure. But there, in the bathroom, he liked shook-up Arthur a lot.

Arthur pushed his glasses up his nose and straightened his coat. "Let me go first. Take a minute. When you come out, you should seem confident, not—"

"Lustful? Thoroughly kissed? Wanton?"

And Arthur smiled, for real this time, and as he ran a hand over his mouth, Ethan noticed just how long and delicate his fingers were.

"Then I guess this is a test of your acting skills. If you truly are those things, then you better act as if you're not."

"Yes, sir," Ethan breathed. He stepped away from the door and reached for the turtleneck, pulling it on over his head and tucking it into his slacks. He turned toward the mirror and began to finger comb his waves. "I truly am those things, thanks to you, and I'd like to be them again, so you should walk out there knowing that you're responsible for all this." He gestured to himself, from his messy hair and flushed cheeks, to the extra bulge in the front of his pants.

Arthur rolled his eyes and reached for the doorknob. "I'll see you in a few minutes."

But as he opened the door, he turned and gave Ethan a onceover, clicked his tongue against his teeth and let out a breath, muttering something about disasters.

Ethan hoped he meant the earthquake and not what they'd just done.

Because kissing Arthur Frye had been the best thing to happen to him since those stupid pictures came out, maybe even longer. And though Ethan had realized quickly that he was entitled to nothing in this life, he had hope that just maybe he was worthy of something good happening to him, and Arthur was something so good. Maybe too good.

He could hope.

Twenty

Arthur

"Oh my God, Arthur, are you all right?"

"Did you feel that?"

"Where's Ethan?"

Questions were shouted at Arthur from all sides, and then Danny started singing, "If the house is a rockin', don't bother knockin'," as he walked around the side of the house with Bronson and Julian.

Arthur held up a hand as he approached his parents, and then he was hit by a hundred and thirty pounds of dog.

"Legs!"

Arthur steadied himself, then scratched the Blacks' Irish Wolfhound behind her ears before she bounded off to Jane, who was sitting with Nora and her sister Connie. Connie was on Alex's lap, looking a little shaken herself.

"I'm fine. Ethan's fine. Is everyone out here okay?"

Jesse clutched at his arm. "We're all good out here. Danny and the guys are checking the gas and what's going on with the neighbors. Jane and Legs came out from her bedroom but she said she didn't see you in the house. It looks like the whole hillside is without power. Everything okay with you two?" She whispered the last part, her eyebrows raised.

And he couldn't pretend with her. He grinned. "Yeah. I think so."

"He's such a sweetheart, Arthur. Be gentle."

He nodded as she moved away, but he took her words in and deposited them in his vault to think about later. Obsess over.

Be gentle? With him?

Could it be that she saw the vulnerable side of Ethan as well? That she didn't think Arthur was evil for considering being more than professional with Ethan?

"Can you believe it?" Bernard said. "That was a five-point-eight. We haven't been in an earthquake this big for some time."

As Arthur rejoined his parents, they were all sharing tales of earthquakes past. It turned out the Bowmans actually lived up north in San Francisco when the quake of 1989 hit, and of course everyone old enough still had the 1994 Northridge quake fresh in their memories, as that one hit less than twenty miles away from Hollywood.

"It was terrible. My son's dorm was damaged. He lost friends in another building." Tatiana brushed her braids back over her shoulder and took another sip of her drink, obviously still grieving with her son after all these years.

"Thankfully they've made improvements to the building codes to keep us safer, but that's not including houses like this," Roland said. "Although, the architect on this project assured me they took extra precautions because of the hillside. I've never...knock on wood...had any damage from quakes up here.

"Hey, everything is good," Danny said as he rejoined them. "I'm going to shut off the gas just to be safe in case we have another, so we'll have to go without the fire pit. Sorry everyone." Danny shrugged.

"That's fine, dear," Ella said to him, patting him on the shoulder. "We've still got the tiki torches."

"True, and there are more in the garage," Nora said. "I've got LED candles turned on throughout the house too, so if anyone gets chilly and wants to come in, you're welcome."

"And you're more than welcome to stay," Jesse said. "As long as you'd like. I'd hate for anyone to be out driving in the dark with no lights to get down this hill. But if you need to go, Cosmo and Jinx are happy to give you rides."

There was some chatter, and folks pulled out their phones and made calls and texts to check on family.

"Hey." Audra approached him. "Everything okay with Ethan?"

Just the name made him grin like a kid with a treat. "Yeah, yeah. He's apparently, ah, allergic to wool. Jesse got him a shirt to wear and gave him some Benadryl."

Audra had an eyebrow raised at him.

"What?"

"Why are you like this?"

"Like what?

"Like...*you*! You're all smiley. Why are you smiley?"

He looked around and leaned close to her ear. "You absolutely have to take lead with Ethan. I cannot have any fingers in his dealings."

"Did you have fingers in his—"

"Audra!"

She snorted, and he pulled her away from the others to avoid being overheard.

"I'm sorry, Arthur, but seriously. What is wrong with you?"

"I kissed him," he whispered. "And I..."

"You kissed that boy and you liked it. Hot damn, boss!"

"Gah, don't call me boss right now! That's it. I'm making Patricia your boss. You're reassigned effective immediately. I can't be trusted."

She put her hands on his arms. "Arthur, take a breather here, man. Look, you can't help how you feel, right? Did you have consent?"

"Yes, I had consent! God, I'm not a total monster."

"But you think you're partially a monster. Look, you had me set up all the paperwork making me his manager. You signed off as my supervisor. If you want me to go through Patricia, I will, but seriously, Arthur, you need to take a breath. You taught me how to do this job, and I am determined to do right by him and make you proud. Leave the work stuff to me, and you just...enjoy yourself, all right?"

He had five more arguments on the tip of his tongue, but then

Ethan was coming out of the house with Spencer and Toby, laughing at something they said.

"Let me go take care of introductions. You just...have a drink. Before you break something in your face from actually smiling."

Audra walked off, flinging her long black hair over her shoulder. She looked sophisticated in black slacks and a cream sweater with boots on, and as she took Ethan by the arm, Arthur saw the confident way she handled him. Like a pro. Soon they were surrounded by Arthur's parents' friends, and Arthur watched as Audra introduced him as her new client, accepting congratulations for taking this important step in her career.

Arthur leaned against the tiki bar and thought his heart was about to leap out of his chest. He needed to let her handle everything. He needed to relax, true. But then he pressed a hand to his chest and felt his heart doing that little hop-skip thing he knew meant he'd probably had way too much caffeine today. Or, maybe he was experiencing a tad bit of stress.

You kissed a pseudo-client in a bathroom during an earthquake.

"Arthur, darling. What are you up to, hiding over here in the dark like a villain?" Toby gave a maniacal laugh as he wiggled his fingers before scooping Arthur up in a hug, lifting him off his feet like the extra friend he was.

"You'd be the last person I'd tell," he said with a smirk.

He accepted a hug from Spencer, and the three of them turned to watch Ethan take a seat in between Arthur's parents on the couch. He spoke animatedly to the guests, who listened with rapt attention.

"He's absolutely stunning," Spencer said. "And he was so good with the boys this week. And his voice, oh, I could listen to him sing for—What?"

Toby raised an eyebrow at Spencer and slipped an arm around Spencer's shoulders. "Careful, love. You'll have me panicking that you're going to run off with a younger man."

"And while I would gladly validate your feelings," Spencer said, wrapping his arms around Toby's waist. "You know better." They kissed, and Arthur looked away, turning to go behind the bar. If he was going to have to watch his friends canoodle all night, he was definitely going to need a drink. Red wine was supposed to be good for the heart, right?

"I mean, if you were *going* to leave me for a younger man, Ethan Bradley is quite the package."

Arthur cleared his throat, not wanting to hear Toby's thoughts on Ethan. It was weird to think about kissing someone who his friend had been intimate with. *Bleck.*

"You two lovebirds want something to drink? I know Danny was getting fancy with the mixed drinks, but I've got some plain old red wine—"

"Nonsense," Bernard said, approaching the bar. "I'll have you know that bottle came from my collection. It's a vintage cava from Pènedes in Spain and it's stellar."

Arthur shrugged and took a big swig from his glass, needing the buzz more than a wine-appreciation lesson. He smacked his lips. "Ahhh. Tastes delicious, Dad. Gentlemen?"

Toby shook his head and looked around the backyard, taking off after Jesse.

Spencer turned with a sigh. "I'll take some. I might need it."

Arthur poured him a hefty serving, noting that his eyes flared a bit as he accepted the glass.

"Your new client sure has that spark, doesn't he?" Bernard said, accepting a glass of wine from Arthur.

"Audra's client," he corrected. "She'll be working with him."

Bernard turned to him and raised an eyebrow. "Well, he certainly has nothing but stars in his eyes when he talks about *you.*" He leaned his elbow on the bar and gave Arthur a pointed look.

Spencer glanced between the two of them and pressed his lips together. "I'm going to go...yeah." He scurried away, obviously aware that Bernard Frye had something to say to his son.

"So what's keeping you busy these days?" Arthur asked Bernard before he had a chance to dig.

"Besides entertaining your mother? Planting, digging up, then replanting various succulents she wants in the yard? Eating out way more often than I ought to be? Nothing, that's what I'm up to." He drained his wine glass and leaned his elbows on the bar.

"Just because you're retired doesn't mean you have to stop doing the things you love," Arthur said softly, not wanting to send his father into a tizzy. "You have so much to offer beyond your desert gardening skills."

Bernard smiled. "She really has made the place cute, you know. You ought to come out to visit, you know, when the boys' show is over."

Could it be that his father missed him?

"I'd like that, Dad." He figured he might not have another opportunity for one-on-one with Bernie that night, so he pitched his idea. "Hey, what do you think about imparting some of your wisdom on up-and-coming filmmakers? You know you have a lot to say, and with media like podcasts, YouTube, or even the Masterclass program, you can reach a significant audience."

Bernard gazed thoughtfully at his son for several long minutes. Then he frowned, and Arthur knew he was hooked.

"You bet your ass I've got things to say. Where are the thoughtful, character-driven films? Why does everything have to be CGI dino disasters and superhero fight scenes? Where's the romance? I'm dying for some really good script to come along and grab me by the guts and... But, I don't know. What if I end up sounding like some old Boomer shouting at kids to get off my...I don't even have a lawn. My rock garden?"

Arthur smiled fondly at his father. Bernard was a proud man who had so much emotion and wisdom packed into his thin frame that he occasionally needed to let it out in a big emotional rant. Arthur got his height and slight build from his father and his delicate coloring and terrible eyesight from his mother. The red hair came from his father's side, but no one had it as shockingly bright as Arthur did.

"I'd love to bring you some ideas. When the show's over?"

"Yeah, yeah. When you're not busy. Although with this Bradley kid...you're gonna have your hands full."

"That's not...Audra is managing him, not me. And she's already got meetings set up—"

"You bet your ass, she does. She's got Tatiana bringing him in to read for a new Western she's casting and the Reynolds' have some ideas for rom coms they're pitching, and if they had a looker like him with the chops he's got? Shoo, he was a knockout in that *Thames* film. Your mother and I both left the theater wishing we were a few decades younger."

Arthur slapped a hand over his forehead as his dad shoved at his shoulder.

"I'm playing with you. Like I said, he's all moony-eyed talking about, 'Oh, Mrs. Frye, your son has such wonderful taste," he said, mimicking Ethan's enthusiastic way of speaking, "and, 'Mr. Frye, that car you gave him is gorgeous.' That's when I knew, you know."

"Knew what, Dad?" Arthur poured himself his third glass of wine. He couldn't help himself, he glanced over to where Ethan was laughing at Jesse's imitation of how timid the boys were touching each other.

"You don't take the Vitesse out for just anyone."

"What are you talking about? I love that car—"

"And you rarely drive it, much less with anyone in it."

"Dad, Ethan is...it would be improper."

"Says who?"

"Says Human Resources! Says the divorce rate in Hollywood. Besides. It's a terrible idea to date the talent."

Bernard coughed. "If that were true, then you wouldn't be here. Wouldn't exist. You'd have never made it past a twinkle in your old man's eye."

It was true. Ella had been the star of one of Bernard's films, and they'd quickly become one of Hollywood's hottest couples back in the days before that sort of relationship was considered poor taste, or like today, might've landed his father in hot water with the studios.

"He's very special," Arthur said, his voice so low, he almost hoped his father didn't hear him.

"The more important determination is whether he's special enough for my son?"

Arthur turned sharply to find his father smiling fondly at him. His parents had been fully accepting of him being gay when he came out in college. He hadn't really been worried about telling them because they'd gone overboard to be the most understanding parents ever. His father had been open about his own bisexuality and the nature of his parents' swinging relationship, which ended after one of his mother's affairs turned serious and threatened their marriage.

As far as Arthur knew, they hadn't revived that part of their relationship, and he hoped that if they had, he'd never find out about it. It was one of the darkest times in their lives together, an experience that shook up Arthur's whole world. It was part of the reason he had his rules, and why he worked so hard to keep his life and the lives of those he managed stable. Or, as stable as possible.

Spencer trotted over. "Oh, Arthur, I'm sorry. Reese texted to say they're not going to make it. Seems Thomas is upset over the earthquake. He sends his apologies."

"Totally understand. Thank you."

"Oh, and Toby brought some of the proofs for you to take a look at." He beamed. "The book turned out amazing. Thank you for setting us up with the printer! They were willing to fulfill a rush order so we'd have them to sell at opening night!"

Arthur grinned. "I'm so glad it worked out."

Spencer glanced at Bernard, then turned his attention back to Arthur. "I know Reese and Toby have been overwhelmed with everything, but I want you to know that they—and I—very much appreciate everything you've done to set them up for success. They couldn't have done any of this without you."

Arthur's eyes burned as he nodded at Spencer. "It's my job," he said, but when Spencer tried to argue, he held up a hand. "I'd do anything for those two. They're my best friends."

Spencer nodded, not quite buying it, and he excused himself.

"He's right, you know." Bernie came around the bar and leaned on his elbows next to Arthur. "You are a fantastic manager. So competent and caring. They're lucky to have you." He put his arm around his son and kissed the side of his head. "*I'm* lucky to have you."

Before he started sobbing like a soap opera star, he exhaled. "Does that mean you'll let me do some information gathering, work up some proposals for you? I don't want to push you, but I want you to be happy, Dad."

Bernard tapped his fingers on the bar. "Do that. And talk to Reese, when he's ready, about the documentary about Thomas. Maybe we can get some behind-the-scenes on the show in the next week or so. I can see opening with preparations for opening night, the transition to the first performance, then zoom in on Reese performing his grandfather's songs...and then Thomas watching fondly. Oh, baby. We're talking Academy Award over here, not to mention a lasting love letter to Thomas's legacy."

Bernard's excitement was contagious.

Someone turned on music, and the group followed Danny and Jesse's lead and started dancing. Ethan was dancing with Ella, and he had moves that had his mother laughing and swooning. The others watched them as they did their own steps to "Waiting For A Girl Like You," Ethan dancing with Ella, and Kevin dancing with Kyra just as he'd done with Lori Singer in *Footloose*. Toby and Spencer danced with them, and Arthur heard Ethan tell Kevin that he'd played Ren in a stage production of *Footloose* in Chicago when he was in college. That led to Kyra, Ella, Spencer, and Ethan doing the choreography to the musical *Chicago*, and Jesse and Ella doing choreography to "One" from *A Chorus Line* while Toby sang the music...

Nora approached the bar and handed a plate of food to Arthur.

"You better sop up that wine with some food," she said, raising her eyebrow at him.

"Nora, dear, we're only on...how many bottles have we opened?" Bernard looked at the bottles behind the bar and then he was called away by Roland.

"Thanks," Arthur said, hungrier—and drunker—than he realized. "And thank you, so much. My parents are having a wonderful time. Everyone is."

Arthur watched as Roland led Bernard into the house, along with their dream team, probably to plot out this documentary. *Good.* His father with a bone was way better than him with nothing to do, and Ella was having the time of her life dancing with the boys, being fawned over.

"Well, Jesse's not going to be okay if I don't get her to take a breather, and Danny better save his voice for rehearsals."

"When did we become the parents, huh?" Arthur asked her, giving her shoulder a bump. He and Nora had bonded on many occasions over wrangling the talent in their keep. When Patricia went on a much-needed sabbatical, it had been Arthur and Nora who kept the Blackened ship afloat. Patricia may have been back as Blackened's manager, but Nora managed Danny, the estate, his daughter, the personal stuff...and she was brilliant. "You know, in another life you would have made a fantastic manager."

She scoffed. "What do you think I've been doing? And making more money, I should add. But in two more years when Janie goes off to college, I'm going to retire. Amalia and I want to travel, and I want to suck the life out of every day I have left with her."

"I admire that," Arthur said, his eyes glued to Ethan on the makeshift dance floor. "I don't even think about retiring. It seems so far away."

"For you, sure, you've got a lot of years left to work, but you have to have dreams for yourself, Arthur. Can't just make everyone else's come true. What do you really want? For you?"

"A nap."

Nora barked out a laugh. "Go on inside, then. I'll keep an eye on these wildlings."

He rested his chin in his hand, barely able to keep his head up, but he couldn't take his eyes off of Ethan. "And miss the show?"

She sighed, and it was a long, drawn-out, resigned kind of noise. "You, too, huh? I thought you were my one shot at having someone else with their head on straight. I guess not."

Arthur stood to his full height, which put the short Black woman at about his sternum, but she had so much power just in that one expression with the eyebrow raised, and that *mmm mmm mmm* she was laying on him.

"I thought I had my head on straight. Then the Earth shook a week ago, he was dropped in my lap, and I was asked to take care of him. I wanted nothing to do with him. A week ago. And now all I want *him*."

"Uh-huh. Then why is he dancing with your mom and not you?"

Arthur laughed. "Because she's the dancer, not me. I'm the rub-your-feet-after-you've-danced-all-night kind of guy. I'm the cook-you-dinner-when-you've-had-a-rough-day kind of guy. Not that either of those have ever happened to me before, because people can't accept the fact that the ugly duckling might have something of value to offer."

Nora slapped his arm, and he turned on her, shocked.

"I better not ever hear that out of your mouth ever again, you hear me?"

"Ow," he said, stumbling a bit. "What did I say?"

"You know exactly what you said. Arthur Emmanuel Frye, you going to make me—"

"It's true, Nora. Look, all I'm going to do is get him work and let Audra handle the details. Hopefully that work will take him far from LA because if he stays here, this place will ruin him."

"Arthur," she said, placing a hand on his arm. "What about you? What about what you want?"

"Right now, I want to watch that beautiful man sweep my mother off her feet. I want my father to find something to be passionate about and run with it. I want Reese and Toby to get through this show in one piece. Then I want to take a nap." He rested his crossed arms on the bar and lay his head down on top of them. He closed his eyes and sighed. "I just want everyone to be happy."

Twenty-One

E^{than}

"Be a darling and get me some water?"

For a woman in her late 60s, Ella Frye was in fantastic shape, and dancing with her had been the most fun Ethan had had in a long time. Well, except for his shopping trip and lunch with Arthur.

"Yes, ma'am," he said, leading her into the house. The power had come back on and everyone was gathered inside, snacking and laughing. Most of the Fryes' friends were saying their goodbyes, so Ethan handed Ella a glass of water and let her mingle.

He needed to sit down and catch his own breath.

"Have you eaten?" Jane asked.

"Hey, where did you come from?"

She shrugged. "I've been hanging out with Legs in my room. She got really nervous when the power went out with that loud pop."

"I don't blame her. Is she still in there?"

"Yeah, she's in her crate. I just came to grab some food. Come on, let's go see what's left."

Ethan followed her over to the trays of food that were still on warmers, and he nearly drooled over the delicious cuts of prime rib and roasted turkey. He grabbed a plate and heaped it with meat and salad and then he followed her outside, where Danny's band members had turned the fire back on and were eating as well.

"God, this food is delicious." Ethan was ravenous, snacking as Jane led him to the fire pit.

"Guys, this is Ethan. I don't know if you met him yet."

And Ethan found himself shaking hands with Julian, Bronson, and Alex from Blackened, along with Nora's sister Connie. Jane asked her where Nora and Amalia were, and Connie told her they'd retired already.

"There you are," Audra said to Ethan. "Hey, I've got to get home, but I wanted to let you know that I've got meetings set up for you Monday, and Tatiana wants to see you Tuesday, all right? So I'll pick you up bright and early. Cosmo said he'll take you back to the hotel tonight, when him and Jinx and Patricia finish cleaning up in the kitchen."

Ethan looked over his shoulder. "I should go help."

"No, it's fine. Finish eating." She leaned in and kissed him on the cheek. "Get some rest this weekend, okay?"

He placed a hand over hers. "Thank you," he whispered. "For everything. I really appreciate you introducing me to everyone tonight, and setting up all the appointments. I promise, I'll do my best."

"I know you will. Tell Arthur I said I'll call him tomorrow."

She waved to everyone and made her way toward the house.

"Where is Arthur, anyway?" Ethan wondered.

The guys all looked at each other, as if none of them wanted to be the one to spill the beans.

"Well," Danny finally said. "We did a sweep not too long ago, and I found my wife about to pass out, so I dumped her unceremoniously in our bed."

"And we found Arthur passed out behind the tiki bar, so we carried him in and put him in the guest room." Julian chuckled.

"That room gets a lot of action whenever we have people over," Danny said. "You guys have all passed out in that bed."

"Uh-huh. Last time, you know, at the fundraiser for the musical, Spencer passed out," Alex offered.

"Yeah, but he's a lunger. He was sick, not drunk like you fucks."

They all laughed and held up their beers.

"God, it's a wonder I've turned out to be a normal kid," Jane said. "Surrounded by all of you."

Ethan laughed. "I don't know if you could be called a normal kid, Jane."

She turned on him with a scowl and everyone laughed. "I go to school like a normal kid."

"Yeah," Danny said, "and then you go to the barn and ride your horse, and you go on tour with your dad in the summer—"

"That's different—"

"And you live in the Hollywood hills."

She groaned. "See, that's why I wanted Bailey to be here. At least he gets me."

"Yeah, he won't be a normal kid for long either," Danny said. "Not once the musical starts up. If they go to Broadway with it? Jesse's already talking to him about how they can work together this summer to finish his diploma before he leaves, like graduate a year early."

Jane sighed. "And I'll be alone for my senior year then. Oh well. Maybe I'll drop out and join a rock band."

Danny started to protest but she held up a finger.

"Not a single one of you can speak to that."

"I could," Ethan said. "I finished high school and went to college before I went to New York."

She rolled her eyes. "Great. None of you are on my side."

"We are, baby," Danny said. "You can do whatever you want. You want to start a rock band, let's do it. But you gotta earn your diploma, however you want to. Don't be a dropout like I was."

"What do *you* want to do, Jane?" Ethan said.

She shrugged and let out a big moan. "I don't know. I don't know if I want music to be my career like Dad, or dance like Jesse, or if I want to do something different. I just have no idea."

"That's the best part about college," Ethan said, looking around, wondering if any of Danny's band had gone. "I tried all kinds of things. I even thought I might want to be an accountant at one point." When she laughed he continued. "I'm serious!"

"What happened?"

He scrunched up his face. "I don't math. Like at all. So I auditioned for every show and thought, well, if I'm sick of acting by the time I graduate, I'll have my decision made for me."

"And were you?"

"If I was, I wouldn't be here right now trying to break into something, would I?"

She shook her head and grinned. "So, you think I'll figure it out?"

"Isn't that what Jesse's been telling you?" Danny asked her.

"Yeah, but she doesn't count. She's my mom now. It helps to hear from someone outside my family. I mean, my mother acted, but it wasn't very good for her, so I didn't have a great example from her."

Ethan frowned. "Who's your mom?"

"Brooke Jones."

Ethan tried to school his face. He'd met Brooke in New York. Her boyfriend, the producer Oliver Beck, had been one of the first film people Ethan auditioned for. In private. In his office. And he felt his stomach roil just thinking about it.

"Oh, sure. I've met her. She's very talented."

His gaze shot to Danny, and they exchanged a knowing look. Brooke's descent into drugs and her need to step away from acting for mental health reasons had been splashed all over the internet a couple of years prior. Ethan had paid attention because he'd met her right about the time things went south. She'd been kind of awful to him.

They were better off without her, that was for sure.

Jane looked like she wanted to ask a question, but she changed her mind. "I'm going to go see if Bailey can play *Among Us*. Goodnight y'all." She went over to kiss Danny's cheek and he hugged her tight, whispering in her ear before letting her go. Once she was in the house, he leveled me with his gaze.

"I take it your meeting with Brooke wasn't good?"

"She was all right," Ethan said, not wanting to shit-talk Danny's ex.

"It was her boyfriend. I read for him and...let's just say I would never recommend anyone be alone with him."

The guys looked at each other and swore under their breaths. "Yeah, we knew something was off about him. Thank God Jane never spent a night under his roof. That was when I got full custody of her. Brooke left him a few months later, strung out, and went to rehab. She's been living with her mom the past couple of years and trying to figure out what to do with the rest of her life. She and Jane don't talk much. It sucks, but yeah. I hate that it gave Jane a bad taste in her mouth about acting because she's actually pretty great at it."

Ethan shrugged and rubbed at his arms. It was getting a little chilly, now that the sweat had dried under the borrowed turtleneck. He wanted to go...home. Too bad he didn't have one of those. But Cosmo and Patricia were in the kitchen together, and they looked like they were in a serious conversation. Ethan didn't want to interrupt.

"I'm happy to talk to her about it whenever. She's a great kid. Great voice, too."

Danny smiled. "Yeah. She's the best thing that ever happened to me." Then he got serious. "So what's up with you? I hear you're out here looking for work."

Ethan leaned back. Reality crashing in after a great night of pretending to be okay with the world kinda sucked. "Yeah. Something. Anything."

Danny rubbed at his chin. "Patricia filled us in on London, man. Fucked-up deal."

Ethan nodded and rubbed his palms on his thighs, really wishing he could make his escape.

"Arthur will take care of you," Julian said, leaning forward. "He interned under my father. He's a fantastic manager. You wouldn't believe the clients he's worked with."

"Actually, Audra is working with me," he said, his eyes darting around. "Arthur didn't want to take me on." And whether that was really because he was attracted to Ethan or because he didn't want to hang his reputation on him, he didn't know which to believe. He hoped it wasn't the latter.

Julian and Bronson frowned. "A catch like you?" Bronson said.

"Well, I guess she's gotta take on a big fish at some point. She'll do great. Patricia and Arthur will be behind her one hundred percent."

"I wouldn't say I'm a big anything, other than a big pain in the ass. But I'm certainly going to try my best for them."

"Awesome," Julian said, and then the brothers stood. "We've got brunch with Mom and Dad in the morning, so we're going to beg off." The guys all shook hands, and Ethan stood, feeling totally out of place. He said his goodbyes and then he wandered into the kitchen. Cosmo and Patricia were gone. Jinx was gone. Okay. He heard voices down the hall, so he crept closer.

"I'll touch base with Arthur tomorrow and then reach out to Reese."

Bernard was showing some notes on a tablet to Toby and Spencer. They were sitting around a very Gothic-looking living room, which didn't quite match the rest of the house's sleek, modern look, but it was awesome. All kinds of horror memorabilia. Roland and Fernando stood and shook hands.

"Call me when you have more information. I'd love to work with you on this. It would be a lovely way to honor Thomas."

Bernard and Roland hugged, then Bernard kissed cheeks with Fernando and they spoke to each other in Spanish.

"Oh, hello, dear," Ella said, returning to the living room from farther down the hall. "I just went to check on Arthur. Bless his heart, he fell asleep. We'd take him with us, but we've got the two-seater. Bernard? Should we leave our car here and take Arthur home?"

"I can drive him home," Ethan offered, wondering where he'd found the gumption to insert himself into Frye family business.

Ella grinned and clapped her hands together. Bernard gave him an atta boy kind of nod and pat on the shoulder.

"That would be wonderful, darling. He's in the spare room, just down the hall there. It was so nice meeting you. Join us for dinner tomorrow with Arthur, won't you?"

"I, um, thank you. I'll speak to him."

They waved, said goodbye to Danny and the boys, who followed them out, and then the foyer was empty except for Ethan and Danny.

"Let's see if Art is awake. You're both welcome to stay. I've got a pullout couch in the library if you want. Roland and Fernando've got their usual room..."

"No, that's okay. Thank you. You've done so much already."

Danny shook hands with Ethan and didn't let go right away. "You're a good guy, Bradley. I'm glad you came tonight. And thank you for talking to Jane. She's been in this 'my parents don't know anything' phase for a while, and while I know it could be way worse, it sucks to not be able to swoop in and have all the answers, you know?"

"I get it. Happy to help."

He still hadn't let go of Ethan's hand.

"And it sure is nice of you to take care of Art tonight. Guy works hard. Sure would like to see him find a nice guy."

Ethan blew out a breath. "He's really great. I just... Yeah, it would be nice. He deserves to be happy."

Danny shook a couple more times, gave Ethan this weird fatherly kind of onceover and then finally let go, pounding on his back. He gestured for Ethan to walk ahead of him and then pointed out the spare room.

"I'm down here on the left if you need anything. I'll check on you two in a few."

Ethan smiled at him and whispered thanks before he opened the door.

And his breath caught.

He'd never seen anything more precious in his life.

Arthur was sprawled out on his stomach, facing the door, his lips smushed and open. His hair was a mess, his feet hung off the far side of the bed, and Ethan wished he could leave him be, but he also thought he should at least make sure he was breathing.

He sat on the edge of the bed and reached over to brush Arthur's hair back. It was so soft, so thick it curled around Ethan's fingers. He allowed himself to run his fingers through it twice, three times, and then Arthur stirred, one blue eye opening.

"Ethan?" He squinted, and Ethan realized he'd never seen Arthur without his glasses.

"Hey, you're in Danny's spare room. Did you want to crash here?"

"No!" He pushed himself up and squinted at the clock on the bedside table next to Ethan. "Elvis! I have to go."

He tried to stand, but he sat down and put a hand to his forehead. "Ugh, spinning."

"I told your parents I would drive you home if you needed to go," Ethan said. "They were worried about you."

Arthur rubbed his hands over his face. "You said you didn't drive though."

"I said I'd never owned a car. I know how to drive. I have a license."

Arthur nodded. He slipped his shoes on and reached for his coat. He picked up his tie and glasses from the bedside table, put the glasses on and put the tie in his pocket.

"The keys?" Ethan asked in a quiet voice as Arthur passed him.

"The keys?" Arthur stared at him as if he'd spoken a foreign language.

Ethan held out his hand and smiled. "The keys? To your car?"

"Don't need them," he said, and he trudged out the door, his feet shuffling over the carpet. Once they hit the foyer, they made a loud clacking sound, so Arthur froze, then tiptoed toward the door, wobbling on his feet as he went.

Adorable.

Ethan caught movement out of the corner of his eye, and Nora came to the door of the kitchen. "Lots of water for that one," she whispered, pointing to Arthur.

Ethan beamed. "Yes, ma'am. I'll take care of him."

And Nora smiled right back.

Ethan trotted to catch up to Arthur at the front door, which he was trying to push rather than pull.

"Here," Ethan said gently, taking the doorknob in hand. He pulled the door and Arthur looked at it like it was a foreign concept. He eyed it suspiciously as he rounded the corner and then nearly faceplanted as he missed the step.

"Hey," Ethan said, sliding his arm around Arthur's waist, wondering how much of this was wine and how much was exhaustion Arthur leaned into him and they trudged slowly toward the Volvo. When they reached it, Arthur tried to go to the driver's side.

"I'll drive you, don't worry," Ethan said, gently leading Arthur around to the passenger side.

"I can't see," Arthur said as Ethan guided him into the seat.

"Because your eyes are closed," Ethan said, and his heart was melting at how precious Arthur was. He really didn't seem all that drunk, more just half asleep.

"You'll take care of me?" Arthur said, turning his face up to Ethan, and *oh*, did he want to kiss him.

"I'll take care of you," he assured. He lifted Arthur's leg into the car and closed the door. When he went around and got in the driver's side, he realized he was in trouble.

He still didn't have the keys.

And he didn't know where Arthur lived.

"Here," Arthur said, pushing the button on the dash that brought the car to life. The screen lit up, and Arthur pushed a navigation button, one marked Home, and then the directions queued up.

Ethan felt around on his left side and flicked switches until he could touch the pedals.

"Knob on your right changes gears."

"Right." Ethan hadn't driven a car in a couple of years, so while he knew how to drive a car, this modern marvel was more like a spaceship.

He turned the knob to D and pulled carefully away from the curb and onto the street, pleased to see there were 360-degree cameras to help him avoid nicking the bumper of the car in front of him.

He turned up the volume so he could hear the navigation voice and above that, he heard Arthur snoring.

At one in the morning, there was more traffic than Ethan would have thought, but then they were on Sunset Boulevard and the clubs were still active. He slowed down as he got close to the turn for Arthur's home, and a few cars honked at him before he could see where to go. He had to turn around the block and was back in the vicinity when a siren went by them.

Arthur sat up and shook his head. "See that driveway? It's right up there."

Ethan never would have seen the entrance next to an office building that led up a steep driveway to a rounded building up the hill. Arthur was awake enough to guide him to his parking spot, and Ethan once again applauded the 360 cameras so he didn't scrape the side of the car on a concrete pole.

"This is nice. It's like you're hidden from the world back here."

Arthur grunted and opened his door. Ethan hurried around to meet him and was pleased when Arthur accepted his arm around his waist. He even let Ethan support some of his weight as they made their way up a set of concrete stairs to a brick patio with a swimming pool and an incredible view of the city, and what Ethan thought was the ocean beyond.

"Wow," he breathed as Arthur fumbled in his pocket for keys and moved toward a set of French doors. The building was a semi-circle, three floors, and the unit Arthur led them into was on the bottom floor.

"Is this all yours?" Ethan followed him in and stood agape at the brightly colored accents that highlighted the white walls and antiqued laminate floors. The place was immaculate, just like a movie set, and he couldn't help taking it in while Arthur flipped the lock on the door. "It's amazing, Arthur."

Arthur only grunted in response as he flung off his suit coat and began stripping out of his shoes and dress shirt in what appeared to be his living room. It was small, the building itself was narrow, and there was a breakfast nook and small kitchen in this room. Arthur stumbled over a cow-print ottoman and disappeared into the next room.

Ethan took a minute to look around at the walls covered with pop-culture nostalgia. There were several prints of movie posters from the '80s, like the Nic Cage classic *Valley Girl*, Val Kilmer's *Real Genius*, and a campy-looking teen comedy titled *Just One of the Guys*. Plus, there were posters from three films Ella Frye starred in, rom coms that had her vying for the title of America's Sweetheart beside Meg Ryan and Julia Roberts. Ethan also recognized two of Bernard's film posters.

Along with the movie posters was the retro furniture, a huge stereo system, a neon sign, and several huge racks filled with cassette tape cases and CDs, including a whole section for Elvis Costello that had Ethan very curious. Just who was this man who paraded around Hollywood dressed like a modern, successful talent agent with all of these treasures in his home?

He heard a thud in the next room, and he hurried in to find Arthur once more face down on the bed, his pants around his ankles leaving him in silk boxers and a white cotton undershirt. He'd had the presence of mind to pull the covers back first, but that was all he'd accomplished.

Ethan pulled Arthur's pants the rest of the way off his legs and hung them over the back of a chair. He only let his gaze wander for a brief moment over the red hair on Arthur's legs, and the skin covered with more freckles, before he pulled the covers over him, tucking them around him as it was chilly in the room. He walked around to the other side and pulled the drapes closed a bit, leaving only a sliver open.

"Are you okay?" He knelt beside the queen-size bed and placed a hand on Arthur's back.

"Tired. Too much wine. Not enough caffeine. Need sleep."

Ethan brushed his hair back from his face and sighed. He carefully removed Arthur's glasses, which were precariously smashed under his cheek and looked as if they were digging into his nose.

"I'll put these by the bed," he whispered and reached back to run his fingers through Arthur's hair again.

"Feelssnice," Arthur murmured before his lips parted and he blew out a long breath, followed by the cutest snore.

Ethan couldn't help himself. He didn't want to stop touching Arthur or watching him sleep. So he pulled a throw blanket off the end of the bed, wrapped it around himself, and sat on the floor. With all of the windows in the place, there was a draft, and Ethan wondered if it bothered Arthur.

Something bumped Ethan's arm as he was about to doze, and it nearly sent him screaming through the floor-to-ceiling window.

He turned to find the fluffiest gray cat he'd ever seen. The rhinestone collar with the E charm was a dead giveaway.

"Ah. You must be Elvis," he said, trying to calm his heart down.

The cat licked a paw, glared at him, and then walked away.

Ethan was just about to start stroking Arthur's hair once more when the cat let out the loudest yowl he'd ever heard. He ran out into the kitchen and found the cat sitting on the counter next to an empty food bowl.

"He did say he needed to get home. Let's see what we can find for you."

He figured if the cat kept up this racket, Arthur would never get to sleep. He found cans of food in a cabinet under the counter. Thankfully it was a pull top, so he yanked it open and found a spoon to dish it into the bowl.

"There. Okay, now let your daddy sleep."

The cat stared at him as he walked away. Ethan darted into the bedroom, glanced back, and the cat was still staring at him. *Whoa.* Intense. He decided to use Arthur's bathroom, where he did his business, put some toothpaste on his finger and made it work to clean his teeth. He drank some water from the faucet, glad his hives were gone, but his skin felt raw.

He was about to peek into Arthur's cabinet for some lotion when he heard an ear-shattering scream from the cat.

He flew out into the kitchen, nearly knocking a picture frame off the wall.

"What?" he scream-whispered at the cat.

The cat stared at him for a beat, and then bent to eat his food.

"Good. Eat your food, silly."

He was about to turn and go back when the cat shrieked again.

Ethan shushed the cat and ran towards him with his hands out. The cat flinched, but kept staring at him.

"What is it? I fed you!"

The cat began to eat, but it was the weirdest thing. He kept watching Ethan as he bent to take dainty bites of his stewed meat.

"You like an audience, huh?"

The cat licked his whiskers and went back to eating.

Ethan sighed and figured he should wait with the cat, but his eyes were getting tired. After what felt like the longest five minutes, the cat hopped down from the counter, gave himself a quick bath in the middle of the floor, then swaggered into Arthur's room.

"Finally," Ethan sighed. He pulled the blanket around himself and went around the bed, just as the cat hopped onto the mattress, walked onto Arthur's back and lay down, claiming his territory, or maybe for protection, Ethan couldn't tell from his glare.

"Fine. I'll leave you two be." He took his blanket and was about to lay on the couch...but no. If this was his one and only night to be near Arthur, he was going to be a creep and watch the man sleep. He wished he had some psychic powers of suggestion that he could send through the ether to Arthur's brain.

Give me a chance.

Break your rules for me.

Let me prove that I can be good for you.

He sank down on the floor next to Arthur's bed, ran his fingers through the man's hair once more, and then rested his head against the mattress and gave in to the urge to close his eyes.

TWENTY-TWO

Arthur woke with a start in bed the morning after his parents' party, completely discombobulated, with a twenty-pound weight on his back making bread and growling.

"Fucking hell, E. I got it, I'll feed you. You're fucking starving. Fine."

He pushed up to his elbows, still not dislodging the cat, wondering where the hell he'd left his glasses, when he saw something next to the bed he couldn't quite make out. He moved closer to the edge of the mattress and reached out to feel whatever the dark fluffy thing was at the edge of his line of sight.

When his fingers made contact with soft, curly hair, the unknown entity flung itself away from the bed with a shout, which caused Elvis to launch himself off of Arthur's back, leaving scratch marks in his wake.

"*Fuuuuuck, E!*"

"I'm sorry!"

Arthur squinted into the gray light of his bedroom. "Ethan? Is that you? What are you doing in my bedroom?" He winced and ran a hand over his back, his fingers bloody when he looked at them. "That cat is a fucking menace."

Ethan stood with a snicker and bent over the bed. "Oh man, he got you good. Want me to clean that up?"

Arthur continued to frown at him, trying to get his bearings.

Ethan. In his bedroom. He did a quick mental recap: the wool sweater, the hives, Danny's bathroom, the image of shirtless Ethan, *kissing* shirtless Ethan...but then there was wine, the encouraging and uplifting conversations with his father, with Nora...

And Ethan dancing with his mother. Ethan effortlessly talking and laughing with some of Hollywood's biggest names as if he did it every day.

And every few minutes or so, he'd search Danny's back patio for Arthur, and when their eyes met, he'd grin.

Arthur had been overwrought about his professional slip, fearing that he'd done a dastardly deed, but despite an earthquake, the ground still hadn't caved in and swallowed him down a funnel to hell. No one seemed all that surprised, shocked, or even concerned that he and Ethan had made some sort of connection. In fact, they'd encouraged it!

So how could kissing Ethan be all bad?

Arthur could very much get his heart broken, a heart that had begun to make space for the sensitive, quirky actor, and a heart that liked being needed for more than what he could do for a career.

You'll never know until you try.

"I can't tell if you're mad or if you need your glasses."

Arthur cursed again, this time with less vigor, and Ethan continued to laugh.

"What's so funny?" Arthur patted around on the bed, prompting Ethan to hurry over to the table to grab his glasses.

"Here," he said, handing them to Arthur. "Stay there. Let me clean up these scratches."

"Fucking menace. Fucking furry feline menace. Fine. There's first-aid stuff bottom right-hand drawer in the bathroom. Fuck." He flopped back down, and Ethan trotted over to the bathroom.

"Is this a pre-coffee thing?" he asked as he returned. "All of this swearing?"

"*Fuuuuuuck.* Yes. I like to get them out of my system before I leave the house in the morning." Arthur buried his head in his pillow and shouted a few more times as Ethan used a cotton ball and some peroxide to clean the scratches.

"Man. He got you with both feet. I'm so sorry."

"You didn't answer my...*fuck that stings*...question. Why are you in my room?"

"There...let me put some antibiotic ointment on these. You want a Band-Aid?"

"No, fucking hell, I need a shower. Why were you on the floor? What happened last night?"

Ethan had the throw blanket from the end of Arthur's bed wrapped around his shoulders, his hair was wild, and his feet were bare. He took the first-aid things back to the bathroom, returned to the far side of the bed, crossed his ankles, and lowered himself to the floor to sit crisscross applesauce in Arthur's line of sight.

"Before or after we kissed in the bathroom at Danny's?"

Arthur was rendered momentarily speechless by Ethan's shy smile. When he finally collected himself, he sighed and let himself sink into the bed a bit more, resting his chin on crossed arms.

"I remember that part, yes."

Ethan's cheeks flushed, and he looked down at his feet, pulling at a thread on the hem of his slacks. Arthur thought he might need to take them back to Mervin.

"Was it something you remember...fondly? Or..."

Arthur fought the urge to grin, figuring he was awake enough to be a little contrary. "My memories of last night *are* a little hazy."

"Oh," Ethan said, his soft, serene expression faltering. "Sorry. Um, did you want—"

"A do-over? Yes. Come here."

Ethan's exhale was a sound of pure relief. He let the blanket fall from his shoulders and he crawled slowly over to the side of the bed.

"I'm a lot less itchy today, so a do-over would be nice." He paused just before the edge and frowned. "If you're sure. I mean, you've had a night to sleep on it. I wasn't sure if a do-over would even be on the table, you know, or if maybe you were thinking more like a *don't*-over."

"Do you take issue with morning breath?"

"What?" Ethan's eyes went wide. "No?"

"Good. Then come here and do me over."

The sparkle in Ethan's eyes was exactly what Arthur had hoped he'd see, they were just like the dream he'd had earlier that morning, replaying the moment he'd kissed Ethan in a bathroom, only in the dream, he hadn't held back, hadn't worried about his rule.

Don't date the talent.

Arthur had told himself in that dream—an actual separate, outside-himself Arthur spoke to him—that his rule had meant to protect him more than anything, more personally than professionally, and since he'd taken steps to avoid career issues for Ethan or himself, and as he was tired of playing it safe and being alone, he needed to get over himself.

And while he'd been exhausted and barely able to keep his eyes open, he recalled every moment of Ethan taking care of him: driving him home, guiding him into his place, helping him into bed, even removing his pants and glasses. And then this morning, the careful way he'd touched Arthur, cleaning the wound with such care, even blowing on it to help the stinging subside.

"I want that so much. But Arthur? Last night you said you couldn't, wouldn't. What changed?" He scooted closer and rested his chin on his hands, six inches from Arthur's face. "I don't want you to—"

"But *I* want *you* to."

"You won't be sorry?"

Arthur pushed himself forward and rubbed noses with Ethan. "Not unless you keep talking and don't kiss me."

Ethan smiled hesitantly. "And you'll still respect me in the morning?"

Arthur curled his fingers around the back of Ethan's neck. "It *is* the morning. I respect you. Now kiss me."

Ethan's lips felt even better this morning, with Arthur's skin feeling hypersensitive. Ethan's stubble had grown in overnight, and it felt deliciously scratchy.

Ethan raised his hand tentatively and brushed the backs of his fingers along Arthur's cheek with a sigh, but then he pulled back. "Your mom."

Arthur laughed. "My *mom*? Oh, honey, we need to work on your pillow talk."

"She wanted you to meet her for dinner. Us. To meet them. I mean. And I didn't tell them I got you home. I'm sorry."

Arthur gave an exaggerated sigh. "Thank you for letting me know, and thank you for getting me home, now please? Can we just spend the day in bed? I want nothing more than to kiss you and touch you—"

Ethan scrambled onto the bed and lay on his stomach next to Arthur, his eyes wide. Arthur realized that he needed to be careful with Ethan. The guy was unbelievably kissable, but he seemed nervous, hesitant, as if he was afraid of any perceivable misstep.

"And get to know you." Arthur turned on his side and propped his head on his hand. He reached out with the other and ran his fingers along Ethan's shoulder. He was still dressed in the turtleneck and slacks from the previous night, and though Arthur wanted access to his skin, he worried about moving too fast and scaring him.

Ethan dragged his chin along his shoulder and gazed at Arthur with those impossibly pale blue eyes. "I want to. Get to know you. More than anything. Because if we're going to...get closer, I want you to be sure you really want me." He sucked in a big breath. "Because I have more than a passing interest in you, and if that's all you have in me, then I'd rather... pass. On anything else." He cleared his throat as Arthur's eyebrows rose. "I've made enough mistakes in my life, and I don't want this to become another one. Which is hard for me to say, because I really want to lick every single one of your freckles right now."

Arthur burst out laughing and rolled onto his back, sucked in a breath, shouted another *fuuuuuck*, and then rolled back to his side.

"That's a lot of licking. You might find yourself a tad parched. Let's do this. You said you haven't spent much time here in Hollywood, right?"

"Right." Ethan nodded, biting on his lip, making it so very hard for Arthur to do the right thing here. He, too, feared making a mistake with this delicate man.

"Well, how about this? We get dressed, I take you out for breakfast, and we do a little Hollywood educational tour, guided by yours truly, as my parents call me, 'the walking encyclopedia of useless Hollywood pop culture,' and then we'll meet my darling parents for dinner. If, after a full day spent with me, you want to come back here for some, uh, freckle tasting, then by all means, I'll give you complete access. And if you don't, I'll take you back to the hotel, and Monday you'll go with Audra to your meetings as planned."

"Arthur," Ethan said turning on his side to face him. "Why are you being so nice to me?"

Arthur cupped his jaw and placed a chaste kiss on his lips. "At first, I didn't want to be. I know I made that clear, and I apologize for my behavior. Then, I couldn't figure out what was real and what was an act until I finally realized that you *had* no act. You are a genuinely sweet and caring man, and I'd forgotten it was possible to find someone like you in a place like this. And now?"

"Now?"

Arthur studied how Ethan hung on his every word. Usually, in his line of work or even in his line of dating, the men were always looking for clues as to how they were being seen, trying to impact Arthur's impression of them, not being genuinely themselves.

"Now, I know better. And I want to know more. Let's go explore. And if you decide you want to go back to the hotel, that will be okay too. I don't want this to be a beginning that I forced on you. I want it to be one we start together."

Ethan smiled and held out a hand. "Deal."

Arthur took it, but instead of shaking it, he lifted it to his mouth and kissed Ethan's knuckles.

Rowl.

Arthur turned to find Elvis in the doorway.

"Fucking menace! Fine, I'll feed your fuzzy butt."

"So you save your f-words for the cat?"

Arthur sat up and stretched, reaching over his head before he stood and walked to the bathroom.

"Don't you think he deserves them? He's the only one who's here to hear them. He was Patricia's cat but he's been with me for three years now, and we've only barely reached...detente."

"He's certainly protective of you. I had to stand with him to get him to eat, but I think it was because he thought if I wasn't standing there I might harm you. When he was done, he climbed on your back and didn't move all night. I was a little afraid he was going to attack me in my sleep."

"He's been known to do that, but he actually wants to be watched when he eats. Shithead," Arthur said from the doorway.

"Did you name him Elvis after Elvis Costello?"

Arthur cocked his head. "Patricia named him after Presley, but it all works."

He hated leaving Ethan alone in his bed, and while he knew he was doing the right thing, it took all of his willpower to walk away. "Thanks for feeding him, by the way. It may have saved both of our lives. I'm going to shower real quick and then we can go by the hotel...unless you want to borrow something? My pants might be a little tight for you but—"

"Whatever's easiest for you. I'm just excited to spend the day with you."

And his smile was completely genuine. Wasn't that just great?

"Me, too. Give me a few minutes."

Arthur took the quickest shower on record, scolding his morning wood, pleading with it to get with the program.

"If you behave, maybe you can come out to play later. But we have to be good to this one."

It worked. Mostly. He still didn't know how he was going to spend the day riding around with Ethan right there within reach. But if they were going to be out in public, they needed to have a strategy.

When he stepped out of the shower, Ethan was in the kitchen whistling to a familiar tune. Arthur had to stop picturing Ethan's lips as he puckered them.

"I'm out if you want to hop in," he called out. Ethan twirled into the room.

"You've got such an awesome music collection! I've heard of most of the bands but haven't really listened to them. You think, sometime, we could listen to your tapes?"

Arthur's heart stuttered, but it was the good kind of hiccup, not the caffeine-induced kind. He hadn't even had any coffee yet, and he actually didn't care for once. "I'd love to share my collection with you."

Ethan took the towel he offered, brushed a kiss over Arthur's lips, surprising him, and then he blushed and chuckled as he skipped into the bathroom, shutting the door behind him.

He sang in the shower. "Sulphur to Sugarcane" by Elvis Costello.

Arthur hoped his heart could take all of the swooning.

He took his time choosing an outfit, eventually dressing in baggy green chinos cinched at the waist and a little short at the ankle, with a wide black belt, and a white t-shirt under a white V-neck sweater adorned with blue and green stitching around the collar that he'd bought at a vintage shop. It was from United Colors of Benneton and was a quintessential '80s look. Every once in a while he liked to take his style back to the era he loved the most; the time when his parents' movies topped the box office and fascinated a tiny red-headed child.

He loved this particular look. He even busted out his Doc Martens and styled his hair a la Duckie in *Pretty in Pink*, though he more closely resembled Anthony Michael Hall in *Sixteen Candles*. It had taken him a long time to get comfortable in his nerdy skin, but once he turned thirty and had achieved success in his career, he was ready to settle in and get comfortable with himself. His business was cutthroat, but he'd learned how to relax in his downtime, what little he had.

"Hey, does Elvis need to eat again— *Wow. Arthur!*" Ethan took in his vintage casual look and pressed a hand to his chest. His naked chest. Arthur really should have given Ethan his big fluffy bathrobe to preserve his own sanity. "You could have just stepped out of a catalog from the eighties. I love that sweater, and those pants, and oh man, I wish I could wear Docs. I tried once, but ouch."

"These are the softer leather ones. I couldn't handle the break-in time for the regular stiff leather. I have some, and I've broken them in, but I prefer these."

"Could you fix me up? I want to go back in time, too!"

Arthur beamed. He was grateful Ethan was willing to have a little fun. "Step into my vault," he said, gesturing to the large walk-in closet he'd created in what should have been a small den attached to the master bedroom. "I've been collecting for...a while."

They spent a good forty-five minutes putting outfits together. Arthur managed to find a couple of pairs of vintage Levi's that were meant to be worn baggy but instead hugged every curve of Ethan's hips, thighs, and calves. They both wore size eleven shoes, and Ethan had been delighted to try on every wacky boot, loafer, and platform shoe that Arthur passed his way. It was way more fun than their trip to the tailor because now they were both able to enjoy what appeared to be their mutual love of quirky clothes.

They settled on a white and navy striped boatneck t-shirt to go with the faded Levi's, with a black leather belt, and Arthur pulled out his favorite navy cardigan with the wood toggles on it—that thankfully wasn't wool—and a pair of Sperry topsiders to round out the outfit.

"I look like a more fashionable version of Robin Williams's Popeye."

"You've seen it? The nineteen-eighty film?"

"Yeah. I've seen every Robin Williams film. He's one of my idols," Ethan said, smiling at Arthur in the full-length mirror. Arthur loved seeing them together. He had a few inches on Ethan, but together? They were hot. They'd turn heads...which reminded him.

"Here," he said, reaching into a drawer where he kept accessories and handing Ethan a pair of sunglasses. "You'll probably be recognized anyway, but damn, those look good on you."

"More swearing," Ethan laughed, turning to face Arthur. He ran his hands over Arthur's sweater and licked his bottom lip. "You are beyond hot, Mr. Frye. I love this side of you."

And that was probably the nicest compliment Arthur had received in a long time. Complimented on being himself, expressing himself in the way he rarely allowed, at least not with many people. It had been years since he and Patricia had gone out dancing, or he'd dressed up in his favorite pieces to go out on a date. Not everyone got it, or they thought he was being pretentious, or that he was trying to be a hipster.

He didn't have to explain himself with Ethan. He didn't feel judged. Ethan had gone along with it, even bounced on his toes and clapped his hands when Arthur showed him his collection of Swatch watches.

"I've read about these and seen posts about them but I've never seen one, like, in the wild. These are so fun."

"Pick one," Arthur said, wondering which one Ethan would like the most.

Ethan ran his fingers over the bands, settling for a moment on the clear watch face with the exposed gears, then he pulled his hand back.

"I'd be afraid I'd break it or lose it. I can't."

Arthur smiled at him and pulled out the last watch he'd touched and placed it on Ethan's left wrist, fastening the buckle gently, taking care not to catch any of the dark hairs on Ethan's wrist.

"Unlike the teens in the eighties who wore whole forearms covered in their watches, I prefer to wear one at a time. This way, with you wearing one, I can look at two of my favorites all day." He winked at Ethan and picked out the green and blue Nautilus model that matched his outfit and fastened it on his left wrist.

"Arthur, I'm so excited I don't think I can stand it. Will you forgive me if I squeal?"

Arthur chuckled and pulled Ethan in for a hug. "Go ahead. My neighbor upstairs is away filming a series in Toronto."

Ethan squeezed him tight and squealed into his shoulder. "This is the most fun I've had since..." His smile fell. "My mom and I used to have so much fun trying on clothes, creating different outfits. It's been a really long time." He kissed Arthur's lips, pausing long enough for Arthur to feel the longing. "I'm sorry, I should really stop kissing you until you invite me."

"You're invited. Kiss me."

Twenty-Three

Ethan

This was the kiss Ethan wished would have been their first kiss. Standing in front of a gigantic full-length mirror, wrapped in his arms, Ethan pressed his body against Arthur's and sighed as their lips came together. No hesitation, no fear it wouldn't be reciprocated, just two men on equal footing exploring each other's mouths with curiosity, vim, and vigor.

Arthur groaned and took the kiss deeper, grabbing a handful of Ethan's hair and positioning his head back to give him more leverage.

Ethan gasped, loving Arthur's enthusiasm. God, the man was so put together, so wound up tight at work, so in control of his people and environment...even dressing Ethan for their day out together had been an exercise in letting Arthur take control, and Ethan loved every minute of it. He knew Arthur loved it too, and Ethan wanted to please him, not just because the man had taken a pretty expensive chance on him, and not because he wanted anything from him other than companionship. Well, and sex. Definitely sex. If they didn't get out of this apartment, soon, playing dress-up was going to lead to taking dress off.

Ethan dropped his head back and groaned as Arthur ran his tongue over his Adam's apple. His knees buckled, and Arthur caught his weight.

"Arthur? If we keep this up, I'm totally going to mess up your hair. Probably your clothes too. And I'm definitely going to be on my knees with your pants open any second—"

Arthur groaned and pulled back, panting, his lips puffy in the most delightful way and his pale skin fully flushed. Ethan loved putting this look on the man. He was this undone from just kissing? Wait 'til Ethan worshipped every inch of his body.

"You're right," Arthur said breathlessly. Knowing he wasn't the only one affected made stepping back a little easier. "You're right. It was a nice taste, but I meant what I said. I want to spend the day together."

And so they did.

It started with a very late brunch at Mel's Drive-in. Ethan was reminded of his economic status as soon as he opened his menu. He could maybe just get a side of eggs? That would tide him over. He started to reach in his pocket but then he recalled giving his last few dollars away.

Arthur reached over and put a hand on Ethan's thigh. "When you're working, you can treat me, Ethan. I don't want you to be over there trying to figure out how to make your last dollar stretch. You'll take care of me when you can. Besides, I've chosen a slate of activities for us that cost little to nothing." He leaned closer. "The thing that would make me most happy would be for you to enjoy yourself. That's all I want."

Ethan blew out a breath but he didn't speak. He couldn't. He had nothing to say. He was so far in debt to Arthur, he was going to have to take on a blockbuster action film to earn enough to pay him back.

He was quiet throughout breakfast, listening to Arthur talk about his first breakfast meeting with his first-ever client, an up-and-coming actor who'd landed a role on one of the longest-running sci-fi series of all time. The kid moved up to series regular and suddenly he was thrust into the spotlight and being offered all kinds of roles, and Arthur had to scramble to keep up with his needs.

"What do you think is the hardest part of your job?" Ethan asked him, because he had a hard-enough time managing himself, much less a bunch of people with busier lives than his.

Arthur sighed. "The hardest part? Knowing what's best for your client, then not being able to convince them, watching them take another path, and then not saying 'I told you so.' Although, most of my clients trust me. Then there are Reese and Toby, who are like 'we want to do this ridiculous thing and make it happen, please, Arthur.'"

"And you do it because you love them."

Arthur shrugged. He was definitely smiling more today than Ethan had seen up to this point.

"I do. But also, they're two of the most talented men I've ever met, and that's saying something, seeing as who birthed me. They've taken chances with their careers that have made me wince at times, but look at them, doing such important things. I'm in awe of them. And Joe Judd, too. Do you know Joe?"

"Wasn't he on *Dance Machine*? I'm afraid I haven't kept up with him since then."

Arthur folded his hands in front of him, neglecting the rest of his chocolate chip pancakes. Ethan had been tickled to see that he'd chosen the smiley-faced pancake meal and black coffee, which he'd had three refills of.

"That's when I first saw him too, and then the show's producers reached out to me because they saw his potential, and I scooped him up. He's done so much. He's magic to watch."

"When did you know you wanted to be a manager?" Ethan was grateful to have Arthur in a sharing mood and wanted to keep him talking. The more he ate and drank his coffee, the more animated he got, and Ethan could absolutely see how he'd risen to the top of Hollywood talent management. He was so compelling to listen to, spoke with such authority, and while he normally stayed out of the spotlight, he commanded your attention when he spoke directly with you, his words carrying more weight than one would imagine for a man of his relatively young age.

"Let's see, I've been basically managing the Frye household since I was a teenager and my parents had their hands full with their careers and their personal issues."

"You managed your *parents*?" Ethan laughed. "Isn't it usually the other way around?"

"Nah. When I was too old for a nanny, I started by putting myself in charge of the mail, paying the bills. I learned how to balance a checkbook from my grandfather, and I told my parents I'd take over the household finances. Horace Manning handled most of their business stuff, but he let me handle the groceries and bills. Then I took on the hiring and firing of handymen, gardeners...getting the pool serviced, you know, that kind of thing. I was good at it. I liked having control over it, and I liked that when my parents were home, they could spend their time with me instead of handling all that stuff. There's something magical about being able to tell your parents, or your clients, 'it's handled.'"

"That's amazing. How old were you? And you were on your own?"

"I think I fired the last nanny after my freshman year?"

"You *fired* the nanny?"

Arthur chuckled and downed the last of his third cup of coffee. Ethan hoped he'd switch to water now. He knew if it were him, he'd be bouncing off the walls after one cup, much less three.

"I did. My parents were away on various film shoots for that summer, and I assured them that I could handle my own transportation and feed myself. When it came time for school to start again, I successfully lobbied for independence. They threatened to sick my grandparents on me if I messed up, so I didn't mess up." His face darkened a bit. "They had their hands full, so it wasn't like they would've noticed anyway."

"So you took that experience and said, 'Huh, I want to boss other people around?' How did that work?"

"I don't know. I spent a lot of time with Horace as a teenager and in college. Had my first job as an office assistant at Slade after my sophomore year. Horace thought I did a good job and kept me on as a paid intern in the summers, and I realized it wasn't a whole lot different than what I already did for my parents. I managed a rock band my freshman year at USC, but at the firm, I realized that with my Hollywood connections, I'd be able to serve clients in the visual media realm more than music. Besides, Patricia had already glommed on to the Manning brothers and became Blackened's manager before they got signed by a label, so my dreams of leftover groupies were dashed."

Ethan nearly spit out his water. "Groupies? Seriously?"

Arthur shook his head, his smile boyish, and for once Ethan could see a side of Arthur that was less than confident about his place in the world.

"Well, it wasn't like I was going to get a date any other way. Of course, I kind of didn't pick the right band if I wanted dates."

Ethan rested his chin in his hands. "You're joking, right? How could anyone resist you?"

Arthur gave him a look Ethan would never recover from. It was a cross between "how stupid are you" and "how could anyone be attracted to me." Ethan feared he would freeze up, so he decided to change the subject.

"Were you out back then?"

Arthur nodded, moving his food around on his plate, creating a neat line of pancake crumbs swimming in syrup. "By college, anyway. My parents knew before I did. I thought I was making a big announcement. I'll always be grateful to them for not making it tough on me. I wasn't afraid to tell them or anything, because I knew they were both queer themselves in a time people didn't really call it that."

"Really? I'd never even met another queer person until I started community college in Chicago."

Arthur leaned back and smirked. "Put it this way, my folks had swinger parties at our house. I saw all kinds of activity at an early age." He cocked his head to the side. "It helped me not feel too weird about being gay, if that makes sense. I think if I hadn't grown up around folks who were out, and those who were only open with their families, I might have struggled more with it."

"I can't imagine." Ethan wished he could have met someone like Arthur when he was first finding himself and exploring what it meant to be a sexual being. Instead, he wound up in a lot of uncomfortable and unpleasant situations that made him leery to get involved with anyone.

"But growing up in the most beautiful place on earth, surrounded by beautiful people looking for perfection, I spent a lot of time just watching folks and not participating."

Ethan wanted to tell Arthur that he was perfect, that he was beautiful, but he could tell that Arthur didn't see himself that way.

"Most of the people who I went out with only wanted me for my connections anyway, so I gave up, focused on building my client list, and worked my magic." He wiggled his fingers as if he were a magician, and Ethan figured that was a pretty fitting way to describe him. Mysterious, powerful, and maybe a little dangerous...at least to Ethan's heart, he was.

"You must have met so many interesting people, seen so many interesting things. I've always been fascinated by Hollywood. It felt separate from what I was doing, especially going from Chicago to New York and then London. It's still surreal to actually be here."

Arthur watched him for a long time, and Ethan could only smile back at him like a loon. It was surreal in more ways than one. The epicenter of his chosen career was here, and now, so was the epicenter of his heart's desire.

"If you're done eating, let's start your Hollywood education. You ready?"

Ethan exhaled. He was more than ready. He was elated.

"Teach me your ways."

"First stop, next door for the Hollywood Museum tour. It takes up all four floors of the old Max Factor building."

"Like the makeup Max Factor?"

"The very same. This place has so much memorabilia it will make your head swim, but it also was the place where the starlets came to get their signature looks created, from hair color to makeup palette, they made miracles here." He held out his arm, and Ethan took it eagerly, following him up the steps that led from the restaurant to the main building.

"Will you let me get the tickets?" he asked Arthur quietly as they approached the ticket taker.

Arthur shook his head and pulled out his wallet. "I'm a benefactor. I sit on the board." He winked at Ethan and showed a card to the worker, who smiled widely.

"Thank you, Mr. Frye. Would you like a guide?"

He held up a hand as he put his wallet back in his pocket. "I got it. Thanks."

And Ethan proceeded to experience an expertly guided tour of this incredible building full of so much history, his head was spinning before they finished the first floor. He loved seeing the costumes, cars, even Pee-wee Herman's bicycle!

"Oh, I love *Big Adventure* so much. I used to watch *Pee-Wee's Playhouse* on DVD in secret because my brothers thought it was dumb, but I loved the show. It was so silly and zany and sweet. I fell in love with Tim Burton after *Big Adventure*. I admired the actors he convinced to take chances on his other quirky characters." He peered around them to make sure they were alone. "My dream role? Something creepy and sweet like *Edward Scissorhands* or *Big Fish*."

Arthur looked surprised. "Yeah? You don't want to be a rom com king like Mathew McConaughey or the next Colin Firth?"

He shrugged, looking at a display of Elvis memorabilia. "I don't know. I'm glad I was able to do such different roles, with such different filmmakers, but a career like Johnny Depp's or Robin Williams', even Tom Hanks' would be phenomenal, although I'm not sure I'd want to play a beloved character from classic literature or film, or a real historical figure. I'd prefer to dig into something weird and wonderful." He laughed. "At this point, though, I'd play just about anything to get back to work."

Arthur put a hand on his elbow and guided him to a corner hidden from view. "But this is exactly the time to be choosy and set a path for yourself. Take risks. *Choose* something weird and wonderful. If that's what you want, that's the direction I'll steer Audra. I'd love to see you do something unexpected." He brushed Ethan's hair back from his cheek. The stylist had left Ethan's hair longish so he could have flexibility in styles for whatever auditions he needed to do. He loved that it gave Arthur a reason to touch him. "Audra wants to see you get dirty."

Ethan's eyes widened, and he stepped farther into the shadows, closer to Arthur. "Really?"

"Yeah. We agreed we'd like to see you dirty up that pretty face."

"You think I'm pretty?" Ethan wasn't above flirting to get another kiss. He never wanted to *stop* kissing this man, actually, and surrounded by all of this movie magic? He was buzzing under his skin, holding in way too much energy. If he didn't let it out, he was going to pounce.

"You *know* you're pretty," Arthur said. "I find you irresistible." Arthur lowered his head and brushed his lips over Ethan's, holding his gaze. His perpetually serious face had been more relaxed today than Ethan had seen it, but now he was back to serious.

"What's wrong?"

Arthur cupped his face and ran his fingers over Ethan's lip. "Nothing. Sorry. Let's see some more. How do you like the museum?"

He took Ethan's hand and led him out of the dark corner, and Ethan tried not to let his disappointment show, especially when Arthur dropped his hand. He hadn't really been careful about touching while they were in public, which Ethan knew a lot of gay men were. He understood Arthur didn't like to have attention on him, and if Ethan were to be recognized, it might cause a scene that Arthur wouldn't like. Not that it happened often. He had several instances of it in London, but so far in LA? Well, he hadn't been out and about in public much. He had no idea whether it would happen.

They were quiet as they went through the special effects displays, and Ethan was blown away by the sheer scope of the collection. Everything from the classics to sci-fi greats like the *Alien* films and *Starship Troopers*, to *X-Men* accessories like Wolverine's bone knives.

"You said you're on the board for the museum?"

"I am. We basically help with fundraising efforts and I occasionally approach folks, or they approach me, to talk about donating memorabilia and artifacts to the museum. If you couldn't tell by my condo, I'm quite passionate about preserving Hollywood history."

"You are, and I think it's amazing. Thank you for bringing me here."

Arthur blinked and his face softened. "I'm glad you like it. I know this old stuff isn't for everyone—"

"No, I love it. My mom used to tell me stories. We watched a lot of old movies together, and she would tell me all about the actors, their origin stories. She read memoirs all the time, and together, we loved contemplating what it was about them that made them so appealing to moviegoers."

"I know people think it's some formula or something, but honestly, it-factor is the only real way to describe it. Charisma isn't quite enough, but it's a start. People who have that ability to draw the best out in others, who make others feel like they're the center of the universe, who are genuinely caring and interested, enthusiastic and optimistic, and who are so riveting when they speak that they can command a room."

He put his hands on Ethan's shoulders and turned him to face a picture of James Dean.

"You know who this is?" Arthur spoke close to his ear.

Ethan nodded.

"Despite being the quintessential all-American boy, he had trouble finding roles in LA, so he moved to New York and hit the stage. He was discovered while playing a gay house boy in *The Immoralist*, which was the story of a married man who can't seem to consummate his marriage with his wife until he's seduced by the young Dean. I haven't seen it. It was way before my time, but all of the reviews said he was completely irresistible, so much so that Elia Kazan was convinced he'd be perfect for the Steinbeck project *East of Eden*. Dean ended up nominated posthumously for Best Actor for that film."

Arthur ran a hand up the nape of Ethan's neck, gently massaged the base of his skull, and leaned closer.

"You have that same irresistible quality as someone like James Dean, without the self-destructive streak. We just have to connect you with the right people, the right project, and then I'll look forward to sitting back and watching you soar."

Ethan turned to face him. "You really think so?"

Arthur pulled him in for a tight hug, obviously not caring who might be looking.

"I know so."

TWENTY-FOUR

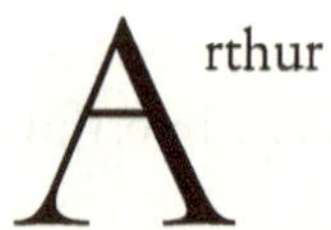

Arthur loved sharing the museum with Ethan mostly because he could tell Ethan was absolutely in love with it. He absorbed the stories of every artifact, picture, and piece of costuming in the place. They spent hours walking and talking, and the experience gave Arthur a much greater understanding of how the boy had become the man before him. If Ethan's mother were still alive, he would have kissed her. She'd given him an extensive background in Hollywood history, but also made sure he'd seen the important films, knew the important players, and had a good head on his shoulders about his looks and abilities, and how he could use them to play the kinds of roles that would make him not only a star, but give him a career he could be proud of.

They left the museum and the sun was already starting to retire for the day.

"What's next?" Ethan asked him, still beaming at his side.

Arthur looked at his Swatch. "We've got a little time before we meet my parents, but how about some more Hollywood history?"

Ethan rubbed his hands together. "Lead the way."

They drove down Sunset Boulevard, and Ethan pointed out all of the hotspots with wonder. "The Whisky! The Rainbow Room! Holy cow, I never realized how close together everything here is. I can't believe it. Did you hang out in the clubs when you were younger? Wait, I don't even know how old you are."

Arthur sighed dramatically. "Old. So old." When Ethan squeezed his thigh, Arthur put a hand over his. "Put it this way, I graduated from high school right before the turn of the century, so I'm a Gen Xer by the skin of my teeth. I finished my bachelor's at USC in two thousand three and went straight into law school, passed the bar in two thousand six...I saw a few bands on Sunset during that time. The Cult, Billy Idol, Depeche Mode. I had a thing for eighties artists even then. I guess I'm kind of stuck there."

Ethan laughed. "It could be worse, I suppose."

Arthur snorted. "How?"

Ethan sighed. "I mean, you could have gotten stuck in a nineties ska or swing phase, or like those big pants? Or you could be totally into Nu Metal and dress like Fred Durst?"

Arthur laughed. "Uh, no. That was not my vibe. I mean, don't get me wrong, I met a lot of those guys. I do like Korn a lot, and Slipknot puts on some of the best shows I've ever seen, but style-wise, I'll stick with my nerd chic."

"You are not a nerd, Arthur. You're one of the smartest men I've ever met and you're hot as hell."

Arthur felt his cheeks flush. "Ethan—"

"Don't argue with me."

"Or what?"

Ethan leaned close as Arthur pulled to a stoplight. "Or I'll be forced to show you just how hot—"

Arthur put a finger on Ethan's lips. "Did I mention we're about to have dinner with my parents? It won't do for either of us if I show up freshly kissed and standing at attention."

Ethan grinned. "From what you told me, I can't imagine your parents would be surprised."

Arthur sighed. "They would be for *me*. The only dates I've ever brought to meet them were incredibly...ordinary. Boring. I know that's a cruel way to describe someone, and perhaps for someone else, they would have been fantastic and amazing, but for me..."

"You were raised around big personalities. You're surrounded by forces of nature," Ethan said, leaning both elbows on the armrest between them. "I can imagine that could get old for you."

Arthur glanced at him and saw his smile had slipped.

"I thought I wanted normal, but what I think I actually want is an ordinary life with an extraordinary person." He flicked his gaze to Ethan before he took off.

"I want that for you." Ethan sat back in his seat and returned to gazing out the window. "You deserve that."

Arthur took Ethan's hand and linked their fingers together, and then brought Ethan's hand up to his lips. "Despite everything those horrible people said about you in the press, Ethan, you deserve that, too."

"I'm not too sure. I'm certainly not great at reading a situation right, and I tend to be impulsive...with everything." His gaze flicked to Arthur and then back out the window. "I've made bad decisions, and I worry those bad decisions will keep me from getting what I really want."

"Besides your career back?"

Ethan nodded.

"What else do you want?" Arthur lowered his voice, sensing Ethan's vulnerability. He was about to pull into the lot for the hotel, and he wanted to give Ethan his full attention, but there were attendants and other cars vying for his attention. "Hang on, let me park."

Ethan blew out a breath and let go of Arthur's hand.

Arthur pulled into the line for valet, wishing he would have brought the Vitesse. It would have meant they were sitting closer together. He wanted the crush of Ethan's weight against him in the tiny cab.

"I know it's soon, we only officially just met, and you're much more experienced than I am at this and I'm probably being impulsive again, but Arthur..." Ethan turned to look at him. "I want a shot with you. A real shot at something nice. I'm afraid you're going to decide I'm not worth the trouble of seeing someone who's an actor, or I'm going to do something wrong." He laughed, but it was a pained sound. "I've been a nervous wreck since I drove you home last night."

Arthur started at his confession. No one had ever put much thought or care into how they treated him. Was Ethan young? Yeah. *Really* young. But old enough to have had some bad experiences under his belt, and Arthur thought he probably knew what he *didn't* want. Could he trust what Ethan said? Or was this just a right-now kind of feeling, and as soon as Arthur was out of sight, he'd be out of mind?

He was starting to have some real feelings himself, and while he thought something nice sounded very appealing...

"I don't want you to be nervous, Ethan. I'm a curmudgeon is all. Stuck in my ways. And you're...surprising. Your life is also in flux, right? Don't let me be one of your worries. You don't need that. Let's just... well, I'd say enjoy this meal with my parents, but you never know what they're going to do. You think *you're* impulsive." He laughed, hoping to move away from this heavy topic. "On a whim, they moved to the desert thinking they were going to have this whole new retiree life. Guess what? Dad's ready to get back to work and Mom's bored."

Ethan shrugged. "They're great people. I'm honored they invited me."

God, this guy was so damned sweet and thoughtful.

Arthur sighed. "You say that now."

They pulled up at the valet stand and got out of the car. Arthur pulled two blazers out of the trunk before the valet pulled away. "Here," he said. "So we're officially dressed for dinner."

"Always prepared," Ethan said with a laugh, accepting the coat. "Here, let me swap out this one." He took off the cardigan, folded it, and placed it carefully in the trunk before slipping on the navy blazer.

He was absolutely stunning. Though Arthur could tell he was nervous, he carried himself with confidence, the only tell being his smile was not the full-powered one he only seemed to have when he was looking at Arthur.

That made his heart stop. Could he really mean what he'd said? Did he even understand what that would mean to a guy like Arthur, who never acted on impulse? Well, not until Ethan had taken off his sweater in Danny's bathroom.

"What?"

Arthur realized he was staring. The valet stood with his hand out for the keys and Arthur really needed to act, but he was caught in a force field, the edges of his vision going all hazy like a cheesy '80s TV show moment.

He handed the key to the valet and cleared his throat. Ethan was still waiting for an answer. He placed his hand at Ethan's lower back to lead him into the hotel.

"Something nice sounds...nice."

Ethan's hopeful smile sped Arthur's heart again, but he had to keep himself under control. They were about to enter a place where they would be under a microscope. Not only would people be paying attention to Arthur's parents, but they'd also see Ethan on Arthur's arm and it could be good for him, for his meetings this week. Impulsivity and flirtatious behavior had to be snuffed out.

They stepped through the front doors of The Beverly Hills Hotel, a Hollywood institution and a place where the movers and shakers still came to make plans and shake things up.

"Ethan," he began, but then he took in Ethan's broad smile and the wonder in his eyes. He realized that he'd never had that wow experience in Hollywood because he'd grown up going to places like this. He really was jaded. He liked that he could experience these firsts through Ethan's eyes, but he had to set some ground rules.

"Ethan," he urged again, pulling him to a stop next to a massive bouquet of flowers in the middle of the lobby. Ethan seemed to be absorbing every detail. "Honey, I need you to focus for a minute."

"Honey?" Ethan turned his full attention on him, and it left Arthur a little gobsmacked. It happened when the beautiful man turned his gaze him, and though they'd been together all day, there were times when Ethan looked at him that Arthur wanted to fall to his knees and promise him the world if he'd only keep eyeing him like that.

"I...Ethan," he said, feeling like the one who needed this speech. "I want you to keep in mind where we are at all times, all right? There shouldn't be paparazzi, but people are going to notice you. They're going to see you with me, and that's going to tell them you're here with management. They're going to see you with my parents, and they're going to think you're here on business. I'm going to try to keep my hands to myself, but I want you to know that's why. I don't want to take anything away from *you*."

"So I shouldn't tell you I wish I could kiss you right now? Right here next to these beautiful flowers?"

"There will be time for that later," Arthur said, turning so he could block Ethan from view.

"You promise?"

And with the way Ethan's blue eyes were wet and so full of desire, Arthur could do nothing else, even if it meant his own demise.

"I promise. Now, shall we?"

He gave Ethan a professional smile and gestured for him to walk in the direction of the lounge, nearly tripping over himself at the skillful way Ethan pulled himself together. He walked with his head held high, looking straight ahead as if he knew exactly where he was going and how good he looked doing it.

Arthur's phone rang and he pulled it out.

"Yes, Mom, have you been seated? Great, we're on our way in."

Ethan raised an eyebrow, and Arthur gestured which way they should walk. It was effortless, how Ethan had shifted from his unsure body language in the car to this star who looked exactly like he knew he belonged in this particular solar system. He even shined a little brighter than the other stars around him, an observation that was only slightly subjective.

Arthur spotted a group of CW starlets, waiting for a table, and they passed a booth with actor Bradley Cooper and his manager David Bugliari, the writer Josh Singer, and actor Matt Bomer sitting together.

"Arthur," Cooper called out.

Arthur turned and smiled, accepting his hand. "How's it going?"

"You know everyone here, right?" And then Cooper looked at Ethan curiously. "Hey, you were in that British film—"

"This is Ethan Bradley," Arthur said. The two of them shook hands with the others and Arthur brimmed with pride at the genuine way Ethan smiled and greeted everyone.

"Great to meet all of you," he said.

"Ethan's in town consulting on Reese and Toby's new show. You ought to check it out if you're in town next weekend. It's going to be a stunner."

Cooper nodded. "I heard. I'm around, so I'll check it out. Good to see you, Arthur. Say hi to your folks for me. I think I saw them come in a bit ago."

Arthur patted his shoulder. "Will do. I'll leave you and your brain trust to your dinner. Take care."

Cooper winked at him, and he knew magic was on the menu at the Polo Club that night.

"I don't think I'll ever get used to the casual way you introduce me to mega stars like that."

Arthur put a hand between his shoulder blades to guide him toward his parents' table. He moved closer and said, "You did good, honey. If you want to join dinner conversations like that, I'll make sure it happens for you."

Ethan turned on him, his eyes wide. "Only with you. Only if you're with me."

Arthur paused, his feet refusing to go forward. Ethan placed so much faith and trust in him, even after Arthur had done so much to push him away. He kept coming back, asking for more, looking to the future.

Ethan realized he wasn't at his back and turned with a curious smile.

And it dawned on Arthur right then that he'd never even considered a future with the actor. He hadn't even bothered to think of Ethan being around after he handed him off to Audra on Monday.

What could even come out of this, an affair with an actor? It just couldn't be done. Wasn't possible. Was against everything Arthur had ever thought of having in his life...and yet as he gazed into Ethan's hopeful eyes, he realized that was exactly what Ethan wanted. He hadn't pushed for sex when Arthur asked to spend the day with him, he hadn't tried anything the night before, when Arthur had been vulnerable. He'd been eager to please him at every turn, had worried over what Arthur thought...

Ethan might have thought himself impulsive, but none of his behavior pointed at that particular quirk.

No. He was playing an end game where he and Arthur not only had sex, but had a...what? A courtship? A relationship?"

"Is everything okay?" Ethan asked, stepping close to him. "If you don't want everyone flocking to you to ask if you've just had a stroke or something, maybe you better walk with me to your parents."

Arthur paused a moment longer and then commenced walking, but he couldn't speak. A swarm of thoughts were vibrating around his brain, like glasses rattling in a cabinet during an earthquake.

"You're scaring me," Ethan whispered, but his smile would have been considered relaxed to anyone not paying attention to the minute details, his lips straight across and not with the playful quirk to them, and his laugh lines weren't engaged around his eyes.

"I'm fine," he said, and he tried to put on a smile for his parents as they reached their booth.

"Darling." Ella stood and held out her arms.

Arthur went to her, and she gave him a quick hug before she reached for Ethan, wiggling her fingers as he hesitated.

"It's my new favorite dance partner. Come here, sweetie." Ella squeezed the life out of Ethan and then patted the booth seat for Ethan to sit beside her.

"Son, you look quite dashing. Did you go into the vault this morning?" His father kissed his temple as Arthur took a seat next to him. He was relieved for the physical distance from Ethan as his thoughts had his heart spiraling out of control.

"Yeah," he admitted. "Seemed like a good idea." Although had it been? In a rare case of self-reflection, Arthur couldn't believe he'd let Ethan so far inside his ecosystem.

His father glanced at Ethan and Ella, already deep into conversation, and then leveled his gaze on Arthur. "You look like you're going to jump out of your skin. What's it about this one?"

"I think *it* is the operative word in your question. He's got *it*, he could *be it,* but what am I supposed to do with *it* right now?"

Bernard chuckled. "Preferably nothing at the dinner table."

Arthur's eyes bugged out and he started to protest.

"We had those conversations a long time ago."

"Dad!" Arthur spoke a little louder than he intended, catching Ethan's and his mother's attention.

"Arthur, darling, are you feeling okay after last night?"

"Yes, Mom. I'm fine."

Ethan lost his smile and he leaned back against the booth, a worried crease forming between his eyebrows.

The server arrived and Arthur ordered coffee, black, and he prayed the guy would keep it coming, because his nerves were shot. He looked up to ask his parents whether they'd be getting their usual—and he caught Ethan's look of panic.

The menu. The prices. *Fucking hell.*

"You know, I'm going to have the McCarthy," Bernard said. "It's been a while. Ethan, you really should try it, it's kind of a signature dish in this place."

Ethan's eyes flicked up, and Arthur tried to offer a reassuring smile as he nodded. "I'll have one too," he said.

"Sure. Can't have too many vegetables," Ethan said, and Ella patted his shoulder as she ordered the fish of the day.

As if Bernard had divined the near-panic Arthur was feeling, he took over the conversation and kept them all enthralled with his stories about the films he did for Paramount in the '70s, when Robert Evans was in charge, and how different things were then.

"I can't imagine what it would be like to have worked with Jack Nicholson, Mia Farrow, Al Pacino, Dustin Hoffman...all at the beginning of what became huge careers," Ethan mused. "Watching their growth, seeing what they became..."

"Well, you live long enough, you're bound to see people achieve all kinds of things. But you work in this *business* long enough, you learn to see that potential from the beginning."

Bernard had such a fond expression when he looked at Ethan, it made Arthur wonder what his father saw in Ethan's future.

Arthur finished his third cup of coffee when his phone buzzed. He tried to ignore it—phones were not allowed at the table with his parents—but after the third buzz, he figured it needed addressing.

"I've got to use the restroom. Excuse me for a minute?"

His father nodded at him and continued telling a story to Ethan and Ella about the time he interrupted a very famous leading man getting serviced in his dressing room. Arthur made his way through the tables, palming his phone in his pocket as it continued to buzz. He nodded at a few folks before he ducked into the restroom and into a stall. He laughed to himself, thinking that these bathrooms had probably been used for more clandestine activities than checking text messages over the years.

Is Ethan with you?
    He's not answering his phone
    Cosmo said he never came back to the hotel last night
    He also said he thought he was supposed to drive him and forgot
    Oh God, no one has seen him! Arthur? Please call me?
    I've lost my first client! Fuck, Arthur, fire me now.
    Oh my God, Arthur are you okay? Are you getting my messages?
    Is this thing on?

Arthur hadn't seen Ethan's phone since he'd first handed it to him. Was he carrying it? That was the point of giving it to him. He appreciated that Ethan had been so attentive, but he couldn't afford to be unreachable, not at this point in their work. *Ethan's* work. Ethan and Audra's.

He decided to put Audra out of her misery. He stepped out of the stall, washed his hands, and dialed her number. She answered as he was looking under the doors to see if he was alone.

"Please say you've found him."

Arthur chuckled. "He's been with me. I'm sorry, we're out with my parents, so I couldn't answer you right away."

She exhaled a long, dramatic breath. "God, I've been scared shitless over here! Is this what I have to look forward to? Constant tachycardia? Wait, what did your doctor call it?"

"Palpitations, and no, most of the time you won't have to worry. I'll ask him to text you."

"Okay. Wait. If he didn't go back to the hotel last night... Did you take him home? Oh, shit. Arthur, am I even allowed to ask you? Wait! I am! He's my client! But you're my boss. How am I supposed to yell at you about my client when you're my boss?"

"Yes, he went home with me, but it's not like that. I fell asleep at Danny's and so Ethan drove us to my house in my car. We had lunch today, then I took him to the museum and now we're out with my parents." He sucked in a breath. "And you don't have to worry about the rest because *you* are his manager. I won't be anything to him after this weekend."

"What do you mean?"

Arthur sighed. "I mean just that. You'll pick him up Monday and he'll deal only with you. It's better that way," Arthur said, knowing he was full of shit. "I have to let him go."

"Oh, Arthur. You sound so sad. If you like him, why—"

"I never told you about Andrew Fleming, did I?"

A group of young men walked in so Arthur made his way outside to the patio. He could see his parents' booth through the window but he was hidden from their sight by palm fronds.

"He was in that twenties gangster movie with your mom, right?"

"Right. And what I'm about to tell you goes no further, got it? It's Frye lore, so technically you're covered under the NDA—"

"Jesus, Arthur, you're not just my boss, you're my best friend. I'd never break your confidence, now tell me!"

Arthur sighed. "There was a period in my parents' marriage when they were...non-exclusive. Mom and Andrew, however, got closer than what was an agreed-upon amount of closeness...this is really hard to talk about without revealing details that I wish I didn't have about my parents' lives—"

"Okay, okay, only tell me the pertinent details. Go."

"When my father confronted her and asked her to end things with him, she was angry, but she didn't want to lose Bernard, so she tried to cut things off with Andrew. He showed up at the house and threatened to kill himself, and my father felt terrible, so he ended up moving Andrew in with us...it was a year of complete emotional turmoil and dysfunctionality. Eventually they got him help, and he moved out and moved on, but it took a long time before they were tight again."

"How old were you when this was going on?"

Arthur exhaled. "I was thirteen."

"Oh, God. And you were in the house? Did they keep it from you?"

Arthur rolled his eyes. "What do you think? Just like now as their manager, I've always been privy to the dirty details of their lives. I couldn't avoid it. After a particularly awful night, I asked my grandparents if I could stay with them. I was gone for a month. That was the catalyst for them to figure things out."

"Oh Arthur. That had to be awful."

"You can imagine, then, why I can't even bring myself to consider getting involved with an actor."

"Well, yeah, but Arthur, your whole life revolves around actors. You've made a living out of it. And I could see you not wanting drama in your personal life, but I've gotta tell you…from the conversations I've had with Ethan so far? He's not drama. He's idealistic, a bit naive, but he seems to want nothing to do with the kind of shit that got him into the tabloids, and I believe him. He's just not that guy. He can handle the spotlight, I believe, but he doesn't seem like someone who will seek it outside of work."

"Maybe not intentionally, but Audra—"

"I learned from you how to trust my instincts. You put me in charge of him, so that makes me think *you* trust my instincts. Do you like him?"

"More than I should. More than I want to."

"That doesn't have to be a bad thing. Be careful, but don't be opposed to exploring possibilities."

"Easy for you to say," Arthur said. "You have no shortage of women falling all over themselves to go out with you."

"And I'm picky, so I understand why you're cautious, but you are too good of a person not to share yourself with a sweet guy like that. Plus, he couldn't stop talking about you, you know."

Arthur couldn't help but smile. He knew he had things to offer in a relationship. But never in his wildest dreams would he have thought an actor of Ethan's caliber would be into him. Simple as that. Didn't seem possible.

Yet there it was. Ethan had made it clear, Audra confirmed it...even Jesse told him to be careful with Ethan, as if she knew something.

"Arthur! Come on, I've worked for you for four years now. You've taught me everything I need to know to do this job. You've also taught me a lot about how to read people. He's good people. You're good people. And the two of you together make hella sense. Just *puleeze* make sure he's at his hotel on Monday morning? I don't want to fuck up my first solo client, you feel me?"

"Your Bay Area roots are showing, darling. Fine. I'll make sure he's ready for you. You're the best and you know it."

"I know it. Go get your man."

Arthur barked out a laugh and looked inside. Ethan was still hanging on his mother's every word, and God, did he look so adorable sitting there. His parents had fallen in love with Ethan. Maybe Arthur had too. Maybe that was why he was so terrified.

Love was a scary, scary thing.

TWENTY-FIVE

E^{than}

Ethan was absorbed in Bernard's story, but he realized Arthur had been gone for a long time. He tried to be inconspicuous as he looked around. He breathed a little easier as he spotted Arthur on the phone outside the window.

"Now, Ethan, dear, before Arthur comes back to the table, we want to talk frankly with you."

Ethan sat up taller as both of Arthur's *very famous* parents focused on him. "Absolutely."

"We know we're biased because he's our only son, as well as our business manager, but you are in good hands with Arthur."

Ethan smiled. *How sweet.* "I know. He's been very kind and generous, even though I know my arrival put a crimp in his plans."

Bernard glanced over his shoulder and saw Arthur outside. He sighed. "He needed a crimp in his plans. He needs a kick in the ass."

Ella bumped Bernard in the belly with her elbow. "Bernie, be kind." Then she turned and wrapped her arms around Ethan's. "What my husband is trying to say is that our son has been through a lot and has been taken advantage of by people in the past. He has his reasons not to trust in others." She gave Bernard a sad look, and then turned her dark blue eyes, so like Arthur's, on Ethan. "We want the best for our son—"

"And he wouldn't know the best for *himself* if it hit him over the head repeatedly with a baseball bat."

"Bernard!"

"What? I'm tired of watching him push people away. I don't want him to end up alone. We're not always going to be here, my love."

Ethan had no idea how to respond. He'd never had someone's parents say, "Here, take our son."

Thankfully Arthur returned before Ethan had to come up with something.

"Did I miss dessert?" he asked as he slid in next to Ethan this time. He smiled at his parents, then turned to Ethan. "Did you bring your phone?"

Ethan's eyes widened. "I did." He pulled it out of his pocket. "Oh no. The battery must have died. I didn't think about charging it. Sorry."

Arthur patted his thigh. "That's all right. Please forgive my absence, but Audra was ready to file a missing person's report. I had to assure her that Ethan was alive and well."

"We have an early morning, so we're going to say goodnight." Bernard scooted to move out of the booth.

"Last night was lovely, darling. Thank you so much. It was wonderful to catch up with everyone, and to dance the night away." Ella pinched Ethan's cheek, and he smiled at her lovingly.

"I took care of the check, Dad," Arthur said as he stood to hug his father.

Ethan started to scoot out of the booth, but Ella pulled him close and spoke in his ear.

"Don't let him push you away," she said. "You could be so good for him."

Ethan kissed her cheek. "Thank you for saying so. I'd like to be."

She leaned back and patted his cheek. "You are such a keeper."

Ethan slid out and helped Ella to her feet. She went into Arthur's arms and kissed his cheek, taking a moment to whisper in his ear.

"Ethan," Bernard said, pulling him in for a hug. "It's been a real pleasure, son. You're going to do fantastic this week. I'll be in touch with Audra to share with her my thoughts about your projects. Arthur is right, you should choose wisely. This is the time to carve your path. Listen to him." Bernard released him, then held out his hand.

"Thank you, sir," Ethan said, shaking his hand enthusiastically, maybe a little too much, but he'd fallen under the man's spell and was so grateful for every piece of wisdom he'd offered.

"We'll look forward to your visit. Soon, Arthur," Bernard said, as he put his arm around Ella.

"Drive safely tomorrow," Arthur said to them. Then he turned to Ethan. "Did you want dessert?"

"I'm okay."

Arthur nodded and gestured for Ethan to lead the way out. Ethan looked around as surreptitiously as possible, spotting a YouTube star, a cast member from *Dancing With The Stars*, and even Laura Dern.

"Ethan Bradley? Is that you?"

Ethan turned, shocked to hear his name in a place like this. And then his stomach clenched. Tightly.

Arthur was at his side, though. He could do this.

"Miranda, how are you?" He stepped toward the booth that held Miranda Robertson, who would have been his co-star in the British period drama he was set to start filming after *Ruby* wrapped. He took her hand and leaned down to kiss her cheek.

"Ethan, meet my fiancé Ben, and my sister, Antoinette, and...oh, well, you may have met Rupert Bancroft?"

Ethan kept any reaction other than friendliness from flitting over his features as he met the actor who'd been hired to replace him. "I haven't, how do you do? And may I introduce Arthur Frye, from Slade Artist Management?"

Arthur was reserved but polite as he shook the hands of those at the table, his smile slipping a bit at Rupert. "How do you do?"

"Are you here working, Ethan?" Rupert asked, only a hint of snooti-ness in his authentic British accent. Ethan had tried not to read too many of the articles written about him after the pictures came out, but Rupert had sure talked about him in the tabloids. He also took the role of Lord George Foster Beaumont in *The Lords of Elizabeth* after Ethan was fired. It was a somewhat true story about a group of nobles who'd plotted against the queen—Beaumont being one who remained loyal to her. He'd been nervous about playing the part, but his manager thought it was the perfect follow-up to *Affair on the Thames.*

Ethan had just been happy to be working, but there'd been a lot of chatter in the press that he was just a pretty face, and that he didn't have the acting chops to handle such a weighty role. Rupert Bancroft had agreed with that opinion more than once in interviews.

"He's here consulting on a musical production and taking meetings. My firm is representing him." Arthur stood close and rested a hand at Ethan's back, which kept Ethan grounded in his performance.

"Splendid," Miranda said. "I do hope we'll be able to work together in the future. I was so looking forward to it."

Ethan patted her shoulder. "I was as well. Have you wrapped?"

"No, actually, we had a stopover here on our way to film some scenes in Hawaii, if you can believe that."

"That's wonderful. I hope it goes well. It was good to see you. I wish you the best of luck."

"Have a nice evening," Arthur said as he guided Ethan away from the table, not dropping his hand. Ethan was grateful as he worked hard to control his walk so it wouldn't appear he was running away. He kept his head held high. He knew he would have done better than Bancroft in the film, but it didn't matter. If the film's producers thought he wasn't right for the role, it would have been a miserable experience. He was better off.

He thought he might throw up.

"You handled that so well," Arthur murmured.

"I think I'm going to puke."

Arthur rubbed between his shoulder blades. "Do we need to detour?"

Ethan shook his head. "No, please. I'll be okay. I just want to leave. I promise I won't mess up your car."

Arthur chuckled. "I know you won't. You're good. In fact, you're fucking amazing."

Arthur dropping the f-bomb was enough to turn Ethan's discomfort to laughter.

"Thank you?" he said, turning to smile at him. "I don't know how else to act when faced with the guy who talked shit about me in the press and then took the role I got fired from."

"You did exactly what you should have. You took the high road. It suits you. You did so good, honey."

"You keep calling me honey and I'm going to get the wrong idea from you." He tried to keep his voice light, but his emotions were all over the place after the day they'd spent together.

Arthur picked up his pace and urged Ethan on toward the valet stand. "No. You won't."

Ethan wanted to protest, but Arthur gave his waist a squeeze before he handed their tag to the valet.

"Arthur?"

"Wait 'til we get in the car."

"Thank you for dinner," he said, thinking it was a safe thing to say. "I'm not sure what the story is about that salad, but it was delicious."

"It's named after former guest Neil McCarthy, a polo player, who asked for that particular combination of ingredients. These days they serve over six hundred of those a week."

"That's...wow. Wild."

It felt like forever before the valet arrived, and Ethan was both elated and terrified to be alone with Arthur. Would he take Ethan home with him? Would he drop him at the hotel and say goodbye? When the Volvo pulled up, he wondered if he shouldn't just take a cab—

Arthur took his hand and led him to the passenger side, opened the door for him, and waited until he was seated before closing the door.

Ethan rehearsed his monologue as he waited for Arthur to make his way around the car.

Thank you for everything. I appreciate it more than you know. I will always remember this day. I will never forget that you believed in me, that you stood up for me.

Arthur climbed in, fastened his seat belt and paused, his hands braced on the wheel for a moment as he blew out a breath.

"Arthur—"

"Can I take you home with me?"

"Oh. *Please.*"

Arthur gazed at him a moment before he nodded, put the car in drive, and pulled out of the lot.

Ethan's heart was racing. It was what he'd wanted all day, but Arthur had been throwing so many mixed signals, Ethan had no idea what would happen at the end of their date.

The radio was down low in the Volvo but Ethan heard a familiar melody. Arthur had it on the '80s satellite radio channel and the song playing was "Space Age Love Song" by Flock of Seagulls. Kathy Bradley used to love to play '80s music, and Ethan recognized the song as one of her favorites to dance to. He could totally relate to the whole falling in love scenario.

"Do you mind if I turn this up?" Ethan asked as he reached for the screen, but then he wasn't sure how. Arthur touched a button on the steering wheel and the cab filled with the synth-pop sound of the new wave era.

Ethan rested his head against the headrest and slid his hands down his thighs, tapping his fingers along to the music. Arthur was tapping his thumbs on the steering wheel and bobbing his head, his lips moving with the lyrics. Ethan got caught up watching Arthur, the way his lips pursed out, perpetually pink and puffy. His freckles seemed to dance on his skin as the streetlights flickered over his face. His eyelashes were thick and sprinkled in varying shades from blond to red. Ethan's own blue eyes were like ice, almost silver, but Arthur had those deep, stormy blue eyes. Ethan was swept away by them every time he let his gaze rest there. He wanted to swim in them, drown in them maybe.

He'd spent all day trying to be on, to be what Arthur wanted, and he was no closer to figuring out if he *could* be what Arthur wanted, or *what* Arthur even wanted.

"We're home," Arthur said what seemed like seconds later, and Ethan realized he'd fallen asleep. "Looks like *I'll* be tucking *you* into bed tonight."

"No, I'm awake. I promise." He pushed himself up in his seat and rubbed his hands over his face. He reached for the door handle but Arthur put a hand on his leg.

"The same agreement, okay?"

Arthur was giving him an out. Did he want Ethan to take it?

They climbed out of the car and Arthur waited for him, taking his hand.

"Then I guess I'd ask the same question?"

Arthur was quiet as they walked up the stairs, but he held Ethan's hand tightly. He opened the door to his place and once Ethan was inside, he pulled the door shut and turned to face him.

"As much as I hoped this would be a passing thing for me, it's not. Ethan, I'm into you, and while I told myself so many times today that when the night was over, I'd take you back to the hotel, that thought made me incredibly sad. I don't want to let you go. It's the smart thing to do, the responsible thing...but it's not what I want."

Ethan stepped closer, hating that Arthur had been fighting his desire so hard, and grateful that his desire seemed to be winning.

"What *do* you want?" He pressed his body against Arthur's and finally slid his fingers into Arthur's curls and filled his hands with all that thick, gorgeous hair.

A shiver ran through Arthur. "God, I want to—"

Rooooooooooooooooooooowlllllllllll

They both turned and looked toward the kitchen.

Elvis sat there, his round fluffy body sitting in judgement, the rhinestones on his collar catching the lights coming through the window.

"We know what you want, you menace." Arthur put his arms around Ethan and sighed. "I want to—"

Rooooooooooooooooooooooooowwwwwwwwwwlllllll

"It appears he doesn't care what you want." Ethan chuckled.

"Fuck off, Elvis," Arthur said. He slid his hands down to Ethan's hips. " I want—"

The cat cut him off every time he tried to speak, getting louder and louder, his yowls growing longer until he resembled some sort of demented siren.

"*Fine! Fuck!* You fucking feline cockblocking menace!"

Ethan took pity on him and patted his face. "Let me take care of him so I can take care of *you*."

As he stepped back, Arthur had that same expression on his face he'd had in the restaurant, like he was dumbfounded.

Ethan smiled at him and turned for the kitchen. "Maybe you can put on some music?"

He took out a clean bowl and a can of cat food, dumped it in the bowl, and then he filled Elvis's dry food and refilled his water bowl. Then he rested his elbows on the counter and stood still. Waiting.

Elvis watched him from a foot away from his bowl.

Arthur fiddled with cassette cases and made a victory motion with his fist as he apparently found the perfect one. He opened the tape deck and slid the cassette in carefully, closing the door with his long middle finger, gently. He hit rewind and stood watching the wheels spin while Ethan remained motionless, waiting for the cat to do his thing.

When the tape was ready, Arthur pressed play and then walked slowly over to Ethan, wrapping his arms around him from behind and nuzzling the side of his neck.

"Go on, fur face. Eat."

Elvis gave one last swish of his tale before he bent daintily over his canned food and began to lick at it.

Ethan gave a relieved sigh, and then Arthur sucked on the side of his neck.

"You think he'll let me speak now?"

"Speak?" Ethan sighed again, his skin coming alive under Arthur's touch. He was hard in an instant and it was difficult to make words.

"Mmm. I don't know where to start with you. I want to f— Oh, God."

Ethan had turned in his arms and had Arthur's belt buckle unfastened, followed by his pants, in a few quick moves. He slid his hands inside and gripped his hips before he lowered to his knees and—

Roooooooooowwwwwwlllllwwwwwllllrllrrrrrr

"What?"

"He can't see you," Arthur said. "Stand up 'til he's done. God, I want you so fucking bad, Ethan. Hurry the fuck up, E."

"You want my mouth?"

"God, yes. I want your mouth. I want…"

"My hands on you? You want that?"

"Yes, yes, please, and I want your…"

"You want my ass?"

"*Fuck*, Ethan—"

"Is he done yet?"

"How am I supposed to watch my cat eat when you say such things? Goddammit, hurry up, Elvis!"

"I could just…do this?"

Ethan reached in the front of Arthur's pants and stroked his incredibly long cock. *Jesus*, fully erect, the tip was barely covered by the waistband of his boxers. Ethan's mouth watered, imaging how it would feel on the back of his tongue, how much he could take.

"Wait…he's done, he's done, oh, fuck, honey, you feel so good."

But as Ethan started to kneel again, Arthur stopped him. "No, the floor will hurt your knees—"

"I can't wait. Brace yourself. I'm going to be here a while."

Silly man, worrying about a hard floor. Ethan was in heaven as he reached his knees and slid Arthur's pants down far enough to reveal his gorgeous cock nestled in bright red hairs, neatly trimmed.

"You're beautiful," he breathed, before he grabbed the base and closed his lips over the tip.

Arthur groaned and leaned forward to brace his arms on the counter.

Ethan pulled off the blazer Arthur had given to him earlier and he eased away from Arthur's cock long enough to pull his shirt off over his head. He tossed both pieces of clothes away and took Arthur deeper, relaxing his throat as much as he could, realizing he couldn't swallow Arthur all the way down. At least not now. It would take practice, and maybe a different angle. He caught the taste of Arthur's precum and was overwhelmed with the need for more, for all of it—

"You're so good at this. Look at you. Your lips wet, your eyes wet, you're the beautiful one, Ethan." He moaned and his hips bucked. "I don't want to come yet—*fuck*, you're so good—but I do want to come on those lips. Would you let me? Fuck, would you take all of me?"

Ethan nodded and moaned around Arthur's cock, using both hands to stroke in time with his lips and tongue, so pleased he was making Arthur feel good. He wanted that more than anything, wanted to make Arthur come apart, wanted to know how it would feel to take apart this incredible man.

Arthur pulled back and cursed again. "Stand up, I want you…"

Ethan scrambled to his feet, and Arthur spun him around and bent him forward over the counter. He gasped, surprised at Arthur's strength. He yanked Ethan's belt free and slid it out with a snap. Ethan shivered. He'd had no idea Arthur would be so—

"Ohhhhh," he moaned as Arthur had his pants down in a few quick motions. He leaned over Ethan's back and ran a hand over his ass.

"Do you trust me, honey? I won't hurt you. I promise. I just want to taste you for a little while and then I want to take you to bed, that okay? I'll stop, all you have to do is ask—"

"Don't. Don't stop. I want—" He tried to turn around, but Arthur had him caged in.

"Hold still," Arthur said. He went to his knees, and Ethan's heart was pounding so loudly in his ears he could barely hear the music.

He felt Arthur's hands on his ass, on the backs of his thighs, then his fingers running over his cock, lightly, gently, teasingly.

"You'll let me taste you, Ethan? You'll let me have this ass? This beautiful, perfect ass?"

"Yes, have me. Whatever you want." He tried to turn again but then Arthur spread his cheeks wide and the next thing he knew, Arthur had licked his hole and *ohhhhhh*, was it such a good, good feeling. His eyes rolled back in his head and closed for a moment as he sank into Arthur's grip and relaxed his body, allowing Arthur to go deeper, which brought a satisfied moan out of him, the vibrations making Ethan's cock weep.

When he opened his eyes, Elvis was right in front of him on the counter, staring at him.

"Oh. Hey, get down." He shooed at the cat but Elvis didn't move. "Arthur?"

"I'm sorry, you want me to stop?"

"Not at all, but unlike Elvis, I don't think I like having an audience when I'm, um, *being* eaten."

Arthur grunted, cursed again and climbed to his feet.

"I swear, Elvis, if you don't take your ungrateful fucking derriere somewhere else, you'll be eating in the laundry room from now on." He waved his hand toward the cat, and Elvis hopped down from the counter with a short yip that let them know he was not pleased to be reprimanded.

"I'm sorry," Ethan said breathlessly. "I just couldn't—"

"May I continue? I was really enjoying myself."

Ethan turned to look at him over his shoulder. "Are you sure? Do you want me to shower? I can move so you're more comfortable."

Arthur patted his ass and shook his head. "You're perfect." He smiled, and Ethan thought it was the most relaxed expression he'd ever seen on Arthur's face. "Turn around. I want to finish my dessert."

"By all means."

Ethan held on for dear life as Arthur turned him into a quivering mess. He'd never imagined in a million years he'd be face down on Arthur's counter, ass in the air, as the man he'd thought he'd never have a chance with turned him inside out with a pleasure he'd never experienced before. His legs were shaking so much and he was trapped by the jeans, which held his ankles in place. He needed to move. He *needed*.

"Fuck, you taste so good." Arthur leaned back and ran his hands gently over the backs of Ethan's thighs, making him squirm. "Is this good for you?"

"God, yes, but I...I need, I can't...I want..." He toed off the shoes and hopped around until he had the jeans off, while Arthur chuckled.

"Yes, I love you like this, naked in my kitchen. But I really want you in my bed—"

"Yes, please—"

"Under me—"

"I...yes."

Ethan's heart was now racing for a different reason. He wanted to give Arthur everything he wanted, but what if...

What if it's like last time?

Arthur stood and cupped his jaw in his hands. "Hey, what's wrong? I told you, we don't have to do anything."

"I want to, I just..." He blew out a breath. He wanted to be honest with Arthur and hoped it didn't ruin the moment. He swallowed hard. "I've only ever bottomed once, and it was…it wasn't a good experience."

Arthur stiffened and his stormy eyes darkened. "Who hurt you?"

"God, please don't ask me that." Ethan's eyes filled with tears, and he wanted to scream at the unfairness. Why couldn't his first time have been with someone kind like Arthur? The last thing he wanted to do was tell Arthur that it had been one of his best friends.

Arthur gathered him close and held his trembling body, cooing in his ear, reassuring him.

"Let me take you to bed, Ethan. I want to hold you. We don't have to do anything else."

Ethan blew out a breath and let Arthur lead him to the bedroom. "No, it's fine, I just need a minute. I'm okay. I just don't want to disappoint you."

Arthur turned on him. "You could never. You've done nothing but impress me. You're so young and so good, *such* a good person, despite how others have treated you. You won't disappoint me."

TWENTY-SIX

Arthur

He guided Ethan to the bed and had him crawl in. Ethan peered out at him from a cloud of white bedding and Arthur took a moment to savor the sight. His bed had never looked so inviting. And yet he had to be very, very careful.

"I'm just going to get out of these pants," he said, not wanting to spook him.

"Please," he said, sitting up. "Take all of your clothes off? You said I could taste your freckles."

He was so damned cute, but there was such innocence there. He gave his affection so freely to Arthur, but under the surface, he was like a scared rabbit. It made Arthur want to break something—or someone.

He unzipped his boots and stepped out of them. He slid his pants off and tossed them toward the door to his vault, along with his sweater and undershirt. He caught Ethan's eyes flare when Arthur's dick was exposed, and it made him chuckle. Arthur may not have had a super fit physique, but he'd never had complaints in bed. He wouldn't push for anything more than cuddling if Ethan wasn't ready. Arthur would never forgive himself if he became one more bad experience.

He slid into bed next to Ethan, who immediately came to him, resting his head on Arthur's chest, wrapping his arm and leg around him.

"What are we listening to, by the way? I like it."

"It's an old mix tape I made of my favorite mellow songs. The Cure, Type O Negative, Peter Murphy, Cocteau Twins...I used to play it before bed when I couldn't sleep."

"After all the coffee you had at dinner tonight, I worry you'll never sleep again."

Arthur sighed. "You caught me. My biggest vice."

"Caffeine?"

"Yeah. Since college. I've cut back a lot—"

Ethan's head popped up, and he gave Arthur an incredulous look.

"I'm serious! Six cups of coffee is nothing. I usually have more than that plus energy drinks and green tea."

Ethan placed a hand over Arthur's heart. "I don't want anything to happen to you," he said quietly against Arthur's chest. "You push yourself really hard. Your parents worry, too."

Arthur sighed. "I know. I'm seeing a doctor. I'm working on it. I promise." He kissed Ethan's hair. "Don't worry about me. But tell me what happened to you. I don't want to hurt you, honey, I *never* want to hurt you. Please tell me so I don't."

Ethan blew out a long breath. "I...I wanted this guy to think I was more experienced than I was. I flirted a little too much, acted like I knew what I was doing, and I fucked up. It hurt. A lot. And I didn't say anything. I didn't want to seem weak, so I took it. I think he knew when it was over. He was a little freaked out, grabbed his stuff and left."

Arthur closed his eyes and held Ethan tighter, brushing his hair back and kissing his forehead. They were quiet for some time, and then Ethan started to fidget.

"Sorry I brought down the mood—"

"No, you didn't." Arthur forced him to look into his eyes. "I'm glad you told me. We don't ever have to have intercourse, if you don't want to. I would never hurt you. He had to have known he was...there's no excuse for that."

Ethan shrugged and looked away. His eyes were wet. "I deserved it. I'd been stupid, flirting with people, trying to make everyone like me. I don't know, when we got to London it was like this whole other world, and I think I let my character carry me away. I wanted to be confident like him, and I wanted everyone to love me. I met some nice guys, I pretended to be really into them, and when we were alone it felt... wrong. So I'd leave and they were always confused, like, didn't I like them? I was a big tease. But I thought I was hot shit, leaving them wanting more, I guess. Stupid. And then...well, I tried that act on the wrong person, and he called me on my bullshit."

"Honey, no. No matter what, if a situation doesn't feel right, you don't owe anyone *anything*. No matter what you said you would or wouldn't do, you can say no anytime and they have to respect that. It's your body. This guy who hurt you—"

"I didn't say no. I didn't tell him to stop. I was fine after a while. I just haven't been with anyone else, hadn't even thought of being with anyone else until I met you, and I didn't want to bring my baggage here. I want to be good for you."

"Ethan," Arthur started, wanting to take this delicate conversation so carefully. "You've said that a couple of times. You *are* good. You're a good person, and I like you a lot. I like being with you. That's all the good I need from you. That, and that you're honest with me, because unlike that guy, if I thought I'd hurt you, it would fucking kill me."

"You wouldn't, I know you wouldn't. And I got tested and everything, and I'm okay. He used a condom...I just thought I'd tell you. I've never topped, only bottomed the once, and yeah. That's what you're getting."

"No." Arthur rolled over on top of Ethan and brushed his hair back from his face. "No, what I'd be getting is the honor and privilege of you sharing your body with me. Nothing else matters. Only what happens between us matters to me, only taking care with you and treating you right matters to me. Only you being real and honest with me matters to me. Don't ever pretend, don't ever *not* tell me when something isn't right."

Ethan nodded, and his smile was tentative. "After all that, you'd still want me?"

Arthur took Ethan's mouth in a deep kiss he hoped let Ethan know exactly how much he wanted him. Deep brushes with his tongue elicited sighs and moans from Ethan, and he let his legs fall open. Arthur let his hips rest between Ethan's parted thighs, loving the way he welcomed him.

"I don't want you. I *need* you, honey. Can I please make you feel good?"

Ethan nodded, his eyes still wide.

"Say it. I need you to say what you want."

Ethan gasped and licked his lips. "I want to come, please."

God, that admission turned Arthur's crank. He kissed Ethan once more and then it was on. He dove under the sheets, making hungry noises until he found what he wanted. Ethan cracked up until Arthur swallowed him down. His thighs were quaking as Arthur was relentless with his strokes. Ethan wasn't long like Arthur, but he was thick, with a curve just before the tip. Arthur loved the stretch it took to keep his lips suctioned, his cheeks hollowing as he sucked and sucked.

"Arthur, I want to watch you," Ethan said, lifting the covers.

Arthur yanked them back down. "I don't want you to get cold."

Ethan pulled them up again. "I'm fine, I'm fine, God, you look so hot. You still better let me lick all of your freckles— Oh my...oh...my oh my...*oh my God*."

Arthur spit into his hand and spread the wetness over Ethan's hole.

Ethan spread his thighs wide and pulled his knees up, giving Arthur access to what he wanted most.

"You want more?"

"Yes, please, Arthur."

Arthur had always been attentive in bed, always the one to make sure his lover was fully sated, relaxed, and comfortable when he was done with them. But with Ethan, he mostly wanted to wipe away every bad experience he'd ever had, wanted to erase his self-doubt and make him realize how special he really was.

He pulled out all the stops, used all of his tricks. Only then did Arthur pull the covers down so he could watch the thing of beauty about to occur. Within seconds, Ethan was sobbing through a full-bodied orgasm that kept coming and coming and coming. The sheer amount of cum on his abdomen when Arthur was finished was something to feel triumphant over.

He moved up the bed next to Ethan and brushed his hair back. "How do you feel?"

Ethan had one hand over his face and with the other, he held up a finger as he continued to pant. He wiped the tears from his cheeks and Arthur was relieved when he smiled.

"You...that...what...I can't... *How*?"

Arthur sighed and kissed Ethan's cheek. "Can I assume that was okay?"

Ethan turned and looked up at Arthur, his eyes still full of tears. "Yeah. It really was. I feel like I've never had sex before that. It's never, I've never..."

"I'll take that as a good thing?" He patted Ethan's chest. "I'll be back."

Arthur scurried into the bathroom on a mission. Warm washcloth. Then to the kitchen for a glass of water. When he came back, Ethan reached for the cloth.

"Oh, thanks."

"Let me." Arthur handed him the glass of water and then he cleaned off Ethan's belly and between his legs. He tossed the washcloth across the room, nailing a three into his hamper, lifting his hands in victory. Ethan laughed as Arthur climbed in bed next to him. He turned to touch him, but Arthur grabbed his hand.

"No, honey, now it's time for me to hold you. I want you relaxed and off to dreamland."

"But what about you?"

"That's not how this works with me," he said, turning Ethan over and spooning him from behind. "You let me hold you, and I kiss and caress you until either you fall asleep, or the sun comes up and then I feed you breakfast. Bottom line? You're going to find out what it really means to be pampered. Are you ready?"

"No, I don't understand. Arthur, why are you being so good to me?"

"Because it makes me happy. Secondarily, because it hopefully makes *you* happy."

"Of course I'm happy. God, you are the most incredible man. I... Arthur—"

"Wants you to rest, honey. Here." Arthur picked up his phone and turned on music through his Bluetooth speaker as the cassette in the other room had finished and he didn't want to get up and flip it over. Spandau Ballet came through, and Ethan sighed, snuggling closer.

They lay like that for a long time, but Ethan never went to sleep. When he started fidgeting, Arthur rolled him over.

"What are you thinking about?"

"I'm sorry, am I keeping you awake?"

"Only because I'm worried about you."

Ethan exhaled. "I don't sleep very well when I'm not...I guess, when I'm in a new place. I haven't had a home for a long time. Then that got me thinking about, if I get hired, I'll be moving again, and I wonder where I'll be, and that led to going through the monologues I've memo-rized so I'm ready if I get asked to do something."

"And it's been like this every night?"

Ethan shrugged. "Pretty much. Well, last night I watched *you* sleep until I couldn't keep my eyes open. I was wondering what would happen when you woke up, whether you'd be mad I was still here—"

"I wasn't mad at all. Only sorry I didn't take advantage of you being here sooner. Despite the fact that you're a fidgeter, you're very nice to cuddle with."

"I've never had much opportunity to cuddle. I think I'm a fan."

Arthur pulled Ethan to him, their bodies pressed together, their legs tangled. "I think you've made me one, too."

Ethan pressed a tentative kiss to his throat and a shiver ran through Arthur. The best kind of shiver.

"Is this the beginning of freckle tasting?" he asked. He still wasn't a hundred percent accepting of this scenario, that a beautiful man like Ethan would find an older, plain-looking-on-a-good-day man, one who was in no kind of shape to speak of, attractive. And yet every time he'd tried to let Ethan off the hook, or give him an out, he remained. Part of him was still waiting for his dismissal.

"I would love to if you'd let me."

Arthur sighed and ran his fingers through Ethan's curls. They were silky, his hair was fine, not as thick and coarse as Arthur's, and the barely there hair on the rest of Ethan's torso was as soft as velvet.

"As long as it's what you want. Please don't think I expect anything from you."

"God, I want to, Arthur. I've wanted to touch you and kiss you so badly."

"Why me, though? Since we're being open and honest. I don't see the attraction."

Ethan pushed up on an elbow. "Are you joking? God, Arthur, what's not to love? You ooze competence and confidence, you're so smart, you're passionate about what you do, you're generous...and you make the world make sense to me. Being with you...I feel safe for the first time since I left home. I showed you all the ugly parts of my life, and you still asked me to come home with you. And to top it off? You believed in me when I was ready to quit." He chuckled. "And bonus? You have more freckles than I do, which I didn't think was possible, and I really, *really* want to taste them all. So can I, please?"

Arthur wanted to believe what he said. In the past, men had chosen him for what being seen on his arm could do for their careers, or for his money, or an introduction to his parents. He'd had an agent friend once who'd told him that the ugly ones worked harder at relationships and that's why, in her opinion, they got the hot ones. "Those of us who aren't hot will always have to wonder if that's why our partners chose us. That's our lot in life."

It was one of those comments someone made in passing that had never left Arthur's consciousness. He couldn't unhear it, despite knowing he had a lot to offer a partner. Some things never go away.

"Say something," Ethan breathed.

Arthur could hardly speak around the lump in his throat. "Okay," he whispered.

Ethan's answering smile was so bright it brought tears to Arthur's eyes. No one had ever looked at him with that much enthusiasm, that much happiness, that much—did he dare believe it?—adoration. He closed his eyes, worried the damn tears would become actual crying.

Ethan loved his body so thoroughly that Arthur was already in heaven before Ethan even put his mouth on his cock. It was so good. All Arthur could do was rock into his talented kiss. He'd managed to find Arthur's most sensitive spot, the one that made his whole body shudder and made it nearly impossible to not let go and—

"Fuck, Ethan, I'm coming!" was all the warning he was able to give. Ethan moaned happily and took all Arthur had to give. It was as beautiful to watch as Arthur thought it would be. Ethan's bright blue eyes were shiny and half-lidded, his lips glossy, his hair artfully mussed. God, he was incredible, smiling as he licked Arthur's cock. His tongue was even beautiful, pointy at the tip and so very skilled.

Arthur couldn't hold up his head any longer, and he laughed as Ethan continued on his quest to lick all of his freckles, eventually giving up.

"I want to save some to explore next time."

Next time. He'd very much like a next time. At this point, he didn't ever want Ethan to leave his bed.

"My freckles are here for your exploration. Anytime. Thanks, honey. Kiss me."

"I'm going to hold you to that," Ethan said as he kissed him deeply, using his position above Arthur to kiss the hell out of him. Arthur was breathless and struggled to make his lips work. He laughed when he realized he was barely reciprocating, just loving Ethan's attention.

"This old man is about to get pulled under by sleep. I'm not going to be able to keep up with you, I'm afraid."

"Let me take care of you, and we'll be just fine."

Arthur's heart hiccupped at Ethan's words, but he realized it wasn't the scary kind of hiccup. That kind had gotten better and less frequent. No, this was a hopeful hiccup, the kind that his heart made whenever Ethan said such things. A hiccup was a hiccup, though, and whichever kind it was, it could still do Arthur in. He just didn't know if he had it in him to take preventative measures when it came to Ethan Bradley.

And with that, Ethan curled himself around Arthur and he ran his fingernails lightly over Arthur's chest until he fell fast asleep.

. . .

Arthur's senses came online the next morning to the following stimuli:

The sound of his phone buzzing.

Ethan's hair tickling his nose.

The bright light of the sun coming through the drapes they'd forgotten to pull the previous night.

And a weight on his very full bladder.

Arthur opened his eyes and peered past Ethan's head to stare into the accusing eyes of Elvis as he attempted to reach his phone. Ethan tried to move, but Arthur held him in place.

"No, honey, stay here. I got it."

He grabbed his phone and glasses, bringing the phone up to his right ear as he stroked Ethan's back.

Yeah, he definitely never wanted to let Ethan out of his bed.

"Arthur Frye."

"Arthur, it's Jude."

Worst-case scenarios filled Arthur's mind. "Everything okay?" he asked, trying to keep his voice steady.

Jude's voice was quiet, letting Arthur know that Reese probably didn't know he was calling. "Mr. Matheson is okay. But Reese..."

"What's wrong, Jude?"

"Reese has laryngitis, and I'm trying to take him for a chest X-Ray—"

"I don't need an X-Ray."

"Oh, God, was that him?" Reese's voice sounded like ground hamburger rotting in a garbage can.

"I'm afraid so. We stayed outside with Thomas for hours after the earthquake Friday night. He was shaken up and worried about after-shocks. Reese lit a fire in the fire pit to keep everyone warm, but then he played guitar and sang for Thomas to calm him down, and I think between the smoke and the damp air...I made him rest yesterday but he's worse today. With the show...I don't know what to do. His lungs sound horrible, he's got a temperature of one hundred and two, and he won't let me take him to urgent care."

"Put him on the phone, please." Arthur blew out a breath, and Ethan sat up. "Don't," he whispered, but Ethan grinned down at him, looking like a goddamned angel with the light filtering through his curls.

"I'm going to feed Elvis before he—"

YOOOOOOOOWWWWWWWLLLLLLLL

Ethan grinned wider and climbed out of bed. Arthur enjoyed the view as he walked naked through the bedroom first to the bathroom, and then out to the kitchen to feed the furry menace.

"Arthur," Reese croaked into the phone.

"Don't talk, just listen. I'm calling Dr. Shah. If he wants you to get an X-Ray, you're going. I'll take you so Jude can get some rest."

"Arthur, I can't be sick. The show—"

"It's going to be fine. Let me get dressed and I'll be over. We can work out a plan."

"Arthur."

"Reese, I love you, but I'm hanging up. Listen to Jude and don't use your voice. Tell Jude I'll call him right back."

Arthur hung up and blew out a long breath.

"Is everything okay?" Ethan stood in the doorway in Arthur's jeans from yesterday. The fly was down and he wasn't wearing anything underneath. If Arthur hadn't been in the middle of a fire drill, he would have been hard as steel and ready for round three with this beautiful man.

"Probably not." He dialed Dr. Shah, a private practice physician who made house calls to Hollywood's elite and would be absolutely frank with him.

Once the doctor heard Jude's take on the situation, he clicked his tongue against his teeth. "Jude is right. He should have an X-Ray, especially if he has a fever, to determine if it's viral or bacterial."

"Thank you. Anything else?"

"I'll text Reese instructions for Jude. Hopefully this is a bronchitis and not a pneumonia. If it's the latter, he'll be down for at least a couple of weeks."

"Perfect. The show is Saturday."

"I'm sorry, Arthur. I'm sending orders to the imaging clinic for the X-Ray, you don't need to take him to urgent care that way. I'm also going to set up a referral for the ENT I recommend. Reese needs to know that if he pushes through this, he could do irreparable damage to his voice and lungs. Make sure you tell him I said that."

"Thank you. If he's going to listen to anyone, it'll be you."

Arthur hung up and resisted the urge to chuck his phone across the room. Once again, a day he was looking forward to was snatched away. But this situation was serious, and they all had a lot to lose.

"What can I do?" Ethan asked, still framed in the doorway like a delicious meal just waiting for Arthur to taste.

"Be standing there, looking beautiful, every morning."

Ethan's eyes flared, and Arthur thought about what he'd said. Ugh, he'd always laughed when people said they knew what they wanted after one night together. Despite his parents and friends having similar experiences, Arthur had always thought it was bullshit. *When you know, you know*, they'd say. Maybe Arthur knew instinctively that Ethan was someone he could see himself wanting in his life permanently, but his rational mind couldn't let go of control.

Ethan crossed his arms and tilted his head against the doorjamb. "I'll be wherever you want me, whenever you want me, if you keep looking at me like that."

Arthur wanted to growl. If ever there were an occasion when a man should growl, looking at Ethan Bradley—who was giving morning-after-great-sex vibes while showing miles of perfect skin and enough happy-trail pubes to be considered borderline obscene—was it.

"Well, then, this is your first challenge as my paramour...being patient through a client emergency."

"Your paramour? I like that."

"Do you?"

"If it means being yours, I love it."

Arthur grinned. He wanted that. Wanted Ethan.

"Seriously, I'll do anything for you, but I'll also stay out of the way if that's what's best. I don't want to interfere."

Arthur sat up and hugged his knees, putting his manager hat on. Unfortunately, it fit differently now that he'd carved a little space in his heart and mind for a...paramour.

"If you came with me, it would go one of two ways. Awkward or comforting. You'll also see me at work and maybe you'll decide I'm a dick, and you don't want to come home with me again."

"You forget I've watched you work all week, and I've already been a part of a production you were involved in. It's too late for me, my mind's made up." He shrugged and pushed off the wall. He stood next to Arthur's side of the bed. "I'll do whatever you want, Arthur. Don't worry about me. Either bring me so you have backup, or I can go back to the hotel."

"No. Not the hotel."

Ethan gazed down at him with a frown. Could Arthur do it? Ask him to stay? Was that a good idea or him being impulsive? So many decisions.

"Stay here," he said before assessing the wisdom of that option. His life was about to get messy if he was going to carve out that spot for Ethan. Might as well get messy now. "Be here when I get back. Use the pool, order takeout, relax. You've got a big week coming up. You could use some time to chill."

TWENTY-SEVEN

E^{than}

Ethan tried not to fidget as Arthur made calls while he made coffee, shaved, only hanging up to get in the shower. Eventually, Ethan hopped up from the bed and started making it. He was tucking in the final hospital corner when Arthur came out of the bathroom in just a towel.

"You absolutely don't need to tidy up. Please." He stepped up to Ethan and put his hands on his biceps. "I want you to relax. Watch a movie or three," he said with a sad laugh, rubbing his wavy hair with another towel. "Make yourself at home."

Ethan wrapped his arms around himself and tried to smile. "I don't know what that means." He laughed. "I mean, I do. I just..."

"Look, I'm hoping to go check on Reese, get him to go have an X-Ray, and calm him down. Then come right back to you. I wanted to feed you, I wanted to pamper you today. After last night...I'm not ready to be away from you yet."

Ethan let his arms fall. "Yeah? You don't want to get rid of me?"

Arthur cupped his face in both hands, and the motion stilled Ethan for the first time since he'd climbed out of bed.

He'd woken up so...happy. Full of joy. Arthur had made him feel special, cherished, and their intimacy had felt...mature. Loving. It wasn't just about getting off. It was about building a fire that could last. Ethan had gone from feeling adrift and terrified when he'd landed in LA to, well, almost a grown-up, and one who could be worthy of the love of a man he so admired. What a difference a day made.

"If you're not careful, I'll never want to be rid of you. You sure you want to take on an old curmudgeon like me? I'm stuffy, I'm grumpy, I drink way too much caffeine, and I'm particular—"

"You're romantic, thoughtful, and so caring. Honestly, if last night was all we had, I want you to know how amazing—"

Arthur kissed him mid-phrase, and Ethan melted against him with a sigh. It was the morning after, and Arthur hadn't made excuses and asked him to leave. In fact, he'd asked him to stay, and he was kissing Ethan like he meant it.

"Fucking Reese. Fucking responsibilities. Please, Ethan. Stay. Make yourself at home in my home. Wait for me. And when I come back, we can talk about what happens next, all right? And if you're still dressed like that, I won't be mad about it."

Arthur let him go and winked at him as he entered his vault. Ethan giggled as he heard Arthur whistling to himself. When he emerged a few moments later, Ethan staggered a bit.

God, Arthur in a suit was all Ethan needed for his spank bank from now to eternity. The sharp line of his shoulders and jaw contrasted with his wavy, barely controlled hair and those puffy, pouty lips that Ethan wished he could suck on some more. His long straight nose and those serious wire-rimmed glasses, his intense eyes, but then there were the freckles, which made him seem playful almost.

"Plug in your phone to charge."

"Right. In case you need me to go or—"

"No. So you can order yourself food, or I've got bagels, eggs, sourdough, avocado, peanut butter and jelly. I think I even have some boxes of kid cereal that I keep for emergencies."

"Cereal for emergencies?"

"Mmm, sometimes that's what you need after a hard day. Eat, crawl back into bed. The remote for the Fire TV is right there. I've got every streaming service. Fucking eat in my bed, leave all the crumbs, I don't even care. I want you here when I get back so I can get you all messy again."

He said all this while expertly tying his tie without even using a mirror. He smoothed it down, straightened his coat, and grabbed his wallet and keys.

"I'll do my best," Ethan said with a laugh, still feeling a bit unsure about all this. Which gave him another thought. "Hey, Arthur?"

Arthur adjusted his cufflinks and slid a pair of black dress shoes on. "Yes, doll?"

God, Ethan wanted to swoon.

"So, we spent the night together, we had dinner with your parents... say someone asked you what was going on, what would you answer?"

Arthur turned and leveled a serious gaze at him. "I don't know. I'd want to tell them that I'm very into you, that you give incredibly good head, and that I want to wake up with you next to me from now on."

Ethan felt light-headed. This was too good to be true. He sat down on the bed. "But?"

"But?" Arthur parroted.

"I'm waiting for the but."

Arthur smiled in a wicked way that made Ethan want to fall to his knees at his feet and wait for instructions.

"Oh, I'll wait for the—"

"Arthur!"

Arthur took a knee next to Ethan and placed his hands on either side of Ethan's hips. "In all honesty, I'm not sure what I'd say. I don't know that it's good for you at this point in your career resurrection to be in an openly gay relationship, especially one with me. You have to decide how out you want to be moving forward. You should talk to Reese and Toby, or I can have you talk to Joe. See what they say. It brings a unique set of potential problems, but it also means not feeling like you need to hide anything."

"Okay," Ethan said, nodding. "You're so good at this. You think of everything. But with friends and family?"

"I would want to tell them."

Ethan's eyes filled, and he blinked a bunch of times. "Really?"

"They all knew how I felt before I did, so yeah, it will give them all the ammunition they need to fuck with me for the rest of my life."

Ethan put his hands over his mouth and laughed. "I can't get used to you swearing."

"Get used to it," Arthur said, leaning in close. "I say fuck a lot in my house." He pulled Ethan's hands away from his face. "If you're going to be here, you're gonna have to put up with it."

"You really want me here?"

"I do." Arthur captured Ethan's lips in a kiss that hinted at other activities he'd done with his lips and tongue, and Ethan shuddered. "What about you?"

"I want to be here."

"Good. But what about your family and friends?"

Ethan winced. "Don't really have any."

Arthur frowned so severely, it made Ethan pull back, though Arthur had a hold of him.

"What do you mean? I know things aren't good with your father and brothers. Any college friends?"

Ethan shrugged. "You know how I came here for a second chance? A fresh start? I meant just that."

Arthur scowled, and then he fucking growled, and he grabbed Ethan into the tightest hug.

"I'm going to give you all of it. Friends, family, a fresh start, and everything you could ever want. Mark my words, Ethan Bradley. Everything you could ever want. Now you need to stop wasting time and start relaxing. I'm pissed I can't feed you, but this is where I need you to be patient."

"Go. Go. I'll be here when you get back." Ethan sniffled, now desperately wanting Arthur to leave so he could have a good cry. "Reese needs you."

Arthur kissed him once more, like he was a treasure he took out and admired, then kept safe in his lair. "Turn your ringer on. I'll keep you posted." He stood and exhaled, shaking his head as if leaving was the last thing he wanted to do.

"Take your time. Wait! Is anything off limits? I don't want to overstep—"

"Nothing of mine is off limits to you." Arthur pressed two fingers to Ethan's lips and then turned to leave. "Elvis will probably yell at you to feed him again, if I'm not back. He can have half a can if that's the case, just know you'll have to watch him eat. Weird fucking cat, I swear. I'll call you, okay?"

"Okay," Ethan called out. He heard the door close and then he heard Arthur whistling outside the window. There was a tap a second later. Ethan stood and pulled open the drape.

"Beach towels are in the cabinet in the other bathroom. Swim trunks are in my vault. It's warm out. Sunscreen is in the medicine cabinet. I'll be back soon." He pressed those two fingers to his lips and to the window, and Ethan smiled so wide he thought his cheeks would break.

God, he was dangerously close to being hopelessly in love with Arthur Frye.

Elvis came waltzing into the room and sat just inside the doorway staring at him, his fluffy gray tail flicking from side to side.

"Guess it's just us?"

No response.

"Well. Shall we find breakfast? What do you think? Should I go swimming? What should I do?"

Elvis kicked up his back leg and started licking his balls.

"Yeah, not that."

An hour later he'd eaten, gone for a swim, and was letting the sun recharge his batteries when his phone buzzed.

Please tell me you're alive?

Audra. Shit, he'd forgotten to text her back last night.

I'm alive and well and terribly sorry for missing your texts. It won't happen again.

The phone started playing "867-5309," and Ethan nearly dropped it, he was so startled.

"Hello?"

"Thank God, where are you?"

"Hi, Audra. I'm so sorry—"

"Yeah, yeah, where are you?"

Here we go. "At the pool?"

"Uh-huh. Which pool? Because you aren't at your hotel."

Ethan squeezed his eyes shut. "At Arthur's pool?"

Audra was quiet for several long beats. "I have two very strong reactions to that statement, and since you're my first client, I have no idea which one is appropriate."

"I'm supposed to tell you everything, right? And you're supposed to advise me. At least that's what we talked about. I can tell you my last manager didn't care all that much for or about me. He took me on, got me into a bunch of projects, took my money, and told me where to go and what to do."

"I'd like to tell *him* where to go and what to do," Audra mumbled. "First off, I want you to trust me and I want to advise you, yes, but I'm here to support you, be a sounding board for you. And to do that, I need to know what you need."

Ethan blew out a breath. "Probably a reality check." He laughed. "Like, how can I be this elated and this terrified at the same time?"

"Just means you're human. Okay, talk to me. What's your status? What do you need for real?

"My status is...I had a delicious breakfast cobbled together in his kitchen. I think his cat doesn't hate me. I had a great workout in the pool and now I've got a tan going for the first time since...I don't even know when? I have no clothes here. Well, nothing clean. Arthur had to go to Reese's, and he asked me to stay here and wait for him. And I think maybe he likes me a little bit."

Audra squealed. "I knew it, and I'm so glad he did something about it! But that's all I'm going to say. Wait, are you happy, Ethan? Are you safe? Are you okay? I don't know, what am I supposed to ask a client who's dating my boss?"

Ethan chuckled. "I'm deliriously happy, very safe, and I just might be okay."

"Good. That's really good. So tomorrow—oh, wait, that's Arthur on my other line. I'm going to put you on hold."

Audra's line went silent, and Ethan kicked his legs over the side of the lounge chair. His sun-neglected skin had probably had enough exposure for now. He gathered up his towel and headed into the house. He wondered about the other folks who lived in this unique building. Arthur had mentioned an actress lived upstairs and she was away on a shoot, but was there anyone else around? Did Arthur own his unit or the whole building?

"Are you there?"

"Yeah, Audra, I'm here."

"Great, okay, I'm coming to pick you up. Your presence has been requested. I'll be there around one. Arthur said to grab whatever you need from his vault and to dress comfortably. This might take a while."

"Sure. I'll be ready." For what, though, he had no idea.

He hung up with Audra, took a quick shower, loving the different fragrances that, all combined, smelled just like Arthur. Loved that he smelled like Arthur when he was finished.

He walked into the vault and proceeded to hang up all of the items they'd left strewn about, put both of the Swatches away in their cases. He went commando in a pair of soft tan chinos and found a plain red t-shirt—it wasn't as much fun getting dressed without Arthur, and he didn't know which items of clothing were special or expensive.

He borrowed a pair of socks and put on his dress shoes. He was watching Elvis have a snack when Audra arrived. She gave him a raised-eyebrows kind of oh-shit look as she walked in the door, pulled him in for a hug, and then held him at arm's length.

"We've got a situation."

Audra drove like a bat out of hell, taking side streets and swerving around cars driving too slow for her taste as she explained what was going on.

"Reese does indeed have a whopper of a case of bronchitis, possibly pneumonia, so he can't sing this weekend for the opener of the show. We're not sure he'll even be able to play."

"That's awful! This show means so much to him, to everyone."

"Right, and the show must go on, so I'm bringing you over so they can talk to you about standing in for Reese on vocals."

Ethan felt a jolt run through him not unlike the earthquakes they'd experienced this week.

"Me? Sing for *Boy*?"

She nodded and then made a couple of complicated lane changes that had Ethan grabbing for the *oh shit* handle.

"Yes, you. Reese is convinced the dancers can get by with the recordings for a couple of days, or just the instrumental, and he thinks based on your work in *Ruby*, you can pick up the songs in time for dress rehearsals Thursday and Friday. Toby is on his way over there as well to work with you. I've seen recordings from *Ruby*. You have a stunning voice, Ethan. But returning to musicals wasn't in our plans for you career-wise, so I don't know if you're—"

"I would do anything for Reese Matheson. If he thinks I can do it, I'll do it."

She nodded and her lips quirked up in a smile. "That's good. That brings me to our dilemma. We've got meetings set up all week—"

"Can I practice in between? At night? Can we make it work?"

She blew out a breath. "We're sure going to try. You're my priority—"

"The show is the priority, though. It has to be."

She nodded, her smile growing. "I knew you were a ten. Now you're going for eleven."

"I'm serious, Audra. The show has to be the priority. I'll do whatever they need me to do."

Which seemed like the right answer, but a half hour later when they arrived, and he got a load of Arthur on the phone with a worried expression, Reese's terrible cough, Jude's hand to the forehead and deep cleansing breaths, Bailey's giant eyes, and, well, *Toby*, Ethan was feeling a little less than confident.

Thomas Matheson's comments weren't helping, either.

"Why doesn't the fairy just sing it? It's about a couple of fairies, after all."

"Grandpa, now isn't the time for fairy jokes," Reese croaked out. "Besides, I don't know if you've noticed, but besides Bailey, you're surrounded by fairies." He coughed, and Jude pleaded with him to go to bed.

"You've heard all the music, right, Ethan?" Reese asked.

"I have. I saw the show run-through about three times, I think. It's so great."

More coughing. Ethan could see how much pain Reese was in and felt terrible for him.

"'Fire' is the toughest song, I think," Reese said. "Can you try it? Here's the sheet music. Let me play it through for you and then let's see, okay? Toby will sing the harmonies with you."

"Reese, why don't you have him sing with the recording?" Arthur asked. "You need to rest." Arthur and Jude had apparently been pleading with him all morning, and now that it was close to two in the afternoon, Jude needed to get lunch made for Thomas, who continued to put his two cents in.

Ethan looked over the sheet music and felt like he had a good understanding.

"He needs to warm up first, right?" Audra asked. "You haven't sung in a while, Ethan, you should warm up."

"Good idea," Reese said. "Let's do some scales, just like we did for *Ruby*. Toby? You do it with him."

Toby and Ethan stood next to the piano in the living room, which was so crowded with people there wasn't a lot of room. As they started going through the familiar warmups, Toby's arm brushed against his, and Ethan moved away, getting a raised eyebrow from Toby. Arthur had just hung up the phone, and he looked at Ethan funny for just a moment before he went back to speaking to Audra. The two of them walked into the kitchen as they were finishing up the scales.

"Good? You ready? Let's do 'Fire,' and then I swear, Jude, I'll go to bed."

Jude brought a tray over to Mr. Matheson's chair with his lunch and the elderly man started eating, though he was still watching the goings-on at the piano, which was next to his chair.

Reese started playing the beginning of the song, and Ethan took a step away from Toby.

"I'm not going to bite you," he said with a laugh. "Again."

"Toby, shut the fuck up," Reese said, dropping his hands on the keys. "Start over. This time just run it through and get the tempo, okay?"

Ethan nodded. He took a deep breath and waited for his line. When he started singing, his voice sounded a little weak, but he didn't want to go overboard on his first try. He wanted to be sure he got all the words right before he put more force behind it. This was the song from the bedroom scene, which was the part he'd helped the boys with in rehearsal, so he understood the intention of the song in the overall story.

When Toby joined in, his voice was strong, higher than Ethan's, and Ethan broke out in goose bumps. He wasn't sure he'd heard Toby really sing before, and when their voices climbed higher together, he understood just what was so important about this show. The feelings were so big, the stakes so high...much higher than they'd been in *Ruby*.

When Reese asked them to do it again, bigger this time, he and Toby both gave it that push and when they hit those high notes together, everyone in the room stopped moving. Audra and Arthur stood in the doorway gaping, and Ethan reached deep inside himself to give just a little more until—

"Whoa." Reese sat staring at them. "That was...wow. Pops? What do you think?"

Mr. Matheson narrowed his eyes and wiped his mouth with a napkin. "These two fairies just might have the balls to pull it off."

Toby snorted, Reese shook his head, and Thomas cackled until the whole room laughed.

"It's going to be okay," Toby finally said, running his fingers through Reese's disheveled hair. "Go to bed. I got this."

Reese pushed himself to standing and Toby put his arms around him, hugging him tight. Then Bailey and Jude were there to help Reese down the hallway to bed. He coughed the whole way.

Toby watched him go, and then he turned on Ethan. "It's a start, pretty boy, but we've got a lot of work to do if we're going to make this show as good as it needs to be. You ready to step it up?"

Ethan wanted to roll his eyes. It was hilarious that Toby was calling *him* pretty boy when Toby had always had supermodel looks.

"I'll do whatever it takes. I owe it to Reese, and to you."

Toby's lip quirked, and he said in a low voice, "Pretty sure you don't owe me anything." Then he got serious. "But we all owe Reese, so let's do this."

Ethan nodded and looked for Arthur. He stood leaning in the doorway, his hands shoved in his pockets,

"We should clear out." Toby gathered up the sheet music and put it in his messenger bag. "Let's go to my place. We can be noisy all we want there."

Toby left to tell Reese what they were doing and Ethan approached Arthur.

"What do you think?"

Arthur looked down at his shoes for a moment and blew out a breath. Then he leveled his gaze on Ethan and spoke in a low voice only the two of them could hear.

Twenty-Eight

rthur

"You're incredible, you know that?" Arthur's heart stuttered, and he cleared his throat, waiting for Ethan's reaction.

Ethan's eyes darted around the room, and when they landed back on Arthur's, they were brimming with excitement. "You think so?"

"You know I do. You sure you're up for this?"

Ethan nodded enthusiastically. "I want to do this for Reese. After everything...I want him to get well. I want to do what I can. And the show is amazing."

"You're so good," Arthur whispered, and he saw the effect his words had on Ethan. His eyes went soft around the edges and his cheeks flushed.

"Hey," Audra said, looking between them. She cleared her throat. "Am I taking him to Toby's, or are you?"

Arthur smiled at her. "I think I'd like to take my boyfriend to this rehearsal." He knew it was a ballsy move, but he wanted to be explicit with her about their situation. He thought it was only fair for her to know what she was dealing with.

She raised her eyebrows and looked between the two of them. "Very well. Can we discuss Ethan's schedule for tomorrow? I need to know where to pick him up."

Arthur gave Ethan an appraising look. "I hate for you to have to give up your entire Sunday," Arthur said. "But would you mind going to the hotel, collecting Ethan's things, and taking them to my place?"

Ethan's eyes flared. "Arthur?"

Arthur wondered at his tone. Was it hope or hesitation?

"Do you two need a moment to discuss this?" Audra offered.

"No," Ethan said. "I'd...I'd like that, if it's not too much trouble."

"Not at all. I'll go right now. Need anything else?"

Arthur rubbed a thumb over his bottom lip. "If you have a chance, pick up some chamomile tea, honey, and lemon? I think Ethan will need it. What time do you need him tomorrow?"

Audra pulled out her phone and opened her calendar. "We have a meeting at Paramount with Wendy Culbert, casting director, at ten. I've got a lunch set up with Tony Brown from the agency, and in the afternoon, I was going to take him on a tour at Warner Brothers to visit with some of our friends there, but I can reschedule that..."

"If you can, that would be great. I have a feeling Ethan is going to need to spend the afternoon and evening rehearsing. I'll bring him to you at the office in the morning."

"Thank you, Audra," Ethan said, surprising her with a big hug.

Arthur was so damned proud of Audra. And he was ready to burst with the amount of pride he had for Ethan. He was glad he'd have the drive with Ethan in the Vitesse to Toby's, to see how he was holding up. Arthur also needed that time to recover from hearing him sing.

Jude came out of the bedroom and gave Arthur a sad smile.

Ethan held out a hand for Jude. "I hope Reese feels better soon. Please let me know if we can—"

Jude grabbed Ethan in a hug and held him tight. "Thank you for doing this. It means so much to us."

Ethan turned his wide eyes on Arthur and squeezed Jude back.

Arthur put his hand on Jude's back. "I'll check in with you later. Let me know if he gets difficult. I'll be the bad guy for you."

Jude's relieved smile let Arthur know he'd most likely be hearing from him.

Arthur followed Ethan over to say goodbye to Thomas Matheson, who was now back in bed.

"Well, if it can't be my grandson, you'll do just fine."

Ethan shook his hand. "Thank you, sir. I'll do my best. The music is incredible. I get goose bumps just listening."

Thomas kept ahold of his hand for a minute longer. "You seem familiar, have I met you before?"

Ethan cleared his throat. "Last weekend? I was here—"

"You might remember him from Reese's last musical. Ethan played Randy in *Ruby in Red Plaid.*" Arthur put a hand on Ethan's shoulder. It was sometimes tough to tell whether Thomas was confused or about to say something inappropriate. He went back and forth between the two states more often these days.

Thomas pulled Ethan a little closer. "I see you like them redheads too." The old man grinned wickedly at Ethan. "Whoever said blonds have more fun ain't never made it with a redhead." He patted Ethan's hand and cackled as he sat back in his bed. "You go practice, now. My grandson needs you."

"Yes, sir."

Ethan waved and Arthur guided him at the door, catching Thomas's wink at him.

Thomas Matheson had been part of the Hollywood elite for many years. Arthur had met him at one of his parents' parties when he was a teenager. He'd had a manager at Slade, and one of the associates continued to manage his music catalog, only now with Reese's approval.

Arthur had jumped at the chance to represent the up-and-coming songwriter Reese Matheson as he was just getting started. When his band The Waves got a deal and started touring, Arthur had already signed him, and eventually got him his deal writing songs for pop star Melinda. Then *Ruby* happened, and Reese had kept Arthur on his toes ever since. But Arthur had a feeling that after *Boy* had its limited run, Reese would need to take a step back. He needed time with Thomas before the man's dementia became so severe, he'd require a more intensive level of care. Arthur would be there to support Reese and his family no matter what.

"Hey, thanks for coming," Bailey said, catching them by the door before they left. "Poor Reese."

Arthur patted him on the back. "Don't worry, kid. 'The show must go on' isn't just a saying, it's a way of life. We make it work. See you tomorrow."

Ethan got a hug too and then they were outside. "Man, this is awful for them."

Arthur put his arm around him. "Not with you here to save the day. Let's grab some lunch and then I'll take you to Toby's."

Ethan blew his hair up out of his eyes as they reached the Vitesse. He grinned at Arthur. "You brought out the fancy car today."

Arthur shrugged. "If I'm coming to the beach, I love to drive it out here. Wanna see why?"

Ethan bounced on his toes as Arthur manually put the top down.

"Are you kidding? I've never ridden in a convertible before!"

"How? How is that possible?" he asked, chuckling as he opened the door for Ethan to climb in. When Arthur climbed in on his side, he was so glad he'd brought out the Vitesse today. The last time he'd had Ethan in the car, he'd been uncomfortable with their closeness. Now, he craved it.

He pulled out of Reese's driveway and made his way through the town of Malibu to CA-1, which had some of the most gorgeous views in all of the United States. Ethan's smile was nonstop as he gazed out over the ocean on this clear, sunny, pristine day. He lifted his face to the sun and looked so at peace. Arthur had to remember this was also a somewhat treacherous road to travel and that the twelve and a half miles of windy, cliff-side highway had claimed many lives. As much as he wanted to watch Ethan, he had to remain focused.

When they got to Santa Monica, Arthur pulled over to park near a collection of food trucks. "Let's grab something to eat here. I know a great place we can park and eat for a bit."

Ethan was game. Arthur went for a loaded burrito, and though Ethan lingered at the gourmet hot dog truck, he opted for a rice bowl.

"I don't want to give myself heartburn if I'm going to be singing," he admitted.

Arthur was impressed with his discipline.

"But if you weren't going to be singing, if we were just hanging out, would you have gone for the foot-long?"

Ethan grinned. "I'll always go for the foot-long."

Arthur laughed as they climbed back into the car and then pulled into the lot north of the Santa Monica Pier. They found a tiny spot overlooking the beach, just right for the Vitesse but not many other cars would have fit.

"This is amazing," Ethan said. "I haven't actually been to the beach here. I went to Coney Island and Brighton Beach when I was living in New York, but the time I was in LA before, I only made it as far as the studio and a gala at the Dolby Theatre."

"I'll bring you back when we have time to spend."

Ethan grinned with his whole body—a little shimmy to the shoulders, legs bouncing, eyes sparking. It was the most adorable thing to watch him get excited about something that Arthur took as commonplace. Arthur had a feeling that extended time with Ethan might just wreck his curmudgeon status. Which might not be a bad thing.

"You can imagine I didn't get to spend a lot of time at the beach as a kid," Arthur said, gesturing to his skin, "but I did have some wonderful vacations with my parents to Hawaii and Central America, where I was allowed out as long as I wore a hat and long sleeves. I hated it, but sometimes you gotta cave in the name of fun."

"You've been all over the world, huh?" Ethan had turned sideways as much as possible in the tiny car. He had his knee resting on Arthur's leg as he picked at his rice bowl. Arthur loved the ease with which Ethan showered affection on Arthur when they were alone. He'd been very cautious about touching him even in passing when they were at Reese's, but as soon as they'd gotten in the car, Ethan had placed a hand on his thigh, touched his shoulder, held his hand when Arthur didn't need it to steer.

Arthur's parents were both very affectionate people, and Arthur was affectionate with his women friends, but he hadn't realized how much he longed for that contact with a lover. None of the men he'd dated in the past had wanted much physical contact outside of sex. Between the loving touch and the cuddling, Arthur's feelings for Ethan were growing stronger by the minute.

"I *have* been to a lot of places, yes, but when I went as a kid, it was usually just to wherever my parents were working with the rare trips like the ones I mentioned. As an adult, sure, I'd go to London to oversee an event, to be a plus-one with a client, awards shows, galas. I've not had a whole lot of opportunity to do the random touristy things. I've got a bucket list of places I'd like to go that have nothing to do with work. Like, I'd love to go to Puerto Rico. Someday."

"What's keeping you?"

Arthur placed a hand on Ethan's knee and caressed him through the material. "Guess I hadn't found the right person to go with."

"Arthur," he breathed, his eyes wide, but his smile hesitant. The sun was sinking into the horizon creating a spectacular sunset. Golden rays and shadows played over Ethan's face.

"Come here." Arthur curled his fingers around the back of Ethan's neck and pulled him forward, their lips and tongues meeting eagerly, as if they hadn't had enough the night before. God, that seemed like so long ago after everything that had happened this morning.

"Ooo," Ethan laughed, pulling back and touching his lips. "Spicy."

Arthur looked down at his burrito. "Are you a delicate eater, Ethan?"

He winced and nodded. "I come from 'pepper is spicy' people." He leaned forward and licked at Arthur's lips. "But I'll brave it for some more of you."

Arthur tuned out the activity around them—surfers taking the opportunity to enjoy larger-than-usual surf this afternoon, tourists taking pictures, families packing up after a day at the beach—and he kissed Ethan like they were the only two people on Earth. That feeling was appropriate, seeing as everything else tended to fall away when he was with Ethan...his responsibilities, his cynicism...and he liked it, wanted more of it.

Unfortunately, they didn't have time for more right now thanks to yet another bit of chaos with his clients...it was more than that, though.

Reese and Toby were his friends, this show was more important than just an event, and while the manager part of Arthur saw it as just that—an important event his clients decided to throw together on short notice, and one that was making him nuts with all of the chaos—Arthur was also a queer kid at heart who had been ostracized and alienated as a young person as much for his bright red hair, weird interests, and awkward social skills as for being queer.

He was grateful in a lot of ways that he'd grown up in Hollywood schools, because at least he was around other kids who were eccentric and odd. If he'd grown up like Ethan, in the Midwest, it would have been harder to be himself. Impossible, even, seeing as Arthur had been a skinny kid, unable to defend himself. Had Ethan ever had to fight?

Ethan pulled back with a sigh and rested his head on Arthur's shoulder. "Is it wrong that I wish we could have stayed in your bed today?"

Arthur kissed his forehead and pulled him closer. "Not wrong at all. I hope you don't mind that I basically kidnapped you. If you don't want to stay with me—"

"Is it wrong that I was hoping you'd want me to?"

"No, honey. It's not wrong. For the record, though, I still feel a little like I've crossed a line."

Ethan lifted his head and raised an eyebrow at Arthur. "Let the record show that no line has been crossed. You don't work for me, I'm not your client, but in bed, just so you know, I like it when you tell me what to do."

Arthur snorted and pulled him into a hug. "Be careful, doll. I might get all kinds of bossy with you."

Ethan pressed his lips to Arthur's ear. "Promise?"

"I *do* promise. I want...I want to be with you, Ethan. I know the timing is tough and we're going to have lots of interruptions and distractions, but...I want this."

"I want you, too, Arthur. So much."

As their lips met once more, Arthur allowed himself to be swept away into the fantasy of a world where he got the pretty boy, and they lived happily ever after. Dreams did come true sometimes in Hollywood.

But seeing as this *was* Hollywood, they had work to do.

"I wish I could kiss you all afternoon, but I'm afraid that gorgeous voice of yours is needed."

Ethan sat back in his seat and let out a breath. "Wow. I really hope I can do this show justice. Reese wrote some pretty wild vocals for this one. If I thought *Ruby* was tough..."

"He wouldn't have asked for you if he didn't think you could do it. You even got the old man's blessing. Look, there are four shows scheduled, two next weekend and two the following weekend. All you've gotta do is get through the first two and then we can breathe and reassess. Maybe Reese will be well enough. We can set up monitors with lyrics, you won't be dancing, so all you need is to nail the vocals. You can do this."

Ethan's blue eyes filled, and he laughed, blinking them hard. "I can with you believing in me."

Arthur pressed their foreheads together. "You know I do."

He started up the car and once he'd backed out of the spot, he gave Ethan's thigh a squeeze. He did believe in Ethan. He also had a lot of eggs in one basket, and they couldn't afford for any more eggs to break.

Three hours later, he was ready to break one of his other eggs.

"*Again*, Ethan. You have to watch the tempo on that verse." Toby was drilling Ethan on the third piece from the first act and losing his temper, which had Arthur ready to scream at him. Toby was frustrated to only be able to play piano one-handed. He still wore a cast after attempting to put his fist through a stone wall, breaking his hand so badly that it required surgery. They were using the recordings for the most part, but he'd been trying to slow things down for Ethan to get the verse right.

"You're right, I'm sorry. I'm not used to that timing."

"Well, get used to it, darling. We don't have time for this." Toby stood from the piano in his living room and stalked off to the kitchen.

"I'm sorry," Spencer said. "Can I get you two anything else? Some more water?"

"I'm okay, thank you," Arthur said. He turned to Ethan. "Want to take a break? You've been going at it for a while."

Ethan's cheeks were a little red, but his voice sounded stronger and stronger the more they worked. "I can go longer. Or if Toby wants to stop, I can just take the recordings and practice on my own until tomorrow."

"You're doing so good," Arthur whispered, wanting to touch him, but Ethan had been jumpy since they'd gotten to Toby's.

He grinned back. "Thank you. Can you tell me where the restroom is?"

"Yeah, it's down the hall to the right," Arthur said, pointing the way. "Take your time. I'll go talk to Toby."

Once Ethan was out of earshot, Spencer stood from the table where he'd been going through the proof of the print book once more, with corrections for the final version.

"He's a powerhouse. I can't believe he can pick up these complicated songs just like that."

Arthur smiled. "He's pretty incredible."

Spencer's eyes flicked to the kitchen. "*He's* not doing too well with this. Maybe have a chat with him? I'm not sure he wants to hear my opinions right now."

Arthur patted Spencer on the shoulder and walked into the kitchen. He found Toby at the sink with his hands on the counter and his head hanging down.

"What's going on?" Arthur asked.

Toby didn't turn to look at him, but he sighed and stood to his full height, which was about an inch taller than Arthur's six-foot-three.

"I know I'm not supposed to say this is my fault, but this is my fault."

"What? Toby, no. Even you don't have the power to cause an earthquake. You heard Jude, Thomas got spooked and they sat outside with him at the fire pit. That's what caused this."

Toby rolled his eyes. "Do I need to remind you that my little breakdown meant leaving all of this shit for Reese to do on his own? He's taken on too much, and I should have been there."

"You had to step back. You did what you had to do for yourself, Toby. We'd all rather have you step back than lose you. You know that." Arthur kept his voice calm. Toby had been keeping a lot of trauma locked up inside him, and his relationship with Spencer, which was arguably the best thing to happen to the moody genius, also unleashed the effects of that trauma. He was getting better, but he'd had to withdraw from the production of the musical, which he co-wrote with Reese, and was doing some intensive therapy, both on his hand and his emotional self. Arthur had tried to be supportive, but he'd been torn. Having best friends and partners as your clients often meant playing referee.

Toby kicked the cabinet below the sink and pushed away from the counter to pace across the expansive kitchen. His beachfront townhome in Venice Beach appeared deceptively small from the outside, but each of the floors was quite roomy. Arthur hadn't spent a lot of time there, as Toby tended to keep his private life separate from his work with Reese. Now, Arthur understood why.

"Toby, if this is too much, maybe I can have Danny work with Ethan? Or Dwayne, since they'll be performing together?"

"Well, shit, you need to line up a piano player regardless! Reese is not going to be up to playing for rehearsals this week, maybe not even up to playing for the show." Toby kicked the cabinet again and Arthur took a deep breath.

"I already talked to Jesse, and she said they're okay with the recordings for rehearsals at least the next two days. I'll ask Danny to be on standby."

"What a horrid fucking time for me to have a fucked-up hand. It's killing me to not be able to fix things for Reese."

Arthur reached for him and put a hand on his shoulder. "It'll work out. Somehow. I'll make some more calls tomorrow and if we need to bring someone in on piano, we will, but I know Reese. He'll somehow pull it together so he can play. If he actually rests, Dr. Shah says he should be well enough to at least play piano by Saturday, but not sing."

Toby blew out his breath. "Fucking Ethan Bradley, huh? What kind of freaky kismet brought him here? *Now?* The fact that Reese and I have completely different ranges makes it work when we're together, but I'm no substitute for him. I wouldn't even be able to sing this shit without totally changing the arrangements, and this kid comes along with his ridiculous range."

Arthur couldn't help but smile. "He's pretty great."

Toby smirked. "You said it. Can't say I was happy to see him again, although Spencer's in love with him." He rolled his eyes. "Awkward much, your past coming back to bite you in the ass."

Arthur stood taller. "Yeah, well, Spencer's not the only one who's fallen for him." Immediately his cheeks got hot, and he shoved his hands in his pocket. He wanted Toby to hear it from him. Not that he gave a shit what Toby thought, but he didn't want things to be any more uncomfortable than they already were.

Toby laughed and his eyebrows went up nearly to his hairline. "No fucking way, *you*? But Arthur, darling, you don't date the talent. Isn't that what you tell me when I hit on you, like, every time we get drunk together?"

Arthur crossed his arms over his chest and leaned a hip against the island. "Seems like I'm not the only one who breaks their rules these days." Toby had a steadfast no-relationship rule, which had lasted until his anonymous vacation fling with Spencer reignited when they ran into each other stateside.

Toby exhaled and shook his head. "I know. But do you blame me? Spencer is brilliant. And totally fucking hot."

"I don't blame you at all. Maybe fate decided you and I wouldn't end up grumpy old bachelors together after all."

"Ethan, huh?" Toby wrinkled his nose. "That's...you know...talk about awkward."

Arthur held up his hands. "I don't need to know any more than I already do. It's in the past."

"Fine by me. Not like I want to give you the details."

"Good. I don't want them. Now, are you going to quit blaming yourself for all the world's problems and work with Ethan?"

He poured himself a glass of water and chugged it down. "I am, but I think he's had enough today. How about you take him...wherever... and I'll meet him tomorrow afternoon at the theater? Audra said she's got meetings set up for him?"

"Yeah. A few promising ones. I'm hoping he'll find something that we can rub in those snobby Brits' faces."

Toby snapped his fingers. "*That's* why you're having her take the lead with him, you dirty dog." He laughed, holding his gut. "Straight-laced Arthur Frye might break a rule, but he's still the most upstanding citizen I know."

"Whatever." He pulled Toby into a hug. "You get some rest, okay? And I don't want to hear you blaming yourself anymore. We'll get through this like we always do. Got it?"

Toby pulled back and wiped at his eye. "You're our rock, Arthur. Thanks for keeping this crazy train on the rails."

"That's what I'm here for. Get some rest."

Toby pulled back and patted his shoulder. "He's a sweet kid. Good luck."

Arthur frowned. "Awkward."

Toby gave him a dude punch, and they both laughed.

Cool, that went well.

Reese would be easier to tell, especially since he was the one who'd dropped Ethan in Arthur's lap in the first place. It was kind of his fault, if he were going with the Toby Griffiths philosophy of blame.

Ethan and Spencer were both leaning over the table, looking at the proofs for the book.

"This is so beautiful. Thanks for showing me."

"Thank you! I can't believe it came together so quickly. I'm just glad I'd already put together a book like this once before. I'm looking forward to actually sleeping, though. We've been going at this nonstop."

"Good night, you two," Arthur said. "Honey, Toby's going to meet you at the theater tomorrow."

Ethan's eyes flared at Arthur's use of the endearment in front of Toby.

Toby gave him a knowing smile and nodded.

"Great, thank you. See you tomorrow."

Ethan and Spencer hugged, Arthur shook Spencer's hand, and he practically pushed Ethan down the stairs to the street level and out the door.

He didn't need to give Toby any more opportunities to make it weird.

"Ready to go home?" he asked Ethan.

"So ready."

Twenty-Nine

E^{than}

Ethan rested his voice in the car on the way back to Arthur's. He ran through the music in his head, committing the lyrics to memory as best he could. They hadn't even gotten through the first act of the show. There was a lot more to work on, which meant more time with Toby.

Ethan shuddered at that thought. It had been harder than he'd thought it would be to work with him. He didn't have the calm and patient demeanor that Reese did. When Ethan was in *Ruby*, Reese had done most of the stage direction and the choreographer had handled the rest. Toby only gave notes occasionally.

It wasn't that he thought Toby would do anything. He was with Spencer now and they seemed solid. And he hadn't been a letch even before Ethan had gone out of his way with a foolhardy plan of seduction.

It had all happened fast. They'd held the wrap party for *Ruby* at The Londoner Hotel. Ethan had downed three glasses of champagne on an empty stomach before he'd seen Toby leaving the room. Ethan had made sure they ran into each other—and made it clear he was available.

No, he didn't want to think about it, not after everything good that had happened with Arthur, who was a kind, patient, and generous lover. Ethan didn't want his past to come back and ruin the good thing that was blooming between them.

Never in a million years would Ethan have thought when he got to LA, the stern manager would become the person he trusted most in the world, who he cherished most.

"You're awfully quiet over there." Arthur turned off I-10 and headed into West Hollywood. "Everything okay?"

"Yeah," Ethan said, stifling a yawn. "Just running through the lyrics, although my brain is pretty full. I think it's reached its peak learning capacity for one day."

Arthur chuckled, turned onto Santa Monica, then onto Sunset. It was still relatively early, but it felt like the day had lasted a whole week.

"I think you need some mindless entertainment and pampering tonight. I can order some dinner, put on a movie and rub your shoulders."

Ethan turned to look at Arthur's profile. The lights glinted off his glasses and Ethan saw flashes of his faint smile. "What about you? I would think all of this is even more stressful for you."

Arthur rolled his fist forward on the steering wheel. "Comes with the territory. I've worked with those guys through a lot of trials and tribulations. They were on tour with The Waves when Reese's parents died in a car accident while in South America, on location. I worked with him and his grandparents to sort out their estate. Then Reese lost his grandmother four years ago, and I helped him figure out care for Thomas, who was in the beginning stages of dementia. In the past, I've worked with clients going through divorces, buying and selling houses and moving, health issues, and of course, the usual negotiating contracts—"

"I thought only agents did that?"

"I'm also an attorney, so I can act as agent and negotiate contracts. We have an agency we work with, but I oversee all the legal issues for my clients."

"Anyone ever get arrested?"

Arthur bit his bottom lip. "Even criminal issues, although I usually delegate that to our outside counsel."

"Wow," Ethan breathed. "I knew you were brilliant, but you're like omnibrilliant, right? Like omnipresent and omnibrilliant?"

Arthur chuckled as he turned into his driveway. He parked in his spot and when they got out, he plugged in the Vitesse.

"I promise I won't be omnipotent or omniscient when it comes to you, doll. I want to help however I can, but you can always say no, and you don't ever have to run things by me—"

They were standing outside Arthur's door when Ethan reached for his arm. "But I would. Right? If we're...dating...I would want to include you in my decisions."

Arthur put his hands on Ethan's shoulders and smiled. "I appreciate that, but I won't ever ask you to choose, and you never need my permission."

Ethan understood that Arthur was trying not to take over, that he wanted Ethan to stand on his own feet, but of course he wanted Arthur's advice and wanted him to take an active role in his career. Even if he wasn't Ethan's manager, if he were his...partner? Was that getting ahead of himself? They'd only just started this thing, and though Ethan wanted to move forward with Arthur, they were not on steady ground yet. A lot could happen.

"So," Ethan asked as Arthur shut the front door. "I don't need to ask your permission to kiss you? I've been dying to—"

Arthur scooped Ethan up in his arms, pulling him in tight, and kissed him so deep, Ethan felt tingles all the way down to his toes.

"You know, in all of this, I don't think I thanked you for helping out my clients and best friends. You didn't have to do any of this, but you saved the day."

"You don't have to thank me. I just made myself useful, working off my debts. And now, I would like to discuss one more order of business before I shut up for the rest of the night."

Arthur released his tight grip on Ethan and his expression was concerned.

"No, it's nothing bad. I know Audra will be there and I trust her, but do you have any words of wisdom for tomorrow? You know who I'm meeting with, right?"

Arthur gave him a rundown of the people he expected to be there as they made their way into the vault. He removed his clothes as Ethan listened carefully.

"The most important thing," he said as he hung up his suit coat, "is that you don't ever verbally agree to anything." Shirt unbuttoned and tossed in dry cleaning pile. "You wait until they put an offer in writing and you always have Audra look at it." Slacks off and hung carefully over a hanger. "Never sign anything unless she's looked at it, and she'll probably show it to me first for a while, just so you know, so your boyfriend will unfortunately be all up in your business." He turned around with the hanger in his hand and frowned. "I should have another attorney or Patricia look at it. Yeah, I'll have Patricia—"

"Arthur," Ethan said, grinning. "It'll be fine. I trust you."

"Should you?"

Ethan blanched. "Why shouldn't I?"

Arthur grinned. "Because I've been thinking very, very naughty thoughts about you all day."

And the stress of the day fell from Ethan's shoulders like new-fallen snow, leaving him warm and definitely willing. Then his clothes were falling, then the two of them were falling into Arthur's bed, and when Arthur covered Ethan with his body, he could see the appeal of an angel falling.

"This show is going to address issues in modern LA, and probably bring up more questions than answers. It'll be West Coast *Friends* but add diversity and reality. High school friends move back to their neighborhood and try to remain close as the issues of the city try to tear them apart. A rookie LAPD officer, a rookie LAFD, a schoolteacher, a community activist, a lawyer with political aspirations, a real estate mogul, and they all meet up at one of the friends' parents' LA restaurant, where they all used to hang out, only to discover it's in danger of closing because of new city ordinances/developers/gentrification all the above.

"The point is for the show to be hopeful but also address the issues. With your physicality, we could look at you for the police officer or the queer firefighter. We've got writers from all perspectives because we want to do this the right way, you know?"

Wendy Cuthbert was probably in her late thirties, with severe bangs and long dark hair. She wore cat-eye glasses that made Ethan feel like he was about to be shushed by a Gothy librarian. He liked her.

"Sounds like you're doing your homework," Audra said. She smiled at Ethan, who was trying not to let his leg bounce under the table. This was exactly the kind of project he wanted to do. Good queer representation, but also looking at problematic behavior and how we're all human. But Audra's smile was cool, so Ethan tried to be cool.

"We're schedule to be shooting the pilot in March—"

"Which is late for a pilot." Audra clasped her hands in front of her on the table.

"It is, but this show is looking to be an off-shoot of the popular *LA One* show. They're filming a crossover episode in two weeks, and we want to have our casting done so those actors can participate on that crossover. Ethan, are you a member of SAG-AFTRA yet?"

"I—"

"We're working on it. He should be qualified based on his work on *Take My Hand*, as preliminary work for the film was done in New York, but if not, we're confident he'll be accepted based on his membership in Equity for his principal role in *Ruby in Red Plaid*. Our attorneys are looking into it."

"Great. I have a couple of other projects I also think Ethan might be right for, based on the package you sent over. We've got a limited series about a Mafia hitman exiled to the Midwest that we need some young actors to play innocent country bumpkins looking to get rich." She flipped through some files on her phone. "We have a couple of roles in established series, I can send you the info and you can decide whether you want to audition for them. Ethan, your prior work isn't as well-known here as it was in the UK, but you do have a somewhat rabid fan base. I don't know if you've looked at the fanfic sites, but there's some quite steamy fanfic about Lord Harrington."

He looked to Audra, who grinned at Wendy.

"I'll make sure to take a look," Audra said.

"Well, it was great to meet you, Ethan. I'll work with Audra to set up some auditions for you. I hope we can find a place for you at Paramount."

They shook hands with Wendy and left her office.

"I totally forgot about SAG-AFTRA," Ethan muttered as they left the studio grounds, some of the air out of his lungs.

"I didn't. I checked. Your Actors Equity Association membership is paid up through May, so we should be covered. This is why you have me, Ethan. So what did you think?"

"The LA show sounds interesting, but what do *you* think?"

She frowned as they reached her car. "I'm concerned with the timing, it leads me to think their casting fell through or the pilot was greenlit late because of some other issue, although with all the new programming the Netflixes and Hulus of the world are doing, the pilot window has become a bit more flexible. I think in the next five years, the typical TV season will fade away and a lot more of the good shows will be snatched up by streaming services. Already the networks are placing programs direct to their apps."

"I feel like I should know more about this. Is there a resource you recommend I check out for news on all the latest industry stuff?"

She smiled at him. "I'll put together a reading list, including the fanfic sites. I can't believe I hadn't thought to check those out."

Ethan stared at her, confused. "Do I really want to read that?" She let out a maniacal laugh, and Ethan shook his head. "Thanks a lot."

Lunch was next and Tony Brown was also very cool. Young, Black, wearing a bright pink suit and wedge sandals that showed off his lime-green painted toenails. He wore his hair in locs pulled back from his face, and he had a silver septum piercing that Ethan couldn't help watching as he spoke. He was only a few years older than Ethan, and he talked a mile a minute. Audra had warned Ethan, but he wasn't prepared.

"I've been over your package and I think you have several directions we can go, including a couple of limited series over on Netflix, they wouldn't be principal roles but they would be great exposure, but the project I *really* want you to consider is a queer retelling of a beloved eighties movie, you might have heard of it. How do you feel about water? Like, can you swim?"

Ethan glanced at Audra, who was nodding and smiling, so he nodded. "Sure?"

"*Splash*? With Daryl Hannah? So good. Tom Hanks has even signed on as a producer. They were thinking of just reversing the roles but the director wants to go with a full queerification and West Coast vibe. Merman rescues a shipping exec who falls off the *Queen Mary* after his fiancé dumps him, but the merman can't stop thinking of the exec so he spies on him up at the Port of LA and decides to go after him, but of course he shows up naked and...then of course Eugene Levy's role was so important to the film and we've got Dan Levy ready to step in as the researcher's son...it's going to be huge. You'd need to bulk up a bit, you don't have a problem with that do you? I can get you set up with a personal trainer so it's all done safely..."

Ethan's head was literally swimming just thinking about playing a merman. Was that even a thing? He couldn't even focus on eating his poke bowl as Tony discussed all kinds of projects he was looking to find the perfect actors on his roster for.

Then Tony wanted to know all about *Boy*, and Audra told him only that Ethan was acting as understudy to Reese in case he wasn't able to perform on Saturday.

"Of course I don't want Reese to be sick, but this could be a great way to get you some visibility. I had your reels from *Hardbody* and *Ruby* on repeat all weekend. You've got such a great voice. Oh, that reminds me, Ethan, I'd love to submit your name for the Switch It Up charity event where Broadway stars perform gender-swapped performances. You've heard of it?"

"I have. I'd like some more information," he said, eager to volunteer. "I'm very interested in doing charity projects like that. Please share the details with Audra."

She raised her eyebrows and nodded, which he hoped meant she was pleased and not going to scold him.

He'd been thinking about how he wanted to repay not only Reese and Arthur for taking care of him when he arrived, but what he could do to help those with food insecurities. Once he made a name for himself—or remade his name—he wanted to look for ways he could help, perhaps even starting his own foundation, or going to work as an ambassador for an existing organization. He wondered what Arthur would think of him going out to sites and helping to cook and serve. Down the road, he certainly wanted to give back...once he had something to give.

The rest of lunch was Tony asking questions about the filming of *Affair on the Thames* and where Ethan had learned to do such a brilliant accent.

"My mom was a bit of an anglophile and we watched a lot of British detective shows together. I also had a British roommate in college, and I hounded him to help me get it right. I've always been able to pick up accents after listening for a while, but I worked with a coach for the film. Today's London accent is quite different than what they wanted for Lord Harrington."

Tony clapped his hands. "Oh, I love it! I can't wait to get you working, Ethan. I'll have you fully booked with auditions within a week."

"Okay, as long as I'm able to work around rehearsals for Reese. I've committed to helping him."

"No, of course. I think it's wonderful that you were able to help out. I'm sure Reese and Toby are incredibly grateful."

Audra and Tony caught up on a few other issues, and Ethan tried to eat a little more of his poke bowl, but it was spicy, which made him think of kissing Arthur the previous day, which made him wish it was Arthur beside him at this lunch. Audra was fantastic, so cool under pressure, but Ethan knew, despite what Arthur said the previous night, he would be discussing all of this with him.

Would Arthur think a merman was hot?

"Sound good Ethan?"

"Hmm? Oh, I will discuss it all with Audra. Thank you."

She chuckled as Tony reached for his hand.

"Glad to meet you and hope to work with you soon," Tony said as he waved goodbye.

And then Ethan finally breathed.

"You did great today."

"I felt like—"

"Like your face was going to break into a million pieces?"

"Maybe? That was a lot. What do you think about all of this?"

She blew out a breath. "I think you should do as many auditions as Tony can set up, mostly for the practice, since you haven't done a ton, have you?"

"Just for Broadway, a few film and TV roles in New York, which I'd rather not think about, and then I met with the casting director for British Films, and that landed me both of the film roles."

"Okay. So the auditions will be good, but were there any projects you were interested in?"

"Definitely the one about the friends. I don't know how I feel about the merman role."

Audra looked him up and down. "If it's legit? It could be really good for you."

Ethan nodded. "Then I guess, do your magic?"

She laughed. "Yes, sir. Did you, ah, get enough to eat? I suppose I should have asked you about your food preferences."

"It was fine, just a little spicy."

"I'll try to remember that if I book us any more lunch meetings. Now, let's get you to the theater. Toby should be there."

Ethan blew out a breath as he stood. "I'll try to bolster myself."

Audra put a hand on his arm as they walked out of the restaurant and to her car. "What do you mean by that?"

He sighed. "Oh, nothing. He was just riding me pretty hard yesterday. I hope I can keep up tonight."

Audra frowned. "I'll be there if you need me. You got this."

Ethan hoped she was right.

THIRTY

On his way out of the office, later than he'd hoped to be, Arthur dialed Dr. Shah, who had been to Reese's to see how he was doing with the medicine he'd prescribed.

"He says he already feels better on the antibiotics, and I think by tomorrow he'll *think* he's better enough to go back to work, but I don't want him anywhere near the theater until Friday at the very earliest, and only if his fever has been gone at least twenty-four hours. I went over all of this with Jude, but you know what a terrible patient Reese can be. He's a lot like his grandfather."

"Jude definitely has his hands full with both of them. I told him I'd bring Bailey home so he doesn't have to worry about it."

Dr. Shah had been consulting on Thomas's case, so he was aware of the living situation at the Matheson abode.

"Keep me posted. If he follows instructions, he should be fine to play piano in the show this weekend. I'd like him to see the ENT before he does any singing. I don't like the inflammation in his throat."

"Thank you. I'll stay on top of it." They hung up and Arthur tossed his phone onto the passenger seat of the Volvo.

The roller coaster that was the musical *Boy* was requiring more of Arthur's wrangling skills than any single operation to date. His small world had become even more intertwined and intricate, and he felt that at any moment, he was going to lose the thread, drop a spinning plate, *something*.

As he drove to the theater, all he could think of was hearing about Ethan's day. What projects did they discuss? Which ones had interested Ethan? How much time would he have before he got to work? Arthur began to have fantasies of stealing him away for a few days, just the two of them, after *Boy* wrapped. It was very possible that whatever Ethan auditioned for, if he got the part, there'd be some time until he had to report to work. It could happen.

He thought about their date at the museum, about Ethan's enthusiasm for everything. Imagine having that special brand of Ethan joy every day? Arthur wanted the opportunity to experience that. Because all of this drama surrounding their meeting was wearing on him a bit.

Bottom line, he wished he could have Ethan to himself, wished he could separate their time from his work, but that wasn't to be, now that the show was in trouble.

Rehearsals were in full swing as Arthur entered the theater. Jesse was onstage coaching the dancers through the scene just before Bailey's character seduces the Boy. It was looking much better, the boys were much more comfortable with each other, and Bailey had even mastered the lifts.

But Arthur's attention immediately went to the right corner of the stage, where Ethan stood. As soon as he opened his mouth to sing, Arthur lost focus on the dancers. Ethan was lost in the song, Dwayne harmonizing with him, and it was stunning.

The stage lights were on Ethan, and he had his head tilted back, his eyes closed. Every eye that wasn't already occupied with a task was on him, even Danny watched him while he played the piano. It had a much different effect than Reese sitting at the piano and singing. It added an element of passion to the already emotional performance.

They hadn't talked about the possibility of having a separate singer and piano player, it was something Reese might want to consider. Arthur would see how this limited run went and then decide whether or not to mention it to him.

The boys completed the scene and ended in an embrace, and the auditorium broke into applause. Arthur was nearly down to the stage when he saw Toby stand from the front row and call Ethan to the front of the stage.

"Watch your enunciation on the second movement and remember, you're the singer, not the star. You're not acting, so tone it down."

Ethan's eyes flared but he nodded.

"Go get some water. Take a break." Toby turned away from the stage, and Ethan stood from his crouch and headed offstage.

"Hey," Arthur said, approaching Toby. "How's it going?" He made eye contact with Danny, who was stretching out his tattooed hands at the piano. Danny nodded and then frowned in Toby's direction.

Toby sighed and pulled out his vape pen. He took a long drag and spoke through the smelly, sweet cloud of his exhale. "It's going. We made it through the first half twice."

"Uh-huh. You doing okay?"

Toby wasn't making eye contact with Arthur, and he didn't like the vibe coming from his friend at all. Toby planted his hands on his hips, winced when he was a little too rough with the hand that was in the cast.

They were all under a lot of stress, and Toby blamed himself for Reese's illness, but he'd agreed to work with Ethan. Didn't mean he was going to handle this well.

"Is there anything you need?"

Toby exhaled. "I just want it to be perfect for Reese."

"I know you do," Arthur said, putting a hand on his shoulder. "What do you think needs work?"

Toby frowned. "I don't know. The kid sings it all great, I just know he's used to being the lead, and the point was not to have the singing draw all the attention from the dancers." He snorted and shook his head. "I always told him his pretty mouth was going to get him into trouble."

Arthur felt a chill down his spine, and he stepped back from Toby, his muscles tense. "What the fuck is that supposed to mean?"

Toby put a hand on his chest. "Do my ears deceive me or did the fuck word just slip from your prim little mouth?" He laughed but his big blue eyes were round. "I just mean sometimes he doesn't know when to quit until someone calls him on it."

Arthur's fingers balled into a fist and before the word "no" could even travel through his synapses and stop him, he hauled off and punched Toby in the jaw.

Toby's head kicked to the side with the force of the blow, and then he clapped a hand over the spot and gasped.

They stood there staring at each other, and Arthur wasn't sure who was more surprised.

"Arthur! While I'm sure I've deserved that on more than one occasion—"

"It was you." All he could think of was Ethan's frightened face.

"I tried that act on the wrong person and he taught me a lesson. I found out what it was like to have someone call me on my bullshit."

Danny hopped down from the stage and got between them, putting a hand on Arthur's chest. "Jesus, Toby. What the fuck is it about you that makes everyone want to hit you?"

Toby was still staring at Arthur, who was shaking and unable to form words.

"It was me what, Arthur?"

"Arthur?" Ethan stood at the front of the stage, staring down at them.

Toby looked between them, but there was still no recognition in his face.

"It was me *what*, Arthur?" Toby demanded.

Ethan gasped and covered his mouth.

Arthur was frozen in his spot, spitting mad at his friend, terrified to add to Ethan's pain by exposing him.

Retreat seemed like the best option.

Arthur turned and walked up the aisle, clenching his fists, his right throbbing from the impact with Toby's stubborn jaw.

He'd never hit another person in his life. What the hell had come over him?

"Arthur, wait!"

Ethan's voice spurred him forward at a faster clip. His heart was doing all the flips and flops, and he was hit with a massive headache. He pushed through the doors at the top of the ramp and looked for a place to—

"Arthur!" Ethan ran up to him and put a hand to his face. "What's going on? Talk to me."

Arthur was panting and he put a hand to his chest.

"Shit! Give me your wrist."

Arthur lifted his arm, and Ethan pressed his two fingers to his pulse point, then looked at Arthur's watch.

"Your pulse is racing," Ethan whispered. He looked up into Arthur's eyes and a worry crease formed. "Can you take some slow, deep breaths? Come on, breathe with me."

Arthur tried to focus on breathing in time with Ethan, tried to get his brain to kick back into gear. "I'm sorry," he whispered.

Ethan raised his eyebrows. "No need to apologize to me. Toby might be another issue."

"It was him, wasn't it?"

Ethan frowned. "What do you mean?"

Arthur gripped Ethan's biceps. "He was the one who hurt you."

Ethan's eyes flared. "Arthur—"

"He's been riding you. You were jumpy around him. It was *him*."

Ethan sighed. "I didn't want to say anything. He's your friend. And really, Arthur, he didn't know. I didn't say anything."

"That doesn't make it all right."

"Did you really hit him?"

Arthur let go and stepped back. "Yes! I've never hit someone before...I don't know what came over me, I was just so mad! He hurt you, and he's being such a dick..."

"He's under a lot of pressure," Ethan said, but Arthur shook his head.

"Don't stand up for him." Ethan flinched at Arthur's tone, which was not at all what Arthur wanted. "I'm...I'm not handling this well right now. I'm sorry."

Ethan put a hand to his face and smiled. "Don't be sorry to me. I don't want to cause a problem between you and your friend, though. You should talk to him—"

"I don't want to break a confidence with you, Ethan. You shouldn't have to have your business put out there because I can't control my temper."

"But if I want to be a part of your life, Toby comes with the package. I need to be okay around him, and you have to explain to him why you're upset. What happened with him...bad experiences happen sometimes. I gave consent. I need you to look at it as the *act* hurt, not that *he* hurt *me*. Okay? It's embarrassing, yes, but I'm at least aware enough to know now that I was in over my head and I made a bad decision, and that I won't do that again. I won't try that again until I'm ready and I'm with a partner who makes me feel safe."

"I don't like this...I don't like feeling like this, and making a scene? I'm acting in the way I can't stand for others to act. What is wrong with me?"

"Do you really want me to answer that?"

Arthur frowned at Ethan, but he nodded.

"You're under a lot of stress. How much caffeine have you had today—"

"Ethan?"

"How much?"

"Too much," he muttered.

"And correct me if *I'm* wrong, but I'm beginning to think that you're just as new as I am at this. You knew that. That's why you made Audra my manager. We're just going to have to keep talking through all of this. Feelings are messy, and sure, we could all behave better. But humans are often governed by their emotions. We have to learn to think with our rational minds first, which requires us to be in good health...have enough sleep...manage our stress. I don't want to be more stress for you. I want to be there *for* you, *help* you when you're stressed. Let me help you do that."

"I'm a grown-ass man. I should know better."

Ethan shrugged. "So we learn together." He stepped closer and snaked his arms around Arthur's waist. "And you need to tell Toby why you hit him."

Arthur dropped his forehead to Ethan's and grunted. "I do. I don't know what came over me, I was just so angry, and he was being a smug asshole."

"Because he *is* a smug asshole. He's also a very talented asshole, and he was right. I did need to tone it down. Don't worry, as much as I've been a bit unsteady this past week, being onstage has brought back a little of my confidence. I have thick skin. I'd just forgotten it for a little while."

Arthur tucked a curl behind his ear. "I'm so proud of you, Ethan. You sound so good up there. Oh! Any prospects from today? Anything sound interesting? I want to hear all about your meetings."

Ethan grinned up at him. "How do you feel about mermen?"

Arthur raised his eyebrows. "They're hot?"

Ethan laughed. "I'll tell you all about it on the way ho— I mean, back to your place."

"Say home, please," Arthur said. "I know it's crazy to even ask in the middle of all of this, but I'm crazy about you, Ethan."

Ethan ran his fingers through Arthur's hair. "I'm crazy about you, too. I want to come home with you, but let's talk some more. As much as you hate the drama, I don't want you to have any second thoughts. Let me...let me find work. Then we can talk about we want to do, okay? Maybe it will help you feel steadier if *I'm* steady. I don't want us to be shaky when we take the next step together. I know we kind of started this in the middle of an earthquake, but I don't want to bring any more natural disasters into your life."

Arthur pulled him tighter. "How do you know the right thing to say?"

"I'm learning."

Ethan brushed his lips over Arthur's, initiating but not insisting. He appreciated that Ethan was looking out for him. Was trying to help Arthur do the right thing, to feel secure. Arthur was so used to doing that for everyone else, he never imagined a young, vibrant soul like Ethan would ever want to do the same for him.

"Now, I want you to go back to the doctor, Arthur. I'm worried—"

The outer doors burst open and Spencer came trotting in. "Have you seen Toby? He just called—"

"I know why he called you.

Arthur kept hold of Ethan's hand as he walked away as long as he could before letting his hand drop.

"What happened?" Spencer asked.

Arthur let out a heavy breath. "I lost my temper earlier. Toby said something that... I need to talk to him. Can you wait for me to do that?"

Spencer cocked his head to the side. "I can. But he's really struggling, Arthur. I hope you're not going to make it worse."

"I already did, and now I need to make it better."

THIRTY-ONE

E^{than}

Arthur walked off in search of Toby, leaving Ethan alone with Spencer.

Totally not awkward.

"I wanted to—"

"I'm sorry—"

They both laughed, and Spencer held up a hand. "May I go first?"

"Please." Because Ethan had no idea how to deal with this.

Spencer took a deep breath. "Toby and I have been together for a rocky, oh...six weeks? Give or take? And during that time, I've gotten used to having my life upheaved. I'm trying to roll with the tide. I say that, fully accepting that Toby had a very active personal and sexual life before we met—which, might I add, was at a gay singles resort in Bali. He's been very open with me as he comes to terms with his past, which he may or may not share with you or Arthur.

"Suffice it to say that I know the two of you were intimate, and I want you to know that I have no negative feelings about that. It just is."

He smiled kindly. "He told me last night after I pestered him as to why he was acting so, well, dickish."

Ethan exhaled and laughed, clutching his chest. "I'm...thank you for telling me, and I'm sorry—"

Spencer held up a hand again. "No need to apologize whatsoever. Like I said, I knew what I was getting into. I don't want things to be uncomfortable between us. I know Arthur and Toby are close friends and colleagues, so we'll likely spend time in each other's company. I hope that's not going to be a problem." He frowned. "I'm currently dealing with the aftermath of a sex-related shake-up in my own friend group, and it's awful. I learned some time ago that the gay community of Southern California is small, despite the miles it covers and the vast amount of people who are a part of it. The likelihood of, ah, overlap of partners has a high percentage rate."

"I'm new to all of this—and I mean *all* of it—but I'm certainly getting that impression. I don't want there to be any discomfort either, and I feel terrible that there was a problem tonight...on top of all the other problems going on around here."

Spencer nodded seriously, but then he grinned. "You sounded *so* good last night. How did rehearsal go today?"

Ethan beamed. "Pretty good, I think? Toby had some good notes for me, so I'll be ready to tackle the second half tomorrow and then the whole show Wednesday. That's the plan, I think?"

Spencer shook his head. "Wow, that's amazing. I was a dancer, and I understand picking up choreography quickly, but singing is a whole other universe. And I understand you can dance as well."

Ethan shrugged. "Mom wanted me to be a triple threat. I'm working on it." His gaze went skyward out of habit. He wondered, was his mother's spirit cognizant of what he'd accomplished? He knew she'd be proud of his performances. Perhaps not how he'd handled himself after she'd passed away, but somehow he thought she'd forgive him.

Especially now that he was trying so hard to walk the right path.

Spencer stuck out his hand. "Well, I'm certainly rooting for Reese to get better, and for you to kill it on Saturday. Let's just hope our significant others manage to work out their issues."

Ethan took his hand and shook it, placing his other one on top. "Thank you, Spencer. That means a lot."

"There you two are," Jesse said, hurrying out as she pulled on her coat, followed by Bailey. "Ethan, you're with me. Spencer? Toby said you guys can drive Bailey home? He wants to see Reese tonight."

"Of course," he said, giving her a hug as she hurried to them. "No problem. Need anything else?"

She hooked Ethan's arm and waved at him over her shoulder. "A hope and a prayer!"

Ethan waved goodbye as Jesse dragged him toward the door. "Is everything okay?" he asked, worried at her speed.

"Besides your new boyfriend socking his best friend in the face at my rehearsal? No, of course not." She laughed as they reached a black Dodge Challenger. "I just need to get away from all of this damned testosterone! Grrr!"

Ethan climbed into the passenger side and shut the door as she gunned the motor to life. "I'm sorry, Jesse."

"Oh, no. I don't blame you. Well, not really. I just cannot tell you how many overgrown boys I've had to deal with since I met Danny Black. At least it's not him fighting this time. Did you know that my darling husband still gets in the occasional bar fight? I could just..."

"Sock him?" Ethan said, biting his lip. Jesse definitely had a teacher vibe, and he absolutely respected her, but she also cracked him up.

"Yes! Anyway, I'm driving you so he can play referee in case anyone else decides to punch Toby in the mouth."

"Is he okay?" Ethan asked, feeling bad for Toby. He didn't deserve this. Ethan should have been clearer with Arthur about what had happened.

"Oh he's fine, just surprised and worried because he didn't know what he'd done. Once they started talking, though, well... Arthur will fill you in. I left before they got into details. Like I was saying, I'm driving you home because Audra called Arthur, and she needs to see you tonight, so she's meeting you at his house. Sounds like she's got some time-sensitive information for you." She clapped her hands together. "That's exciting, right?"

"I don't know. Yes? I mean, our meetings went well today. I wonder what's up?"

Jesse pulled out onto Sunset and she frowned. "I always miss the driveway."

"Right? Isn't it such a weird place for a condo?" He pointed it out, and she put on her blinker. Traffic was coming fast so she gave the car a bit too much gas and peeled out as she made the turn. The engine growled as she gunned it up the hill, and she shouted, "Woohoo! I love this car. Don't get me wrong, I also liked my little old economical and environmentally friendly Honda, but when it broke down, Danny said, 'You're driving my car from now on, got it?'" She rolled her eyes. "He's so bossy."

Ethan cracked up as she pulled into the spot next to the Vitesse. Audra's car was parked on the other side.

"But is it a bearable level of bossiness?" he asked.

"It is. I just...well, I didn't come from money, in fact I was unemployed and nearly broke when I started working with him. He was trying to earn his high school diploma, and I'd just been laid off from the school district. Anyway, he browbeat me and bullied me and then he fired me—"

"He did *what*?"

She laughed. "I'm sorry, I love to tell it that way. Makes me feel better. No, we fell ridiculously in love, and we went through a whole-ass soap opera full of drama for a year until I finally agreed to marry him. I hated the fact that I wasn't bringing anything financially to the relationship, and I *haaaaated* accepting gifts from him, but I finally accepted— after many scoldings from Nora, Patricia, and even Arthur—that a relationship is made up of many facets, and money is only one of them."

She said the last in a snotty singsong voice that made Ethan laugh.

"I brought a lot to the relationship that made up for the fact I barely had anything when we got married. And now? I see us as co-owners of a business. He plays guitar and sings for money, I take care of things that keep the household running when Nora is away, and together, we make sure Jane has everything she needs. I contribute."

"Wow, I hadn't thought about it like that. I appreciate you saying that."

"Good. Because I know you've had a rough time. I don't know everything, but I've picked up a bit of your story through conversations, and I just wanted you to know that we're all glad Arthur found you, or you found him, or—"

"I kinda got dumped on him." He laughed. "Reese had his hands full, and Toby, well..."

"Yeah. But everything happens for a reason, and I think the reason was to be here for Reese, for the show, and to bring Arthur some joy. I've never seen him so happy."

Ethan smiled at her. "Thanks for saying so. He's wonderful."

They sat smiling at each other. "He is. And I'm super glad I got to drive you, because I'm totally raiding his movie collection. Let's go."

Jesse practically ran up the steps ahead of Ethan. He had no idea how she could have so much energy.

"As soon as the show is over, I'm going to spend like a week in Danny's home theater binge-watching movies, and I know Arthur has a bunch of old ones I can't get on streaming." She knocked on the door.

"Oh good, you're here! Come in, come in." Audra waved them inside and shut the door. Then she turned on Ethan with an eyebrow raised. "I need you to strip."

"Excuse me?"

"Hurry up, I've got a whole lighting setup in Arthur's bedroom. Just strip and I'll explain." She pushed him into the bedroom while Jesse laughed. "Here," she said, shoving something at him. "Put this on. Tell me when you're done."

Audra shut the bedroom door, and Ethan looked down at the fabric in his hands.

Oh. My. God.

"No way. You've gotta be—"

"Just put it on. I'll explain in a minute."

When Arthur and Danny showed up an hour later, Jesse and Audra were hysterically laughing at Ethan as they drank Arthur's wine.

"Okay, roll over onto your belly," Audra instructed him.

He did as she asked and groaned, his eyes burning from the bright lights and screens she'd set up all over Arthur's bedroom.

"Wait, don't come in yet," Audra shouted. "Jesse, he needs more spritzing."

Jesse hurried over with the water bottle and sprayed his naked torso, the water droplets standing up on oil-coated skin. Jesse fluffed his hair up with the blow dryer, making his curls fan out around his face.

"Okay, okay, I think that's good." She stood behind Audra, who'd brought over a professional camera. Apparently, photography had been Audra's undergrad minor, along with business, and she, too, had a JD from USC.

Arthur walked in—and his jaw dropped.

"Hi?" Ethan said, trying to smile. He wiggled his feet, which were encased in a super-tight mermaid suit, and the tail flicked at him.

"What in the Creature From The Sparkly Lagoon kind of fucking shit is this?"

Jesse went to him and kissed his cheek as he stared at the scene on his bed in shock.

"Audra let me help with the shoot. I'm the...what did you call me? The fluffer?"

Arthur put a hand to his forehead, and Danny burst out laughing.

"A spritzer," Audra said. "We have to keep him wet. Sorry, Arthur, you're gonna need to wash your duvet. We kinda spilled this sparkly oil shit all over it."

"It's fine," he said, and Ethan was relieved when his shock turned to a warm smile.

"Tony talked to the producers and they were excited about having Ethan read for them but they wanted to have some pics to see—"

"They wanted to see him naked with a tail. I get it," Danny answered. "Fucking weird, man. As long as I've lived in fucking Hollywood, I'll never not be shocked at the fucking weird in this town."

Jesse rolled her eyes. "Next time you're over, Ethan, remind me to show you our engagement pictures. Danny, you can tell him about the time your rock 'n' roll bestie had you over for a photo shoot—"

"Ah, shit, now I'm itchy just thinking about it. All right, babe, can we leave them to their...are those actual scales? Fuck me. Good luck, Ethan. See you tomorrow."

"Bye."

Arthur continued to stare, his eyes dragging over Ethan's naked torso and the sparkly fabric that hugged his—

"They wanted to see his physicality, and they were wondering about tattoos—"

"Which I don't have," Ethan answered.

"No, which is helpful in this case. They're looking to cast this next week. We lucked out because they haven't been happy with any of the auditions so far. Tomorrow, I need to get some film of him in the water—"

"May I ask what the project is?"

Audra put her camera down and her eyes bugged out. "You haven't told him yet?"

Ethan smiled. "We hadn't had a chance to talk. It's, um—"

"A queerified *Splash* but on the West Coast. Filming will be here, and I'm not sure where they're planning to do the water shots, potentially travel for that. All the names attached are top notch. They've got —wait 'til you hear this—Pedro Pascal slated to play the shipping exec. And Dan Levy is set to play the scientist's son...how fun would this be?"

Arthur sat on the side of the bed and reached for Ethan's hand. "It means a lot of time in the water. Daryl Hannah had a helluva time in her tail. I read some of the interviews."

"I understand. It's quirky, though, right? And it would be fun to be a part of making a big-budget gay rom com."

Arthur nodded. He went to touch Ethan's face, but Ethan pulled back and wrinkled his nose. "You'll get all greasy."

Arthur smiled and leaned down to kiss him. "I'll take my chances."

Ethan sighed into the kiss, hoping it meant they were okay.

"So tomorrow—excuse me, hello, let me finish so I can get out of here."

Arthur pulled back to give his attention to Audra, and Ethan wished they were alone...and he was out of his tail.

"Tomorrow?" Ethan asked and gave her a big smile.

"I'll be here at nine. We'll do the water shots, then get you cleaned up.

Tony has you scheduled to read for Wendy for that *Friends LA* show. Then I need to take you over to meet with Tatiana, I'll feed you, and then I'll take you to the theater. I'm working on getting some of your photos over to be considered for the watch ads. Oh," she said, putting down her camera and sitting on the other side of Ethan on the bed. "I also have some *very* good news."

Ethan perked up and flicked his tail. "I like good news."

Audra cracked up and Arthur shook his head with a smile.

"I dug around and found out that you haven't been paid your residuals. Like, *anything*, from the two British films. Your former agent has been holding on to the funds since they dropped you."

"What? Really?"

Audra nodded. "They're claiming you left them no forwarding address, so I took care of it. We should be getting a wire transfer tomorrow. They didn't want a lawsuit. It's not hog-wild money, but it should cover any expenses you've had since you arrived in LA."

Ethan sighed and smiled at Arthur. "I can pay you back."

Arthur held up a hand. "No way. I told you, not until we get you work. I want you to have a cushion. You'll pay back your expenses when you sign a contract for work."

"Right, so Ethan, I'm going to open a new bank account for you, and I'll get you all the particulars on Wednesday, all right?"

"I could just hug you," Ethan said, his eyes filling with tears. Things were looking up, in so many ways. He hadn't dared to hope for an outcome like this.

"Maybe not while you're covered in oil, m'kay?"

"Okay," he said, fanning himself. "I can't even wipe my eyes."

"I'll get you into the shower, hang on," Arthur said.

"And that's my cue. Wait, let me get my lights—"

"You're going to need them in the morning," Arthur reminded her. "Just leave them."

"Great." She clapped her hands together. "We had a great day, Ethan! I'll get these pictures ready for you to look at in the morning too. You're gonna love them. Kay. Byeee! Oh, Arthur, I left the extra keys on your table like you asked."

"Thanks, doll. See you tomorrow."

Audra scurried out of the bedroom and out the front door. Arthur waited until he heard the *clack-clack* of her shoes pass by the bedroom window before he stood.

"What happened with Toby? Is everything okay?" Ethan had been so worried, but Jesse wouldn't take no for an answer and scooted him out of the theater.

Arthur shrugged and brushed a piece of Ethan's hair out of his eyes. "He forgave me for hitting him, though I'm not sure he should have," he said, losing a bit of the softness around his eyes. "And he feels terrible for what happened with you. He had no idea. He was...well, he was using a lot of drugs at that point. He's sober now, thank God, but he's had quite a struggle with his mental health. We nearly lost him just a few weeks ago."

"Oh God. Arthur..."

"I know. I think we all need to just get through this weekend. The creation of the show has been healing for both him and Reese, but they're both going to need time to recuperate when it's done." He smiled down at Ethan. "He wants to talk to you...eventually. But for now, he promises he'll try to curb his dickishness to get through rehearsals. Will you be okay with that?"

"Yes, I told you. I'm doing much better. I can take it for the good of the order." Ethan leaned his face into Arthur's hand and closed his eyes. "And you? Are you going to be okay with all this...mess?"

Arthur sighed. "I think we'll have to sleep in the guest room tonight. I don't think I have it in me to clean all this up."

Ethan rolled his eyes. "You know what I mean."

Arthur continued to stroke Ethan's cheek. "So this is what it's going to be like, huh? Dating a—"

"Merman? Yeah, I think so. Although, I think we can go a little lighter on the oil."

"Come here," Arthur chuckled, shaking his head. "Let me help you."

Arthur took his hands and Ethan scooted his legs around and sat them on the floor. He kicked the flipper out in front of him and wobbled as he got to standing.

"Arthur?" Ethan was still worried. Was he still shaken up by his behavior earlier?

"It's going to be an adjustment. I worked really hard to keep drama out of my personal life, but in the process, I think I kept everything of worth out, too. I don't want that life. I want *you*, honey. Fins and all."

Ethan breathed deeply for the first time since he'd stepped out onto the stage and seen Arthur and Toby facing off. "If the movie doesn't work out, maybe I can get a job at one of those mermaid bars, or, like, do they still have the underwater shows?"

"You are adorable." He tried to pull Ethan into his arms, but he sucked in a breath.

"What?"

"Your suit! Maybe you should, um, undress first. Or help me out of this tail."

Arthur smoothed his hands down Ethan's sides, and Ethan heard the tiniest moan. "Boy, this thing is...form-fitting."

"Uh-huh. It also doesn't hide anything."

Arthur looked down and saw that Ethan had a situation going under his...appendage?

"I wonder, how do real mermen deal with this sort of thing?"

Arthur slid out of his suit jacket and tossed it aside. Tie was off with a flick of his hands, and then he unbuttoned his dress shirt as he took a knee in front of Ethan.

"I'm not too sure. I'm guessing there has to be some way to...procreate, right? Baby merpeople have to be made somehow."

Arthur slid his fingers under the elastic and began to peel the fabric down Ethan's hips. He winced when he caught a few hairs.

"I, uh, didn't have time for a full shave."

"I'll be careful," Arthur said as he continued his work. He leaned forward and pressed kisses into the area he'd freed from the clingy suit. "I'll be so careful with you."

And he was. As soon as Ethan's cock was freed, Arthur caught it with his lips and somehow managed to give a phenomenal blow job while peeling the rest of the stretchy fabric down to Ethan's ankles, which were so tightly pinned together he couldn't move, and he was afraid he would topple over.

"Arthur, please," he gasped, his hands shoved into Arthur's hair. "I gotta move, baby."

Arthur grunted and continued his attention, using one hand to slide the elastic over Ethan's feet. Once he was free, he tugged at Arthur to stand up.

"Please, let me wash this off. I want to be all over you."

Arthur grinned and took his hand. "Right this way, Mr. Bradley."

THIRTY-TWO

"Look at you, handsome."

Patricia and Arthur stood outside the theater alongside the red carpet, set up for arriving guests on opening night. They were on meet-and-greet duty, and seeing a dapper Thomas Matheson, a cane in one hand and with his other he was on the arm of a tuxedoed Jude De La Torre made all the chaos they'd been through worth it.

Thomas let go of Jude's arm and leaned in for Patricia to kiss his cheek. "Seems a shame to not have a hot redhead on my arm, what do you say?"

Jude rolled his eyes and let Patricia lead Thomas to his seat in the balcony.

"Hello, Mr. and Mrs. De La Torre, and Brianna," Arthur said, shaking hands with Jude and Bailey's parents and sister, and he continued to greet De La Torres for the next several minutes. If this show got picked up, there was a good chance Arthur would approach the family about taking on Bailey as a client. The kid was incredible, and even though he needed some professional training, Jesse had already taught him so much.

"Thank you for everything, Mr. Frye," Bailey's mother said, squeezing his arm. "Jude let us know that this wouldn't have happened without you and Ethan. I'm so happy that Reese is well enough to play piano. He would have been so disappointed."

"Yes, ma'am. We made it. Enjoy the show."

She winked at him, and Arthur felt another presence at his arm.

"Arthur, man, you seen Patricia?"

Arthur turned to spot Cosmo wearing a burgundy velvet suit with no shirt underneath. He shook his head as he shook his hand. The guy pulled it off with his dramatic good looks and his long, curly dark hair.

"I'm afraid you're too late," Arthur said. "She's already spoken for."

Cosmo's eyes bugged out until Arthur took pity on him. "She's walking Thomas Matheson to his seat."

Cosmo grinned. "Guess I can let the guest of honor have her for the evening." He winked at Arthur and made his way inside.

"Darling!" Arthur's mother and father were next to arrive, and they complimented him on his suit before asking after Ethan.

"He's nervous but he's going to do fine. He managed to learn all the music in a week. Doesn't even need the monitor."

Bernard leaned close. "Can't wait to tell him congratulations on the contract."

Arthur shushed him. "He doesn't know yet. Audra and I are going to surprise him tonight after the show."

"I bet you will."

"Get inside, you two," Arthur said, patting his father on the shoulder. "And thank you for coming."

There were camera crews everywhere inside and outside of the theater, and they'd been around for the past three days, catching footage for the documentary on Thomas. Once Reese's illness had improved enough for Arthur to approach him with the idea, Reese was one hundred percent for it. All the cast signed forms, authorizing filming of the final rehearsals, and a few gave interviews. Roland and Bernard were heading up the project, and Fernando was making calls to folks interested in investing.

Arthur would be heavily involved with the project, which was good. After *Boy* wrapped in a week, he would have a lot more time on his hands.

He greeted a whole slate of Hollywood royalty—including one Bradley Cooper, who made good on his promise to come. Joe Judd happened to be in town, and he arrived with several of the dancers from the reality show *Dance Machine*.

"Good to see you," Arthur said, giving Joe a hug.

Then there were folks like Melinda, the pop star Reese wrote songs for; several of the musicians Thomas had played with over the years; Spencer's friends; Danny's fellow band members; Nora, Amalia, and Nora's sister Connie, with Roland and Fernando; and Horace and Grace Manning.

Arthur was waved over to be interviewed by Maria Menounous, who was covering the event for E! Television. He never loved being on camera, but he gave her all of the pertinent information on the show and tried to be charming.

Then it was time to head inside and hopefully give his boyfriend a good-luck kiss.

Backstage, everyone was buzzing. Dancers were stretching and having last-minute adjustments to their costumes, and the venue's staff was doing a great job taking care of everything.

Arthur found Ethan and Dwayne warming up their voices with Toby and Reese in a sound room in back. Reese had cried when he saw the full dress rehearsal the day before.

"Thank you," he'd whispered. "You have no idea how much this show, how much this *story* means to me and my family. I cannot thank you enough for all of your sacrifices to make this show happen."

"All right. It's almost time. Bring it in." Reese pulled the three men into a hug, and he pressed their heads together.

"Arthur, get in here," Toby called out, and Arthur joined the lovefest.

No one said anything for several beats, and then Dwayne started humming and snapping his fingers. Toby's voice rang out high and clear, "Love, the kind you clean up…"

"With a mop and bucket," Dwayne answered.

"Oh my God," Arthur said, bending at the waist, he laughed so hard.

"What is it?" Ethan asked, putting a hand on Arthur's back.

"On the Discovery Channel…"

"It's 'The Bad Touch' by The Bloodhound Gang," Arthur finally got out, as Toby, Reese, and Dwayne started doing the bump and finished singing the song.

"Not this again," Jane said from the doorway. Then Danny and Jesse pushed past her and joined the melee.

"What even is this song?" Bailey stood behind Jane in the doorway. She turned to smile up at him and gave him a hug

"What we thought was great music in nineteen ninety-nine. It's the official pre-show sing-along for every gig." Arthur put his arm around Ethan and drew him away from the ruckus. He whispered, "Are you ready?"

Arthur had been blown away by the dramatic look the costumer had given Ethan for the show. His dark hair was dramatically slicked back with a severe part, he wore stage makeup, complete with heavy black eyeliner; a charcoal suit with a black shirt and tie; and black lace-up dress shoes. A fedora rounded out the look, which he'd use as a prop in sync with the dancers.

Arthur was looking forward to taking everything off of him after the show.

Ethan beamed at him. "I am. Full house?"

Arthur nodded. "Every seat. I'm going to head out. I'm going to watch at least the first half from the box. Break a leg?" He kissed him lightly on the lips and Ethan shuddered.

"Thanks, baby."

Arthur strolled away from that room with pride puffing up his chest. He allowed himself this private moment of victory. He'd lifted his clients up and helped them achieve their dreams. They'd pulled off a miracle, writing, producing, choreographing, and staging a musical in just under thirteen weeks. They sold out the theater for all four performances. Arthur was already fielding calls from prospective producers from Broadway.

Oh yeah. And he'd fallen in love.

Life is good.

The house lights were flickering as he entered the box and sat behind Thomas Matheson.

"You need anything, sir?"

Thomas turned and placed a hand over Arthur's. "Just to hear my music." The old man's eyes were watery as he smiled.

The lights went out and the applause of 2,700 guests filled the house.

Reese, Dwayne, and Andre started to play, and Ethan walked out onstage, tipping his hat to the audience. Arthur sighed, leaning forward and resting his chin against his fingers. He had a monologue that kicked off the show.

"Good evening guys and dolls,
And all my friends within these walls,
we'd like to tell you a story about love.
Yes, love, that far-out feeling
that makes your heart keep beating
and your breath keep stealing.
That's right, have you been in love?
Ever dreamed about it, only to discover
it wasn't quite what you thought it was,
or didn't look like you thought it would
Well, let me tell you friends,
love comes in all kinds of shapes and sizes,
and sometimes it surprises us.
But that don't mean you don't still grab ahold
with both hands, yeah, real tight, ya dig?
I'm here to lay it on ya, give it to ya straight.
You better hold on before it's too late.
Because love, when it comes, fills you with joy.
Now here's a little story of boy meets Boy."

. . .

Arthur was grateful to be sitting in the dark at the back of a balcony box, because he was swooning over Ethan's words, and when his voice filled the auditorium, Arthur's heart began that hiccup dance, the happy one, not the scary one, although it was still a little scary. Was this really his future? Dating, living with, and someday marrying an actor he'd then have to share with the rest of the world? With his clients, he could sometimes step back and know that when he went home, the drama would subside for a while...

But did it ever really? With his parents, Reese and Toby, and now Ethan?

He was a goner, and he needed to face it.

He wanted this swoon, he wanted this pride, and he wanted the beautiful man who would be waiting for him backstage after the show with a special smile meant just for him. He'd sworn he'd never date the talent, but that was before he'd met the talented man singing his heart out onstage.

Swoon-worthy indeed.

He took a moment to look around the box and the one next to them, to gauge the reactions of friends and family.

Jude's parents were both crying as they watched their son Bailey light up the stage. Sean's mother sat in the box on the other side with her girlfriends. Thomas had a mischievous smile on his face, and every once in a while he'd lean close to Jude and say something naughty that would make Jude shake his head, but he was smiling too.

Arthur couldn't tear his gaze away from the boys when they began their tap number that had them literally tiptoe-tappety-tapping around their attraction, circling each other on the stage, gazes locked until they were so close...then Sean pulled away and fell to his knees downstage, his confusion apparent.

He covered his face with his hands and Bailey wrapped his arms around him from the rear. He lifted Sean from the floor, and Sean kicked his legs and arms forward as if reaching for an escape—then he flung his arms back, wrapping them around Bailey's head, and wrapped his legs around Bailey's.

Bailey spun him in several circles and let him go in front of a table upstage. Sean stared down at the table as Bailey bent him forward. Sean spun around to protest, and Bailey pressed a finger to his lips, pressing him backward onto the table, and as Ethan hit the high note of the music, Bailey was supposed to lean forward over Sean and hover until the lights went dark.

But he kissed Sean instead.

Arthur heard gasps in the boxes, murmured surprise from the audience, and then Thomas cackled.

The lights went dark, then the house lights rose for intermission.

Mrs. De La Torre turned to Jude from the box next door. "Was that supposed to happen?"

Jude shrugged and shook his head.

Bailey's parents seemed a little concerned, but his aunties started to giggle and then the whole box was laughing.

Jude sighed in relief.

Arthur leaned forward and touched his shoulder. "I'm going to go backstage and check on everything."

Jude turned with wide brown eyes. "Do that."

Arthur left the balcony and made his way backstage to find Jesse talking to the two giggly boys and Toby.

"As long as you're both okay with it, I think it shocked the audience, but it worked."

"I mean, that bicurious twat you had working on the choreography kissed my Spencer in that spot, so you shouldn't be *that* surprised."

Jesse turned on Toby with her mouth hanging open, and Sean and Bailey covered their mouths as they kept giggling.

"Julian isn't a twat—"

"Yeah, he is," Danny said, joining the circle. He was dressed in a tux and on standby in case Reese got too tired, but Reese seemed fine after the first half. "But he's my...I guess he's not *my* twat. He's my bicurious pain in the ass."

Jesse put a hand to her forehead. "Can we please focus? Look, you guys are doing great, I just don't want your parents having heart attacks, Bailey, so let's not get carried away in the second act."

He pressed his lips together to hide his big grin. "I promise."

Sean was watching him with big eyes and a bigger smile.

Oh boy.

"Just go," she said. "Too much testosterone in this show, I swear to God."

"Yeah, but that kiss was hot," Toby said, pulling her into a hug.

"It was great, Jesse," Arthur said. "The De La Torres were laughing and carrying on when I left the box, so I think you're safe."

She exhaled. "Oh, thank God."

Reese, Andre, Dwayne, and Ethan turned the corner, and Arthur was swooning once more. Sure he was biased, but he couldn't help but feel the supernova-strength stardom coming at him as Ethan approached. He was a fucking blinding force of nature.

And he swore he wanted to belong to Arthur.

"Hey," Ethan said, running to Arthur as soon as he spotted him. He stopped right in front of him and gazed up at him with those big blue eyes. "How was it? How's everything sound? Did I tone it down enough?"

Arthur put his hands on Ethan's waist. "You did so good," he murmured against his lips before pressing a kiss there. "How do you feel?"

Ethan licked his lips. "Like I wish we were alone right now?"

"Get through the second half and you can have that wish."

"I want to hug you but I'm all sweaty. Thank you, Arthur."

Arthur frowned. "For what, doll?"

"For believing in me. Kinda helps me believe in me, too."

"You *better* believe in you. Now get back out there and kill it. I'm going to make sure Thomas isn't making ball jokes in front of the De La Torres." Arthur kissed him once more and Ethan stepped back with his fingers on his lips.

"Arthur," he whispered.

"See you soon, gorgeous."

Ethan's answering smile let Arthur know he was just as affected.

"This show has really played cupid with the lot of us, hasn't it?"

Reese and Toby stood there grinning at Arthur.

"Don't get me started," he grouched, but he wasn't mad one bit.

"You two make sense," Toby said, and Arthur was so grateful they'd mended fences after their blowup this week. He loved these two clowns more than he cared to admit.

"Sure, like Jude and I," Reese said, rolling his eyes. "I still don't know how I got lucky enough for him to forget about my disastrous tendencies."

"*Your* disastrous tendencies? I think my storm cleanup was a lot worse than yours," Toby said, and Reese and Arthur both agreed.

"Don't hold back, now," Toby said as they teased him.

"Hey, wait, I'm not a disaster like you two," Arthur said. "I'm FEMA."

"Right," Toby said, "but even FEMA can get caught up in the storm."

"Or in your case, Arthur, an earthquake," Jesse said. She was attempting to shoo everyone back to their places. "Now, say your good-byes. It's showtime."

Arthur hugged his friends and they slapped him on the back.

"Thanks for always taking care of us," Toby said.

"And thanks for making our vision a reality," Reese said. Then they kissed his cheeks and messed up his hair. It got weird, and Arthur had to bat at them with his hands to get them to go back to their posts.

"Do your job," he yelled at them as he hurried away.

By the time Arthur got back up to the box, Jude was working his magic with Thomas to get him to drink water and eat some string cheese.

"You need to keep your strength up for the next act."

"Why? Is there going to be more kissing? Anyone losing their drawers?" He snickered and took a sip of water as Jude groaned.

"Jesse and the boys assured me that the rest of the show will go as planned, and that means no, Mr. Matheson, no one will have an intentional wardrobe malfunction."

Thomas wrinkled up his nose. "You know, for a redhead, you sure are a party pooper." Then he was laughing about saying poop, and Jude reached for his hand to quiet him as the lights flickered, signaling the end of intermission.

Arthur sat back in his seat and crossed an ankle over his knee, his gaze focused on the spot his new love would be standing momentarily, and he sighed.

Life, and love, were good.

The rest of the show went off without a hitch and when it was over, the crowd rose to their feet. The applause seemed to go on forever. There wasn't a dry eye in the house as the light swung around to focus on Thomas, who waved and blew a kiss to his beloved grandson. He'd made it, and had been lucid enough to see his hard work over the years come to fruition. His music was the basis for Reese's lyrics and storyline, his experiences in the 1960s the inspiration for the play…and then Reese made it reflect his own life.

It was a beautiful story with incredible dancing and a phenomenal score. Arthur felt honored to have been a part of bringing it to fruition.

Reese and Toby took to center stage with their arms around each other.

"For many reasons, this show almost didn't happen," Reese started. "I want to thank Toby for being my writing partner. Thank you for continuing to make beautiful music with me." They embraced as the crowd went wild, and were both sobbing when they separated. Reese pulled himself together to finish his thank yous.

"We could not have done this without the outrageously gifted Jesse Martin-Black." Jesse stepped onstage, and somewhere Danny shouted, "That's my woman," leading the whole audience to crack up.

"And thank you to Danny Black, Nora Benson, and the whole Blackened organization, including their manager, Patricia Wilson. Thank you for supporting us. To our frequent collaborators, Dwayne and Andre, thank you for stepping up. And a huge thanks to Ethan Bradley, for saving our asses."

The applause was deafening, and people began stomping on the floor as Ethan stepped out and waved, bowing his head.

Good. Arthur wanted Ethan to have this moment.

"There're so many people to thank, but most of all, our manager— where are you, Arthur Frye?"

Arthur stood and waved, hating the spotlight.

"Arthur has held our hands through all of the hijinks and tomfoolery we've gotten up to over the past decade, and I'm sure he'll be there for us through many more. We love you."

"Stop it," Arthur said through his teeth as he continued to smile painfully. He loathed this part. He took his seat and thought perhaps that was it, they could get on with the post-show events. He wanted to get on with Ethan's surprise. It was killing him, the waiting.

But then Reese cleared his throat.

"The real hero behind this show is my beloved, Jude De La Torre. Thank you, baby, for believing in this, in us, and for handling everything at home with grace. You let me borrow your brother, which, thank you to the entire De La Torre family for putting up with all of the chaos. I swear he's doing his homework."

The De La Torres laughed and waved back at Reese.

"I love you, Jude. I hope I made you proud."

Jude was crying now, and Arthur slipped him a tissue as the light shone on their box once more.

"I'm going to kill him," Jude muttered as he smiled and waved. When the light was gone, he turned to Arthur. "I'm so going to kill him."

"Get used to it," Arthur said, patting him on the shoulder. "I have a feeling this won't be the last time he's thanking you like that.

Reese thanked Spencer, Toby blew him a kiss, and then they both had lovely things to say about the cast, especially Bailey and Sean, who looked incredibly proud of themselves. They'd been absolutely stunning. The entire cast of dancers, who'd filled in the scenes in the lounge, were fabulous. Then finally the cast took one more bow—Arthur's hands were tired from clapping at this point—and the house lights came on.

"Mr. Matheson, are you up for a visit backstage? We've got cake and punch."

The old man got to his feet on his own and straightened his coat, using his cane to support himself. "Wouldn't miss it."

"You sure, Grandpa?"

"Yes, Jude, my boy. I feel better than I have in years. Let me have tonight, then you can fuss at me all you want. I won't even argue."

Jude put an arm around him and helped him out of the box. Arthur walked back with them while the others waited for the auditorium to clear out. He'd scouted his route ahead of time and was able to descend the back stairs from the balconies that led to a corridor off the backstage area.

Harvey was already there with her assistants, getting things arranged.

"Bless you," he said to her as he entered the green room. "It's perfect. I should have come down and helped."

"Nonsense. This is my new favorite creation to date! I had it set up fifteen minutes ago, and I got to see the end of the show. I'm totally coming back tomorrow to see the whole thing."

"And I'll gladly get you tickets." He kissed her cheek and went to open the door for the cast, who'd been told to wait in the hallway.

"Attention everyone," he called out, foolishly, because while he had a strong, deep voice, it took way more than that to get a bunch of squealy actors and dancers in line.

Jesse let out an ear-piercing whistle using her fingers, and the hallway got quiet.

"Guys, dolls, and friends within these walls," Reese said, "our fearless leader has an announcement."

All eyes turned on Arthur, and he rolled his. "Thanks," he said sarcastically. "My dear friend Harvey has created a fantastic confection to celebrate all of your hard work these past few weeks. Before we dig into what I can guarantee you will be the best cake of your lives, we're going to take some cast photos—but first, I need y'all to let Ethan Bradley through."

He caught sight of Ethan making his way through thirty-plus bodies of dancers, musicians, crew, and the like to come to the front.

"Hi," he said, giving Arthur a salute. "Reporting for duty, sir."

Arthur felt his cheeks get warm. "Don't call me sir in front of all these people," he whispered. "Do you trust me, honey?"

"Of course I do," he said, his smile slipping a little. "What's wrong?"

"Nothing's wrong. Step this way."

THIRTY-THREE

Ethan
The sweet smell of buttercream hit Ethan's nose as soon as Arthur opened the door.

"Oh my God," he gasped, his hands over his mouth.

Harvey stood beside a several-layer cake that, like her jungle-themed design for the Fryes' party, had a central waterfall, but instead of vines and jungle animals, there were mermaids and mermen posed on rocks at the different levels. The words, "Way To Make a Splash!" were done in rainbow frosting on the top layer, and there were tiki torches along the top.

Arthur placed his hands on Ethan's hips and spoke close to his ear. "Before we let the rest of the cast in here, Audra has something for you."

Audra stepped out from behind the cake and gave Ethan a big hug. Then she handed him a folder.

"What is this?"

"A contract for *Plunge*. Go ahead and take a look at the front page." She opened the folder, and the words all blurred before Ethan.

"I can't. What does it say?" He gazed up at Arthur, his eyes filled with tears.

Ethan had been really nervous for his audition three days ago, despite Audra's attempts to reassure him. He'd wished Arthur could be there, but he knew he needed to stand on his own two feet if he was going to make this Hollywood dream happen.

He'd done his best to hide his shock when he'd entered the room and discovered he'd be reading with Pedro Pascal and his business partner in the film, played by Melissa McCarthy, who was taking on the John Candy role. And not only did Ethan have to read with those two powerhouses—but producer Tom Hanks and the original director of the film, Ron Howard, were there as well.

Thank God Audra never left his side. Knowing she was rooting him on, knowing a role like this would absolutely put him in a great position to not only repay his debts, but that he'd feel as if he were finally worthy of all the sacrifices people had made for him along the way...

That knowledge gave him courage he hadn't known he had. From his mother to Reese and Toby, and now his beloved Arthur, all of them had believed in him and given him a chance.

The reading went well. The casting director loved the pictures Audra had taken, and after the reading, they let her know they needed to sort out a few things and they'd be giving her a call. It seemed too good to be true, so Ethan tried not to get his hopes up, and he threw himself into preparing for *Boy* and his auditions for the following week.

"It says," Arthur spoke softly, "they want you for the role of Madison, they're going to pay you a considerable amount of money, and you report for work in two weeks." Arthur lifted Ethan's chin with his finger, and he had to blink back tears.

"I did it?"

Arthur smiled and cupped his cheek. "You did so good, honey. Congratulations."

Ethan nearly tackle hugged Arthur, who laughed in surprise.

"Actually, you should be hugging Audra first—"

Ethan grabbed her up in a hug and spun her around, a little too close to the cake for comfort, but she laughed the whole time.

"We did it!" he shouted.

"No, babe." She shook her head. "*You* did it. Though I *will* take congratulations on negotiating my first freaking feature film contract!"

They high-fived and hopped around in a circle, again too close to the cake.

"Okay, okay, can we let the rest of the cast in before they knock down the doors?"

Ethan paused, then he ran over and flung the doors open. *"Let's eat cake!"*

When the group heard what they were celebrating, cake was everywhere. People ate it, they smashed it onto Ethan's face—thankfully they'd all changed out of their costumes—and Jesse was frantically going around telling them all to be careful, they couldn't afford injuries, yada, yada, until Toby smashed *her* in the face with cake.

Then it was on. Someone hit Reese, Bailey and Sean got each other, and soon everyone was hugging and singing that ridiculous Discovery Channel song again.

Ethan looked around for Arthur and when he couldn't find him, he went out into the hall.

"Yeah, everything's great. Thank you for coming. It meant a lot that you were here."

Arthur must have seen Ethan approach, because he turned and smiled.

"I'll tell him you said so. Good night. Love you, too." He hung up and slid his phone into his pocket. "That was Bernard. He said to tell you that you have the voice of a very naughty angel and he loved the show. He also said congrats on the merman gig." Arthur chuckled. "I think he was secretly hoping you'd get it."

"I can't believe this is happening," Ethan breathed as Arthur pulled out a tissue and wiped some of the frosting off his forehead.

"Believe it, and you've still got more work ahead. If I were a betting man, I'd say you're going to get an offer to do the *LA One* crossover episode and be asked to do the spinoff show. If it works with your schedule, that is. I'm sure Audra will advise you what to do."

Ethan rolled his eyes. He had a feeling Arthur would be like this, sharing some of his thoughts, but then deferring to Audra's opinion. He was so good at his job, and though Ethan wished Arthur was his actual manager, he understood why he'd done what he'd done. He needed that boundary, and Ethan would do his best to respect it...until it wasn't necessary anymore.

Ethan was terrible about getting ahead of himself, and he knew he needed to work on it, but he was determined to keep Arthur in his life. He wanted to work just as hard at his relationship as he did at his career. But he had to admit he was worried about what this busy filming schedule was going to do to them.

"What's wrong?" Arthur asked, sensing as he always did when Ethan was upset.

"I'm so happy to be getting to work, don't get me wrong...but I'm going to miss you. Audra said there would be some filming in LA, but we'd probably be in the Gulf of Mexico for at least a month filming the underwater scenes." His eyes burned with tears once more, but these weren't the "I'm thrilled with my life" kind. "I just found you, Arthur. I don't want to—"

Arthur pulled him into his arms. "Don't even say it, honey. This will be the first of likely many times we'll be separated, but we'll be fine. You'll be so busy, you'll hardly know I'm not there, and if my schedule permits, I'll come and visit you on set if you want me to. That is, if it's okay with your manager."

Ethan pinched his side and frowned at him.

"I can't take you seriously with frosting all over your face and in your hair."

"That's too bad. I asked Harvey to put some aside for us. I want to take it back to your place and...eat it with you. Preferably with no clothes on. Preferably—"

Arthur kissed him, groaning when he tasted frosting. He licked at Ethan's lips, then down his jaw and neck, while Ethan laughed and squirmed.

"Can you take me to your place?" Ethan whispered. "I really think I should get some rest before tomorrow night." He grinned wickedly at Arthur.

"Can it be *our* place?" Arthur asked, losing his smile. "I want to be your home base, Ethan. I know it's fast, and I know it's impulsive—"

"Which is usually my territory."

"Please, Ethan? If we're going to be apart, I want to spend whatever time—"

"Yes, baby. If you want me, I'm yours."

"I want you," Arthur groaned.

"Good. Then let's say goodbye."

"And grab our cake? That tastes amazing."

Ethan pulled him toward the green room. "I think she even saved one of the mermen for you. She said they're edible."

"The only merman I intend to eat tonight is you."

EPILOGUE

Six Weeks Later…

Ethan was equal parts elated and exhausted to be finished with their filming in Mexico. He'd learned how to snorkel, seen some incredible fish, eaten amazing food—he'd even adjusted to the spice level. But the work had been the most difficult thing he'd done in his life.

He was not born to be a fish.

His skin was dry and irritated from the constant waxing…everywhere…and the tail was a beast on its own. He'd spent hours in costuming and makeup daily, and not only was the tail constricting, but it chaffed. He'd read interviews Daryl Hannah had done, talking about not being able to pee for more than eight hours at a time, which, thankfully, he had different plumbing and they'd created a workaround in his costume, but it took time to get the opening undone, and he had to have help, which was just not cool.

They'd also wanted him to bulk up a bit, so he'd been eating and working out on a strict regimen, but the amount of swimming, along with the workouts, meant he was either eating all the time or starving, and in the end, he hadn't been able to gain as much as they wanted. There was talk of fixing it with CGI later, but the director said no, he wasn't after Aquaman or a superhero, he wanted an Adonis, and he'd gotten one. Ethan had been relieved.

By the time his plane landed in Burbank a month into shooting, he was absolutely on a mission to get home. To Arthur's. Sure they'd talked, and Arthur had come out for a weekend, but it had been torture to be away from him, and some days it took all of his acting ability to pretend like he was happy as a, well, a fish in water and in love with his co-star. Which he was, but not at all in the same way. He'd been blessed with incredible actors on this film who mentored him at every turn, as well as an understanding and patient director in Silas Howard.

It took forever for him to deplane and the wait at baggage claim was delayed by a snafu with the boards. They'd all been waiting at the wrong carousel, and his entire flight had to trek across the arrivals area...it was a nightmare. Audra told him to text her when he had his bags, as she was waiting for him in the cell phone lot.

He had sworn her to secrecy. Arthur didn't know he was coming in that day. He knew Arthur was at an event with Joe Judd, and he wanted to get home, unpack, shower, and be waiting for him.

That had been the plan, anyway.

By the time they sat in LA traffic, she'd stopped and picked him up some food, dropped him off at Arthur's, and he'd dragged his bags inside, he'd barely had time to shower before he passed out. He did manage to prepare one thing for Arthur's arrival, whenever that would be, but he couldn't keep his eyes open.

He sprawled out in Arthur's bed naked, after thoroughly moisturizing his irritated skin, and fell fast asleep.

Arthur

"Another phenomenal routine, Joe. You keep giving *Dance Machine* EMMY gold like this and I'm going to negotiate you a fat raise."

Joe groaned and reclined his seat. He had an ice pack on his hamstring and another one on his left shoulder. "I'm going to need it. Do they even have insurance coverage for nursing homes for thirty-something broken dancers? I swear, I never thought this job would kill me."

"I'm so sorry. At least you have a break. I'll get you appointments set up for massage, your acupuncturist, and we'll see if you need physical therapy, all right? I think we can hold off the nursing home 'til you're at least my age."

"And how old is that?"

"Ah, oh…thirty-eight. My birthday was last week."

"Oh! Happy birthday, man. Did you do anything fun?"

Arthur sighed. "Saw my parents. I finally got out to see them in the desert. Cute place they've got, but they're going to rent a place in the city. Dad's working on the documentary about Reese's grandfather Thomas, and Mom is being courted to do some limited-series roles. It's good, they need to be active."

"What about your boyfriend?" Joe asked. "I thought you said you were seeing someone."

"Ethan," Arthur said, and just saying his name made him smile and wince at the same time. "He's been on location in Mexico. Hopefully they'll be done in the next week or so. I guess there were some weather delays? Anyway, yeah. It's been rough with him gone."

Joe whistled. "Separation is a bitch. It's gotta be tough."

"It has been. I'm looking forward to taking care of him." And he was. He'd looked up some new recipes to practice, since he knew Ethan was on an eating regimen and he was a bit of a picky eater. On their long conversations that sometimes lasted late into the night, Ethan confessed that as much as he loved the shoot, he was struggling a bit with the physicality of the role. It killed Arthur to not be there. He felt like Ethan had finally found some stability with him, and then had been literally cast back out to sea once more.

He'd been so brave. Arthur couldn't wait to praise him.

He'd been worried about what separation might do to their newfound romance, but they'd talked every day, sometimes more than once, and it was just like before he'd left. They had a lot to learn about each other, and they took this time of physical separation to do just that. Arthur felt like they were more solid than ever.

Which was why he really wanted to get Joe back to his apartment and get home. He wanted to call Ethan and see if he had any news about his departure date.

But Hollywood traffic being that it was, it took an hour to get from the *Dance Machine* set to Joe's—which was 3.4 miles exactly—and then another hour to get back through the traffic snarl to Arthur's. It was eleven at night, and he knew Ethan would be going to bed soon, so he took his driveway a bit too fast, squealed the tires when he parked, then trotted up the stairs to his condo.

And he heard the house settle. Water sloshed in the pool. The outdoor lights went out, as did the city lights below.

Well, shit. Another earthquake.

It had been a particularly active year or so in Southern California. Lots of people had opinions about it, but Arthur tried not to fret too much. Nothing he could do. His life, his friends, family and work, were all in LA. Soon, his lover would be too.

Once things settled, he unlocked the door and walked inside. He thought he'd get an earful from Elvis, but the feline menace was nowhere to be seen. Arthur set his things down and hoped the damned cat hadn't gotten wedged behind the couch again.

"Hey, E? You okay buddy?"

Nothing.

He set down his messenger bag and his industrial-sized Yeti mug next to his kitchen table, nearly missing the surface in the darkness. He'd been drinking two to three jugs of water per day and was now taking blood pressure medication, but his last blood tests showed improvement, so he'd avoided adding cholesterol meds and anything else to the mix. He had to take care of himself if he was going to continue taking care of everyone else.

He walked into his dark room, and Elvis was in the middle of the bed, which looked awfully lumpy. Arthur didn't always make his bed perfectly, but he usually at least spread out the duvet nicely.

"You mess up the bed, you little beast?" He sat on the edge and reached for the cat...but the whole bed moved.

"No, I did."

A black mop of hair appeared, and Arthur sprang off the bed with a shout.

"Oh my God, Ethan! Honey!"

He rolled over, and Arthur bent down close so he could see him clearly. "Surprise?"

Arthur flung himself on the bed and wrapped his arms around the man he loved with all of his being. Ethan squeezed back, but not quite as enthusiastically.

"What's wrong?"

"I crashed so hard. I'm sorry, I'm trying to wake up. I'm so happy to...well, not really *see* you. Why's it so dark?"

"Power's out. We just had an earthquake a minute ago."

"We did? I didn't even feel it! Is everything okay?"

"Yeah, I don't have any gas on the property and it wasn't a really big one. I'm sure we're fine."

Ethan lay back and pulled Arthur close, kissing his lips tenderly at first.

"Wait, let me get out of these clothes. When did you get in?" Arthur stripped out of his clothes and tossed them into his vault, determined to deal with them later.

"I don't know. Audra brought me here around six, maybe?" He yawned and held his arms out, wiggling his fingers. "Hurry. I have something for you."

Arthur came back to the bed in his boxers, unsure what kind of a homecoming Ethan was up for, and he slid into bed to find him gloriously naked.

"All I need is you, honey. I'm so glad you're home. Are you okay? Did shooting wrap up without any issues?"

"Mostly. It's fine. I don't want to talk about it. I want to kiss you silly."

Arthur chuckled, pulling Ethan on top of him. "By all means. Commence kissing."

Ethan seemed to shake off sleep a little more with every sweep of his tongue. He tangled his fingers in Arthur's hair and moaned softly as he straddled his hips.

"I missed your freckles so much," he said, sucking on Arthur's collarbone. "I've been waiting for this moment for weeks now."

Arthur let his hands slide over Ethan's hips, surprised by the changes he could feel. "Wow, you've really packed on some muscle here," he said, running his fingers over Ethan's glutes. "You feel so g—" His fingers slid over something...unexpected. "What is..."

Ethan pushed up onto his hands and smiled down at Arthur. "I told you I had something for you." He ground his erect cock against Arthur's own awakening erection.

"What did you do?"

Ethan sighed. "I set out to do a little education. I wanted to be ready...for *you*. When I came home. I read some articles about how to prepare yourself to bottom so it's less likely to hurt."

Arthur gripped his hips to keep him still. "Honey, I told you we don't ever have to do that—"

"And I appreciate it," Ethan interrupted, rubbing his nose against Arthur's. "And if this little experiment doesn't work, then I'll be grateful you feel that way. But I've been...practicing. Here," he said, taking Arthur's hand and placing it over the plug. "Take it out. Let's see if I'm ready for you."

Arthur was completely speechless. He gripped the plug and gave it the slightest tug.

Ethan moaned. "Mmm. More."

Arthur ran his other hand over Ethan's back and arms and felt no tension. He was relaxed. It was tough to not be able to see his face clearly. He wanted to make sure he didn't hurt him.

"You won't hurt me, baby. I've been using these for a couple weeks. I got a set after you left that last time. What else did I have to do when I was alone and *thinking of you?*"

"Fuck, Ethan. You didn't have to do this, but *fuuuuuck*. The of you touching yourself in your room? I could come just thinking about it."

"Well, don't come yet. Take it out. Let's see what happens, okay? Oh...oh, it feels good when you move it. *Oh!*" he gasped, as Arthur slowly worked the plug free. Ethan had used a lot of lube, but Arthur reached over to the bedside table drawer and got some more. He fumbled with the bottle and spilled a little on them both, making Ethan squeal and laugh.

"Use it on yourself. I want you inside me, Arthur. Please, baby."

"Do you want me to use a condom?"

Ethan tilted his head. "Not if it's just us. It is, right?"

"Fuck yeah, it is. I only want you." Arthur slicked himself up and gripped Ethan's hips. "You promise me, Ethan, that you'll tell me if it's not working for you. Say it."

"I promise, now let me...just..." He gasped as he found the head of Arthur's cock. He rubbed it against himself and moaned softly. Arthur helped him line it up, and then Ethan lifted and slowly, steadily, lowered himself.

"Breathe, honey," Arthur said, though he should have been following the same order. He was shaking so hard, totally overwhelmed with the sensation. Ethan was all tight heat, and Arthur wasn't going to last long at this rate.

"It doesn't hurt," Ethan said, lifting a little, then taking a bit more. "It feels...good. Oh God, Arthur, it feels so good!" He started rocking, taking more each time. Arthur tried to stay perfectly still, until he felt Ethan's ass rest against him, now fully seated.

Ethan was breathing hard, but he was smiling against Arthur's lips. "I can't believe it. It's happening. It's...God, move, Arthur. Fuck me. I want you."

Arthur let go of the tension in his body from holding still and began making small thrusts, his brain about to short circuit on him, the pleasure was so intense. He had no rhythm to his movements, his hips and thighs trembled as he tried to control his thrusts, keep them slow.

"God, Arthur, I love it...it's so good. Arthur, baby, please."

Ethan rose up and began using those powerful thighs to ride Arthur, taking him deep with each fall, throwing his head back and bouncing with abandon. He was such a thing of beauty, and Arthur was so moved by the trust Ethan had placed in him that he was overwhelmed.

He wanted to touch Ethan's cock, heighten his pleasure, but then he felt his orgasm building and he lost all thought.

"Ethan, I'm coming...!"

"Arthur!"

His belly was covered with Ethan's slick, hot spend right as he felt himself go, filling Ethan up. Arthur was seeing spots, every muscle in his body tense as he curled up off the bed.

Ethan collapsed on top of him, gasping for air and laughing. "We did it," he slurred. "We did it!"

"*We* didn't do anything," Arthur said. "*You* did it. I just held on for dear life. My *God*, you are beautiful. I love you, honey."

Ethan lifted his head, and Arthur swore he could see the whites around his pale blue irises. "Do you really?"

"Yes," Arthur said, cradling his face. "Oh my God, yes, Ethan. Did you think I didn't?"

"No, well, we just hadn't ever said it."

"But I felt it every day. I knew I loved you before you even left, Ethan. Were you worried? While you were away?"

Ethan dropped his head. "Not... A little? I tried not to worry about it, but it felt like so long, and like it would never end. But I got through it knowing you were on the other end, and your calls, the cards you sent, the flowers...it kept me going. If I knew you were thinking of me, then I didn't worry. But I didn't want to tell you I loved you while I was away."

"I'm so proud of you. I love you so much."

"You sure?"

"Say it," Arthur said, sucking Ethan's bottom lip. "Tell me."

"Fuck, baby, I love bottoming for you."

Arthur wrapped his arms around Ethan and laughed heartily, rolling them onto their sides, his cock slipping from Ethan's body in the process.

"I'm glad you loved it. I loved it too, but that's not what I meant. *Say it.*"

"I love—"

Roooooooooowlll

They both jumped at Elvis's appearance on the bed next to their heads.

"Oh no, I should have fed him before—"

Rooooooowwwwwrrlllllllll

"All right, all right, fucking give me a second. I'm an old man, I need to recover—"

ROOOOOOOOWWWWWWLLLLLL

"Let me feed him," Ethan said. "You rest, *old man*." He chuckled as he started to get up, but Arthur reached for his hand.

"Hey. Say it. Please."

Ethan bent down and kissed him once more, so tenderly it made Arthur's heart pound a healthy rhythm in his chest. No more scary hiccups. Only the good, healthy ones from now on.

"I love you, Arthur Frye."

"Thank you. Now go deal with the menace while I clean up our mess. Then I'm going to cuddle you for at least fourteen hours."

"Fourteen?"

Arthur climbed out of bed and tore the sheets off. "I figure that's the max amount of time we'll be fortunate enough to be left alone. It's all right. I'll take it if it means having you to myself."

Ethan came back and stood in the doorway with the can opener in his hand. The lights flickered on, illuminating his sated smile.

"God, it's so good to see you," Arthur said, moving toward him. He leaned forward to kiss him as Elvis yowled at him pitifully.

"He needs me to watch him. What can I say?" Ethan turned and walked into the kitchen, and Arthur was glad he hadn't gotten a load of him naked in his new, beefier body before they'd done the deed. He wouldn't have lasted as long as he had with that fucking incredible body to look at.

Barring any more work trips to Mexico, Arthur would have that body to look at as much as he wanted for the time being.

And wasn't that a precious gift.

June 2018
Feedback Magazine
Sammara Gunderson

The Rise, Fall, and Resurrection of Ethan Bradley

. . .

Everyone loves a good comeback story, and Ethan Bradley's is one that will hit close to home for many living in the urban city centers of America. Countless Americans have experienced economic hardships that take them from making ends meet to feeling like they've met their end. Health scares, medical bills, and unemployment are just some of the issues that can negatively impact folks in ways they cannot come back from without intervention or assistance. The narrative that houselessness is primarily caused by addiction and mental health issues has been proven wrong in recent years, and we are now living in a reality where many of us are a car accident, cancer diagnosis, or natural disaster away from house and food insecurity.

As the number of houseless folks in Southern California continues to climb, a number of Hollywood faces have been popping up at unexpected places serving those who need it the most. Feedback Magazine *heard about a new effort to bring relief to the streets, and the actor at the head of the organization is none other than Ethan Bradley.*

Former stage actor turned British film heartthrob turned Hollywood It boy, Bradley channeled his personal experiences into action. Bradley was in London two years ago performing in the musical Ruby in Red Plaid, *written by Reese Matheson and Toby Griffiths, when a series of unfortunate events occurred, including the loss of his mother and a series of pictures and stories in the tabloids that got him unfairly fired from his UK film jobs. Ethan went from sharing a penthouse with a group of actors to a youth hostel, and then finally the streets of London.*

Growing up in a working-class family in Iowa, he'd never worried about where his next meal would come from, and finding himself on the streets let him know very quickly that he didn't have the resilience to survive there for long. He scraped together enough money to fly back to Los Angeles, where his now-fiancé, Hollywood talent manager Arthur Frye of Slade Artist Management, assisted him in getting back on his feet. He landed the role of a lifetime in Plunge, *a gay retelling of the '80s classic* Splash, *which starred Tom Hanks and Daryl Hannah, and he's been busy working ever since.*

But Ethan made a vow to himself that as soon as he paid off the debts he incurred during his time of unemployment, he would look into starting or joining an existing organization dedicated to ending food insecurity.

"When I got to Hollywood, I saw such a disparity between those seeing the sights, and those clinging to the shadows of Hollywood Boulevard, hoping someone who was paying twenty to fifty dollars to take a picture with Captain America might have some spare change to share so they could eat something that day. Then when I was on set with the Plunge *crew, I started having conversations with the catering folks, to get an idea of what the costs would be to feed a large group of people. I spoke to my manager, Audra Diaz from Slade, and we started to collect more information. We formed a 501c3, hired a board of directors made up of community activists and philanthropists, and did initial fundraising to purchase two catering trucks and the equipment needed to set up feeding sites.*

"There's a lot involved, including permits, security, and supplies, of course, so it took us a good eight months to get off the ground, but now we've got our friends showing up to work, we're recruiting volunteers, and we're looking to expand to mobile hygiene stations, and even haircuts and shampoos, shaves... Look, I spent a few weeks on the street. A lot of these folks out here have spent years not knowing where their next meal is coming from. It's impossible for me to ever have peace if I don't do all I can to alleviate some of the suffering in my community."

Feedback Magazine *will be contributing financial and labor support to the cause, and we'll be publishing Feeding Hollywood station locations and schedules on our website for those looking for assistance.*

Stay Tuned for More...

***While this is a fictional story, people are experiencing food and housing insecurity at alarming rates in our country and the problem is growing daily. If you or someone you know is struggling, please know that there are resources. If you are in a position to help, supporting your local food bank goes a long way to making sure fewer folks go to sleep hungry at night. Thank you for reading Earthquake Ethan.**

.   .   .

Feed America: https://give.feedingamerica.org/
Covenant House: https://www.covenanthouse.org/aboutus

Want to read more about the characters in Earthquake Ethan?
Check out the following:
Hurricane Reese
Typhoon Toby
Teacher
Teacher: Act Two
Teacher: The Final Act
Everything's Better With You
Here's a sneak peek at my next release: Under His Sheets: Accidentally Undercover. Join me, Layla Reyne, Allison Temple, Linden Bell, M.A. Grant, and Cari Zee for this fun and sexy queer romantic suspense series! You can find the books on Amazon!

Under His Sheets
Sneak Peek

November 13, 2019

10:53 PM Las Ramblas, Barcelona, Catalonia, Spain

All crowds were not created equal, nor did they evoke the same sensations.

Standing shoulder to shoulder with thousands of music fans at the rail on a rainy day in Nuremburg at Rock am Ring after playing a wild set with my band, MoonCraft, was one of my favorite experiences.

Standing back to front on Las Ramblas in Barcelona, with hundreds of protestors shouting in Catalan their desire for independence from Spain and justice for the separatists while police barricaded the side streets, not allowing anyone in or out of the protest, getting shoved and stepped on in the sweltering late-summer heat, wasn't likely to rank in my top ten of anything other than terrifying.

"Por favor. Soy americano," I shouted to one of the officers dressed in riot gear. "No quiero estar aqui." I thought that was the right way to tell him I didn't belong anywhere near this damn protest. I just wanted to get to a bar and lose my worries in a bottle of something strong enough to wash away the stench of what my life had become in the last two weeks since we'd come to Catalonia.

The cop pushed me back into the crowd of protestors who were waving yellow flags with red stripes and a blue triangle with a white star and into...

A frowning Spaniard with short, curly hair, long sideburns, a hard body, and a deep chin dimple covered in dark stubble.

"Cuidado."

"Lo siento," I said before another wave in the crowd pushed me into him again. I lost my balance and was about to go down when he caught me under the arm.

"Ves amb compte."

"I'm sorry."

My English must have startled him because he pulled me back in close and his eyes widened in surprise.

"You're the American."

Not *an* American, but *the* American? And he wasn't asking. When I kept gaping like a fish out of water, he adjusted his grip and yanked me forward, somehow making the crowd part for us. I tripped more than once as he dragged me through the chanting crowd that was yelling "independencia," and I ended up draped over his back as he dragged me toward the barricades on the far side of the corridor. He said something to the cop, who moved aside just enough for my savior to slip through with me in tow.

"Where are we..." I started to ask when he stopped to punch in a code in an alcove of a building a block or so off of Las Ramblas.

"You'll be safe inside."

"Thanks, but I was just trying to get to a bar—"

"I have drinks upstairs."

He led me up three flights and down a dark hallway to an apartment door. Another keypad dealt with and he opened the door, moving inside quietly and disappearing into the darkness.

Should I follow? The last time I'd followed a stranger into a dark, unfamiliar apartment... Okay I'd never done this before. You'd think as a musician who'd been touring the world with his band for the past four years, I'd have had wild, adventurous experiences like that. If you did, well, you'd be sorely disappointed.

"Ven aquí, guiri."

"Excuse me?" I asked. "What did you call me?"

I walked down the entry hallway into the apartment and into the dimly lit living room with sparse furniture and no decor to speak of. Not even a wall calendar or a plant.

The man stood in front of a large window, which overlooked the chaos we were just in. The lights from police vehicles bounced off the bare walls, giving a red hue to the place.

"¿Hablas inglés?"

"Yes, I do, better than you speak Spanish." His words were soft though, so I didn't take offense.

"Thank you for getting me out of there," I said, looking down into the crowd. It was much denser than I'd thought and went on as far as I could see. "I shouldn't impose."

"You're Randall, right? From that band MoonCraft?"

That was the last thing I thought he'd say. "I was. We broke up. Now I'm just Randall."

"Why break up? You were good."

"Have you seen us?"

He nodded. "I have. At Sala Razzmatazz. It was a good show." He opened a bottle of wine and poured two glasses. "I loved the cover you did of that Mike Patton song, 'Deep Down.' Wasn't expecting that." He handed me a glass and when I paused, he gestured to it. "I said I had drinks. You look like you could use one."

"Thanks." I accepted the glass and pushed all thoughts of stranger danger out of my head. "Yeah that Mike Patton stuff is a vibe." And super niche. How did this guy know the album *Mondo Cane*?

He nodded once and turned his gaze back to the street below the window. There was surprisingly little noise from the protest inside his apartment, and though it had been a sultry night outside, it was cool, probably due to the ceiling fans.

"It is lucky I saw you. You could have been arrested. Being American might have made things difficult for you."

"Losing my passport would do that too." I finished my wine and without missing a beat, he refilled it.

"How did you manage that?"

"The same reason my band broke up. We got robbed two weeks ago, right after that show that you saw. All of our gear? Gone. Most of my personal stuff gone. That was the last straw. We were on our last few Euros we'd budgeted for the tour and couldn't play the rest of the gigs we'd booked without buying all new instruments and equipment, so the guys decided to bail. I've been sitting around my hotel waiting for my appointment at the embassy, trying to figure out my next move. It was not my plan to get involved with a protest, I was just looking for a bar to spend my last night in Spain, potentially, before my appointment tomorrow. Then I can go home, not that I'm looking forward to that."

Last sip. He refilled. I didn't know why I was unloading my tale of woe on him, but he was the first person I'd spoken to in a couple of days and he carried himself like someone who...cared. I still wasn't sure why he'd brought me to his home, though. No red flags had jumped out, but I was still a bit...confused.

"I suppose I was in the right place at the right time, then. Can't have you being detained. Though it's too bad you're leaving."

I was halfway through my third glass of what was exceptional wine when his words struck me. "Why's that?" It almost sounded like he was flirting?

He moved my way with the bottle, filling my glass before I could finish.

He shrugged. "Seems a shame for you to leave España on a low note."

For the first time, he made prolonged eye contact with me, and while I wouldn't call it a smile, there was definitely humor in the curve of his lips, his dark red lips that cut dramatically into his olive skin. His short, dark brown, curly hair was lightly sprinkled with gray, making it tough to tell how old he was. Maybe he was prematurely gray? But I felt like, the way he carried himself, he was older than my twenty-seven years old. But not like *old* old.

The weight of the past two weeks seemed to dissipate as I looked at this incredible specimen of Spanish finery. He wasn't much taller than me, maybe 5'10", but the way he filled a pair of jeans made me want to weep, and when I'd been draped over his back, I'd felt his powerful grip, his exceptionally large deltoids, and he hadn't faltered under my weight, which wasn't insubstantial.

I'd been told I had a pretty face, pretty hair, and a stunning voice, but I certainly wasn't built like most rangy, lanky singers in rock bands. My DNA meant no matter what I tried, I always carried extra padding around the middle and my ass *really* didn't quit. It hadn't mattered to me much until MoonCraft fell prey to the number two band killer: number one is feuding siblings; number two is members getting romantic. In a moment of weakness, I blurted out my feelings for my guitar player, Rig, and two years into our tenure, I fell into his bed.

Such a cliché, hoping to make harmony with a bandmate. I should have known better. It wasn't like MoonCraft was my first band. Our affair didn't last long before he'd moved on, leaving me to pretend everything was okay. Now Rig and our drummer, Halo, were *together* together and headed back to the U.S., most likely making plans for a new band without me.

Four years I'd invested in them. I'd told myself that if I could manage to keep us focused, this could be the project that launched my career into the stratosphere. Perhaps band killer rule three should be European club tour.

"What do you suggest I do?" It must have been the wine, or maybe he was responding to my downtrodden forlorn look, but as he gazed back at me intently, I thought, *It sure would be nice to not be alone tonight.*

He took my glass and set it down, then tugged gently on the lapel of my cardigan, frowning at a small hole in the seam where the shoulder met the sleeve. Yeah, I looked exactly as if I'd seen better days. "You could use a little comfort tonight, no? Save your worries for tomorrow?"

"You make it a habit of rescuing American musicians from trouble?"

"Most certainly not." His voice had a breathy tone, and it was higher-pitched than I would have thought by the way he got us out of a sticky situation. "I definitely don't make it a habit of kissing American musicians in trouble, but sometimes..."

"You make an exception?"

"Sí. Do you make a habit of needing rescue?"

"Not really? But I appreciate what you did tonight." I stepped closer to him, prompting him to put a hand on my waist, which, whatever, if this was going to happen he'd likely get a glimpse of what I *didn't* have going on. I might have winced though.

He gripped me a little tighter and his expression turned serious.

"You're safe here. That protest and the aftermath will likely go on for hours. You're welcome to stay, no expectations."

"But possibilities?"

He smiled then, and there was a mischievous glint in his soulful brown eyes.

"Endless."

Under His Sheets: Accidentally Undercover is out April 9th!

Acknowledgments

Mr. Ro has been wonderfully patient with me as I attempt to take advantage of my empty nest (well, with Velma it's not an empty nest), and I'm eternally grateful to him! I swear I'll get the taxes done. And to my college kids, I love you and I'm so stinking proud of you.

This year marks nine years that Kelli Collins has been my editor and I've learned so much from her. Thank you, Kelli, for all of your encouragement and LOLs as well as your "oh, honeys." Here's to many more. LOLs, that is.

To my assistant Rachel, you continue to be a rock goddess. Thank you.

Thanks to my writing communities sponsored by Rachael Herron and Jen Graybeal for providing the support I needed to meet my authory goals.

To my pals in BAQWA, thank you so much. And special thanks to Richard May for beta reading and giving such great feedback. Much appreciated. (Gingers rule!)

This time around I was grateful to have a large group of beta readers: Fedora, Robin, Tricia, Michele, Jamie, Lisa, Ruth, Staci, Mary, and Julie. Thank you all for taking the time to give me feedback.

Thank you to everyone who has read my books, but especially my Forces of Nature series. You've patiently awaited this final book and I hope I did the story justice.

And as always, to the SBC. You lot are such a vital support network and I love you all dearly.

To my bestie, NLOD, I look forward to more adventures with you...

About the Author

Whether she's writing contemporary romance featuring quirky and relatable characters or diving deep into the paranormal and supernatural to give readers a shiver, R.L. Merrill loves creating compelling, diverse, and inclusive stories that will stay with readers long after. Winner of the Kathryn Hayes "When Sparks Fly" Best Contemporary award for *Hurricane Reese*, Paranormal Romance Guild's Best Rockstar Romance for *You Can Do Magic*, and Daphne DuMaurier finalist for *Connection*, Ro spends every spare moment improving her writing craft and striving to find that perfect balance between real-life and happily ever after. You can find her connecting with readers on social media, advocating for America's youth, cruising around town with Great Dane Velma, cuddling with twin black cat familiars Frankenstein and Dracula, or headbanging at a rock show near her home in the San Francisco Bay Area! Stay Tuned for more...

Newsletter: www.rlmerrillauthor.com
Facebook: www.facebook.com/rlmerrillauthor
Instagram: www.instagram.com/rlmerrillauthor
TikTok: www.tiktok.com/rlmerrillauthor1342
BookBub: www.bookbub.com/profile/r-l-merrill

OTHER BOOKS BY R.L. MERRILL

Haunted Series: (Contemporary Romance)

Haunted

Fated

Bated

Jaded – (Coming Soon)

Minded Series: (Paranormal Spinoff of Haunted Series)

Minded

Blossomed

Father F'in' Christmas

A Peculiar Prom Night

Magic and Mayhem Universe: (Funny Paranormal Romance in the universe created by Robyn Peterman)

Shifted

Ghoul Me Once

Gator Me Twice

Magic and Mayhem/Shifted Collection

Fang Me Three Times

Fangtastic Four

Five Fanger Witch Punch

Hollywood Rock 'n' Romance Trilogy: (Contemporary Romance)

Teacher

Teacher: Act Two

Teacher: The Final Act

Contemporary Romance Series:

The Rock Season

Road Trip

You Fell First

The Heart Knows (Re-Releasing Soon)

A Match Made in Spain

LGBTQ Romance

Pinups and Puppies (Originally in Love Is All Vol. 2)

I Want, More – Bolder Breed Studios #1 (Originally in Love Is All Vol. 3)

Love and Pride – Bolder Breed Studios #2 (Originally in Love Is All Vol. 4)

Everything's Better With You: An MM Sports Romance

All I Wanna Do — Bolder Breed Studios #3 (Email Ro for your copy)

Under His Sheets: Accidentally Undercover – Out April 9, 2024

Road To Rocktoberfest 2024 (Coming Soon)

The Banes of Lake's Crossing (Historical Horror Romance)

The Fourth Man (The Banes of Lake's Crossing) (Historical Horror Romance)

The Redemption of Nathaniel Bane

<u>The Absolution of Jonah Bane</u>

The Gifted Series: (Supernatural Suspense/Paranormal Romance)

Healer

Connection

<u>Protector</u>

Sundowners (M/M Paranormal Romance

<u>Sundowners Book One</u>

Sundowners Book Two (Coming Soon)

Forces of Nature Series: (Gay Contemporary Romance)

Hurricane Reese

Typhoon Toby

Earthquake Ethan

Summer of Hush Series: (Gay Contemporary Romance)

Summer of Hush

Brains and Brawn

You Can Do Magic: Carnival Of Mysteries (A Summer of Hush Tie-In)

Carnival of Mysteries 2024 (Coming Soon)

Anthologies:

Thanksgiving Day Parade From Hell (Worst Holiday Ever) (Gay Contemporary Romance

Valentine's Day From Hell (Worst Valentine's Day Ever) (Gay Contemporary Romance)

Salty and Sweet (Summer Fair) (Lesbian Contemporary Romance)

The Fourth Man (The Banes of Lake's Crossing) (Historical Horror Romance)

A Piece of Him (Gone With The Dead) (Horror)

Breaking Bread—Dark Divinations from HorrorAddicts.net Press (Horror)

Exchange (Renewal) (Science Fiction)

Tap-Tap-Tap (Impact) (Horror)

Human Sacrifice (Innovation) (Horror)

The Sitter (Clarity) (Horror)

Joy Is A Phone Call Away – A More Perfect Union (Lesbian Contemporary Romance)

The House Must Fall – Haunts and Hellions from HorrorAddicts.net Press – May 2021 (Horror)

A Kept Woman – BAQWA Presents: Horror Show 2021(Lesbian Horror Romance)

Gods of Rock 'n' Roll (Free on Wattpad)

How Bittersweet is Karma? Free on Wattpad)

Let Me Stand Next To Your Fire (Queer Cheer)

Midnight in the Renaissance Elevator

Holiday Romance

A Peace Offering (Re-release)

Love and Pride – Bolder Breed Studios #2

Once Upon A Holiday Story 2024 (Coming Soon)

Audiobooks

The Rock Season (Kiss App)

Brains and Brawn (Kiss App)

Teacher (Kiss App)

Hurricane Reese (Kiss App)

A Match Made in Spain (Audible)

Healer: Gifted Book One (Audible)

Under His Sheets (Audible Coming Soon)

Non-Fiction

Horror Addicts Guide To Life Volume 2 - Edited by Emerian Rich

Death's Garden Revisited - Edited by Loren Rhoads (Out Fall 2022)